"It seems that an astonishing number of people who earn their living by putting words on paper in an appealing way have tried their hands at putting a little white ball into a cup cut into a very large and very green lawn. They also like the notion of writing about it and the violence it can engender.

"There is a long and distinguished history of golf in mystery fiction, with such giants of the genre as Agatha Christie, James Ellroy, Ian Fleming, Michael Innes, and Rex Stout having produced classic works in which golf figures prominently. You will encounter in these pages some fascinating motives for murder and any number of memorable characters created by the champions of today's mystery writing world."

—Otto Penzler, from the Introduction

PRAISE FOR *DANGEROUS WOMEN*, EDITED BY OTTO PENZLER

"I'm not usually given to superlatives, but *Dangerous Women* may be the best, most varied, and colorful mystery anthology of all time."

—Janet Evanovich

"Wow, what memorable dames! What terrific short stories! *Dangerous Women* is a winning collection."

—Susan Isaacs

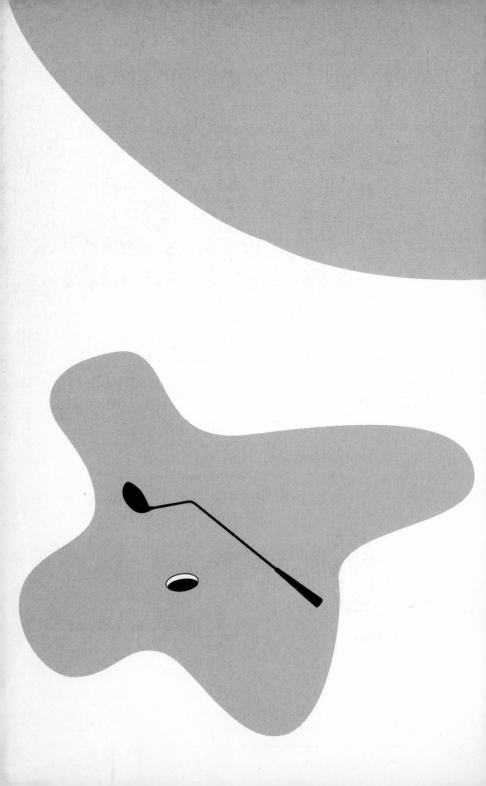

MURDER IN THE ROUGH

EDITED BY
Otto Penzler

NEW YORK   BOSTON

The events and characters in this book are fictitious. Certain real locations and public figures are mentioned, but all other characters and events described in the book are totally imaginary.

Mysterious Press

Hachette Book Group USA
1271 Avenue of the Americas, New York, NY 10020
Visit our Web site at www.mysteriouspress.com.

The Mysterious Press name and logo are trademarks of Warner Books.
Mysterious Press is an imprint of Warner Books, Inc.
Printed in the United States of America
Published simultaneously in hardcover by Mysterious Press

First Trade Edition: June 2006

10 9 8 7 6 5 4 3 2 1

Warner Books is a trademark of Time Inc. Used under license.

Library of Congress Cataloging-in-Publication Data
Murder in the rough / edited by Otto Penzler.— 1st ed.
    p. cm.
    ISBN 0-89296-017-5—ISBN 0-446-69741-9 (pbk.)
    ISBN-13: 978-0-89296-017-0—ISBN-13: 978-0-446-69741-5 (pbk.)
    1. Golf stories, American. 2. Detective and mystery stories, American.
I. Penzler, Otto.
PS648.G64M87 2006
813'.087208357—dc22   2005053435

Book design by Fearn Cutler de Vicq
Cover design by Bradford Foltz
Cover illustration by Stanislaw Fernandes

For Michael Malone,
with affection and admiration for
his abundant measures of kindness, generosity, loyalty, and talent

CONTENTS

Introduction   ix
Otto Penzler

Welcome to the Real World   1
Lawrence Block

The Man Who Didn't Play Golf   21
Simon Brett

Spittin Iron   39
Ken Bruen

His Mission   47
Christopher Coake

Water Hazard   120
Stephen Collins

Those Good Days   160
Tom Franklin

Death by Golf   182
Jonathan Gash

Room for a Fourth   219
    Steve Hamilton

Miss Unwin Plays by the Rules   233
    H.R.F. Keating

A Good **** Spoiled   257
    Laura Lippman

The Hoarder   271
    Bradford Morrow

Graduation Day   298
    Ian Rankin

Lucy Had a List   322
    John Sandford

Unplayable Lies   352
    William G. Tapply

The Secret   369
    John Westermann

Golf Mysteries   395

INTRODUCTION

It has famously been written that the smaller the ball, the better is the literature involving that sport, which would suggest that the greatest sportswriting should be about golf. Or Ping-Pong.

Try as I might, I could not convince my publisher that a book collecting Ping-Pong mystery stories was just what the world is waiting for, which is just as well, because when I raised the subject with some of the world's top crime writers, they looked at me as if I had finally taken that last step over the edge of sanity.

Golf is a different kettle of mackerel, however. It seems that an astonishing number of people who earn their living by putting words on paper in an appealing way have tried their hands at putting a little white ball into a cup cut into a very large and very green lawn. They also liked the notion of writing about it and the violence it can engender.

There is a long and distinguished history of golf in mystery fiction, with such giants of the genre as Agatha Christie, James Ellroy, Ian Fleming, Michael Innes, and Rex Stout having produced classic works in which golf figures prominently. At the back of the book is a comprehensive list of titles for further reading or collecting—the most complete bibliography of golf mysteries ever compiled.

Mystery writers have used numerous golf course settings as homes for their corpses: in the rough, in a sand trap, even right there on the green. And the methods and devices used to finish off their hapless victims have been as varied as your previous ten tee shots, including exploding balls, exploding golf clubs, an exploding cup, and even an exploding golf course. Victims have been speared with a flag stick, clubbed with a, yes, golf club, and murdered in a sabotaged golf cart. Most bodies attained their status as the formerly living in more ordinary ways, such as being shot, garroted, or stabbed on a golf course before, during, or after a game.

Happily, none of the authors in *Murder in the Rough* have used exploding devices to dispatch their victims, but you will encounter in these pages some fascinating motives for murder and any number of memorable characters created by the champions of today's mystery writing world.

Lawrence Block has received the two top awards it is possible to receive in the mystery community: a Grand Master Award from the Mystery Writers of America and the Diamond Dagger from the (British) Crime Writers' Association, both for lifetime achievement.

Simon Brett has remained a popular crime novelist for thirty years, most memorably for his work featuring Charles Paris, a frequently out-of-work actor who enjoys the bottle as much as he enjoys solving mysteries; he made his debut in *Cast in Order of Disappearance* (1975).

Ken Bruen, one of the hardest of the hard-boiled writers

working today, is the author of twenty novels. He has been nominated for an Edgar and won the Shamus Award from the Private Eye Writers of America for *The Guards,* which introduced Jack Taylor, his Galway-based P.I.

Christopher Coake, who recently got his M.F.A. from Ohio State University, has already published a short story collection with Harcourt, *We're in Trouble,* which contains "All Through the House," which was selected for *Best American Mystery Stories 2004.*

Stephen Collins is the author of two suspense novels, *Eye Contact* (1994) and *Double Exposure* (1998), but is best known as an actor in the long-running television series *7th Heaven* and in such films as *All the President's Men, Star Trek: The Motion Picture,* and *The First Wives Club.*

Tom Franklin won the Edgar Allan Poe Award for his short story "Poachers" in 1999; it became the title story for his first book, *Poachers and Other Stories,* which was followed by his critically applauded first novel, *Hell at the Breech.*

Jonathan Gash, a physician in real life and one of England's foremost experts in tropical diseases, is most famous for his series about Lovejoy, the not-overly-scrupulous dealer in antiques, portrayed for several seasons by Ian McShane in the popular television program.

Steve Hamilton's first novel, *A Cold Day in Paradise,* won the Edgar and Shamus awards. Like his subsequent novels, it featured Alex McKnight, the former northern Michigan cop who reluctantly becomes involved with cases to help or protect friends.

H. R. F. Keating is one of the Grand Old Men of the detective novel, having written several distinguished critical works about Sherlock Holmes and crime fiction, plus more than fifty novels, most famously those featuring Ganesh Ghote of the Bombay police force.

Laura Lippman, formerly a reporter and feature writer for the *Baltimore Sun,* has been nominated frequently for all the major mystery awards, winning the Edgar for *Charm City* in 1998. All of her books are set in her much-loved Baltimore and feature Tess Monaghan.

Bradford Morrow was described by *Publishers Weekly* as "one of America's major literary voices." The founder and editor of the literary journal *Conjunctions,* he was given the Academy Award in Literature by the American Academy of Arts and Letters.

Ian Rankin and his series hero, the Edinburgh policeman John Rebus, have become so popular that Rankin is in *The Guinness Book of World Records* for having seven books in the top ten in England at the same time. He won the Edgar in 2004 for *Resurrection Men.*

John Sandford, a Pulitzer Prize–winning journalist, is a perennial on the best-seller list with his *Prey* novels featuring Lucas Davenport, the Twin Cities policeman who is unlike most cops in that he likes to work alone, drives a Porsche, and creates video games in his spare time.

William G. Tapply has a successful career as a columnist for *Field & Stream* and as the author of several books on fly fishing, but it is his series of novels about Brady Coyne, the kindly Boston lawyer who functions as a private detective, that endears him to mystery readers.

John Westermann is of the Joseph Wambaugh school of writers about police officers, except that he focuses on dirty cops and corruption. His novel *Exit Wounds* was filmed with

Steven Seagal as Orin Boyd and opened in 2001 as the number one box-office hit in America.

So it seems appropriate to say welcome to the Masters (though *Murder in the Rough* allows women to participate).

—Otto Penzler
New York, June 2005

WELCOME TO THE REAL WORLD

Lawrence Block

Kramer liked routine.

Always had. He'd worked at Taggart & Leeds for thirty-five years, relieved to settle in there after spending his twenties hopping from one job to another. His duties from day to day were interesting enough to keep him engaged, but in a sense they were the same thing—or the same several things— over and over, and that was fine with him.

His wife made him the same breakfast every weekday morning for those thirty-five years. Breakfast, he had learned, was the one meal where most people preferred the same thing every time, and he was no exception. A small glass of orange juice, three scrambled eggs, two strips of bacon, one slice of buttered toast, a cup of coffee—that did him just fine.

These days, of course, he prepared it himself. He hadn't needed to learn how—he'd always made breakfast for both of them on Saturdays—and now the time he spent whisking eggs in a bowl and turning rashers with a fork was a time for him to think of her and regret her passing.

So sudden it had been. He'd retired, and she'd said, in mock consternation, "Now what am I going to do with you? Am I going to have you underfoot all day every day?" And he established a routine that got him out of the house five days a week, and they both settled gratefully into that routine, and then she felt a pain and experienced a shortness of breath and went to the doctor, and a month later she was dead.

He had his routine, and it was clear to him that he owed his life to it. He got up each morning, he made his breakfast, he washed the dishes by hand, he read the paper along with a second cup of coffee, and he got out of the house. Whatever day it was, he had something to do, and his salvation lay in doing it.

If it was Monday, he walked to his gym. He changed from his street clothes to a pair of running shorts and a singlet, both of them a triumph of technology, made of some miracle fiber that wicked moisture away from the skin and sent it off somewhere to evaporate. He put his heavy street shoes in his locker and laced up his running shoes. Then he went out on the floor, where he warmed up for ten minutes on the elliptical trainer before moving to the treadmill. He set the pace at twelve-minute miles, set the time at sixty minutes, and got to it.

Kramer, who'd always been physically active and never made a habit of overeating, had put on no more than five pounds in the course of his thirty-five years at Taggart & Leeds. He'd added another couple of pounds since then, but at the same time had lost an inch in the waistline. He had lost some fat and gained a little muscle, which was the point, or part of it. The other part, perhaps the greater part, was having something enjoyable and purposeful to do on Mondays.

On Tuesdays he turned in the other direction when he left his apartment, and walked three-quarters of a mile to the Bat Cave, which was not where you would find Batman and Robin, as the name might lead you to expect, but instead was a recreational facility for baseball enthusiasts. Each of two dozen batting cages sported a pitching machine the standard sixty feet from home plate, where the participant dug in and took his cuts for a predetermined period of time.

They supplied bats, of course, but Kramer brought his own, a Louisville Slugger he'd picked out of an extensive display at a sporting goods store on Broadway. It was a little heavier than average, and he liked the way it was balanced. It just felt right in his hands. Also, there was something to be said for having the same bat every time. You didn't have to adjust to a new piece of lumber.

He brought along cleated baseball shoes, too, which made it easier to establish his stance in the batter's box. The boat-necked shirt and sweatpants he wore didn't sport any team logo, which would have struck him as ridiculous, but they were otherwise not unlike what the pros wore, for the freedom of movement they afforded.

Kramer wore a baseball cap, too; he'd found it in the back of his closet, had no idea where it came from, and recognized the embroidered logo as that of an advertising agency that had gone out of business some fifteen years ago. It must have come into his possession as some sort of corporate party favor, and he must have tossed it in his closet instead of tossing it in the trash, and now it had turned out to be useful.

You could set the speed of the pitching machine, and Kramer set it at Slow at the beginning of each Tuesday session, turned it to Medium about halfway through, and finished with a few minutes of Fast pitching. He was, not surprisingly, better at getting his bat on the slower pitches. A fastball, even when you knew it was coming, was hard for a man his age to connect with. Still, he hit most of the medium-speed pitches—some solidly, some less so. And he always got some wood on some of the fastballs, and every once in a while he'd meet a high-speed pitch solidly, his body turning into the ball just right, and the satisfaction of seeing the horsehide sphere leap from his bat was enough to cast a warm glow over the entire morning's work. His best efforts, he realized, were line drives a major-league center fielder would gather in without breaking a sweat, but so what? He wasn't having fantasies of showing up in Sarasota during spring training, aiming for a tryout. He was a sixty-eight-year-old retired businessman keeping in shape and filling his hours, and when he got ahold of one, well, it felt damned good.

Walking home, carrying the bat and wearing the ball cap, with a pleasant ache in his lats and delts and triceps—well, that felt pretty good, too.

Wednesdays provided a very different sort of exercise. Physically, he probably got the most benefit from the walk there and back—a couple of miles from his door to the Murray Street premises of the Downtown Gun Club. The hour he devoted to rifle and pistol practice demanded no special wardrobe, and he wore whatever street clothes suited the season, along with a pair of ear protectors the club was happy to provide. As a member, he could also use one of the club's guns, but hardly anyone did; like his fellows, Kramer kept his own guns at the club, thus obviating him of the need to obtain a carry permit for them. The license to own a weapon and maintain it at a recognized marksmanship facility was pretty much a formality, and Kramer had obtained it with no difficulty. He owned three guns—a deer rifle, a .22-caliber target pistol, and a hefty .357 Magnum revolver.

Typically, he fired each gun for half an hour, pumping lead at (and occasionally into) a succession of paper targets. He could vary the distance of the targets, and naturally chose the greatest distance for the rifle, the least for the Magnum. But he would sometimes bring the targets in closer, for the satisfaction of grouping his shots closer, and would sometimes increase the distance, in order to give himself more of a challenge.

Except for basic training, some fifty years ago, he'd never had a gun in his hand, let alone fired one. He'd always thought it was something he might enjoy, and in retirement he'd proved the suspicion true. He liked squeezing off shots with the rifle, liked the balance and precision of the target pistol, and even liked the nasty kick of the big revolver and the sense of power that came with it. His eye was better some days than others, his hand steadier, but all in all it seemed to him that he was improving. Every Wednesday, on the long walk home, he felt he'd accomplished something. And, curiously, he felt empowered and invulnerable, as if he were actually carrying the Magnum on his hip.

Thursdays saw him returning to the gym, but he didn't warm up on the elliptical trainer, nor did he put in an hour on the treadmill. That was Monday. Thursday was for weights.

He did his circuit on the machines. Early on, he'd had a couple of sessions with a personal trainer, but only until he'd managed to establish a routine that he could perform without assistance. He kept a pocket notebook in his locker, jotting down the reps and poundages on each machine; when an exercise became too easy, he upped the weight. He was making slow but undeniable progress. He could see it in his notes, and, more graphically, he could see it in the mirror.

His gym gear made it easy to see, too. The shorts and singlet that served so well on Mondays were not right for Thursdays, when he donned instead a pair of black spandex bicycle shorts and a matching tank top. It made him look the part, but that was the least of it. The close fit seemed to help enlist his muscles to put maximum effort into each lift. His weight-lifting gloves, padded slightly in the palms for cushioning, and with the fingers ending at the first knuckle joint for a good grip, kept him from getting blisters or calluses, as well as telling the world that he was serious enough about what he was doing to get the right gear for it.

An hour with the weights left him with sore muscles, but ten minutes in the steam room and a cold shower set him right again, and he always felt good on the way home. And then, on Fridays, he got to play golf.

And that was always a pleasure. Until Bellerman, that interfering son of a bitch, came along and ruined the whole thing for him.

●　●　●

The driving range was at Chelsea Piers, and it was a remarkable facility. Kramer had made arrangements to keep a set of clubs there, and he picked them up along with his usual bucket of balls and headed for the tee. When he got there, he put on a pair of golf shoes, arguably an unnecessary refinement on the range's mats, but he felt they grounded his stance. And, like the thin leather gloves he kept in his bag, they put him more in the mood, as did the billed tam-o'-shanter cap he'd put on his head before leaving the house.

He teed up a ball, took his Big Bertha driver from the bag, settled himself, and took a swing. He met the ball solidly, but perhaps he'd dropped his shoulder, or perhaps he'd let his hands get out in front; in any event, he sliced the shot. It wasn't awful—it had some distance on it and wouldn't have wound up all that deep in the rough—but he could do better. And did so on the next shot, again meeting the ball solidly and sending it out there straight as a die.

He hit a dozen balls with Big Bertha, then returned her to the bag and got out his spoon. He liked the 3-wood, liked the balance of it, and he had to remind himself to stop after a dozen balls or he might have run all the way through the bag with that club. It was, he'd found, a very satisfying club to hit.

Which was by no means the case with the 2-iron. It wasn't quite as difficult as the longest iron in his bag—there was a joke he'd heard, the punch line of which explained that not even God could hit the 1-iron—but it was difficult enough, and today his dozen attempts with the club yielded his usual share of hooks and slices and topped rollers. But among them he hit the ball solidly twice, resulting in shots that leaped from the tee, scoring high for distance and accuracy.

And therein lay the joy of the sport. One good shot invariably erased the memory of all the bad shots that preceded it, and even took the sting out of the bad shots yet to come.

Today was an even-irons day, so in turn he hit the 4-iron, the 6-iron, and the 8-iron. When he finished with the niblick (he liked the old names, called the 2-wood a brassie and the 3-wood a spoon, called the 5-iron a mashie, the 8 a niblick), he had four balls left of the seventy-five he'd started with. That suggested that he'd miscounted, which was certainly possible, but it was just as likely that they'd given him seventy-six instead of seventy-five, since they gave you what the bucket held instead of delegating some minion to count them. He hit the four balls with his wedge, not the most exciting club to hit off a practice tee, but you had to play the whole game, and the short game was vital. (He had a sand wedge in his bag, but until they added a sandpit to the tee, there was no way he could practice with it. So be it, he'd decided; life was compromise.)

He left the tee and went to the putting green, where he put in his usual half hour. His putter was an antique, an old wooden-shafted affair with some real collector value, his choice on even-iron Fridays. It seemed to him that his stroke was firmer and more accurate with the putter from his matched set, his odd-iron choice, but he just liked the feel of the old club, and something in him responded to the notion of using a putter that could have been used a century ago at St. Andrews. He didn't think it had, but it could have been, and that seemed to mean something to him.

His putting was erratic—it generally was—but he sank a couple of long ones and ended the half hour with a seven-footer that lipped the cup, poised on the brink, and at last had the decency to drop. Perfect! He went to the desk for his second bucket of balls and returned to the tee and his Big Bertha.

He'd worked his way down to the 6-iron when a voice said, "By God, you're good. Kramer, I had no idea."

He turned and recognized Bellerman. A coworker at Taggart & Leeds, until some competing firm had made him a better offer. But now, it turned out, Bellerman was retired himself, and improving the idle hour at the driving range.

"And you're serious," Bellerman went on. "I've been watching you. Most guys come out here and all they do is practice with the driver. Which they then get to use one time only on the long holes and not at all on the par 3s. But you work your way through the bag, don't you?"

Kramer found himself explaining about even- and odd-iron days.

"Remarkable. And you hit your share of good shots, I have to say that. Get some good distance with the long clubs, too. What's your handicap?"

"I don't have one."

Bellerman's eyes widened. "Jesus, you're a scratch golfer? Now I'm more impressed than ever."

"No," Kramer said. "I'm sure I would have a handicap, but I don't know what it would be. See, I don't actually play."

"What do you mean you don't play?"

"I just come here," Kramer said. "Once a week."

"Even-numbered irons one week, odd ones the next."

"That's right."

"Every Friday."

"Yes."

"You're kidding me," Bellerman said. "Right?"

"No, I—"

"You practice more diligently than anybody I've ever seen. You even hit the fucking 1-iron every other Friday, and that's more than God does. You work on your short game, you use the wedge off the tee, and for what? So that you won't lose your edge for the following Friday? Kramer, when was the last time you actually got out on a course and played a real round of golf?"

"You have to understand my routine," Kramer said. "Golf is just one of my interests. Mondays I go to the gym and put in an hour on the treadmill. Tuesdays I go to the batting cage and work my way up to fastballs. Wednesdays . . ." He made his way through his week, trying not to be thrown off stride by the expression of incredulity on Bellerman's face.

"That's quite a system," Bellerman said. "And it sounds fine for the first four days, but golf . . . Man, you're practicing when you could be playing! Golf's an amazing game, Kramer, and there's more to it than swinging the club. You're out in the fresh air—"

"The air's good here."

"—feeling the sun on your skin and the wind in your hair. You're on a golf course, the kind of place that gives you an idea of what God would have done if he'd had the money. And every shot presents you with a different kind of challenge. You're not just trying to hit the ball straight and far. You're dealing with obstacles, you're pitting your ability against a particular aspect of terrain and course conditions. I asked you something earlier, and you never answered. When's the last time you played a round?"

"Well, as a matter of fact—"

"You never did, did you?"

"No, but—"

"Tomorrow morning," Bellerman said, "you'll be my guest, at my club on the Island. I've got tee time booked at 7:35. I'll pick you up at six. That'll give us plenty of time."

"I can't."

"You're retired, for chrissake. And tomorrow's Saturday. It won't keep you from your weekday schedule. You really can't? All right, then, a week from tomorrow. Six o'clock sharp."

• • •

Kramer spent the week trying not to think about it and then, when that didn't work, trying to think of a way out. He didn't hear from Bellerman and found himself hoping the man would have forgotten the whole thing.

His routine worked, and he saw no reason to depart from it. Maybe he wasn't playing "real" golf, maybe he was missing something by not getting out on an actual golf course, but he got more than enough pleasure out of the game the way he played it. There were no water hazards, there were no balls lost in deep rough, and there was no score to keep. He got the exercise—he took more swings at the driving range than anyone would take in eighteen holes on a golf course—and he got the occasional satisfaction of a perfect shot, without the crushing dismay that could attend a horrible shot.

Maybe Bellerman would realize that the last thing he wanted to do was waste a morning playing with Kramer.

And yet, when Kramer was back at the range that Friday, he felt vaguely sorry (if more than slightly relieved) that he hadn't heard from the man. He knew how much he'd improved in recent months, hitting every club reasonably well (including, this particular day, the notorious 1-iron), and, of course, it would be different on a golf course, but how different could it be? You had the same clubs to swing, and you tried to make the ball go where you wanted it.

And just suppose he turned out to be good at it. Suppose he was good enough to give Bellerman a game. Suppose, by God, he could beat the man.

Sort of a shame he wasn't going to get the chance . . .

"Good shot," said a familiar voice. "Hit a few like that tomorrow and you'll do just fine. Don't forget, I'm coming for you at six. So remember to take your clubs home when you're done here today. And make sure you've got enough golf balls. Kramer? I'll bet you don't have any golf balls, do you? Ha! Well, buy a dozen. They're accommodating at my club, but they won't hand you a bucketful."

• • •

On the way there, Bellerman told him he'd read about Japanese golfers who spent all their time on driving ranges and putting greens. "Practicing for a day that never comes," he said. "It's the cost of land there. It's scarce, so there aren't many golf courses, and club dues and greens fees are prohibitive unless you're in top management. Actually, the driving-range golfers do get to play when they're on vacation. They'll go to an all-inclusive resort in Hawaii or the Caribbean and play thirty-six holes a day for a solid week, then go home and spend the rest of the year in a cage, hitting balls off a tee. Well, today's your vacation, Kramer, and you don't have to cross an ocean. All you have to do is tee up and hit the ball."

It was a nightmare.

And it began on the very first tee. Bellerman went first, hitting a shot that wouldn't get him in trouble, maybe 150 yards down the fairway with a little fade at the end that took some of the distance off it.

Then it was Kramer's turn, and he placed a brand-new Titleist on a brand-new yellow tee and drew his Big Bertha from his bag. He settled himself, rocking to get his cleated feet properly planted, and addressed the ball, telling himself not to kill it, just to meet it solidly. But he must have been too eager to see where the ball went, because he looked up prematurely, topping the ball. That happened occasionally at Chelsea Piers, and the result was generally a grounder. This time, however, he really topped the thing, and it caromed up into the air like a Baltimore chop in baseball, coming to earth perhaps a hundred feet away, right where a shortstop would have had an effortless time gathering it in.

Bellerman didn't laugh. And that was worse, somehow, than if he had.

·   ·   ·

By the third hole, Kramer was just waiting for it to be over. He'd taken an 8 on the first hole and a 9 on the second, and at this rate he seemed likely to wind up with a score somewhere north of 150 for the eighteen holes Bellerman intended for them to play. That meant, he calculated, around 130 strokes to go, 130 more swings of one club or another. He could just go through it, a stroke at a time, and then it would be over, and he would never have to go through anything like this again.

"Good shot!" Bellerman said when Kramer's fourth shot on 3, with his trusty niblick, actually hit the green and stayed there. "That's the thing about this game, Kramer. I can four-putt a green, then shank my drive and put my second shot in a bunker, but one good shot and everything feels right. Isn't it a good feeling?"

It was, sort of, but he knew it wouldn't last, and it had begun to fade by the time he reached the green, putter in hand. He was some thirty feet from the cup, and his first putt died halfway there, and he overcompensated with his second, and, well, never mind. He took a 10 on the hole.

"Still," Bellerman said as they approached the next tee, "that was a hell of an approach shot. That was a 9-iron, right?"

"An 8."

"Oh? I'd probably have used a 9. Still, it worked out for you, didn't it?"

·   ·   ·

By the end of the seventh hole, he'd lost four of his new golf balls. Two were in the water on 6, out of anybody's reach, and one was in the woods on 5, where it would take sharper eyes than his or Bellerman's to spot it. And another was somewhere in the rough on 7; he saw it drop, saw it land, walked right to the goddamn thing, and couldn't find it. It was as if the earth had swallowed it, and he only wished it would do the same for him.

On the eighth hole, the head of his Big Bertha driver dug a trench in the earth behind the teed-up golf ball, and the ball itself tumbled off the tee and managed to roll three feet before coming to rest. "I don't think we'll count that one," Bellerman was saying, but he stopped when Kramer lost it and, enraged, swung the club at a convenient tree. That was the end of the club, if not quite the end of the tree, and Kramer stood there looking at the ruined driver, embarrassed not only by what he'd done but by the unseemly feeling of satisfaction that stirred him.

"Probably not a bad idea to use the 2-wood off the tee," Bellerman said gently. "You gain in accuracy what you sacrifice in distance. Hey, you're not doing so bad, Kramer. This is real-world golf. Nobody said it was going to be easy."

• • •

Nor did it get easier. The good shots, fewer and further between as the day wore on, were no longer even momentarily satisfying; Kramer was all too aware that they were just a brief interruption to the parade of bad shots. He used his brassie off the tee, and every time he drew it from the bag it was a silent rebuke for what he'd done to his driver. At least he didn't get mad at his brassie. He hit the ball—never terribly well—and returned it to his bag, and went off to look for the ball, and, if he found it, hit it again with something else.

On the sixteenth hole, a 140-yard par 3 on which he'd miraculously hit the well-protected green with his tee shot, his putter betrayed him. He'd brought both putters, of course, had in fact brought every club he owned, and he was using the antique wooden-shafted club, the one that might have been used at St. Andrews.

He stood over the ball. The cup was eight feet away, and if he could sink this putt, he'd have a birdie. A birdie! He'd been writing down 7s and 8s and 9s, he'd carded a hideous 14 on one endless hole, but if he could actually sink this putt—

It took him six putts to get the ball in the hole.

He couldn't believe what was happening. In his hands, the trusty putter turned into a length of rope, a strand of limp spaghetti, a snake. He poked the ball past the cup, wide of the cup, short of the cup, every-damn-where but into the cup. Bellerman tried to concede the fifth putt—"Close enough, man. Pick it up"—but Kramer stubbornly putted again, and missed again, and something snapped.

And not just within him. The graceful wooden shaft of the old putter snapped when he broke it over his knee.

· · ·

The last two holes were relatively uneventful. None of his shots were good, but neither were they disastrous. He drove with his brassie, and each time kept the ball on the fairway. He took four putts on 17 and three on 18, using the putter that matched his other irons. He didn't utter a word during the last two holes, just playing doggedly, and Bellerman didn't say anything, either.

They didn't talk much on the way back to the city, either. Bellerman tried a couple of times, but gave it up when Kramer failed to respond. Kramer closed his eyes, replaying a hole in his mind, and the next thing he knew they had reached his house. He got his clubs from the trunk.

"I know it was a rough day for you," Bellerman said. "What can I say? Welcome to the real world, Kramer. You can get that putter repaired, you know."

Kramer didn't say anything.

"There are craftsmen who fit old clubs with new wooden shafts. It's not cheap, but it's worth it. Look, you played real golf today. This was the genuine article. Next time it'll come a lot easier."

Next time?

"And before you know it, you'll be hooked. You'll see." A hand on Kramer's shoulder. "I'll let you be, buddy. Grab a shower, get yourself some rest. We'll do this again."

• • •

That was Saturday.

Sunday he stayed in and watched sports on TV. There was golf on one channel, tennis on another. Ordinarily, he much preferred watching golf, but this day, understandably enough, it got on his nerves. He kept switching back and forth between the two channels and was grateful when they were both done and he could watch *60 Minutes* instead.

Monday he went to the gym, warmed up on the elliptical trainer, then put in his time on the treadmill. There were runners, some of them men as old as he, some of them older, who entered the New York Road Runners races in Central Park, trying to beat others in their age group, trying to improve their times from one race to the next, trying to up their mileage and complete a marathon. That was fine for them, and he could applaud their efforts, but no one would fault a man who ran just for exercise, no one would argue that he wasn't doing it right if he never took it outside of the gym.

Tuesday he went to the batting cage and took his cuts. He hit some balls well and missed some of them entirely, but he wasn't so invested in results as to lose his temper with himself or his equipment. He never had the impulse to slam his bat against an unyielding metal post or smash it over his knee. And he never for a moment saw his activity as a second-rate and laughable substitute for joining a team and playing baseball in the park.

Wednesday he went to the gun club, Thursday to the gym again, this time to lift weights. And Friday found him at the driving range at Chelsea Piers.

He hadn't yet replaced his Big Bertha. It would be easy enough to do—one Big Bertha was essentially indistinguishable from the next—but he hadn't yet had the heart for it. He hit his drives with his 2-wood, as he'd done on the course, hit a dozen balls with it, then continued to work his way through his bag of clubs and through two buckets of balls.

It wasn't the same.

Memories of the previous Saturday kept getting in the way. "The wonderful thing about golf," Bellerman had assured him, "is the way memory improves it. You remember the good shots and forget the bad. I suppose that's one of the things that keeps us coming back."

Wrong, dead wrong. He'd already forgotten the handful of good shots he'd managed to achieve, while the awful ones crowded his memory and got in the way of his practice today.

He couldn't take a club from his bag without recalling just how horribly he'd topped or sliced or shanked a shot with it. His mashie, which he'd hit solidly on 12, only to send the ball thirty yards past the damned green. His 3-iron, which he'd used from the rough, visualizing a perfect shot to the green between a pair of towering trees. And, of course, the ball had struck one tree dead center, rebounding so that it left him further from the hole than he'd started, but with the same shot through the trees. Second time around, he'd hit the other tree . . .

"Want to go out tomorrow?"

Bellerman, damn him. He drew a breath, forced himself to be civil. "No," he said. "Thanks, but I can't make it tomorrow."

"You should, you know. Kid gets thrown from a horse, best thing he can do is get right back on him."

And get thrown again?

"You obviously love the game, Kramer. Otherwise you wouldn't be over here after a day like the one you had Saturday. But don't try to make this take the place of the real thing. You've had a taste of golf and you want to keep at it, you know? Say, did you find somebody to put a new shaft on that putter?"

"Not yet."

"Well, you will. Are you sure you can't make it tomorrow? Well, then, maybe next week."

• • •

The weekend passed. Monday he ran on the treadmill, and afterward he went online and ordered a new Big Bertha driver. Tuesday he had a good session at the batting cage, and afterward he took his putter to an elderly German gentleman somewhere on the border of Brooklyn and Queens who repaired old golf clubs and fishing rods in his basement workshop. The price was high, more than he'd originally paid for the club, but it was worth it and more if it could erase the evidence of his bad temper.

Wednesday he went to the gun club. He fired the deer rifle and the .22 at his usual targets, then took a break and sipped a cup of coffee. The weight machines tomorrow, he thought, and then the driving range on Friday, and Bellerman would show up, dammit, and what was he going to do about that, anyway?

The real world. There were, he supposed, fellow members of the gun club who hunted. Had country places in Jersey or Pennsylvania, say, and tried to get a buck in deer season, or a brace of pheasant at the appropriate time. But the majority of members, he was sure, just came to practice marksmanship. They didn't think of their activity as a pale substitute for the real thing, and neither did anybody else.

He went back to practice with the Magnum, selected his usual paper target. Then something made him switch to a target he'd seen used by other members—law enforcement personnel, for the most part. The target was a male silhouette, gun in hand.

It was strange at first. He'd always aimed at a bull's-eye target, and now he was aiming at a human outline. It, too, had a series of concentric circles, centered upon the figure's heart, so you could see just how close you came. And it wasn't a person at all, it was just a piece of paper, but it still took a little getting used to.

And an odd thing happened. *Welcome to the real world,* said a voice in his head, and it was recognizable, that voice. It was Bellerman's voice, and he steadied the big handgun and squeezed off a shot, and the gun bucked satisfyingly in his hand, and the bullet found its mark in the silhouette.

He kept hearing Bellerman's voice in his head, and the two-dimensional generic silhouette began assuming three-dimensional form in his mind, and the face began wearing Bellerman's features.

He spent a longer time than usual at the range, and his hand and forearm ached by the time he was done. The real world, he thought. The real world indeed.

He returned the rifle and the target pistol to his locker. No one noticed that he walked out with the Magnum tucked into the waistband of his trousers, and the remainder of a box of shells in his pocket.

Would Bellerman show up again at the driving range Friday?

Perhaps not. Perhaps the man would have gotten the message by then and would leave him alone, having done what he could to ruin Kramer's life.

But somehow Kramer doubted it. Bellerman was no quitter. He'd be there again, with the same abrasive drawl, the same smile that was never far from a sneer. The same invitation to a round of Saturday golf, which this time Kramer would accept.

Only this time there'd be something new in his bag. And, on one of the more remote holes at Bellerman's club, Kramer would bring out not his brassie or his mashie or his niblick, not his sand wedge, not his (and God's) 1-iron, but a .357 Magnum revolver, cleaned and loaded and ready.

Welcome to the real world, Bellerman!

THE MAN WHO DIDN'T PLAY GOLF

Simon Brett

Leonard Wensam thought he had been very clever. Whenever his wife, Amanda, asked him how he'd spent his Thursday, he'd start to tell her about the round of golf he'd played up at the Westmacott Golf Club. That invariably shut her up. And soon she stopped asking.

When he'd first started talking about golf, when he'd spent all that money on a complete set of clubs in a red and white leather bag that zipped over the top, Amanda had tried to show an interest. She'd bought her husband a golf book that Christmas, and some little knickknack to hold tees for his birthday. But she couldn't sustain the illusion of showing an interest for long.

Theirs was a marriage that ticked over all right. At thirty-six, Amanda was fifteen years younger than her husband. She might have liked children, but Leonard had never been keen on the idea, and as usual his view was the one that counted. What he wanted from his wife was regular sex and a decorative presence at business functions. Leonard Wensam didn't really like women, preferring the rough shallow heartiness of male company. He thought husbands should have secrets from their wives.

And Amanda believed in wives having secrets from their husbands. One of the secrets she kept from Leonard was the fact that, as she had got to know him better during the early months of their marriage, she had found that she didn't like him very much. And as he got older and chubbier, she found she liked him less and less.

But the marriage ticked over all right.

And she'd read in a magazine that husbands and wives having different hobbies was the recipe for a successful relationship. Amanda sang in a local choir, and Leonard, who was immune to any form of classical music, never considered attending any of her concerts. So she felt no obligation to attend any of his tournaments at the Westmacott Golf Club.

Neither did Leonard ever ask her how the concerts had gone, so, having suffered an excruciating hour of tedium the first time she asked him how his round of golf had gone, Amanda subsequently felt no guilt about never again even making the inquiry. As the magazine had said, it was husbands and wives pursuing different interests that kept marriages alive. Amanda felt reasonably happy with the arrangement.

It was doubtful that she would have felt quite as happy had she known from the start the interest that her husband was actually pursuing: a thirty-nine-year-old red-haired divorcée called Juliette. Every Thursday, when Leonard Wensam said he was playing a round, he was, in fact, playing around.

He had semiretired from the accountancy business he had inherited from his father. With no perceptible effort on Leonard's part, the firm had grown satisfactorily over the years and made him a wealthy man. When his rapidly aging mother

died, he would be even wealthier. He could afford to buy anything he wanted, and could have afforded to buy Amanda anything she wanted too. But it was not in Leonard's nature to be
overgenerous, so he bought very little for either himself or his
wife. He was, in fact, extremely mean.

Even Juliette was becoming aware of this shortcoming in
her older lover. In the early days, when he had been trying to
winkle his way into her bed, Leonard had lunched Juliette lav-
ishly at up-market restaurants, but increasingly he abandoned
this expensive foreplay in favor of bringing sandwiches and a
bottle of wine round to her place. Not liking this diminution
of her pampering, the woman he didn't play golf with on
Thursdays looked forward to the moment when she would
dump Leonard. But she was in no hurry. She liked sex, she
liked the attentions of a man—even a man as mean as this
one—and she was not going to get rid of him until she had a
successor firmly in place.

Leonard was unaware of these thoughts going through his
mistress's mind. He was too self-centered to be aware of the
thoughts going through any mind but his own. He thought he
had his life well organized—financial sufficiency, the secure
marriage, the "bit on the side."

He was getting a bit fat, true. Last time he'd been to the
quack he'd been told he ought to take more exercise. And
that was something he intended to do . . . when he got round
to it.

Amanda had even once observed that Leonard's regular
golf did not seem to be making him any fitter. But he had
avoided the moment of potential embarrassment by the deft
assertion that golfers needed to cultivate a low center of gravity. He hadn't put on weight; he had just redistributed muscle.

And Amanda appeared to accept that lie as readily as she had accepted all the others.

Oh yes, Leonard Wensam thought he had been very clever.

• • •

It was his mother's death that provided the first potential threat to his nice cozy little setup. The news was phoned through from the nursing home one Thursday morning, when Amanda was alone in the house. She didn't expect Leonard to be emotionally affected by his bereavement, but, uncaring though he undoubtedly was, she knew he wouldn't want to be seen as uncaring by other family members. He needed to be told quickly, so that he could start dutifully phoning round and making funeral arrangements. Leonard never took his cell phone with him on Thursdays ("the one day a week when I can really forget about the office"), and the information was not the kind that could be passed on in a message. So Amanda decided she would have to go up to the Westmacott Golf Club in person to break the sad news to her husband.

Though she had driven past the entrance many times, she had never been inside the grounds. Many of her friends used to walk up there (the club permitted that, so long as the walkers kept off the fairways), and in one of his moments of good resolution about getting fitter, Leonard had even spoken of exercising there. But that was before he started the golf. Amanda felt strange being in a venue that must be so familiar to her husband, so much a part of his life. She parked amid the rows of Jaguars, BMWs and Mercedes in front of the high mock-Tudor clubhouse, and looked around for someone who might know Leonard's whereabouts. A sign reading "Floyd Carter, Professional" seemed the most promising starting point. The young boy who was minding the shop said that Floyd was out on the practice greens and pointed Amanda toward a tall, rangy figure of about forty hunched over a putt. He had a row of six balls in front of him, and he moved along, slotting in each one with unerring accuracy.

As the last ball perched on the edge of the crowded hole, the professional looked up at her, squinting against the sunshine. He had strong teeth and his face was tanned, revealing as it relaxed a tracery of white lines around his bright blue eyes.

"You do that very well," said Amanda.

"I've practiced it a few times." The voice had a slight antipodean twang. "I can usually hit the target." He grinned easily. "What can I do for you, madam? You want to arrange a lesson?"

"No. I'm Mrs. Wensam." The name didn't appear to mean anything to him. "I'm looking for my husband. Mr. Wensam," she added unnecessarily.

The second name didn't prompt any more recognition than the first.

"My husband's a member here. He plays a round every Thursday."

"Wensam?" Floyd Carter shook his head. "No member of the name of Wensam here."

Amanda couldn't believe what she was hearing. Seeming aware of the potential ramifications of what he'd just said, Floyd Carter immediately went to the defense of a fellow male. "You probably got the name of the club wrong. A lot of other clubs around. Maybe he plays at one of them?"

"I know it's the Westmacott Golf Club. That's the one he always talks about."

The professional gave an easy shrug of his shoulders.

"Well, I know the names of all the members—even the mid-week hackers who spray balls all over the course—and I tell you, not one of them is called Wensam." Still, in the cause of male solidarity, he added tentatively, "Maybe he plays under a false name?"

"Why should he do that?"

"There are a lot of members whose golf's so bad they *should* play under false names."

In spite of herself, Amanda smiled. There was something very engaging about Floyd Carter. She had to force a bit of hauteur into her voice as she said, "I can't imagine my husband ever using a false name for any reason. He's not deceitful."

But even as she said the words, Amanda Wensam wondered whether she was telling the truth.

She watched as the professional gathered up his golf balls and again laid them out in a line in front of him. "Going to get them all down the hole again?" she asked.

"No, done enough putting for today. Have a go at that now. Just a few trick shots." He pointed to the other side of the practice green where a wooden arrow on a pole pointed toward the first tee.

Selecting another club from his bag, Floyd Carter moved forward to the first ball. An effortless flick sent it up to clatter against the arrow. Before it hit the ground, the second ball was in flight. Then the third, fourth, fifth, sixth hit the arrow and bounced back.

"Can you do that every time?" asked Amanda breathlessly.

Floyd Carter gave a wry, self-deprecating smile. "Not every time, no. Can't guarantee it." His grin became more confident. "Often, though."

● ● ●

The following morning, Amanda woke up earlier than Leonard. Now she came to think of it, he did always seem particularly sleepy on a Thursday night. Previously, she'd put it down to the physical stresses of a round of golf. Now, though . . .

Amanda went down to the garage and put on the light. She rarely drove Leonard's Lexus, but he did grudgingly allow her a spare key "for emergencies." She opened the boot.

The red and white leather golf bag lay there, gleaming, pristine, clean. The clubs revealed when she unzipped the top looked equally unscarred by ball or divot. And that wasn't just the result of post-round cleaning; the cellophane was still tight about their heads. The whole set could have been returned to the shop whence it was bought and the owners could not have refused to refund the money. Everything was as new. Nothing had ever been used.

Amanda was pensive as she closed the car boot. And a plan began to form in her head. A plan that would provide a very effective revenge on her errant husband.

●   ●   ●

Leonard was jaunty as he returned home from the office one Wednesday a few weeks later. He had had a very cheering meeting with his solicitor that afternoon. Though always knowing that his mother had been left wealthy by his father's death, he had only just become aware of how much her judicious investments had increased his inheritance. Leonard Wensam would soon be a very rich man indeed. This knowledge gave him enormous satisfaction. There was nothing he wanted to buy with his newfound wealth; he just liked the idea of all that money sitting there. His.

When he walked in, Leonard was surprised to find a visitor in the house. He knew that Amanda occasionally invited her female friends for tea and, though they interested him not at all, he was quite capable of being polite to them.

But it was the first time he'd found a tall, tanned young man rising from the sofa to greet him in his own sitting room.

"Leonard, I'd like you to meet Floyd Carter."

"Hello," he said, mystified, as he shook the firm, tanned hand.

"Floyd's wife sings in the choir with me, and I thought you'd love to meet him . . . because he's terribly interested in golf too."

"Ah." Leonard nodded at his wife's words, playing for time. He sensed trouble.

"In fact," Amanda went on, "Floyd's the professional at Westmacott Golf Club. But I don't need to tell you that, do I, Leonard?"

"No. Of course we've met," her husband mumbled uncomfortably.

There was a long silence. Amanda looked excited, almost triumphant, waiting to see her plotting come to fruition.

Then, to her apparent amazement, Floyd Carter said, "Too right. Of course I know Len."

Leonard gleefully watched the dismay grow in his wife's face during the ensuing conversation. She tried to hide it, but without complete success. Amanda had set up this interview, he knew, to show him up. The Westmacott Golf Club professional, she had calculated, would be bound to expose her husband's lies. But she seemed not to have reckoned with the enduring strength of male solidarity. Women might shop errant husbands to their wronged wives; but no man would ever behave like that to a fellowman. The masculine reaction to hearing of another man's infidelity was always, "Good on you, mate . . . you dirty dog. Anyway, it's not my business."

Aware of his strength, Leonard pushed the conversation even deeper into golf, for the sheer pleasure of watching Amanda's discomfiture grow. He initiated discussion with Floyd Carter on the idiosyncrasies of golf club members whose names he'd only just invented. He summoned up Woffles Rimington, who kept a liter of whiskey in his golf bag and had always emptied it by the end of the round; Tugboat Clark, who was so rich that he bribed all his opponents to lose to him; and Roly Crooke-Winterburn, who'd had to leave the club after being found bunkered in a compromising position with the lady captain.

As each of these fictional figures emerged from Leonard Wensam's lips, Floyd Carter provided further recollections of their quirks and misdemeanors. The two men laughed a lot, as Amanda looked coldly on.

Leonard's invention didn't stop at the names of golfers; he let it spread into golfing terms too, confident that Floyd still wasn't going to show him up.

So, for example, when the professional said, "I always think the fourteenth is an easy par. I can usually reckon on an eagle there," Leonard riposted gleefully, "Oh, I'm afraid I usually get a pelican."

Or when Floyd Carter recommended the use of a spoon to get out of the kidney-shaped bunker at the back of the seventh green, Leonard confessed that he got his best results with a knife and fork.

And Floyd's assertion that he always used a 5-iron and re-duced backswing to guarantee getting over the water hazard at the short third was greeted by the news that Leonard had been remarkably successful using a 17-aluminum and a limp wrist.

He hadn't a clue what he was talking about, but he felt supremely confident. Whatever nonsense he spouted, the professional would play along. And Amanda was looking more uncomfortable by the minute. Her little plan had become horribly derailed. And there was all that money coming from his mother. Leonard Wensam could hardly prevent himself chortling with glee.

But he exercised control until, leaving a fuming Amanda in the sitting room, he saw Floyd Carter out to his car. On the driveway, in the summer evening dusk, Leonard guffawed heartily. Everything was working out so wonderfully well for him.

Floyd joined in the laughter but stopped before his host did. "That was all right tonight," he said, "but a bit risky."

"Not at all." Leonard chuckled on. "Amanda doesn't know the tiniest thing about golf—or anything else, come to that. She may suspect she's being sent up, but she can't prove it."

"Maybe not. And you're all right with me, I'm on your side. Could be awkward, though, if your alibi was questioned in the company of other, less sympathetic golfers."

Leonard, seeing the sense of that, stopped laughing. "You have a point." He looked into the professional's honest, friendly face. "Have you got some suggestions as to what I should do, Floyd?"

"I think you ought to learn a bit about golf."

"But I have no interest in the game. I don't want to take it up."

"I know that, and I'm not suggesting you should. But if you knew the rudiments, knew enough of the proper jargon, then you could hold a conversation with other golfers without raising any suspicions. Your alibi would more likely be water-tight then."

Leonard nodded slowly. "That would make sense. So how am I going to learn?"

"I'd be very happy to take you round the course, Len, show you what's what. Half a day and you'll have picked up the essentials."

"That's incredibly generous. Why are you prepared to do this for me?"

Floyd Carter smiled the duplicitous smile that men have used over the centuries to exclude women from their lives. With a roguish slap to Leonard's shoulder, he said, "We chaps have got to stick together, eh?"

• • •

Though his offer had been genuine, the professional was heavily booked with tournaments and lessons, so the first available date was a Thursday morning a couple of weeks after their first meeting.

This was fine by Leonard. He even felt a glow of right-eousness when, informing Amanda that he'd be off playing golf, he realized he was telling the truth. Juliette was left a message that he wouldn't be able to join her until the after-noon of that day. "After lunch," he said, planning to have something to eat on his own and then exact his sexual sat-isfaction without even the outlay of sandwiches and wine.

Seven o'clock seemed a rather early start, but Floyd was the one who knew about golf, so Leonard turned up on time.

"Better now," said the professional, greeting Leonard as he emerged from his Lexus, "before the hordes of incompetents start their rounds. I tell you, it's like being on a rifle range out there once that lot get going—balls flying in every direction. You see, you only get the quality players here Fridays, Saturdays and Sundays. Midweek it's the rubbish—the retired, the learners—and the women."

The contempt he put into the last word got its predictable knee-jerk chuckle from Leonard, and the golfing virgin moved round to remove his virgin clubs from the car boot.

"You won't need those, Len. I'll lend you a set when we actually start playing. But first I just want to take you through a few of the technical terms and get you familiar with the Westmacott course."

In the pro shop, Floyd Carter outlined the basics. He showed Leonard the different clubs and explained the situations in which each should be used, how the angle of each clubface affected the trajectory of the ball. "Thing to remember is that the numbering starts from the vertical. The nearer the clubface is to a right angle from the ground, the lower its number will be. Got that?"

"I think so," Leonard replied uncertainly.

"Don't worry about the detail. The clubs have got numbers on them, anyway. You can't go far wrong." The professional then went through a few of the basic golfing terms, so that his pupil could tell the tee from the green and the rough from the fairway. Floyd did a little on the etiquette of the game, and concluded, "Well, I think that's about it. All you need to know. The next important thing to do is—"

He stopped himself, and a hand shot up to his mouth in alarm. "Ooh, Len, something I should have told you. More

than etiquette—it's a safety measure too. Do you know what
'Fore?' means?"

"For? Well, yes, obviously. It means sort of 'on behalf of.'"

"No. 'Fore' with an 'e.' You must know what that means in
a golfing context."

"I'm afraid I don't."

"It's incredibly important. Not knowing the meaning of
'Fore!' could cause you the most terrible problems."

And Floyd Carter told Leonard Wensam what "Fore!"
meant.

The older man nodded. "Right, with you. Now, do we start
playing a round?"

"Not yet. In fact, you don't need to play a whole round at
all. With a complete novice, that'll take forever. No, I'll show
you the basics—how you hold the club and so on—when you
come back."

"When I come back? Where am I going?"

"Ah, you're about to do the most important bit of your induction. You're going to walk round the entire course."

"Without any clubs?"

"Too right. Without any clubs. You see, you really must
know the geography of all the Westmacott holes. Then you
can sound authoritative when other golfers ask questions like,
'You know that clump of gorse halfway down the fairway on
the fourth?'"

"But, Floyd, shouldn't I also sound authoritative when
they ask me what stroke I used to get over that clump of gorse
halfway down the fairway on the fourth?"

"No worries about that. The golfer hasn't been born who
cares what stroke anyone else played. They only wanted to tell
you what stroke they played themselves. That's why what

you're doing today is so easy. You need the bare minimum of information to pass as a golfer, because with golfers you don't have to say much. There'll always be someone present who wants to tell you about *his* round."

The professional reached to the counter for a sketch map. "Now, this shows you the layout of the course. As you see, the fairways zigzag all over the place. What I want you to do is start at the number 1 tee and walk from tee to hole, tee to hole, all the way round until you get to the eighteenth green, then come back and find me."

"Won't I get in the way of the golfers?"

"No, you'll be ahead of most of them. And, since you're not playing, you'll go round a lot quicker than they will. Go on, Len, it always works."

"What always works?"

Floyd Carter grinned mischievously. "My instant half-day induction course. Don't imagine you're the only man who uses golf as an alibi. You'd be surprised how many little wives are out there in blissful ignorance of the fact that their husbands aren't playing golf."

On a wave of complicit masculine laughter, Leonard Wensam set off on his walk around Westmacott Golf Club.

• • •

It was a bright summer morning, and Leonard felt good. He was making his Thursday alibi absolutely impregnable against Amanda's suspicions. And he was going to spend the afternoon in the arms of Juliette, telling her to do a variety of particularly enjoyable things to him.

What's more, all that money from his mother would soon be his. Life was excellent.

As he crisscrossed the course along the fairways, Leonard became vaguely aware of golfers starting their rounds. As Floyd had promised, there was very little competence on display. Balls flew in every direction, there were sounds of turf-sized divots being dug up, constant cries of "Sorry!" and "Fore!"

Leonard felt rather superior. Thanks to Floyd Carter, he knew exactly what "Fore!" meant, and each time he heard it, he obeyed the command.

The fifteenth fairway ran alongside the fourth, where there grew the famous clump of gorse. Leonard Wensam was in the rough of the fifteenth, feeling on top of the world, when he heard the shout of "Fore!" He did exactly as he had been instructed.

Then he was hit on the temple by a flying golf ball, and died.

As a golfer might have put it, Leonard Wensam "went out" in a state of euphoria. Sadly, he "came in" in an ambulance.

• • •

The coroner was very regretful about the appalling accident which had taken away "a man in the prime of life, depriving his young wife of a companion, helpmeet and breadwinner." The coroner recommended greater vigilance by walkers who took advantage of the grounds of the Westmacott Golf Club, and suggested that more strongly worded warning notices should be erected on the course.

But there was a note of contempt—almost of "served him right"—in the way he spoke of Leonard Wensam. The coroner, himself an avid golfer, could not understand people who did not share his obsession. And the deceased had clearly had no interest at all in the game. He had never been seen at the Westmacott Golf Club by any of the members, having only gone up there on the day of his death in the cause of fitness.

"And just walking isn't going to make anyone fit," said the coroner. "You need a few good rounds of golf to achieve that."

The verdict of "accidental death" was a foregone conclusion.

But the coroner made it sound as if such a fate was only just deserts for a man who didn't play golf.

He also stressed the point that no blame should attach to the unfortunate novice golfer who had shouted "Fore!" and played his shot immediately prior to Wensam's death. The player had been aiming at the fourth green; he couldn't even have seen his victim in the middle of the fifteenth fairway. The young man should not let this regrettable incident put him off playing the fine game of golf. He should blank it out from his memory.

But the young man, wracked with guilt, found such oblivion difficult to achieve. He even asked the Westmacott professional what he could do to make amends for the tragic incident that he had caused.

The professional recommended that he should move his right hand a little further down the shaft of the club.

• • •

Floyd Carter himself didn't feel any guilt. The moment he fell in love with Amanda Wensam, when he first saw her on the practice green, he knew that something was going to have to be done. And he was very happy to play his part in the plan she formulated.

He'd used her spare key to remove the red and white leather bag of clubs from the Lexus, so that after his death Leonard no longer had any connection with the game of golf. And Floyd later sold the set, as new, in the pro shop. Which made him a nice little profit.

But nothing like the profit he made when he married Amanda and took his share of everything she had inherited under her late husband's will. (It was his first marriage; Floyd's wife in the choir had been one of Amanda's necessary inventions.)

The will's provisions left nothing to Juliette, who, knowing how tightfisted Leonard Wensam had always been, was unsurprised. Anyway, she had since met another rich man, who was more prepared to shower his largesse on a sexy red-haired mistress, so Juliette was fine.

Floyd Carter had left the catapult in the middle of the clump of gorse on the fourth fairway as soon as he had used it to propel the fatal missile at Leonard's head. Amanda, wide-eyed in her confidence in his skills, had expected him to use a golf club to send the ball, but Floyd knew better. Even he couldn't guarantee to deliver a mortal blow to a potentially moving human target at twenty meters. No professional was that good.

Floyd Carter was good by most standards, but when he saw his and Amanda's first son pick up a golf club at the age of three, he reckoned they had a potential world number one on their hands.

So, while Amanda produced more wonderful babies, Floyd set out to teach their son everything he knew about the magnificent game of golf.

Everything, with the exception of a piece of misinformation he'd fed Leonard Wensam. He didn't tell his son that the shouted instruction "Fore!" means "Move immediately to the middle of the fairway!"

SPITTIN IRON

Ken Bruen

ACTION TAKES PLACE IN INTERROGATION ROOM. WE ONLY SEE ONE MAN, SITTING AT A BATTERED TABLE. HE LOOKS SERIOUSLY WORN, BUT WITH ATTITUDE. THE ONLY VOICE WE HEAR IS HIS.

I hate fuckin' golf, I hate fucking golfers, I hate a whole mess of shit but golf really tops the list. You want to set me off? Light that fuse I got up my ass, all you gotta do is, like, mention . . . say, a 9-iron, that'll do it, I'll have you eat the goddamn thing.

Yada yada.

. . . like you give a flying rat's?

But you know what, gimme a cigarette, decent cup of java, I'll tell you why, 'cos then we'll have us what's called Deal City. You want me to sign that confession, then you gotta hear me out.

Sound of Zippo cranking.

Then,

Deep inhale.

To . . . long inhale of breath.

Man, that's fine.

Two days they had me in county lockup, not one goddamn smoke. They had a spic in there, one of the homies, with the Crip colors? The pack of Marlboros tucked under his rolled-up sleeve, Jimmy Dean, right?

I ask him for one, real polite and all, go, "Shoot me a smoke, bro."

Would he fuck? . . . Hard-ass punk gangsta, looks at me like I'm something he trailed on his Converse, unlaced of course. What's with that shit?

He goes, blowing me off, "No habla inglés."

Giving me the smirk, the dead eye. They practice that, yeah, in front of the mirror, in their mama's mirror, pimpin' and preening, get that nine-yard down right. But you know, I been in Tijuana, got me some of the lingo and a dose of the clap. I ask him a second time, making the nicotine motion, using some nice spic manners, and he snorts, "No way, José."

I like to play, long as it's not golf. You know what I'm saying, you know where I'm going here, buddy?

Sound of brief chuckle.

I put his head in the toilet, ram that sucker in among the turds, the crap, hasn't been flushed since Reagan was president.

Pause.

He's thrashing around in there, I get his pants down, let him figger I'm gonna bitch him. I got him so far in the bowl, the Marlboros shook loose, yeah, soaked in piss and stuff, wouldn't light worth a damn. What are you gonna do? You go with the flow, no pun there, partner. I was thinking, what's that fancy word? Irony, that it?

No answer.

You don't say a whole lot I guess you want the confession signed, get your ass on outta here, am I right? Grab yourself a cold one. Tell you what, buddy, have one for me, wash it down with some Maker's Mark. Dude, I love that stuff. Yo man, you got a little smile burning there, you're thinking, going to be a time before I get to have me a cold one. Okay, time to fess, yeah? I used to be a caddie. I'm not shitting you. Hauled them clubs for the fat cats, took shit from lard asses like you wouldn't believe, me and Ellroy, you know the mystery guy? Don't read, huh? Like, who's got the time, me neither. The *National Enquirer,* I like that, get down in the trash, out them fuckers, gives me a rush.

Zippo cranks again, twice.

Getting a little low on gas there, pal. So like, after being a caddie, I swore I'd, like, never have me no connection to golf again and then my main man, Sean, yeah, the dead guy, we celled down in Dade County, had my back and those micks, man, they're crazy mothers. Little red-haired bastard, couldn't go out in the sun and it was hot there, bro, in every sense. He had that Irish face, like a ghost, and freckles, a spade made fun of him. The runt, he gets a shiv, tears that nigger from sternum to scrotum in one swipe. SNS we called it. We learned the words from the Discovery Channel. You know my rep, I've done some bad shit, but this mick, he was the craziest fuck I ever ran across. He'd gotten a five-year jolt for car theft, said to me,

"I like feckin cars."

Thing is, he liked to drink, too, that Jameson gig. So he'd load up on that, grab a car, and the cops, they grabbed his ass or as he'd say, me arse. The judge was going fairly easy on him, and the mad fuck, he goes,

"You talking to me?"

He loved De Niro, looked a little like him, too, and the judge, who was a movie buff, rammed five hard on his jacket.

Sean goes,

"Thanks a lot, yah cunt."

Balls? The guy had cojones big as the British Isles.

Reading, what's with the Irish and that?

He had a battered copy of some dude called, lemme see, Blake . . . no, Beckett, and his nose always stuck in there when he was making hooch. The stuff they brew, blind you. He'd quote the guy to me and I heard it so often, I know the guy my own self. How weird is that?

I don't do buddies. I'm a lone wolf—learned that when I was a caddie, no one to watch your back. You hear this horseshit about the comradery of caddies, the fuckin' downtrodden hooking up. What a crock. You get a guy, he's hauling the bag for some suit and the guy slips him a couple of bucks, guess who now owns his ass? But this skinny mick, he got under my radar and he saved my neck one time, so we get to hanging out, walking the yard, him quoting whole chunks of that there Beckett, so I tell him about the golf. The time this CPA tried to get me fired, said I had me an attitude, got my wages docked and a warning.

I got a 9—no, not that nine, a 9-iron—got a real swoosh to it and go over to his house, big ol' colonial heap on the best side of town. Set about rearranging his decor. Fuck came home early, claimed I tried to kill him, one lousy swing I took, had had me a shot of his sauce, a little sour mash I found in his drinks cabinet, so I caught him on the shoulder, did six months on that rap.

Accountants, they got the juice.

The mick is laughing and I go,

"You think that's funny?"

He tells me about their national sport, hurling? A cross between baseball and homicide, says,

"You can be drunk as a fart and swing that piece of wood, you're going to do damage."

Round that time, he began teaching me Irish-English, I ain't kidding.

Sound of barely suppressed laughter.

You're laughing, right? Got some of that mick blood in you, that it? I tell you, God's truth, it's a whole other deal. They twist English till . . . fuck, I dunno, till it sings. That's when he tells me about *spittin iron.*

Means you're seriously pissed, got a rage on you that's murderous. You shoulda heard that skinny guy say it, spittle flying out of his mouth. They have a way with them, them micks. I mean, they're deranged ten ways to Sunday but, like, cool with it. You ever listen to the Floyd? Pink Floyd, of course, my mistake. You cops, what is it, country and western, day of mourning when Garth Brooks hung it up? You should get yourself a copy of that band, get down, bro. Grab some of that good weed from the evidence room, do a tote, expand your horizons. See, you're laughing again, having you a time. Boy, get us some liquor in here, we'd really whoop it up. Anyway, *Dark Side of the Moon,* that's where those micks live, but they don't give a rat's . . . yeah, there's one of them Irishisms right there. Feel free, use it with your old lady, give her a thrill.

And here's the kicker. For such hard bastards, they're real sops at heart. Straight up, who'd have believed it? Sean, his old lady, named Kaitlin, great name or what? He'd given her one of them Irish wedding bands, with the two hands and shit? He's halfway into his first year in the joint and she fucks off with an attorney. Best bit, the attorney plays golf.

Long sigh.

Dumb mother, he adored that woman. The guy was in real

pain about the bitch. Me, I go, "Fuck her," and he went for me, spittin iron so to speak, and I get him cooled off, say,

"Whoa, buddy, bring it down a notch, what do you say? I'm like . . . sorry. I was, like, outta line, okay?"

I don't get it, she's a broad, you know what I'm saying, but the guy, he's lost. The dame has him all fucked-up so I tell him some golf stories, get his mind offa that. Later he told me she's shacked up in North Carolina, fancy house, fancy guy, and he's dying as he tells me.

Me, I don't do drama. I take it real mellow, no biggie, you hearing me? But I gotta tell you, the little guy, he's hurting, and like I said, he's my running buddy. I gotta watch out for him. Those micks, they'll go through medieval shit, and not raise an eyebrow, then a goddamn woman breaks them like piss on the wind. He said to me,

"Malone dies."

Like that's supposed to make an iota of sense.

Did I mention he'd been caught up in the hooch making? Sure, a mick, if there's booze, he's gonna be stuck in it. And there was some ruckus with the White Supremacists. I told him steer clear of those crazies. They got a whole other agenda going, but would he listen?

Would he fuck.

Said,

"No bollix takes me drink."

They got him in the shower. I was shooting eight ball with one of the Crips and they bled him like a pig. Did that hog gig on his ass too. I was let in the infirmary with him, being his cell bro and all. Took the poor bastard near two days to die. He was weeping, going,

"Mate, they stuck their things in me."

I was trying to hush him. He reaches out his mangled hand, yeah, they broke all the bones, and tries to grip mine. Shee-it, I can't be holding no dude's hand, like some kind of pillow biter, but I let him think it was, you know, cool. He whispered,

"Krapp's Last Tape."

Krapp? . . . Like crap?

And asked me to golf with the attorney, I go,

"What the fuck?"

And he smiled, all his teeth nothing but, like, bloodied stumps. He says—tried to say—

"Use the 9, let her see it."

Then made some sort of awful twisted sound, like he was feeling acid in his gut, coughed up a flood of blood and croaked.

The Aryans, come to me, go,

"You down, bro?"

Like, am I gonna make some waves? And I smile, ask,

"Me?"

The guy, big dumb redneck ox, gives me the look, like he's got the Militia behind him, says,

"Bidness, all it is, nothing personal."

Fuck couldn't even pronounce business.

Night before I get my release, I get in his cell. Had me some Drāno, made him drink it, said,

"Only bidness."

And you know, way I see it, he got to be white inside too, cleansed him through and through.

First thing you do when you get out is get shitfaced and get a hooker. I did that till it got lame and then moseyed on down to the Carolinas. Nice country down there, even if they talk kinda funny.

Took me a few days to locate the house, and all the time, I'm running her name in my head . . . *Kaitlin.*

Sunday evening they were home. He arrived round six, the golf clubs on his shoulder. Mr. Sport, looked like he had a few brews with the guys, what is it, they call it? "The nineteenth hole."

I let him go inside, maybe give the missus one, get them relaxed, and then I went in.

She was a looker. After I tied her up, turned my attention to him. He was just recovering consciousness. I'd taken him out with the 9, just under the chin. You've got my ass for the other gig so I'm going down, shit, I know that, so I might as well let you have the rest of it.

I did her in front of him, and you know, I think she got off on it, bit of rough and all.

When I took out the knife, began to hack at her throat, he screamed,

"For the love of God, why, why are you doing this?"

I tried my best imitation of that brogue, went,

"'Cos I'm spittin iron."

HIS MISSION

Christopher Coake

Pete answered Rachel's call on Saturday afternoon; after a bit of small talk she asked him if he wouldn't want to drive out to Clarksville, to meet her for dinner. She told him she knew she hadn't called in forever, but Allen—her husband—was on a mission in Africa, and she was sitting around lonely, and had gotten to feeling bad because they hadn't talked in so long, and they were due for a catch-up sometime, didn't he think so? Hadn't it been a long time?

It had been, Peter figured, over a year. He listened to her naked, dripping wet, crouched beneath the sill of his living room window; he'd left his curtains open and some of the kids in his apartment complex were skateboarding in the parking lot just outside. He looked back toward the open door of the bathroom, where the shower was still running. Steam licked out around the edges of the door, and the dark wet stains of his footprints, spaced wide, arrowed from the tub toward him.

He told Rachel that yes, it had been a long time, and that dinner sometime sounded great. And—because he always did so when he heard Rachel's voice on the other end of the line—

he remembered the two or three nights back in college when they'd been naked together in his room; the taste of her mouth (the hint of strawberry bubble gum); the way her whispers used to tighten into quick, surprised sighs. *Oh, Pete,* she'd say, stretching his name between spinning wheels of lust and panic. He thought of her voice, flat, saying, *Yes;* he remembered a rustle of silk.

"You're sure Maya won't mind?" Rachel asked him now.

Pete hadn't told her yet about Maya; he'd been trying his damnedest to avoid that call. He shifted on his aching calves. His wet hair dripped across his eyes; the phone was slick next to his ear.

"Maya left me," he said. "About a month ago."

"Pete! No!"

"Yeah."

"What happened?"

"Jesus, Rach," he said. "That's a long story."

"But you two—you were so—"

He had to hand it to Rachel. She'd called him, he knew, because she was in some kind of trouble—when things were fine in Rachel-land, he never heard a peep from her. But whatever her trouble, she sounded, now, genuinely shocked. Sorrowful, even. She'd always loved Maya, never realizing (or ignoring, for his sake) Maya's distaste for her. *I swear, Pete, I don't know what you ever saw in that little drip.*

"I'll tell you about it at dinner," he said.

"But is there—do you think—?"

"We're getting divorced," he said. "Soon as the lawyers work it out."

He could picture Rachel: she'd be sitting on her couch next to a stack of balled-up tissues, eyes as pink as the blotches on her cheeks, wearing something shapeless—pajamas, probably, like the ones she'd had in college, with the little blue flowers on them—her feet tucked under her. Thirty years old and she'd look just like a teenager rejected for prom. For a moment— just a short one, but a moment nonetheless—Pete was glad. Never mind her dumbfuck husband, Allen, and whatever clumsy thing he'd done to her feelings. Maya leaving Pete— that was real trouble. He tried to imagine sitting across from Rachel at dinner, telling her the ugly parts: *So then I told Maya she was a selfish cunt—yeah, I actually used that word, but I've never been so mad in my whole life, and it just came out—and then she called me a spineless cocksucker, and then she got up and left and everyone stared. And you know what? She's living with a guy already! She won't tell me who. Whoever he is, he's good in bed—she made a point of telling me that. Seemed pretty proud, too. And last night? Last night I drank so much I can't quite remember what happened, but according to my cell phone I called her number for five minutes. I spent the time either calling her names again or begging her to come back, and either option makes me feel sick. But that didn't stop me from running out of the shower to answer the only fucking call I got today. Just in case, you know?*

But, hey, Rachie, enough about me. What about you?

He remembered his hand on Rachel's breast, squeezing, heard her voice saying, *Pete,* in that way—warning him, urging him on, as she arched into his palm.

"You should have told me," Rachel said.

"It just would have upset you," he said. "I'm sorry."

She was crying noisily now.

"You okay, Rach?"

"No," she said, her voice barely more than a blotch of static. "Oh, Pete, I need to talk to you so much."

He'd wanted to call Rachel. Every night since Maya had left

him, he'd thought about telling her. He was surprised he hadn't logged a call to her last night, too, when everything had gone fuzzy—or the other nights (more and more of them lately) when he'd lost some hours. But he never had. It was a comfort, he supposed, that even at his worst he'd been able to resist trying to open up all the old doors, to avoid spreading whatever ailed him to Rachel, too. But now—he'd loved two women in his life, and one had told him she wished he was dead, and now here was Rachel again, crying and telling him she needed him, saying his name. The hope that pulsed in his throat was so pure and cruel he almost began to cry, too.

"When can you meet?" he asked her, rubbing down the lump inside his stubbled throat.

He heard her sob. She said, "Tonight?"

Pete told her: "I can leave in an hour."

• • •

He'd met Rachel in college, just as he had Maya—making him, he often thought, one of those sad guys who'd left everything interesting in their lives behind when they trudged, diploma in hand, away from the hallowed halls. (But that was just self-pity speaking, wasn't it? He wouldn't have thought such a thing if Maya was still in his bed—would he?) It was funny to think about, really: he'd gone from a childhood in the middle of cornfields to school in West Lafayette—which was, face it, hardly a metropolitan sprawl, and which housed a school that prided itself on teaching ag science—but for Pete, Purdue was a revelation. In high school he'd been a brainy oddball, tolerated at best. But in his first year at college he found enough fellow oddballs to form a tribe. He started smoking pot in ways he could only describe as constructive. He started playing bass in a terrible band, and doing so made him popular with women, despite the fact that he'd started going bald during his senior year of high school, and was short and hairy, and had— he'd always thought—the squat, bandy legs of a chimp. Didn't matter. He grew a soul patch and wore a baseball cap backward and was generous with his weed and could anchor a groove on-stage; he knew how to dance; he was funny. Women ate it up. His sophomore year he switched majors from history to music education, and then a year later to art—he took a photography class on a whim and got hooked. Sometimes he wondered if he'd done all that casting around just to extend his stay. Only Maya's urging had gotten him to his degree.

But it was in a music ed class his third year that he saw Rachel. He still remembered her taking the seat next to him, which—since he was wearing sunglasses and a Che Guevara shirt, and since the rest of the class was comprised of prim, plump church-choir-type women—was empty.

(He sometimes tried to remember the first time he'd seen Maya. They'd met while working together in a movie theater— almost a year after the debacle with Rachel had played itself out; after she'd married Allen and moved back to the country-side whence she'd come. He remembered his and Maya's easy friendship: cracking jokes with her in a back room, helping her clip her bow tie, smelling her perfume. But that was later. There had to be a time she'd first walked into the room and he'd noticed. But he couldn't. But then he was depressed, stoned or hungover or both more often than not.)

But Rachel . . . she appeared in the doorway of the class-room, blond and tall, round and lush. Her eyes were wide and blue like a cartoon girl's; she wore her hair pulled back in a rib-bon; she wore a buttoned blouse and jeans and sensible tennis shoes. She crossed the room, smiling and chatting with other women—and then she was smiling at Pete, too, asking if the seat was taken, and ignoring (or not noticing) his stammer. Introducing herself: I'm Rachel Beauleaux—she pronounced it Booley. He remembered slipping off his sunglasses when she wasn't looking. He saw her engagement ring—it was a doozy; how could you not notice?—but it was just part of the Rachel package, another dazzle among many. At some point that first day they had to face each other and do breathing exercises, which was just about the cruelest shit in the world—asking a guy like him not only to breathe deeply but to concentrate on Rachel's diaphragm and posture. He remembered the crucifix hanging down between the open buttons of Rachel's blouse. A mole on her collarbone, right next to it. He cracked a desperate joke, and her laughter was immediate and genuine. "See you Wednesday!" she said when class was over.

He asked around about her.

She's not real, a trombonist told him.

So engaged it's not funny, said another man, a tympanist, who'd asked her out only because he'd lost a bet. She had, he said, let him down so nicely he felt a little grateful afterward, like he owed her.

His friend Dave's face crumpled a bit. "Rachel Beauleaux," Dave said, "has no idea how dangerous she is. The girl's good, right? She's pure good. Not a mean bone in her—except her fiancé's, maybe, but c'mon." (Pete agreed—if there was one thing Rachel projected, it was an almost blinding purity. Turned out he was right—even when they were right on the verge of it, the mention of sex almost always made Rachel cringe.) "She has no idea," Dave said, "how many guys just drop dead in her wake."

Then Pete heard about Daniel—a tall violinist, one of the brilliant grad students who hovered over the music program like archangels. The story came to him in pieces, from Dave, from others. During her freshman year, Daniel had fallen for Rachel, and hard. He sent flowers to her dorm room; he dedicated a recital to her; he broke off a near engagement with a pianist in New York. Rachel was touched by him, befriended him; they became so close people assumed they were lovers. She spent one night in his apartment; what happened there was, still, unknown. Then one weekend her fiancé—studying theology somewhere in Pennsylvania—came to visit. People saw the three of them together, Allen and Rachel sunnily in love, holding hands, Daniel trailing behind them in pale, stoop-shouldered shock. In the wake of that weekend Daniel was ruined. His playing suffered; it took him a year, some said, to regain his footing. He shaved his head like a monk.

(And two months later Pete observed—as he walked with Rachel to the library—her greeting Daniel the violinist. They stopped and spoke; Rachel smiled at him brilliantly, sadly. She touched his arm. Pete walked past them, gave them a bit of space, but he heard her say, *Oh, Danny, I know you'll do great,* and saw Daniel shy away from her, as though he were a dog and had memorized kicking more than kindness. And Daniel gave Pete a look, one full of deep suspicion, of pain, and maybe—though Pete might have imagined this—full of warning.)

After hearing the stories, Pete resolved to enjoy Rachel from a distance. He was dating a small, pale, chain-smoking woman who sometimes sang with his band, and they were happy enough; and anyway, he wasn't stupid. If Daniel the brilliant, handsome violinist couldn't pry Rachel away from Allen, then little chimplike Pete Shumaker wasn't going to be able to.

He knew, as they said, to stick to AAA ball; his bitter myopic girlfriend was much more his speed.

But: Rachel, to his shock, wanted to be pals. She kept taking the seat next to him, kept smiling at him in class, kept cracking jokes. (*Oh, Pete,* she'd say, *you're hysterical.* Or she'd say, *Oh, Pete, you look so classy in a button-down.* Or: *Pete! You shaved! You have dimples!* She was awesome in her obliviousness.) Once, standing in front of the class, ready to sing some scales, she gave him a wink.

Then, midway through the semester, they were assigned a project together. And so one night she called him to talk about it, and they chatted for a long time, and then he found himself calling her, talking to her, finding her in no hurry to hang up; and one night he happened to call her right after Allen had hurt her feelings, and she was crying, and told him she could use a friend, and Pete said he'd be right over, and not long after she opened the door to her apartment, she was crying, and he put his arm around her shoulders and she leaned into him and shook, and he spent the next hour stroking her hair and telling her that it would be all right, everything was going to be just fine. She made them tea. *It's late,* she told him. *It's fine,* he said, *I don't live that far away.* She told him, *Just crash here.* She smiled. *I trust you. You're a good guy.* He nodded and spent the night awake on her couch, looking at the dark outline of her bedroom door, smelling her on the sheet she'd given him. In the morning he pretended to be asleep when she walked into the room. He felt her pause next to him and forced himself to breathe. Then she pulled the sheet up beneath his chin; he sensed more than felt the brush of her fingers on his shoulder.

And after that he was lost, lost.

• • •

Traffic was light, and Pete was restless; he reached the diner almost an hour early. It was late June and insufferably hot already—that stupid sweltering Indiana heat Pete had been swearing he'd leave someday, and never had. Out to the west of the interstate a spring thunderstorm was piling itself up; the insides of the clouds glowed greenly. He bought a *Star* from a box outside the diner and sat at a booth and read it twice through, drinking free refills of coffee. He turned to the wedding announcements. One of his photos was pictured: this was of Amy Prosper and Jacob "Jake" Giddens, of Beech Grove. Amy was smiling like a lunatic—she'd wept throughout the photos, and in this one, shrunk to black-and-white, she looked a little demented. You couldn't see it in the picture, but Jake, stoic and mulleted, was propping her up. After they'd posed for him, Pete had started drinking from the open bar, way more than he should have. That the candids came out all right was a small miracle.

Five minutes before Rachel was due to arrive, he bought breath mints from the diner's counter and then ducked into the bathroom to wipe the shine off his forehead.

Outside, the storm had broken; rain fell in sheets across the interstate, and a couple of times he watched hail drum on the hoods of the cars in the lot. Fifteen minutes after the hour she pulled into the lot, in a small white sports car. He watched her back in and out of her parking space, trying to get aligned. He chewed up one of his breath mints and watched her progress toward the doors.

Then she was inside, smiling at him and waving and trying to fold her umbrella all at once. Her smile was as he remembered it: there'd always been an element of surrender in it, a dropping of pretension that made him feel, at the same time, unique and intrusive, as though she smiled like this only for him—and yet was hurt by him, too, in a way only he could hurt her.

She was dressed in a long denim skirt, a long-sleeved blouse, black high-heeled boots. Her hair was a little shorter than he remembered, a little more stylish, with highlights and flipped-up ends, but it was the same beautiful, cheerleader's honey blond. She wore no makeup, never had. Yet she was different somehow—and when he was close enough to her to speak, he saw what it was: her skin, always pale, was now too white, as though drained. Pete saw evidence of his own aging, his own troubles, every time he faced the mirror. But this was the first time he'd ever seen the years taking Rachel down with him—this seemed to him a little obscene.

Rachel threw her arms around him, hugging him fiercely, and as always he was unprepared for the physicality of her, for her leap from his imagination into the reality of her skin, for the scent of her perfume—she always used too much, she had a horror about her own sweat—for the way she always seemed to realize she was embracing him too strongly and then suddenly pulled back, looking embarrassed, leaving only a chaotic pulse in his groin as evidence he hadn't imagined the whole thing. He led her to the booth, and they sat.

"It's good to see you," he said. "You look great."

Ordinarily she would have complimented him, too. Instead, she reached for his hand. "Peter," she said. "Pete, I'm so sorry about Maya. How awful. I can't believe it." Rachel's face had a way of amplifying any pronouncement; she gazed at him with a dictionary-definition expression of sorrow. "Are you okay?"

He couldn't lie to her. "It's been rough," he said.

Already they'd fallen into their old habits: they stared at each other, Rachel looking down at her coffee only occasionally and with confusion, Pete catching himself scrabbling for his own cup without tearing his eyes away. He felt the brush of her boots against his calf under the table. He'd told her once, back in college, that he thought she might have her own gravity; his hands seemed to want to float up and touch hers, his head wanted to incline to hers. He could feel every inch between their fingers, wrapped around their separate mugs of coffee.

"Do you want to—to talk about it?" Rachel asked him. Her eyes, he saw, were bloodshot, her eyelids swollen.

He didn't. But he told her, anyway.

He and Maya had grown distant. She spent time with her friends, he with his. At home she read on the couch, and he messed around in the darkroom. She wanted to move to Boston, and he wanted to go to California, and since they couldn't compromise, they ended up staying put, hating Indianapolis, and then hating each other keeping them stuck. Little things—Pete's belly, her spending habits—grew into big things. And then—he still didn't know exactly when it happened—she met another man. Some guy she worked with at SysTech. Pete had seen him once, well after they were separated; he'd been checking out at the grocery and saw Maya leave the cleaners next door and get into the guy's car, parked at the curb. He looked slight, had glasses and hair that was rumpled and spiky—the way the hip kids liked, these days. Maya laughed and kissed him. It stung. If the other man had been some beefy weight lifter type, one of those dangerous bar studs Maya'd spent her single life chasing, Pete could have chalked everything up to sex. But this was a nerd: a skinny programmer who might have spent some time complimenting her and making her laugh. It might just be love.

Rachel listened to the story with her hand over her mouth. "Oh, Pete," she said.

He sipped his coffee and said, "I guess I knew we were in trouble, but I never figured she was the type to cheat on me. You know? I thought she was stronger than that. Like if she was that unhappy, she'd just come out and tell me."

One moment Rachel stared at him saucer-eyed, and the next she dropped her face into her hands and began to sob.

"Rach?"

She shook her head and fumbled at the napkin dispenser. Their waitress looked over at them; Pete did his best to ignore her. He took out a handful of napkins and pressed them into Rachel's cold hand. This wasn't just Rachel's typical overkill. He was touched by her tears—touched that, even after all this time, she could still care so much for his happiness. His own throat closed, a little.

"Rach, it's okay," he said. "We're better off this way."

She shook her head.

"You okay? What is it?"

She said something so softly he could barely believe he'd heard her words at all. She glanced at him, blue irises swimming in pink. Her face then was as lost and pitiful as anything he'd ever seen.

"I can't hear you," he said.

She looked around the restaurant, then pulled a notepad from her purse. She scribbled on it quickly and slid it across the table to him.

He read the sentence there twice, then sat back and let shock slide over him. He felt almost as though he'd traveled back in time—as though it was Maya now sitting across from him, staring him right in the eye and saying, once again, *Yeah, it's true. You caught me, and I'm not sorry.*

Rachel had written, in her wide looping script: *I cheated on Allen, and I'm in a lot of trouble.*

• • •

He'd asked Rachel once, and only once, as they lay together in her bed: *Why me?*

This was two months after they'd met, a few weeks after he'd first spent the night on her couch. Since then they'd been inseparable. They talked daily, on the phone, over coffee, sitting with their knees brushing on Rachel's couch. (Unlike Pete, always maneuvering past his slovenly roommates, Rachel had an apartment to herself, kept so clean he was often afraid to touch anything.) He'd flipped with her through ten different photo albums full of pictures of smiling, blond Allen, listening as Rachel either narrated reverently (*Look at him, he just radiates love;* or *He's known since he was a boy that he wanted to be a pastor, like he's got a mission;* or *I fell in love with him when I was a little girl—I knew, I just knew, it was God's hand*) or wept over him (*He forgot my birthday;* or *He's going on a prayer retreat in Florida instead of coming to visit—and he told me I shouldn't be sad about God's will;* or *He told me we can't touch for a while, because . . . because we feel too much lust*—and when she said this, her voice lowered to a willowy rasp; her cheeks burned). All her picture albums were decorated with lacy hearts cut from doilies; she'd written "Allen" on each of the covers, in elaborate calligraphy. Pete looked into her bedroom once: her bed was barely visible underneath a creepy mass of arranged teddy bears. Gifts from Allen, she told him. Pete couldn't help wondering if she spent a lot of time kissing the one that sat on her pillow.

But despite Allen's constant presence in their talks, Pete came to understand—as much as he tried to deny it—that Rachel was attracted to him. That this attraction might very well be growing. He knew this was trouble, tried to blame it on his own wishful thinking—of which there was a lot—but he wasn't an idiot, either. Rachel stared at him, right into his eyes—and not just when they talked (though that was dizzying enough). Sometimes, when they were studying together, he felt her eyes on him and looked up to see her steady, liquid gaze, her slightly parted lips, her flush of embarrassment at being caught. She complimented him constantly—he'd told her, once, how ugly he thought he was, and she'd made it a mission to demonstrate to him he was wrong. She hugged him whenever she could, and kissed him on the cheek whenever they said good-bye (the first of those nearly left him deaf and blind). When they walked, she'd often grab his hand and pull him along by it. Once, on the bus, she tipped her head against his shoulder and closed her eyes. The back of her hand rested alongside his thigh; he was sure his quickened breath, his juddering heartbeat, would wake her, but it didn't.

It wasn't just him. Others noticed, too; people in the music program had begun looking at him with a mixture of awe and pity. Daniel the violinist stared at him darkly.

But then Rachel would say something like, *I told Allen all about our trip to the park. He's so happy God gave me such a close friend.* And what the fuck was he supposed to do with that?

God, like Allen, was never far from Rachel's conversation. Pete had told her from the get-go that he wasn't religious and wasn't likely to change. This troubled her, he knew. She told him she prayed for him; he told her she could if she wanted to, but that it wasn't going to make a difference. Every Saturday she asked him if he wanted to go to church with her the next morning, and he told her no thanks. This was all very civil, and he hated to say no to her—especially since when he did, her avid stares would turn inward, turn troubled—but he wasn't going to lie to her, either. With her, in fact, he found himself being scrupulously truthful, thoughtful, about everything they discussed. It was as his friend had told him: Rachel was pure good. If he lied in front of her, he sometimes thought, she'd be burned by *his* corruption.

Eventually he composed a theory: Rachel liked him fine, and maybe was attracted to him, but not in the ways he wanted. She was naive about flirtation, that was obvious. Whether she knew it or not, she was probably trying to make Allen jealous, but she wasn't trying to use Pete—the thought was laughable. She might think she was going to save him, and he'd keep an eye on that. But he told himself to enjoy the time with her; she was a good person, and maybe a better friend than he'd ever had. And if the price for that friendship was that he'd have to stumble out of her apartment stammering and half-erect— well, that was what masturbation was for.

Yet when Pete's girlfriend broke things off—*I think,* she told him, *we'd better just make it official. And don't think you can crawl back when she's done with you, okay?*—he wasn't sorry, either, no matter how hard Rachel cried for him.

And then—as Rachel had always done—she surprised him. Allen went on his prayer retreat, and Rachel spent that entire week clingier, needier, than she'd been before. Pete spent every night keeping her company. That Friday they saw a movie, a thriller. And halfway through, during a particularly brutal murder, Rachel took his hand. This wasn't unusual—she didn't like scares or blood. But when the scene was done, she laced her fingers through his and held tight until the movie was over. He ceased to care what was happening on-screen; he could see her fingers in his mind while he stroked them, as though they were under a spotlight. When the credits rolled, she squeezed his fingers; they stared at each other until the theater cleared. Pete told himself to relax. To be realistic. Rachel smiled and dropped her eyes. They walked slowly back to her apartment, still holding hands; with every other step their hips bumped together.

In her living room she said, "I'll make coffee, if you want to hang out for a bit?" He thought he heard a tremor in her voice and understood that he could no longer credit anything to his imagination. Rachel Beauleaux was making him a nightcap. He wondered if she'd ever made coffee at midnight for Daniel the violinist.

Pete sat in the living room and took deep breaths. He looked at the framed picture on her coffee table: Rachel and Allen hand in hand on the shore of a lake, feeding two swans: two Precious Moments babies in grown-up clothes. With a start he realized ten minutes had passed. He called Rachel; she didn't answer.

In the kitchen he found her standing next to the coffeemaker, as though frozen, a pot of water in her hand. The fluorescent ring buzzed overhead. "You okay?" he asked, his voice catching on its way out.

Rachel's eyes brimmed over.

He did what, by then, had become common: he walked to her and embraced her. She put her arms around his neck. He felt her body soften, curve to his. His mouth was touching the lobe of her ear.

"Tell me what's wrong," he said.

"I don't know why God gave you to me," she said. "I don't know what to do."

Pete couldn't have controlled himself then, even if he'd tried. He put his hands on either side of her face and turned her mouth to his, and they kissed. She didn't hesitate.

He'd spent hours imagining what Rachel's kiss might be like—and, he found, he'd never come close. This wasn't chaste, this wasn't a little-girl kiss; no. Rachel opened her mouth wide and sighed and flicked her tongue against his; she put her fingers into his hair and pressed her breasts, her hips, against him. He'd had sex before that wasn't as good as that first minute in her arms.

They spent an hour kissing in her bed—teddy bears pushed quickly and roughly to the floor, legs tangled, Pete's cock so stiff in his jeans he thought it might be in danger of cracking. Rachel was aware of it, too; she rubbed slowly against him. He took a breath and pressed his hand to her breast and was shocked when Rachel unbuttoned her blouse and arched her dark, stiff nipple into his mouth and moaned, "Oh, *Pete*"—but even as she said this, he heard her tone change; he felt her pull away, return to herself.

They lay side by side, his hand on her stomach. She pulled a blanket over her chest.

"Rach—"

"I love Allen," she whispered.

He listened to Rachel breathe. She stared straight up into the webs of darkness in the room's upper corners and, he supposed, asked her questions of God.

He felt strange: calm, assured.

"Rachel," he said, "I'm not afraid to tell you this. Not anymore. I love you. I've loved you since I met you."

She nodded, sniffling. Say it back, he thought, but she didn't.

"I'm afraid to move," she said. "Like anything I do will be wrong."

He understood that, he supposed.

"If you want me to leave," he said, "I will. But just answer something for me, okay?"

"Okay."

"Why me?"

She didn't speak. Maybe she didn't know. Maybe she didn't know how to say it. He felt a hole open in him—but then Rachel turned to him and put her palm against his cheek and poured her gaze into him, sweet with sympathy and under-standing and—there was no other word for it—love.

She touched his lips and kissed the spot she'd touched. Then she put her face against his chest and said, "I don't know what to do. But I know I don't want you to leave."

And he hadn't. Not then, and—not really—never since.

·   ·   ·

After Pete read Rachel's note, she said, "We can't talk here." So they sprinted through the rain and sat in Rachel's car. In no time at all the windows fogged over. Rain beat heavily on the roof and windshield and trickled in warm slug trails from Pete's scalp down his chest and back. He listened as Rachel told him what she could.

"It was awful," she said. Her hands were in her lap, but they kept twisting at each other, or drifting up to touch the steering wheel before falling back. Her perfume, in the close confines of the car, was strong enough to blur his vision.

"I can't believe this," Pete said, which was the truth.

"I can't, either," she said, tearing open a travel pack of Kleenex from her purse.

He didn't know what to ask. No. He knew a hundred things to ask: What did he say? Why him? Was it like *us*?

He settled on "Who is he?"

Rachel shook her head. "He's . . . he's younger. A lot."

"How young?"

She looked out her window. "Twenty."

Twenty! The knife jabbing in Pete's gut took another quarter turn.

"How—how'd you meet him?"

Rachel shook her head; her lips quivered. Pete took a deep breath and then reached to her, put a hand on her shoulder, and she leaned her forehead against her window. He looked at the dash. A cassette protruded tonguelike from the slot above the ashtray; its case was in the cup holder beneath: *If Jesus Is Always There, Why Can't I Feel His Arms?*

Rachel's shoulder quaked beneath his hand.

He couldn't resist any longer. "Rachel, come here," he said, his words a croak.

And then he was holding her; her arms tight around his neck, her cheeks wet, her knees pressed against the dash. How long had it been? Maybe ten years since they'd shared more than a quick embrace of greeting or good-bye. She moaned now against his neck, and he rocked her, rubbed the small of her back—even under her sweater, she was as lithe as always. Some man had held this back, not too long ago. No: a boy. Some stupid lucky twenty-year-old boy. Whoever he was, he'd felt her back, too. All of her.

And then Pete was crying, too. He felt for Rachel—he'd never been able to bear her misery—but mostly he cried because Rachel's breath against his ear made his skin prickle, because he could think of nothing, while she was in his arms, but his memories of her. How much he'd always wanted this, how he'd missed it. Her. Because losing Maya hadn't just been about the end of his marriage; it meant he'd spent a month remembering he'd lost Rachel first. He was alone, and Rachel was alone, and yet he knew: even if Rachel wanted his embrace now, she'd trade it in a bare second for the embrace of Allen or her lover or Jesus—whose arms, apparently, she was missing, too. Pete might as well not even exist, and yet exist he did, his body a lead weight around an empty hole.

Because he could feel no worse, he said, "Tell me."

And after a moment Rachel did, whispering as though Allen himself was crouched outside the car:

The boy was a student at a small Bible college in Georgia— "just like Allen was," she said, and if she meant any irony, he couldn't detect it. She'd never met him before. He was new in Clarksville, staying with an uncle for the summer, working as a caddie outside of Wakefield, a county over—Pete knew where: a semiprivate course he'd once played with a college buddy. He remembered the caddies there: a bunch of fit, smirking Young Republican types. The boy, she told him, studied in the same bookstore where Rachel shopped—where she went, a lot of mornings, to sit in the café and eat a muffin and read the newspaper, because Allen was gone and she sometimes got lonely—

And Allen's where?

Allen was on a mission to Africa. Building a hospital in Liberia. Pete remembered—their church had been planning this for a while; Rachel had mentioned it last summer, the last time they'd spoken. Allen had been gone now seven weeks; he was due back on the twentieth. Rachel had planned to go with him, but in the end she'd stayed in Indiana because she needed to earn credits for her license, and—

"And . . . oh, Pete . . . I didn't *want* to go. I could have done those credits during the year, but I didn't. I knew Allen was going to Africa, and I just got more and more upset, and—and things weren't great, you know, with us, and—oh, I know it's awful, I know how prideful it is, but I wanted him to have to choose between staying or going. I wanted him to choose *me*—or—or maybe I *didn't,* I might have just wanted him to go alone, I don't know—and I thought at least we'd fight, but he just nodded, and—"

"You should have called me," Pete said, his voice hoarse.

"I was scared," she said. He wanted to ask her, *Of what?* so badly his throat clenched. But he didn't.

Allen was in Liberia and Rachel was alone, and she kept seeing the nice boy at the bookstore coffee shop, and for a couple of weeks all they did was smile at each other, exchange pleasantries. She knew right away he was a Christian, and they talked about that, and had a lot in common, even though she was Church of the Harvester and he was Southern Baptist. And then one day she started crying. She was sitting two tables over from him, holding her coffee, and she just *lost* it.

"Why?"

A shudder went through her shoulders.

"Allen was supposed to call me the night before—it's not easy to call from there—but he hadn't, and it wasn't the first time, and I was thinking, I don't know—"

And anyway, the boy was there, and saw her, and came over to her to ask what was wrong—

"What's his name?"

Rachel looked up from his shoulder, stricken; her face fell into itself. "I can't say it," she said.

"You can't say his name?"

She shook her head. "I can write it down."

Rachel sat up and gazed at the fog swirled on the windshield. Outside, the rain had slowed. She sighed and said, "I don't want to tell you all of it. And that feels . . . I've always told you everything, I know, and if I don't tell you, it feels like I'm cheating on you, too. I know that."

That, and being married to Allen for ten years. That had always felt a lot like cheating, too. Pete ran his hand over his scalp.

"Did he ever hurt you?" he asked.

"No! No. If anything, he was a gentleman. He's—" She reached for a tissue and wiped her nose. Her next words were full of a disgust he'd never heard from her before. "He didn't—I went to *him* as much as he came to me." She glanced at Pete. "He's very pretty. I was . . . weak."

"Rachel—"

"It—it only happened a few times. And each time I felt so terrible after, I couldn't even remember why I'd—why I'd ever . . . and so I'd meet him and just cry and cry." She threw the balled-up tissue onto the floor. "I can't even remember the last time I wasn't crying."

Pete offered her his hand, and she took it. His left hand. He felt her touch the space where his ring had been. Did she pause there? He couldn't tell.

"Just as I was about to tell him we had to stop," she said, "he told me—he told me he was in love with me. He wants to leave college and run away with me."

Pete closed his eyes.

"I told him no," she said, looking up. "Of course I told him no. But now"—her voice cracked on the next words—"now he's *threatening* me. He left a letter under my windshield wiper. It was there when I came out of the store."

"What did it say?"

"It said—it said he wanted to *see* me. And that—and that if I didn't meet him, he'd write a letter to Allen when he gets back. He said he knew I wasn't happy. He said—he said he was doing it for my own good."

Pete's mouth was dry. He'd drawn up plans along those same lines, back when he and Rachel were entangled. When she insisted she couldn't leave Allen, that a life with that cardboard piece of shit was going to be better for her than whatever Pete could offer. Pete had spent sleepless nights imagining visits to Allen at his little college out in the Pennsylvania countryside. He'd knock on Allen's door and push Allen back and say, *Look. You don't love her like I do. If you love her at all, you heartless sociopath. Let her go.* Or: *I'm taking her. We're not coming back.*

Even an imagined Allen was insufferable; he sat in a chair and folded his hands and smiled and looked right through the back of Pete's head. *God leads,* Allen said. *We follow.*

Pete made himself think of Rachel instead. As much as he didn't want to picture the boy, her—the two of them—he tried. The need that drove her to him, the guilt that must have swum up. The sounds she'd have made—no. No. He imagined her reading the boy's note, there in the parking lot. Her fear. It would be all she could do to live with the idea that she was unfaithful. A sinner. But for Allen to know, too—that territory, to Rachel, might as well be outer space. Her panic would be total.

"I don't know what to say," he told her.

If only she'd called him when she was lonely, and not after . . .

He made himself say, "Maybe—"

She turned to him, too fast.

"—maybe you should be honest with Allen," he said.

Her face fell. "No," she whispered. "Oh no."

"Do you want to be with him? What are you protecting here?"

"Allen's my *husband*." She said this in the pious, good-soldier tone that had always made him want to shake her. "We made *vows*."

"Rachel, he also vowed to keep you happy. I was there, I heard him."

That was cruel, he knew. Her eyes flickered to meet his, then away. Neither of them had talked about her wedding since it had happened.

"I *do* love him," she said, "and—I can't. I *can't* tell him. He can *never* know. You don't know him, you don't know what this would do to him—"

"Given all that he's done to you, I don't really give a shit."

Her cheeks were flushed now. "Well, *I* do. We've always fixed things. Always. And I've been so unfair to him already." She glanced meaningfully at Pete, just enough to shrivel his insides. "I just want this to go away. I want to start over. I just—"

She tried to pull her hand back, but he said, "Hey. Hey," and pulled her closer—and then she collapsed against him again, sobbing. "I know," he said. And even though he wasn't, he said, "I'm sorry," and brushed his lips against her hair, softly enough he didn't think she'd be able to feel it.

"Oh, Pete." Her voice was soft, broken, tender. For all its hopelessness, there was love in it still. She'd never convince him otherwise, no matter what she'd been able to convince herself. She'd told herself she wanted to cry about Allen, but there was a reason she'd called *him*. A reason they were sitting here. This wasn't the first time she'd cried out love to Allen and then fallen into Pete's arms. Not by a long shot.

If she was ever to admit anything to him, it would be now: *I'm so sorry. I made a mistake. I don't want to make any more. I love you and I've always loved you—*

She took a breath and said, "I'm sorry, too. I'm not forgetting what—what happened with us. I won't ever forget. I know it probably hurts you to hear this."

"Yeah," he said. "Yeah, it does."

"Especially now," she said. "It's not easy for me to do this to you. I hope you can believe that."

He sighed, nodded.

"And I hope—I hope you'll forgive me for what I'm going to ask you. But I don't think I have any choice. Please understand that."

She met his eyes, and he saw then: he'd misjudged her. Of course he had—the Rachel he'd always known would never have fallen into this trouble in the first place. And when the trouble had happened, she'd sat and thought and thought, and she hadn't called Pete just for comfort. He had no idea what she'd ask, but she was going to ask for *something*. And already his hopes began their long, slow sink.

She began to speak, softly and carefully, and he listened.

• • •

"We can't do this," she'd told him—of course—the day after he spent the night in her bed. "Pete, we can't. I feel *awful*."

She'd taken a long shower after they woke, and all the while he sat at her breakfast table in the kitchen, reading the newspaper and eating a bowl of her Miniwheats and playing with her cat, inexplicably named Terrence. He'd done his level best not to think about the night before—but of course he did, and he spent several minutes staring in disbelief at the sight of himself in his boxers at Rachel's breakfast table. He stood and did her dishes—and then, to his horror, listened as the phone rang, and her machine picked up, and the voice of her fiancé filled the room.

"Hey, Rachie," Allen said. His voice was deep, polished, like a radio announcer's, under a sheen of pure country twang. "Just had a minute to myself and thought I'd call. I'm surprised you're out. Isn't this study time? You and Terrence?" Allen laughed. "Hey, kitty kitty. Well, anyway. I've been thinking that I should apologize about the retreat—not about going, because it's been awesome—but I know it made you sad that I did. I prayed on that, and then I made some calls and freed myself up next month. The weekend of the fourth. I hope that makes you happy. I love you. God bless you."

Pete looked at the mug he was drying. He set it carefully on the counter.

Never mind what had happened the night before. Never mind the instant, oily hatred he'd felt for Allen's voice. Rachel was *engaged*. At no point last night had she said she'd leave Allen—if anything, she'd only set aside her guilt for a few hours' time. Pete heard the shower stop.

Rachel walked slowly into the kitchen a few minutes later, wearing a long bathrobe. Her eyes were wide and sorrowful. Don't see the message, he thought, please—but she did, right away.

"Was it Allen?" she asked in a small voice.

"Yeah."

"I'll listen to it later," she said.

"Okay."

"We can't do this," she said.

She kept stammering, clutching her hands in front of her. The cat slunk across the counter to her, and she picked him up, cradling him in front of her breasts. Pete barely heard what she said, but it was predictable enough: she loved Allen, they were enagaged, she didn't—

A different Pete might have left her then, slunk catlike away, but he was still tingling from her touch. He remembered the way she'd looked at him. How she'd asked him to stay. What she'd said the night before, leaning against the same counter. He walked to her and took the cat from her and dropped it on the floor. Then he cupped Rachel's face in his hands. Her wet hair was cool on his skin and smelled of green apples. She stopped talking and closed her eyes, leaned perceptibly forward. He kissed her. "We can't," she said.

"Rachel," he told her, "we sure can. That's not the problem."

So began their pattern. They spent the same amount of time together they always had. They studied together, went to movies together. They sat on Rachel's couch. She stared at him, laughed nervously at his jokes. She'd make some of her own: "How about tonight we try not to kiss?" And then he'd say, "Okay," and lean across her folded legs and kiss her, and she'd resist for a second and then make the sound he loved— a sigh of nearly pure pleasure—and dig her nails into the back of his neck and pull him toward her. And an hour or so later she'd push him away from her breasts or pluck his hand from the smooth warm inside of her thigh and say, "We can't. We can't. It's so *wrong*."

He learned to avoid certain questions. Like: *What are we doing?* Or: *Do you love me like I love you?* He thought he knew the answers to them, but not with enough certainty to bring them into the open. And anyway: apart from her guilty tears at two, three in the morning, the rest of his time with her was near bliss—better than music, better than drugs.

They didn't have sex, but he'd begun thinking the odds weren't entirely against it. She knew the motions, anyway. She knew to press against Pete's erection; she knew to wrap her legs around his thigh when they kissed and rock gently back and forth, eyes closed, her fingers laced with his. And she'd begun asking him questions about his own past, curled into his side in the dark morning hours:

How many women have you slept with? Five. *Did you love any of them?* Two, I thought. *What about the others?* I don't know. We just kind of—agreed on it. Sometimes we were both pretty drunk. *Does that bother you?* It does now. *Why?* Because I love you. *Why does that make a difference?* Because I know what love's like now. What I was doing with those girls—it's just not the same. *But you—you liked it?* Yeah! Of course. *Even though you didn't love them?* Rach—sex feels good, that's just all there is to it. *How good?* How good? Seriously? *Yeah.* Better than anything, really. Don't you know? *Pete! You know I haven't—* No, I mean . . . haven't you ever had, you know, an orgasm? *No. Allen and I don't, we don't—* Not even by yourself? *No! No, that's a sin.* But when we're . . . when we're fooling around, you get close. I can tell. *I think so.* Rach. *Pete—oh, Pete, no.* Let me give you one. *Pete . . . I can't.* It's okay. *Oh, Pete . . .*

He learned to do it through her pajama bottoms. And when he remembered their time together, sometimes those moments seemed the most appropriate of his memories, the most symbolic: his fingers seeking her out, separated from her most private place by a piece of fabric so soft and thin it might as well not be there at all—but which, by being there, made all the difference in the world.

But all the same he loved to lie beside her and feel her thighs part, feel her hand touch his, guide it to her; he loved to listen to her gasps come quicker and quicker; loved the moment she lifted her head off the pillow, eyes shut tight; loved to feel the muscles in her stomach tighten. He loved to hear her whisper his name.

"You're so giving," she'd say, panting.

"My pleasure," he'd tell her.

"I want to make you feel like that."

And she'd rub him through his boxers, slowly—she was afraid to touch him too hard, even though he'd told her it was all right. He learned to close his eyes, to concentrate on her caress. It took a long time, but that was fine. He'd lie still, Rachel's hair falling across his face, and forget that in the morning she'd tell him all over again, *We have to stop,* that she'd remind him once again Allen was coming to visit—in two weeks, in a week, in two days. Pete learned not to think of it, to feel only the delicate moment in which he lived: the softness of the bed, Rachel's weight across his thighs, the soft touch of her hand, her breath, the feel of his own release building and arriving— and Rachel's gasp of delight, of pride; he breathed her smell in deep and told himself it was love, it was like nothing else, and that love like this couldn't help but survive, no matter what was coming for them.

• • •

He told Rachel yes.

As Pete drove home from the diner, he wondered why— why the fuck he'd ever agreed to such a terrible, crazy plan. He loved Rachel, it was true, but she lived in an entirely different universe than his. They'd made that clear enough to each other over the years, hadn't they? He should have told her no. For her own good, maybe even for Allen's, he should have told her he was sorry, let her go. She wasn't going to come back to him— he knew that, of course he knew it. She'd chosen against him years ago. He knew this now and he knew it when she asked him her favor, and still:

He'd said yes.

She'd whispered the idea to him, nestled in his arms, while he listened in growing disbelief:

She wanted Pete to meet the boy, her lover. To visit him where he worked, where no one knew her or Allen.

And here was the kicker: she wanted him to pretend to be Allen.

"Tell him I told you everything," she said. "Tell him he should go away."

She'd never sounded more like a child, like a girl scheming with dolls at the corner of the playground.

He pushed her off his chest. "No," he said, "no way. Absolutely not."

Rachel explained it again, as though he'd missed something the first time around. She told him she had no choice. She'd made a mistake, and that was her sin to bear, but she didn't want it to be Allen's. She couldn't go to her friends—they were all members of the church. She couldn't tell her family. Who else did she have?

"Give me one reason," he'd said to her. "Seriously. What makes you think I'd do this?"

He had to give her credit. Rachel gave him the truth.

"Because," she said, head bowed, her hands folded in her lap, "you're the only person on earth who loves me enough to help me."

He sat for a long while in the passenger seat of her little car. He inhaled her perfume and watched her wide red-rimmed eyes. Did she know what words like that would do to him? She did—she'd told him so. This was Rachel; she was still good; that she'd cheated on Allen didn't automatically cut out her heart. How much would she have had to suffer—and suffer for him—even to consider asking? Even if he and Maya were happy together, Rachel's request would have been unthinkable. And then for her to hear he'd lost Maya, and to ask this of him, anyway . . .

"I'll be honest with you," he said. "I don't know if I can."

She pressed her lips together.

"I hate Allen. You know that."

She nodded.

All his truths were close to the surface then. He wondered if spilling them—telling her everything—would be an even exchange. If he could say, *I'll do this, but first you have to listen. You shouldn't be with Allen. You should have been with me. We both know that, and I won't lift a finger until you tell me you loved me all along.*

Or he could be worse. Ask for more. *Kiss me, and I'll do it. Come home with me, and I'll do it.*

Give me one night of what you gave that boy. What should have been mine all along.

He closed his eyes. That would just solve everything, wouldn't it? Answering blackmail with blackmail.

"I want you to answer one question," he said. "And I want you to be honest with me."

Her shoulders hunched. "All right," she said in a tiny voice.

He wanted to ask her, once and for all, about her wedding night. About what they'd almost done. But he looked at her eyes, her see-through skin, her raw red nose. She was afraid of him now. What he might ask. That in itself was an answer: if she was afraid, didn't that mean she knew she was lying to herself? That there were truths, yet, to speak?

That she'd been wrong?

He changed his question. "What'll happen to us if I do this?"

"I don't know," she said.

But she did know. He figured he did, too. And it would be true no matter what he answered. He'd climb out of her car tonight and never see her again. The weight of all their secrets, already creaking and vast, had just been made unbearable. How could they ever face each other again? And Rachel had known all along. She'd known when she hatched this crazy plan. Yet she'd dialed his number and cried and thrown what was left of them to the fire, anyway.

So. Helping her was a matter of pure charity, unless he dragged something unpleasant from her in exchange.

His mind summoned up a picture of her straddling him, right there on the passenger seat, her skirt bunched around her hips, her mouth open to his, his hands pressing the curves of her hips down and down—

No. *No.* He loved her. He always had, and no matter how much he'd wished for more to happen, she'd never had to fuck him to keep it. He'd always just given it. And if there was anything he was going to leave her with—anything that would make their whole sad history worth its own pain—it was the idea that his love, unlike any other she'd found, came for free. Pete didn't owe her that—but that was the point, wasn't it? She'd been right: he *did* love her enough.

And maybe, a month from now, a year, maybe she'd look over at Allen and see what she'd saved, and what it cost, and she'd finally, finally understand.

"Okay," he said, and felt a tightness in his chest that could only be grief. "I'll do it."

•   •   •

For all the time Pete spent imagining Allen, envying Allen, hating Allen's pious oblivious guts, he'd only met him twice. Once on Allen's visit to Purdue and again at his wedding to Rachel. Everything else Pete knew of him came through speculation or through Rachel—from her photo albums, from the calls she'd made to Pete since she'd married: roughly one a year. And even the Allen he'd met in the flesh, whose hand he'd shaken, seemed to loom over Rachel. Pete remembered: Allen standing in front of the chapel, straight as a plastic groom atop a cake, smiling at Rachel's slow, ghostly approach; standing with his arm around Rachel's waist as they waited to enter a West Lafayette restaurant; waiting patiently for Rachel to unlock the door to her apartment, before kissing her briefly on the cheek.

Pete stayed at his own apartment the night before Allen's visit to campus; he'd tried for Rachel's bed, but she was in too much of a tizzy, scrubbing and dusting her already antiseptic apartment, alternately hugging Pete and pushing him away.

"I can't face him," she said just before he left for the night. "He'll know right away something's wrong."

"So tell him," Pete said. "Break it off." He meant this as a joke—it just slipped out—but once the words were in the air, Rachel froze, her eyes meeting Pete's in terror.

"I can't. I *can't.*"

Pete could have punched himself. He'd been so careful, and now—

"Oh, Pete." She put her face into her hands. "I can't see you anymore."

"You don't mean that."

"I do. I've been—I've been meaning to say it for a long time now." Her voice had dropped to a rasp. "I hate myself for leading you on. You mean the world to me, but—I think we have to say good-bye."

His anger surprised him—weeks' worth of unworldly calm drained from him like blood. He wasn't mad at her—he was mad *for* her. For what she was doing to herself.

"You can't say good-bye to me," he said.

"I can. I have to."

He reached for anything he could.

"Is this the same way you said good-bye to Daniel?" he asked.

Rachel's mouth opened. "No," she said. "Don't you try to hurt me. You're better than that."

He held up his hands; her vehemence had scared him a little. "Okay. *Okay.* Listen. Can we just talk after the weekend?"

"We can't. Not anymore." Her grief returned. "I'm too weak."

"So loving me is *weak?*"

She sagged. "No, Pete. I'm sorry. I'm so sorry. I've been so happy with—"

He walked to her. "I just don't think we're done."

She put her forehead against his. He wrapped his arms around her waist.

"I can't imagine leaving him," she said.

"Have you tried?"

She didn't answer—which, Pete had begun to learn, was a reliable answer of its own.

"Don't worry," he said. "I'll stay away this weekend. Just—"

"That's the problem," she said, shuddering. "He wants to meet you."

Pete didn't want to. Nor did Rachel want the meeting to happen—and even now Pete couldn't understand how she managed to survive it. But they minimized the damage: Pete would pretend to be on his way out of town. He and Allen would shake hands, say nice things, and it would be over.

And that was what happened. Pete met the two of them Friday night, outside the restaurant where they were going to have dinner. They all stood on the sidewalk. Allen was tall, straight-backed, so blond his eyebrows were barely visible on his forehead. He was a handsome man—as handsome, Pete had to admit, as Rachel was beautiful. He wore a dark green suit and tie; his shoes were shined. Next to him Rachel—in a long dress—smiled with the corners of her mouth turned down and looked as though she might, at any moment, be sick.

"Pleased to meet you," Allen told Pete after a strangely soft handshake.

"Likewise," Pete said.

"I know you're in a hurry. Just wanted to say thanks for being such a good pal to Rachie here. She tells me you're a blessing." He gave Rachel a hearty squeeze around the waist.

"Well," Pete said, "that goes both ways."

Allen grinned, showing very straight white teeth. Pete thought he looked exactly like a giant ear of Indiana corn, and had to swallow back hysterical laughter.

They all smiled at each other. Pete said, "Well, you kids have a good weekend," and they said good-byes. And, because he had nothing better to do, Pete went to his apartment and played the bass into his headphones for hours, distortion cranked. He told himself he wasn't the sort of guy who went and spied.

But apparently he was. Across from Rachel's apartment was a small bar, which he guessed was a safe place not to be seen by two churchgoing lovebirds. He sat nursing a beer and watching Rachel's apartment building through the smudged front windows. At midnight she and Allen appeared, walking down the sidewalk hand in hand. They were too far away for him to see Rachel's face. They kissed good night—more like brother and sister than lovers—and Allen walked away, hands in his pockets, back straight. For a moment Pete's heart thumped mightily—he wasn't staying?—before he remembered. Of course. Allen was still worried about lust raising its scaled head between them. He'd be staying in a hotel, somewhere safe from the corruptive influence of Rachel and her curves and her breathy voice and beautiful beating heart.

Pete argued with himself for half an hour and then left the bar and knocked on Rachel's door.

She was already in her pajamas. She saw him, and her face was swept with panic.

"You can't be here."

"Allen's in a motel, isn't he?"

He walked past her, into her living room.

"You've been in a bar," she said.

"I had a beer. I'm not drunk."

"Seriously, Pete—"

"So. Have a good time?"

She closed the door. "No. I had an awful time. I spent all night trying not to throw up."

He went to her, put his arms around her.

"You smell like smoke."

"Sorry. I had to see you."

"Please go home."

He stroked her hair. "I want to hold you." He said that to her a lot then.

She leaned into his arms. "This is crazy. It's so wrong. He's right here in *town*."

"And I'm right here in your apartment."

They fell into her bed. She cried for a while, but then they were twisted together. And then she was gasping, and writhing, and finally crying out. She fell against his shoulder.

In a better world than theirs, Rachel took his hand then and said, *Oh, Pete, I love you, too. I'm leaving him.*

Instead, she bent her head, and he heard her whispering underneath and between her sobs. And when he asked her, "What's wrong?" she told him she was praying.

"Praying?"

"Because we've sinned."

His history with Rachel was one of small moments like this—little turns of phrase that might as well have been turns of fate. Like his whole life, all his actions, had skidded sideways on the smooth marbles of her words—words like "we" instead of "I." If she'd said "I," he might have let it go.

Instead, they argued. Maybe this was inevitable. She was, after all, a Christian, and he was, after all, not, and he'd come to her at a time that highlighted any number of her quote-unquote sins. And, for all the deep and heartfelt conversations they'd had about respect for the other's beliefs, this was a deep canyon. Maybe, no matter what had happened, an uncrossable one. (How relieved had Pete been, after all, when on their first date together Maya had looked up from her coffee and said, *You're not some Jesus freak, are you? 'Cause that's a deal-breaker.* How glad had he been not to have God in the room when he first unbuttoned Maya's jeans? When she'd groaned and slid him into her? He'd spent the year after Rachel's wedding celibate, and the return of sex to his life was as close as he'd ever come to having a religious experience of his own.) It was easy to forget, when Rachel was pressed close to him, cooing his name, that she saw him as flawed—that for all his doltishness, Allen had one advantage over him that Pete would never overcome: Pete could make her come, but Allen could bend his head and grab Rachel's hand and talk about Jesus and mean it. He could sin and talk of absolution, all in one night.

An hour later they sat on opposite ends of Rachel's bed; he still remembered the sickly look on Rachel's face, the way she crossed her arms over her breasts. Their terrible circular argument: "Rach. Tell me this. Am I a good person?"

Her anger, softening: "Pete. Yes."

"Do I care about you?"

Her eyes turning inward. Thinking, no doubt, of something Allen hadn't done. "Yes," she whispered.

"Do I care about other people?"

"Yes."

"Would I ever hurt you?"

A pause. "No."

"But if I die tonight, I'm going to hell?"

She turned her head toward the closet door, her lips pressed tight together.

"Say it," he said. "I want to hear you say it."

"Pete."

"Say it. Eternal torment, right? I use the brain your God gave me, and the heart he gave me, and I make the decisions I've made, and I've fallen deeply in love with someone sweet and good, and yet if I die tonight, I'll spend all the rest of time burning in—what—a pit of lava?"

She closed her eyes. "Yes," she whispered.

"Some God," he said.

"Don't," she said, turning to him again, her face drawn.

"Don't. I believe what I believe, and you believe what you believe. Let's just leave it."

He couldn't resist, not now. "Do you love me? Answer, Rachel."

She began to cry.

"I think you do," he said. "And you can't tell me, because you think God wants you to love Allen—"

She raised her eyes to him, and this time he saw no equivocation. He'd crossed a line. But that was just too fucking bad.

"God wants you to love a guy who's good at praying but not much else. Right? That's some God, isn't it? To condemn you to a life with him? You spend your life with him, Rach, and you'll be miserable. But if you spend it with me—"

"I'll what?" Her voice quivered, and her cheeks had gone white. "You think I'm *happy*? When every time you leave me I fall over and—and cry myself to sleep? I can't eat. I can't think. You want to take the credit for that, you go right ahead, Peter."

"You know I'm right," he said. "You cry yourself to sleep because you know Allen's not the guy. You *know* it. The hellbound asshole you're so mad at is the one who knows you best. You won't be happy until you admit it."

She got up then and began searching on the floor for her blouse, sniffling furiously. He watched the knobs of her spine, shadowed by the bedside lamp, as she bent over.

"Leave," she said, buttoning herself up. "You leave right now."

He didn't believe her, not then—if he had, he would have panicked. But instead, he stood and went to her. He did know her. He'd always known her. He put his hands on her shoulders and she stiffened, but he pulled her to him, anyway. He bent to speak into her ear. He smelled her perfume, her sweat, felt the smooth lines of her thighs against his. Even now she couldn't resist pressing against him.

"Let me ask you this," he said. "If I got saved tomorrow, what would you do?"

She went completely still.

"Would you leave Allen then?"

After a long moment she said, "You won't. It's just some—some game you're playing."

"No. It makes a point. If I prayed like Allen, would you love me then?"

"I mean it. Go."

"Rach, you know I'm right. You love me. You fell in love with a guy who's wrong for you. Why is that?"

"I don't love you," she said. She was crying now, so much he could barely hear her words.

He saw right through her. "You do," he said. "And when you're talking to God later, ask him why. Ask him for me. Tell him we're both curious."

He stalked home, where he drank half a bottle of a roommate's wine he found in the refrigerator, and passed out sometime in the early morning.

Pete spent the following day in bed; he cracked his eyes at the sunlight and knew, immediately, that he'd made a terrible mistake. The line he'd been so proud of crossing had probably done worse damage than he could imagine, to him and maybe to Rachel, too. He'd be lucky if she ever spoke to him again. For the first time since he'd met her, he cried for her, over her. He held his pillow and talked to it as though it were Rachel lying in the bed beside him. But what could he do? He couldn't apologize for what he believed. Her anger didn't change the fact that he was right. He'd gone after Rachel's one unalterable belief, and now he had to wait to see if she could forgive him that. If she loved him more than God.

She called him on Monday. "I want to see you," she said—but her voice was clipped, tired.

They met at a coffee shop they both liked. Immediately he saw she hadn't slept; she'd never looked so worn, so close to collapse. He imagined he looked the same way to her. He gave up.

"I was out of line," Pete told her. "I'm sorry."

She nodded, then covered her eyes and began to cry.

"Rach? What is it?"

And she told him: she was saying good-bye. She had to. And it was worse, even, than that.

She told him she had talked to Allen on Sunday, and they'd decided: they'd be married in the summer, and she'd transfer to his college as soon as she could.

"I'll never forget you," she said, not meeting his eyes. "But we were doing something wrong. We threatened both our souls. You have to understand—everything I believe tells me this is wrong. That we're damned for it." Her voice had dropped to a whisper. "I'm doing this for *us,* Pete. I hope someday you can understand."

He looked over her shoulder at the others in the shop, at the couples sitting across from each other, the people laughing at the counter or reading over class notes with their hands in their hair: all the world. He was about to become just another part of it.

"We love each other," he told her. "I believe *that.* What you're doing is a mistake. And I think you understand that already."

She winced.

He stood. He thought about kissing her, once more, but he was angry, and he wanted, finally, to make his point, and he was tired and hungover and ready to weep. But the moment he walked past her—and again, when he stepped onto the sidewalk and zipped his jacket against the cold fall air, and with every step, and years later—he wished with all his heart he had.

• • •

He and Rachel had decided: Pete should confront the boy—whose name, which Rachel had finally written down, was Everly, Ben Everly—where he worked. The bookstore where she'd met him was too public. He lived with his family and couldn't be approached there. And the golf course was a county away from Clarksville, where no one knew Rachel or Allen or their church. Pete had told her he'd played there, knew the place—if he went early Monday morning, he'd probably be able to get Everly as a caddie and have him alone anywhere on the course he wanted. And even if other people were around, Everly wouldn't make a scene. Not where he worked.

"What should I do?" Pete asked her. "You don't want me to—threaten him, do you?"

"No," she'd said. "He's a Christian, and he knows Allen's a pastor." Her face twisted with shame. "It won't be hard to make him feel guilty."

The next day, Sunday, Pete slept in, then woke and spent the better part of the day planning, all the while telling himself he was an idiot, that he'd never be able to pull this off.

Allen wasn't even human. Pete had no idea what went on in his head, except maybe the turning of a few shiny gears. His insides were his outsides. He was tall, straight-backed, had a full head of hair. He'd spent all his life drenched in moral authority.

Pete was short, tubby, nearly bald. He couldn't choose a soda from the refrigerator without due deliberation. Allen was a teetotaler; Pete was drinking himself into blackouts. Allen had the love of the world's most perfect woman. Pete had lost her in the worst way, and a wife besides.

And how was he supposed to *confront* Everly? He wasn't sure he could do it even if he was going as himself. Pete could count on the fingers of one hand the number of times he'd ever raised his voice—and two of them were with Rachel. The only fight he'd ever been in he'd lost. A drunk had said something to Maya on one of their first dates, and Pete had swallowed hard and told the man—a reedy guy with a ball cap and a farmer's tan visible even in the bar—to fuck off, and the guy had looked him over almost wearily. "All right, then," the man had said, and had punched Pete so hard he nearly passed out. Pete scrambled for his legs, but the man kicked him in the gut and then left—maybe he was ashamed. Pete sat in Maya's kitchen later, trying not to wince as she swabbed at the scrape on his cheekbone. "It's okay," she said. "I don't want a bruiser." She'd kissed him delicately on the tip of the nose.

What was he supposed to do to Everly? Make him feel guilty, Rachel had said. So was Pete supposed to open up a Bible and point out to Everly where he'd broken the rules? A ten-year-old who'd been to Sunday school could win that argument with Pete.

But the more he thought it through, the more he wondered if he wasn't overthinking things. Everly didn't know Allen. All he knew was that Rachel had a husband. That husband, if he showed up in person, only needed to be scary, hurt, aggrieved. A man who'd discovered a secret, who'd suffered a loss. That wasn't that hard, was it? Pete looked himself over in the mirror. He pointed at himself, tried to keep his face stoic. "Quit fucking my wife," he said.

His voice sounded soft already, like he was pleading. And had Allen ever cursed in his life?

No. But he might curse now. Let Everly know how serious things had gotten.

He deepened his voice. "Quit fucking—"

This was going to be a disaster.

Rachel had told him where Everly went to school; he looked up its Web site. Kirkwood Baptist Bible College and Seminary, in Worley, Georgia. The Web site showed a bunch of white boys in polo shirts smiling serenely at the camera. He read the information page for new students. Women had to wear skirts at least four inches below the knee. Men and women could speak in a dormitory room, provided the door remained open and the visitor logged in with the floor's "upperclassman spiritual adviser." All this, and then Mr. Ben Everly had found Rachel crying in his arms. No wonder it had happened quickly.

Pete dressed the part. It took more effort than he'd first supposed.

The clothing, at least, was easy. Golf clothes weren't a hundred miles removed from good-Christian-pastor clothes, and he had an outfit already, from his yearly golf game with some of his old buddies from Purdue. He looked at his sorry old shoes and decided new ones were in order. Allen always looked fresh.

He went to a thrift store down the street and bought a crucifix on a thin gold chain—Allen, he remembered, had one that matched Rachel's. He bought a gold wedding band, too. He'd thought of using his own, but—despite everything, despite the ridiculous tarnished mess of his marriage to Maya— he couldn't do it. He heard her voice: *Pete, I never thought you could get more spineless, but here you are.* He slipped on the new ring—it was a little big, but wouldn't slide past his knuckle. He turned his hand in front of the mirror. Only a month without his old one, and already the feel of the ring on his finger was alien, like a growth on his flesh he couldn't help prodding. He shaved his stubble and dressed in his golf clothes. Should the crucifix hang out? No. Allen wasn't ostentatious about it. Just a hint of chain at the neck.

The fact remained that he was bald and Allen wasn't. And that was only one of a hundred ways in which Pete didn't look a thing like Rachel's husband. Allen had six inches on him, straight white teeth. He didn't wear glasses. Rachel was sure this Everly kid had never seen Allen. But how did she know? The kid was obsessed, and Rachel was, even now, as naive as they came.

Pete ran another Internet search, this time on Allen. His church had a Web site, but no pictures were posted. Good, humble Allen Purcell—he'd emphasized the church and not his own face. But surely he'd been photographed somewhere. In the house? No—Rachel said she and Everly had only ever used a motel or the car. What if he'd looked in her purse? Their wedding picture had run in the paper. Maybe the kid had gone to the library, looked up the announcement, sizing up the competition. Pete would have.

But still—a photograph was different from flesh. And he'd have the advantage of surprise.

Pete settled on a cap. He also shaved the dense black fur off the backs of his hands and his forearms. Without the hair his arms looked spindly, sick. He'd still better wear a long-sleeved shirt, just in case. And, for good measure, he rushed down the street to a hairdresser. He caught them a half hour before they closed, and talked them into dyeing blond what little hair he had left.

"I'm an actor," he told the stylist. "I need it to look pretty real."

He and the stylist looked at himself in the stylist's mirror; both of them, Pete thought, looked dubious.

"So is it for, like, a movie?" the stylist asked.

"A little independent thing," Pete said. "For a friend of mine. Can you do the eyebrows, too?"

Pete went home and dressed and put on his new shoes and his cap and the crucifix. He looked at his white-blond eyebrows, the pale tufts just above his ears. He'd have to shave pretty close, but early in the morning he just might be able to pull off blond. He remembered Allen, in his tuxedo, waiting to be married. The knowing little smile on his lips. Pete stood straight. "I'm Allen Purcell," he said. "And I know who you are."

He tried the smile and had to admit he came close to nailing it.

• • •

After Rachel told him good-bye, Pete tried his best to forget her. He couldn't, so he began to drink as heavily as he could. He kept away from the phone. Rachel lived on the other side of town, but all the same he stayed inside; he couldn't bear running into her on the sidewalk. School was harder. He talked to the professor of the course he was taking with Rachel and explained that he was having an emergency and needed to drop it. He thought the professor looked as though she might know why, but she allowed it.

He called his ex-girlfriend, who listened to him for five minutes and said, "I'm hanging up, Pete."

And—his worst moment—he ran into Daniel the violinist reading in the corner of a study lounge in the library. Pete, hands sweating, went up to him.

"I'm Pete Shumaker," he said.

Daniel gazed at him. "I know," he said.

Pete sat next to him. "I don't need to know the details," he said. "But how'd you get over it?"

Daniel stared at him for a while, his bald head gleaming under the bright fluorescents. With precision, with bottomless contempt, he said, "Get over what?" Then he closed his books and stood and walked out of the room.

By the time the semester ended, Pete had lost fifteen pounds. He'd taken up smoking. He'd met a newly divorced woman at a bar, and they sometimes met for sex that made him want to weep with distaste. The woman's smell was wrong. Her hair was too coarse, her fingers too stubby. He caught her looking at him sometimes in a panic, probably thinking the same things. He took a job stocking supermarket shelves after midnight, which allowed him to sleep away the sunlight.

When Rachel called him in early July, he was sure he was imagining it.

"Peter," she said, "I've missed you."

He was lying on his bed, naked. It was four in the afternoon.

"I missed you, too," he said, voice cracking. He was ready

to tell her anything then. Whatever she asked of him, he'd agree to. He'd go to fucking church if she'd only hold him again. If she'd say his name one more time.

"I just—," she said. "I'll understand if you won't, but—"

Yes. He'd take her back. Of course. He'd come and get her right now. They could go anywhere—

"You've meant so much to me. I wish I could see you at my wedding."

He almost threw the phone across the room.

"Can we send you an invitation?"

"Jesus Christ," he said. "Will Daniel be coming? He and I could share a room."

She was silent. "Nothing happened with him," she said softly. "Not like with—not like that."

He began to weep. "You're something, Rachel. Really something."

"I want us to be friends," she said. She was crying, too. "Remember—remember before? When we used to talk? That was—I've never had a friend like that—"

He covered his eyes.

"I was thinking it wouldn't hurt us to—to talk on the phone every now and then."

"Rach, I don't know—"

"Can I at least send you an invitation?"

He had to get off the phone. Now. "Sure. Whatever you want. Good-bye."

He hung up and screamed into his pillow. She didn't call back.

The invitation came a few days later, typically complicated and lacy. He could just see Rachel, pouring all her energy into designing it, Allen nodding benevolently over her shoulder.

The wedding was in two weeks, a few hours away in the hinterlands near the Kentucky border.

Rachel had included a handwritten note:

It's too late to RSVP. But please know I miss you. You're a good person, Peter. It breaks my heart that you think I'm unhappy. And that you're not as happy as you deserve. Please come.

He looked over the note. Read it a hundred times, looking for coded messages. The woman he was sleeping with looked it over, too. "You should go," she said. "If for no other reason than to bury her. Maybe you just need to see it end."

That made sense. Or maybe he'd entered a state of mind which called for even more pain. A chance to find the bottom. He watched himself prepare as if in a nightmare. He booked a room at the hotel listed on the invitation. He drove home for his suit, still in the hall closet at his parents'. He set the alarm. He gassed up his car. He stopped in a grocery off I-74 and bought a card and signed it with a pen he found rattling in his glove compartment. He wrote on the envelope: *For Allen and Rachel.* He drove the interminable interstate and told himself the same thing he would ten years later, after another horrifying request: that he loved her, and this was proof. His gift to her.

He arrived at the church a half hour before the wedding. He knew only a few faces—some of Rachel's churchy friends he'd met only once or twice at Purdue. One—in a pink bridesmaid's dress—saw him and bolted. He sat down in a back pew, and then a few minutes later the same bridesmaid knelt next to him and squeezed his hand and said, "She's so happy you came."

What was he supposed to say? That he was happy for her? That he was glad he'd come, too? It was all he could do not to weep.

"Tell her I said hi," he told the bridesmaid.

A few minutes later the music started. The groomsmen filed in. Pete watched as Allen took his place, ramrod-straight, followed in lockstep by his father and his carbon-copy brothers and friends from his college—all of them with identical haircuts and beatific smiles. All of them staring at the doors to the chapel, except for Allen. The disgusting fucker looked straight up. As though God was up there nodding, mouthing, *You're welcome.*

And then everyone stood up, and Rachel was moving down the aisle, tidally slow. She passed Pete's row, and he tried to see her face through the veil. *Look at me,* he urged. She didn't.

The pastor actually asked the old movie question: *Does anyone here know any reason . . . ?*

Pete's throat ached. His throat tightened, his mouth opened. But he couldn't do it. He looked at his scuffed shoes throughout the rest of the ceremony.

He was sure he couldn't watch them kiss—but he did; he watched Allen's face descend, Rachel's rise; he knew her body, her posture, well enough to see her melt into the kiss as the church applauded; he saw Allen's eyes glitter. Because it was okay now. Because God had said, *Go ahead.* Pete wished Allen's throat was collapsing under his thumbs.

They marched out of the church. Pete hung his head until they were gone.

Everyone in the chapel stood and began to file out. He realized then, with numbing panic, that he'd have to pass Rachel in the receiving line. And he couldn't. He couldn't. That was asking too much—even Rachel would have to understand that. He spotted an exit sign near the front of the chapel and shouldered his way down his row. "I'm going to be sick," he told an usher—one of Allen's brothers—and then fled for the doorway beneath the sign.

It let him into a hallway. He followed it, vision blurred, and, naturally, got lost; stairs led him down into a warren of hallways and rooms in the basement, where the air was thick with the churchy smells of old paper, varnish, bad punch. He found an empty room—where they taught Sunday school, from the looks of things—and sat in a child's chair, knees to his chin. He'd wait until the place cleared and then sneak out. He'd drive back to West Lafayette that night. Maybe farther. Maybe he needed to go stare at mountains in Canada.

Forty minutes later he heard footsteps in the hallway outside. He sat still in the dark, watching the doorway, until he saw the silhouette pass—the wide shimmering bell of a dress, the shadow of a trailing veil. Her footsteps stopped down the hall; he heard, he thought—he knew—Rachel's tears.

He almost believed then in miracles. How could a bride slip so far away from the crowd upstairs, to so dark and secret a place, without being seen? The guests must have all left for the reception. Maybe Allen was holding forth, being worshipped, and she'd found a brief window. But she'd done it.

Pete found her sitting on a folding chair, just inside the open door of one of the side rooms—or rather, he saw the ruffled hem of her dress, her slippered feet crossed at the ankle and tucked under her chair.

He said her name, and she looked up at him. He could see her eyes in the shadows but not much else, though he knew, just by the angle of her neck, the expression that would be on her face.

"You didn't go through the line," she said. "I was watching for you."

"I couldn't do it," he said.

She buried her face in her hands and shook.

He knelt in front of her, put his arms around her. He lay his cheek against her bare smooth shoulder, and she wrapped her arms around his neck, squeezing with her elbows. Her cheek was damp against his. She smelled not like her single, simple perfume, but rather hundreds—flowers and fruits and musks and her own astringent sweat—like she'd been ritually anointed, prepared for mummification or the bier. He felt her convulse, once, twice, a dozen times.

He knew then, but even so, even holding her, he had to convince himself it was true. Rachel knew she'd chosen wrong. She'd loved Pete more, after all. He rubbed his hands up and down the ruffled sides of her bodice, along her ribs, across the thin satin straps that crisscrossed her pale shoulder blades. He found the mole underneath her left shoulder with his thumb, felt its downy raised surface, stroked it.

He whispered her name to her, over and over.

She clung to him harder. He touched, delicately, the complicated pattern of her hair, settled for tracing a strand that waved artfully down in front of her ear.

And that was, he thought, when he lost her. It was easy to see now what she needed, why she'd ever been with him at all. It should have been easy to understand then. She had kept him close not just because she loved him, or because he loved her. That wouldn't have been enough.

No: he did more than love her. He *told* her he loved her—and, unlike Allen, he acted like he meant it.

And if he'd told Rachel then, one more time, that might have been enough. The sign she'd waited for, maybe had been praying for. She would have told him she loved him, too; and then he would have been able to show her. He could have taken her hand, led her up out of the church to the back parking lot—surely she knew the way. They could have been twenty miles away from the church before anyone was the wiser.

All he had to do was say he loved her. But he didn't. He said instead the words that would do the most harm, the other sentence he'd said to her a hundred times, but the one whose time was long past: the one phrase that would send her running.

"Tell me what's wrong," he whispered.

His mistake was awful, total. Rachel could not have told him what was wrong, because what was wrong was *everything*. They were past explanation; talking was for the Allens of the world. To demonstrate his love, all Pete had to do was demonstrate that he *knew*, that she need say nothing more. After all the times she'd pushed him away, had withdrawn herself from him, she was ready, this time, to submit. To let him fix things. To take her hand, to pull her to her feet, to say, *Come with me and it'll be fine*. Just as Pete knew now that—no matter what she'd told him—sometime in the last few weeks, in a small motel room, she had sat still and wide-eyed while Ben Everly moved closer and closer; that she'd given herself to him because Everly had done what Pete hadn't: led her where she could never lead herself.

Rachel was right. She *was* weak. After all these years he understood. Everything had happened because Rachel was weak. And because Pete was, too.

"Tell me," Pete had said—and Rachel had only sobbed in the circle of his arms. Then she moaned and clung limply to him, while he stroked her back, which was now a little clammy.

"I'm sorry," she said then, her voice quivering.

"Don't be."

"I should get upstairs," she said, close to his ear. "They're probably looking for me."

Then, of course, he was surprised. He struggled for anything to say, and his words came desperately: "Are you happy?"

With anguish, he felt her standing up. He grabbed at her fingers. "I can't let you go unless you tell me you're happy."

Insane. He'd give anything to erase that sentence from his life, all its hopeless cowardice.

"Are you?"

Rachel hugged him, briefly, and then pulled away; he felt her looking quickly across his face in the dark, not seeing him—dismissing her last chance at love and contentment as a trick of shadows, maybe, but dismissing it nonetheless.

"Yes," she said in the flattest and deadest voice he could imagine, and then walked out of the room, away from him, in a rustle of silk.

•   •   •

Pete set his alarm early. He showered and dressed and then dug his clubs out of his apartment's storage unit. He spent a few minutes wiping the spiderwebs from them, then put on his cap and his fake ring and his crucifix. One look in the mirror left him a lot less confident than he'd been the day before. He looked like Pete Shumaker with an awful dye job.

He drank two cups of coffee on the hour-long drive north to the course. He thought over what he'd say, what the boy might say in return. The sun rose into a rich blue sky: it was good golf weather, at least.

He reached the course when he'd planned: at seven, just as

it opened. His was the only car in the lot. Beyond the parking lot the course glistened, still wet with morning dew and the nighttime work of the sprinklers.

Pete walked up to the desk and paid his greens fee: an exorbitant hundred bucks. The man at the counter asked, "Do you want to hire a caddie?"

"A friend of mine told me to ask for Ben Everly," Pete said. The words came out like bricks. He smiled at the man; it felt like a grimace.

The man checked a clipboard. "Ah, young Everly," he said. And he left the desk and walked to a door behind him and leaned in. "Ben," he said, "you've been requested."

And a few seconds later the door opened again, and Ben Everly appeared, smiling in the same deep artificial way the man at the counter was smiling. And—maybe Pete had imagined it—his face might have fallen, just a little, when he saw Pete. He'd heard the call and expected Rachel.

"Morning," Everly said.

He was small—Pete had been expecting someone a bit more imposing, someone Allen's height. Everly, though, could look Pete straight in the eye. He had a thin, narrow face, with wide, arching eyebrows and a mouth that didn't seem to stretch far enough on the sides. Like he was sucking in his cheeks. His eyes were dark to the point of being black. His hair was styled so that it looked unwashed and uncombed—Jesus, the fucking kids and their hair! Peter hadn't known that kind of cool extended to theology students from Georgia, but here was the evidence.

Everly wasn't handsome. No. He was *pretty*. Almost feminine. In a different kind of life, minus the suntan, he could have been a model, pouting with other thin boys in the front pages of *Esquire*. Maybe Pete thought this only because he knew the kid had been fucking Rachel—but he thought it all the same: Everly was *sexy*. Pete's fingers squeezed in on themselves. Everly wasn't so different from Allen, after all. Virtuous or not, he knew to prop his big Bible open in front of him in coffee shops and to style his hair and trim his nails, whiten his teeth. Pete could see it, just in the way Everly said, "Ben," and held out his hand: he knew what he put out there into the world. And he knew what he'd get. He knew he could walk up to a woman like Rachel Beauleaux and look soulful and virtuous, and ask what was wrong, and she'd tell him and be grateful.

Pete shook his hand and made himself smile and told Everly the lies he'd practiced: "My buddy Dick was out here a few weeks ago, said you did a pretty good job. Said to ask for you if I ever dug my clubs out."

"Dick . . . ," Everly said, and glanced at the man behind the counter.

"Dick Baldwin?" Pete said. "Tall guy, gray hair . . . ?"

Everly grinned so that his eyes crinkled. "Dick, right! Right. Nice guy! Good golfer."

"That's being too kind," Pete said. "I can see why he recommended you."

They all laughed, fake as a sitcom.

"And your name, sir?"

"I'm Al," Pete said.

"Good to meet you, Al," Everly said, and pumped his hand again. "By yourself today?"

Pete nodded and squinted out at the course. "Yeah, I'm rusty. Figured I better not let anyone see me while I shake it off."

Everly grabbed his clubs and shouldered them, without any effort. He wore a polo shirt; his arm muscles flexed. "Well," he said, "your secrets are safe with me. Shall we?"

They walked out onto the course. Pete told himself to breathe deeply, to act like he was enjoying himself. He wouldn't say anything until they were away from the clubhouse. But then, he was the only golfer out this morning—even at the first tee they had complete privacy.

Not yet, not yet. He'd play for a while, find out more about this Ben Everly.

Pete was an awful golfer, but at least that part of his story fit. He triple-bogeyed the first hole, double-bogeyed the second. Everly hung back, making nothing but absolutely noncommittal small talk on the walks between holes, offering him nothing but encouragement before and after each shot. His accent was buttery—studied, Pete thought. Playing up the southern-boy thing. Pete found it hard to say more than a syllable to him at a time. He kept thinking about Everly's mouth, Rachel's mouth. The smooth curve of her bare white ass under his hand. Everly chattered along, smooth and shallow. Professional. What had he said to Rachel? He'd have had a line. A man like him probably had a few. He probably drawled along in bed, called her *sugar, baby, darlin'*.

On the third tee, Everly shaded his eyes and said, "So did ol' Dick warn you about the trap at the dogleg?"

"No," Pete said, shading his eyes, too.

"You can't see it, but it's there. Right past that stand of oak catching the sun."

"Nasty." Pete took out his driver.

Everly said, "Lots of guys have better luck with a 3-wood."

Pete wanted to shoot back—*Oh, do they?* This was perfectly

sensible advice—Pete was spraying balls every which way—but all the same he ground his jaw when he took out the wood.

"Try not to wallop it," Everly said. "Lay it up a little short of the trap—right out there where that shadow is—and you got a pretty good line to the pin. Ground slopes back a little."

Pete followed Everly's advice and watched the ball thump down almost where he'd aimed it, right in the middle of the fairway. Everly watched it, too, even gave a little Tiger Woods fist pump, like there was a TV camera on the two of them. The kid was good—for a second there he'd felt like a golfer.

But. Hadn't Pete seen a few cracks, too? And not just in the kid's frantic eagerness to lie about ol' Dick. Pete sneaked a glance at Everly as the boy shouldered his clubs. Were those shadows under his eyes? Did his lip droop when he thought Pete wasn't watching? He thought of Daniel the violinist, thought of himself walking stunned around campus—and almost, for the space of a minute, felt sorry for Ben Everly.

After all, what had Everly done that Peter hadn't? To be scientific about it: Everly had put his cock in Rachel. Less than five times, Pete guessed, knowing Rachel and her conscience. Everly had given her nothing more than animal pleasure, and not enough of it to overcome the guilt she hauled around with her like a twin. Not enough, in the end, to make her keep him—and so here Everly was, sorry and sleepwalking, doing his best working his job, trying not to think about how many days it'd been since he'd left Rachel the note.

Everly didn't know about Rachel's history with Pete, all that they'd done together. All they'd *had.* He knew only that she was unhappy with her husband—but he didn't know her fears, her soft spots. Not the way Pete knew them. He bet Rachel had never pulled a sheet up underneath Everly's chin. He bet she'd never looked him in the eye and said, *I don't want you to leave.* By any reckoning Everly didn't have Rachel's love. That Rachel had slept with this—this *boy*—and not Pete was a matter of circumstance: when she'd met Pete, she was young and not fucking anybody, and now she was married, had at least a rudimentary sex life, and knew what she was missing, when it went missing. And she hadn't called Pete at first, because she thought he was happily married—because, in her way, she loved him still and didn't want to hurt him—the same reason Pete hadn't called her when Maya left him. Everly had been right in front of her; that was all.

He was lucky. Pete couldn't hate him for that, could he?

"Yessiree," Everly said over his shoulder, coming up on the ball. "One heck of a shot there, Al."

But he did hate him.

He watched Everly stride easily down the fairway—like the fit little twenty-year-old he was—watched him stride off into the sunlight, and felt his fists clenching. Poor sad little Everly with his bedhead hair and his tan and his muscles. Poor little Everly, who could have just about any woman he tried for— but who had tried for the big time. He'd known all along Rachel was married. Just as he'd known he was a long way from school, a long way indeed from his studies and the rules about open doors and long skirts and fucking chastity belts. Rachel hadn't told him the details, but Pete could see them play out easily enough. Everly talked with sad, lonely Rachel and saw immediately what he could do, saw immediately what she was: a woman who was just married enough to know how to fuck, but who was really just a girl, underneath, still a sweet country girl who'd fall apart for a pretty face and a few mentions of Jesus. Why wouldn't she? She'd married a pastor, after all. All he had to do was stand in the right place, work his charms, and in return he'd gotten from Rachel something precious—something Pete had been ready to die for, once.

So Everly had fallen in love. So what? Falling in love with Rachel was hardly unusual. It didn't make Everly *special*. And then, when Rachel took herself away, he threw a big ol' ungentlemanly tantrum. Poor, poor Everly. Pete followed him down the fairway and imagined him praying, late at night: *Oh God, why me? Why did you put her in my path? Why did I sin? What have I done to deserve this torment?*

He imagined Everly crying, snuffling, hearing nothing at all but his own puling weakness.

He imagined Everly going down on Rachel, those thin panties thrown aside at last, knowing her taste, feeling her fingers twining in his perfect messy hair. Imagined him looking down at Rachel's wide blue eyes while she sucked him off, while she gazed up at him, expectant, frightened. Prayerful.

Pete looked up and down the fairway. They were as alone as they could be. Everly deserved everything that happened to him now.

Everly stopped and dropped the bag; he hunkered down and looked at the ball. Over his shoulder, for the first time, Pete saw the sand trap the boy had warned him about. Maybe fifteen feet across and as well hidden as a tiger pit.

"Straight shot," he said to Pete. "And I have a feeling you're warming up."

"I guess so," Pete said. His heart was thumping; he could feel the roots of his teeth.

"So, Ben," he said, "Dick tells me you're a Christian."

Everly looked up, surprised. He smiled, a little uncertainly. "Yes, sir," he said. "That's right."

"Baptist?"

"Southern Baptist, yes, sir." Everly, Pete could tell, was doing his frantic best to remember ever telling imaginary Dick any of this. "I'm studying theology at Kirkwood Seminary, actually. Down in Georgia. I'll be a pastor someday, good Lord willing."

"That's a fine calling," Pete told him, looking off at the green.

"So—you're a Christian, too?"

Pete took his 7-iron out of the bag. "As it happens, I *am* a pastor."

The kid actually said, "Well, I'll be! What denomination?"

Pete told him, and when he did, he saw Everly pause, for just a moment. That's right, he thought.

"I respect your church a lot," Everly said.

"Not too different, are they?"

"No, sir, Al—I didn't catch your last name?"

"Purcell," Pete told him, looking him right in the eye. "Allen Purcell."

Everly's eyelids fluttered; he stood too straight, too still, hands jammed deep into his pockets. Pete held his stare, feeling his own cheeks flush. Everly looked him over, calculating, trying to see a way out. And not, Pete guessed, coming up with much.

"Well," he said finally, "it's a pleasure to meet you, Mr. Purcell—"

"I can't imagine why that would be."

Everly swallowed. Pete tapped the head of the club against the deep green grass.

"I mean," Pete said, "I'd have to imagine Rachel's told you some unflattering things about me."

The mention of her caused Everly to wince. Pete could

barely name what filled him, seeing it. His arms pulsed; his fist tightened slickly around the club. He took in a great noseful of the thick grassy air. The boy seemed to shrink; Pete felt himself growing. Maybe this was how Allen felt all the time.

Everly stammered. "So—"

"So I know. So I know just about everything."

"Mr. Purcell—"

"I know, for instance, that you tried to blackmail her."

Pete thought that maybe be could see the boy shaking a little.

"Did you think she wouldn't tell me?" Pete asked. "Really?"

"No—"

"What did you expect? Did you think she'd keep climbing into your bed? Did you think you'd have yourself a slave?"

"No," Everly said. "That's not it at all." He lifted his head and gazed at Pete. "I just thought—she told me she wasn't happy." He swallowed. "With you. I thought—"

"Let me guess," Pete said. "You thought she wasn't strong enough to leave me on her own? That all she needed was a little boost?"

Everly looked at the green and then back. "Yeah," he said. "That's about right."

"Rachel and I have our problems," Pete said. "As I guess most couples do. It's fair to say we have big problems, Mr. Everly—or else why would we be here talking?"

"But—"

"Shut it," Pete said. He looked at Everly dying a thousand deaths inside. He made himself think of the boy naked, sweating, Rachel kneeling in front of him. The boy's come dripping down her neck. "Don't go thinking you have *rights* here. We're not having that kind of talk."

Everly's mouth snapped shut.

"Some Christian you are," Pete said. "Threats. Carnal relations with a married woman. Kirkwood Seminary must have a little something to say about the Commandments, right? And you want to be a *pastor*?" Pete barked the last word, leaning forward on the balls of his feet to do it.

"No!" Everly said, taking a step back. "That was—that was a lie. To you. I'm not some fool kid. I knew—I knew I was throwing it away when I—when Rachel—"

"Yeah," Pete said. "That's something, at least."

"Mr. Purcell," Everly said.

Pete did his best to stare the boy into silence.

"You said I didn't have rights, Mr. Purcell," Everly told him. "I know why you're angry. Believe me, I know why. I'd be angry, too."

Pete took another step toward him. "You're saying we're alike?"

"Yes. In some—we both love Rachel."

"I tell you what," Pete said. "I'll not hear my wife's name in your mouth again. Boy."

There. Everly was mad now. He saw the kid's jawbone outline itself against his neck.

Everly's voice was quiet now. "I know you hate me. But you better understand I love that woman. You'd better."

Pete laughed. He couldn't help himself. Screw whatever Allen would say—this one he could field himself.

"I got a couple of things for you," he said. "One. You love a woman you've known a month. You love a woman who threw you under the wheels for her husband. She might think she loves you. She might have said so when you were fucking her—"

Everly's eyes nearly bugged out of his head.

"Yeah. I said it. Because to my mind, son, that's all Rachel was doing with you. You know what she told me? I asked her why—oh sure I did—and you know what she told me? *Ben's pretty, and I was weak.* You like that?"

Everly's tan had faded to the color of dried-out clay. Pete felt his words vibrating in his chest, even before he spoke them.

"It's true. You might love Rachel, but not for any good reason. She used you and came back to *me*. No matter what you heard, she made her choice. And I was in *Africa*. She could have been anywhere in the world with you by now, if she wanted. And yet here you are, and here I am, and Rachel's back at *my* house."

Everly was staring at a spot on the grass between them, his eyes wet.

"And I'll tell you something else, boy. So you know what she looks like naked. So you know what she feels like, inside. Good for you. You have it. It's not mine anymore."

Pete was surprised to feel his throat close on the words, to feel the sting in his eyes. He stepped closer; he moved himself in front of Everly's pale stunned face.

"Look at me."

Everly lifted his chin, looking for all the world as though Pete held him at gunpoint.

"You stole some things from me. I'll admit it. But there's ten years of her life with me you know nothing about. *Nothing.* Ten years of secrets. I know the name of her first pet. I know what she dreams. I know what it's like to hear her say, *I love you.* I know what it's like to hear her say, *I do.* To say—to say, *Yes.*" Pete was nearly choking now. He whispered: "I know what she sounded like the first time she ever came. Do you?"

Everly tried to turn his face away. He smelled like bad aftershave and thin, piercing sweat. Pete couldn't help himself—he reached out and grabbed Everly's chin with his thumb and forefinger and turned the boy's face back. "You look at me when I talk to you, you little shit."

Everly's eyes bulged, and he swatted Pete's hand away. Without thinking much about it Pete brought up the golf club's handle between Everly's legs, with all the strength he had. Everly groaned and dropped immediately to his knees, bent over himself, the back of his neck and ears turning a sudden firecracker red.

Pete took a quick look around them. He could just see back to the clubhouse—the entire course was still empty.

"It's a hard lesson," he said to Everly. "But you best learn it. She's my *wife*. She'll be my wife tomorrow. And I want you out of here. I want you out of my life and Rachel's. You'd be best off running back to Georgia in the morning. And you'd best beg Jesus for help, every fucking step."

Everly took a gasping, whistling breath. "Some man of God you are," he said.

"I'm not perfect," Pete said. "But let me remind you I never fucked another man's wife."

"You're—" Everly shook his head and sucked more air. "You're just what I expected."

Pete stood over him.

"How's that?"

"From what—from what she told me. You're not that different."

Pete couldn't think of anything to say now.

"She told me a lot," Everly said. "She told me about the first time. How she begged you to stop—"

The bottom dropped out of Pete's stomach. "Shut your fucking hole," he said.

Everly grinned at him. Pete could see—his eyes were crazed. He didn't have any weapons except this one, and no reason at all not to use it.

"She begged you. Begged you. And she told me what you said." Everly put a hand down and, wincing, lifted himself onto his haunches, eyes squinted shut.

"Quiet," Pete said thickly. But he wanted—needed—to know. He felt a tremor in his leg.

Everly stood, hunched, and said, "She was crying. She was in pain. And you told her: *Bear it.*"

Everly raised his chin and smiled. Pete swayed on his feet. She turned from him in a rustle of silk. He heard her voice, heard her crying on the phone—how many times had it been? She'd called him, three months after the wedding, and told him, *Everything's fine, I'm so happy.* And all he'd had to do was open his mouth. And tell her. And because he hadn't—

"I'll tell *you* something," Everly said, smiling, tears coursing down his cheeks. "I might have fucked her, but I sure as heck never raped her."

Pete closed his eyes.

If only Everly had stopped. But he didn't. He was snorting, blinking, drawing up a zealot's strength. He was going to say everything.

"She begged me, too," the kid said. "Want to know what for?"

"Stop," Pete said. His blood was moving strangely, his heart knocking harder and harder.

Everly smiled, just a little. His hair hung across his forehead. "The first time? When we were done? She said, *It's never felt so good.* We did it over and over. I told her it wasn't safe for us to stay all night in the motel, but she grabbed onto me and said, *Don't leave, please, don't leave me—*"

Pete swung the club as hard as he could. The head whispered around and caught Everly on the side of the chest; Pete heard a quick, bright snap. Everly dropped and scuttled on the grass, wheezing; he reached for Pete's legs. Pete sidestepped him. He saw the sunlight above him, filtered green and warm through the leaves of the oak. He felt himself, his own skin, a burning weakness in his shoulder. He heard a moaning sound that, he knew, was coming from inside his throat. But everything else, all the world apart from the boy on the ground and Rachel's face, was gone. Stop, he told himself, but his arms were still made of iron, his teeth still grinding. Everly, snuffling, grabbed hold of Pete's pant leg. Pete lifted the club with both hands and brought the head down onto Everly's skull. The club and his arms thrummed up to his elbows. Everly let go, and because Pete still had the strength, he performed the same motions again.

Then he returned to himself; the wrongness of what he'd done gushed into his stomach. He was gasping, his shoulder was aching. And Everly lay before him on the grass, jerking, hands curled at his chest, blood leaking from his open lips. His dark eyes flickered up to Pete's. They weren't angry, not now.

Pete dropped down next to him. The left side of Everly's face was swelling. The skin over his temple was split, where Pete had caught him the last time with the club.

Everly's hands clutched at the grass. His eyes rolled up.

"Get up," Pete said. Even as he said the words, he knew they were stupid, useless. Fear slid down his throat and turned in his belly like a silvered shard of mirror glass. He put his hand on the boy's shoulder. Blood bubbled at Everly's lips and outlined his bottom teeth.

"You stay here," Pete said, rasping. "I'm going for help."

But by the time he was done saying it, Everly had died. His tremors stilled. He exhaled—a long sputter—and Pete waited and waited for the next breath. It didn't come. Something changed in Everly's eyes—Pete couldn't have said how, but one second they stared out, and the next they didn't.

Pete looked at the bag of clubs, the dead boy. He took two or three breaths and stood and looked back at the distant clubhouse. Other golfers had appeared now, were loading their clubs into a pair of carts.

He wasn't getting out of this. He knew that right then and there. No collection of miracles could point to anyone but Pete. He wanted to plead with the distant golfers: it wasn't me. But who was it instead? Who'd done it instead? Allen? The empty man who'd swung the club was him. It was him.

But all the same he grabbed two fistfuls of the boy's shirt and, grunting, weeping, he dragged Everly to the nearby sand trap and heaved him into it. Maybe if the guys coming through were any good at all, they'd miss it. Pete might have a little time.

He threw his clubs in after Everly—even the one that had killed the boy. Then he ran for the trees at the edge of the course, not looking back. He climbed a waist-high fence and jogged back through a meadowful of waist-high grass toward the parking lot. No sirens wailed in the distance. The sun overhead was still warm and beautiful, the tall grass cool and wet against his slacks. He reached the lot, a hitch in his side matching the one in his shoulder. A car pulled in past him; the driver didn't even glance his way. Pete dug for his keys and unlocked the door of his car. He put his hands on the wheel and saw for the first time that they were covered with a sticky net of Everly's blood.

He turned the key in the ignition and drove away, doing his best not to speed.

· · ·

Pete drove deep into the countryside outside of Wakefield— taking turns by instinct, doing his best to keep heading away from the interstate, on narrow county roads with mottled pavement and no center lines. Endless cornfields flickered past his windows.

He thought about what Everly had said. The words that had clicked off the rational part of his brain, that had lifted his arms: *Don't leave me*—

He thought about his first night in Rachel's bed. And his last. He thought about her wedding night.

After Rachel turned away from him in the basement, he'd meant to drive home, but a desperate thought had come to him. He had gone to his hotel room, upstairs from the reception, doing his best to avoid all the other guests, the buzzing party static from the hotel's ballroom. Maybe Rachel would reconsider. If she changed her mind, she could find him in his room. He could still get her out of there. The memories were fuzzy— he'd stopped at a gas station and bought a bottle of very bad wine—but he could still feel the crazy spinning hope. And he could remember what lay beneath that hope: the cold weight in his chest, the haze of shock drying his eyes and throat.

For two or three hours he kept wait in his bedroom. He paced and clapped his palms together and sweated a sour smell. A floor below, the reception was in full swing; Rachel would be cutting cake. Dancing. Hearing the teary speech from her maid of honor. He took a few sips of wine. Ten o'clock passed. Eleven. Things would be winding down. He sat on the bed, and watched the door to his room. *Knock,* he thought, he wished. He wished with his eyes closed. He thought of God— Rachel's God, that smug asshole, that vast handful of string. He wouldn't pray. He knew he was drunk. He imagined the bride and groom downstairs, making their way out of the reception hall, hearing dirty sniggering jokes from all corners of the room. Allen getting his back slapped enviously by his groomsmen. Taking Rachel's hand. Rachel's eyes wide with fright, regret. Pete wouldn't pray. She'd come to him. She'd know now—it was for real. He watched as the digital clock in his room turned to midnight. They'd be upstairs in their suite now. Allen would be undressing. So would Rachel. He'd touch her and she'd realize. She'd think of Pete and come running. No way would she go through with it. No way. The world didn't work like that.

Please. *Please.*

And now Pete knew: sometime that night, while he'd waited and drunk and begged, Rachel had been begging, too.

At four in the morning, his bottle empty, he crept down the top-floor hallway in his bulging cocoon of skin and sadness and put his hand on the crack between the double doors of the honeymoon suite. He laid his ear to the door and listened, but heard nothing. He sat cross-legged just outside the suite and wept as softly as he could, for what seemed like hours. Let someone see, he thought. Fuck it. But no one came. The hotel was quiet, soft and cottony quiet, and his blood was thick and sorry in his temples and eyes. He saw Rachel turning from him in the basement, the empty pits of her eyes. *Yes,* she said, in the dead voice. She moaned: *Oh, Pete—*

He woke the next morning on the floor of his room. This did not surprise him. Even drunk, he'd picked himself up and crawled away from her. Like a coward. Like a dog that had the good sense to sneak away to die in the tall grass, where no one would be bothered by the stink.

Pete thought, as he drove now, that he wouldn't run. Not this time. Not even if he had someplace to go.

He stopped the car at the top of a barely-there rise in the road. He stood, shoulder aching, staring out at the vast cornfield to the east, the short stalks rippling in a breeze just strong enough to move the tassels. A little white farmhouse sat a half mile down the road: the kind of place where he'd grown up, where both Rachel and Allen had grown up.

He took out his cell phone and dialed Rachel's number.

She answered right away: "Pete?"

He swallowed, then told her: "I took—I took care of it." He didn't know if the police could listen in on a cell phone call, so he added, "I told him to leave you alone. I think he will."

She began to cry immediately. "Oh, Pete, thank you, thank you."

He cradled the phone against his ear and looked out across the rows of corn. He took several steps and watched the vanishing point shift, the converging rows seeming to turn, as if they were spokes of a giant wheel. He'd thought he might cry, listening to her, but he felt emptied out, spent.

"I can't talk long," he said. "But I want to ask you something. It's important, and I want you to be honest. The answer means—it'll be the most important thing you've ever said to me. And I'm asking now because—because you owe it to me."

He listened to the static on the line, his voice and her breath bouncing back and forth in space.

"All right," she said. She'd never sounded smaller, more distant.

"Here's what I want to know," he said. "I want you to think about that night in the church. Your wedding night."

"Pete—"

"Could I have done it differently?"

The power lines buzzed, the field rotated slowly as he paced forward, back. He'd wanted to ask the question for years . . . but now that he'd said it, he saw how it had changed on him. All it could mean. He almost laughed. But that was how things had always gone with Rachel, hadn't they? She had a way of changing the meaning of everything he'd ever done or said.

Then, at last, she answered, her voice rich with tears: "Yes."

A day before, the word would have filled him with hope, or despair, or both in equal measure. But now?

He could only think of one response he knew to be true.

"I have to go now," he told her. "You might not always think so, but I love you with all my heart."

Before she could speak again, he closed the phone, then switched it off. It was better that way. No amount of talking could fix them, and he couldn't pretend otherwise. And she should have another few hours before she understood what had happened. A last burst of happiness, hope.

He sat behind the wheel of his car. *Yes.* In the baking heat he flexed his hands; he watched the lines of blood in the folds of his skin stretch, then contract.

He'd be honest when they asked him what happened. He'd tell them everything. And Rachel would hear, soon, and then Allen would hear. Their church would hear. The newspapers.

The thought filled him with some comfort. No marriage

could survive such a thing, no pastor such a scandal. Pete smiled at the thought of it. The story would come out. And then Rachel and Allen could spend their days doing just what Pete would: opening their eyes to this strange, changed world, and all the new truths it would have them believe.

WATER HAZARD
Stephen Collins

Fifteen miles north of Manhattan in the sleepy village of Hastings-on-Hudson, Annie Bridget was hitting a bucket of practice balls. It was one o'clock on a muggy Sunday in mid-June, the sort of day the heat index was created for. In less than an hour, the final round of the LPGA Ladies Invitational would begin. Annie, whom some called Golf's Bad Girl, while others claimed her as its undisputed queen, felt queasy. She was hearing the Voice again.

Criminal, it had whispered when she opened her eyes this morning. *You should be locked up.*

Momentarily free of the viciously familiar, punishing sound in her head, Annie drove a ball far and straight into the middle of the driving range of the venerable St. John's Golf Club. She wiped her forehead and glanced at the sun. Nothing short of a total eclipse would keep the temperature from hitting ninety by tee-off time.

That wouldn't be so bad, she thought, a total eclipse. Then maybe I wouldn't have to play today.

The twenty-eight-year-old natural honey blonde was carrying a three-stroke lead over Janet Deeter heading into the last round, with Gail Fahr two strokes behind that. It was anybody's tournament, but even her enemies seemed to be rooting for Annie Bridget this weekend. Her incredible streak of three straight major wins had catapulted her to the first ranks of all-time women golfers and made sudden fans for her everywhere. If she could hold or improve her lead today, she would earn a permanent spot in the record books, and the Hall of Fame, right alongside Tiger Woods and Nancy Lopez.

Fat chance.

There it was again. She called it, simply, the Voice. No one else knew about it. There was no way to tell anyone without explaining where the Voice had come from, and that had never been an option.

With the edge of her 3-wood, Annie separated a ball from the forty or fifty she'd emptied onto the patch of worn Astro-Turf. As she rolled the Day-Glo-yellow sphere toward her feet and lined it up quickly off her left shoulder, she inhaled slowly, taking in the sweet smell of magnolias that were flowering along the outskirts of the driving range. Determined not to overthink today, Annie went into the coiled, controlled backswing that had helped her to the astonishing feat of three straight LPGA major wins.

She struck the ball cleanly, sending it high and straight toward the white sign in the center of the range that read "250." Her ball smacked the metal sign, ringing it like a church bell, and the crowd that followed her everywhere these days erupted into rapid-fire applause for their newfound heroine.

Luck. That was luck. You're almost out of it. You were five strokes ahead after the second round, now it's only three. It's fitting. You don't deserve to win.

She grabbed her light bag of practice clubs and abruptly started walking toward the chipping green, keeping up a convincing smile for the gallery. Hundreds followed. Her short game suffered the most when the Voice took hold, and she had to be ready. A pale, horsey-faced AP reporter in his late twenties struggled to catch up with her. He couldn't help but notice that her navy wraparound short skirt might have looked more at home on a tennis court, clinging as it did to her round but narrow hips, setting off her long, tanned legs. She nodded noncommittally at him and maintained her stride, hoping to avoid another interview. The reporter, flustered and a little starstruck, straightened his thick glasses nervously and gathered his thoughts as best he could.

"Uh, Miss Bridget?" he began.

"That's my name," said Annie, who was smiling in spite of herself, grateful to find his awkwardness charming, even pleasantly distracting.

"Uh, how do you feel?" he asked, as though it were the most original question on earth.

"Well," she said, sensing his discomfort, "that's a tough one to answer, believe it or not."

"Sorry," he went on, fumbling. "I just wondered . . ."

You're a total fraud. Stop trying to charm him.

"Look . . . Chris," said Annie as she lay down her clubs in some medium rough about fifty feet below the practice green. "It *is* Chris, right?"

"Yes," said the reporter, delighted that she remembered.

"Chris. Could you do me a favor? Can I possibly talk . . . off the record?" she asked. Her eyes seemed to be pleading.

"Sure, sure," he replied, touched, shielding the sun from his forehead. His heart, apparently unschooled in journalistic objectivity, thumped.

"Okay: off the record," Annie went on, " 'cause I really need to talk to somebody. So here it is, just between you and me."

She took a pitching wedge from her trusty old canvas and leather bag and lined up a shot. "I feel more excited than I've ever felt in my life. I feel like I want to throw up. I feel like a fraud. I feel like the best player in the world . . . today. Might not be tomorrow, probably won't be. But, well, I feel good . . ."

You stink.

"I also feel like I stink. I feel like I want to die—and I've never felt more alive. And I'm really sorry that you can't print any of this, but you've always been kind to me, Chris, and, well, you asked." She looked into his eyes. "I just really needed to say that out loud, and my caddie, frankly, doesn't want to hear it, and if you don't print it, well, I owe you, and I won't forget. Deal?"

Blushing and trying to think of what to say next, Chris noticed beads of perspiration bobbing up along Annie's furrowed brow. Strange, he thought. She looks like she might cry.

"Okay," he said. "Sure. Mum's the word. But, listen, could you maybe give me something I *can* print?"

"Well, let's see," she began as she chipped a shot out of the rough, dropped her wedge, and pulled out a 9-iron. "I've had this bag since I was ten. How's that?"

"You always use it to practice," Chris said, nodding, reciting a bit of Annie Bridget lore back to her. "It has a familiar, worn-in smell that calms you down. You're very into scents and aromas."

"Okay," she said, blushing. "You've done your homework."

"I saw your A & E *Biography*," he said gently. "So—anything else?"

"Well, everybody knows I grew up on this course. I could play it with my eyes shut. Just say that . . . I feel . . . great." Her shot landed a few feet shy of the pin.

You feel like you're going to explode.

Annie overswung at the next ball, Chris noticed, slicing it like a 20-handicap club hack. It traveled thirty feet out-of-bounds and disappeared down a steep bank.

That's the real you. That's what you deserve.

Not looking at the young reporter, she quickly chipped a shot that flew into a steep arc toward the pin, one-hopped straight for the hole, and dropped into the cup as though on automatic pilot.

"Wow," said Chris quietly. "Nice one."

"Thanks," she said, meaning it, squinting in a way that Chris felt only added to the cover girl appeal that had made her the biggest thing in sport—male or female—in the still-new millennium. He scribbled a note that she looked as though she'd stepped out of a catalog that was half Ralph Lauren, half Victoria's Secret. The shoulder-length blond hair that had just landed her a half-million-dollar-a-year endorsement from Traité gleamed in the dappled early afternoon sunlight. Annie leaned over for her next swing and Chris wondered if she could tell that he was looking down the front of her scoop-neck sleeveless pale blue sweater. He told himself to look away but hesitated, noticing that her lacy bra was serving up the kind of cleavage that made him wish he worked for a less respectable news outlet. She glanced up for a split second—just enough to bust him—and smiled nonjudgmentally, which had the effect of cementing his crush.

"Maybe you better leave me to this," she said. "I need to shut up and concentrate."

"Sorry," he said, backing away. "Of course. Sure. Yes. Good luck today." Okay, he told himself . . . leave her alone . . . don't say another word.

"It's great that you're so familiar with the course," he said, ignoring his own advice. Shut up! he ordered himself again, finally moving away.

Yes, she had grown up on this course and played hundreds of rounds on it. She hadn't mentioned that she'd lost her virginity on St. John's seventeenth green one June night almost exactly nine years earlier, an hour and two mai tais after her senior prom. With her queen's tiara slightly askew but still pinned to hair that was breaking free from its yearbook perfection, she and her date, prom king and peerless senior heartthrob David Strickland, had slipped away from the party in her new Saab convertible, a graduation present from her father. She'd handed David the keys with a twinkle in her eye that had made him drive faster than the manual suggested for a brand-new engine, and they'd parked on a dirt service road that ran behind St. John's. As they approached the seventeenth's wide and notorious pond in the summery moonlight, she had stunned David by stepping casually out of her strapless white gown—a moment she had rehearsed in her mind for weeks. Freezing the scene in his memory, David Strickland, tanned and mustachioed, had the happy thought that this would be the last thing he would think of when he died.

She smiled at David over her shoulder as the pond's cool water overtook her ankles, then her knees. David managed to appear unruffled and enjoyed the view as long as he could, but soon he had stripped and joined her in the shallows of the little lake.

She moved close, draping her arms around his wide shoulders, inviting him for a kiss, then teasingly backing away. "This is a water hazard, you know," she said, laughing softly, licking his ear.

"Doesn't seem too hazardous to me," whispered David.

"It will be if you don't get me home on time." Annie laughed, finally kissing him deeply, running her hand down his back to the curve of his hip, pulling him to her.

"God," David said, laughing softly as she touched him. "Take me now."

"Everyone says you're a heartbreaker, David Strickland," she murmured with a trace of sadness that she pushed out of her mind before it could fully surface. "But I don't care. I love you. Forever."

"You and me," he breathed. "Forever."

They made out to the agonizingly pleasurable point of no return, and Annie took his hand and led a dripping, extravagantly excited David toward the seventeenth green. Tall evergreens shaded the soft grass from the bright moonlight. Annie laid him down and made good on her fantasy, their bodies joining to the sounds of night sparrows, the soft hum of distant sprinklers, and the scent of fresh-cut grass.

To this day, the smell of a newly cut lawn made Annie think of sex. On a golf course, far from being a distraction, it seemed to energize her with picture-perfect memories of that picture-perfect night.

But two years ago, shortly after her and David's third wedding anniversary, the scent of just-cut grass became associated with a new memory for Annie, no less heart-pounding in effect.

• • •

Early in the second round of the Virginia Slims Classic near Charlotte two years before, Annie had severely twisted her left ankle clambering toward a bad lie down a rocky slope off the third fairway. The sprain forced her out of the tournament. David, who now ran a thriving Lexus dealership, had flown in late the night before for moral support. He had slept in, promising to join the gallery to watch her play the back nine. On crutches, Annie had struggled back to their Holiday Inn room unannounced. When she opened the door, she discovered her shining knight, her perfect husband, dressed only in an open, short-sleeved madras shirt she'd given him, spread out on one of the room's two king beds, lying beneath a naked young brunette who'd apparently delivered a still-uneaten breakfast. In shock, Annie gathered her things before David and the woman managed to dress, left the room, and grabbed a cab to the airport.

The next day, David's brunette, sensing that her fifteen minutes was upon her, rubbed salt on the wound by leaking her version of the story to the *Star,* whose next week's headline read ROOM SERVICE FOR ANNIE'S HUBBY. The story managed to paint Annie as a slut who had cheated so relentlessly on David that he had finally been moved to cheat back.

The discovery of her husband's affair not five hours old, Annie landed in New York, rented a car at La Guardia, and drove north to her father's house in Yonkers, her ankle throbbing mercilessly. She blamed herself, as was her habit, certain that her endless weeks on the road had led to David's infidelity. Her mother had been killed in a car accident when Annie was nine. She had been speeding through suburban streets to catch Annie in a school play, and been sideswiped by a van. Despite all the logical explanations in the world from her father and a well-meaning therapist, Annie blamed herself for her mother's death. And worse, Annie had lost her confessor. She had always told her mom everything. After her death, she started to keep secrets to herself.

Johnnie Bridget, Annie's father, was a former PGA pro who had never won on the Tour but now made a decent living coaching a private school golf team and giving lessons at a nearby club. His boyish good looks had gone somewhat puffy with drink, and his slightly lopsided, toothy grin had caused people all his life to say how much he resembled a fellow Oklahoman, Mickey Mantle. Annie drove down her old street, lined with once healthy, now struggling oaks, and parked outside the musty, eighty-year-old, two-story stucco house where she'd grown up, a quarter mile from the Yonkers-Hastings border. She silently opened the never-locked front door and soon, amid the comforting aroma of Johnnie Bridget's pipe tobacco and the hint of bourbon that was always on his breath after six o'clock, Annie was telling him tearfully about David and the waitress. When she finished, Johnnie took a long sip of his now iceless drink and sat, blinking his eyes, looking into the distance.

"I never liked him, you know," he finally said, quietly.

"You're a dad. He was my first love. Of course you didn't like him."

"No," said Johnnie, shaking his head. "It's a guy thing. He's just not, you know, someone I'd take down the river."

"Down the river" was Johnnie's favorite metaphor: people going down a torrid river on a tiny raft. You either wanted someone on that raft or you didn't.

"Go ahead," she said, blowing her nose. "Say 'I told you so.' "

"Nahh," he answered, wishing he'd kept his mouth shut. "I didn't want to be right. Who knows . . . maybe I'm not right. Maybe it'll all work out." He hoped she wouldn't check his eyes and see how little he believed it.

"We were too young," said Annie. "I knew it when we got married."

"So did I," agreed Johnnie, rocking her gently.

"But you were always so nice to him."

"You loved him. I could never say no to you, kiddo. Not that you're spoiled. You're not."

"You gave us that beautiful wedding," Annie said, dabbing at her eyes, "and you didn't like him?"

"Hey, it's tough being a dad. Especially when your kid is beautiful. And talented. You're right, I probably wouldn't have liked anybody who swept you off your feet."

"Daddy," she said, crying softly into his shoulder. "What should I do?"

"How 'bout I call Vito and have David's arms broken?" suggested Johnnie, almost merrily.

She laughed in spite of herself. "Who's Vito?"

"You know—Vito. Generic, plain-wrap Vito. Some guy who'd break an arm if the price was right. Probably a lot of 'em in the greater Yonkers area. Let me see." He got up and opened a drawer at the bottom of the sofa's end table and made a show of pulling out a well-thumbed copy of the yellow pages, opening it with a flourish. "'Legs: Broken.' Yeah, okay, here it is: Vito." He looked up to make sure she was smiling. "No last name. 'Open 24/7,' it says. 'Heartbroken?' it says. 'Let Vito break a leg.'" Annie's smile was widening. "Sounds perfect," he said conclusively. "Let me call." He picked up the phone.

"Stop it," she said, chuckling slightly and elbowing him as he held his finger on the cutoff button and pretended to dial.

"Hello. Is this Mr. Vito?" Johnnie said cheerfully, as though someone had answered. "Oh, just 'Vito'? Okay, sure."

All her life when she was upset, Johnnie had tried to make her laugh, with mixed results. It wasn't as good as a mother's shoulder to cry on, but the effort always meant the world to her.

"Vito, tell me, uh . . . what does a castration go for these days?"

Annie snorted unself-consciously.

"No, no," Johnnie went on as though he were ordering flowers. "It's for my daughter's husband. Oh, great. Lemme tell her." He cupped his hand over the mouthpiece. "They have a castration special for unfaithful husbands: two balls for the price of one."

Annie's laughter, part relief, part embarrassment at Johnnie's crudeness, became borderline hysterical.

"Daddy, stop!" she begged, trying to catch her breath.

Johnnie hung up, a little less anxious now that her tears had been momentarily stayed.

"Vito's got an early bird special," he said. "But I have to order before dawn."

"Stop," she repeated, chuckling in spite of herself, almost guilty not to be crying.

"He'll castrate *and* make that miserable son of a bitch disappear."

"Does he take American Express?" she sighed, quieting down.

They sat still for a few minutes, looking out the window as an elderly couple walked a small dog under a streetlight.

"You know," he said, his voice far away, "there actually *are* Vitos out there."

She dabbed at her eyes. "If only it were that easy," she said.

They talked until Annie fell asleep on his shoulder, and

Johnnie carried his only child upstairs to her old bed, tucking her in with her clothes on, propping a pillow under her swollen ankle. In the morning, he canceled his golf lessons for the day. He hadn't spent concentrated time with his daughter since her marriage, and, gloomy as he felt, he was grateful for her company.

After a few days, she began to snap out of it and started the process of rehabilitating her ankle and getting back on the Tour.

She succeeded, but failed to make four straight cuts. A magazine unearthed yet another affair of David's. Annie decided to cut her losses and began divorce proceedings. One of her attorney's paralegals leaked news of the divorce to a clerk in the county courthouse. The clerk, his face digitally smudged out for the cameras, turned up on *Access Hollywood.* The interview told of how David was countersuing for divorce on the grounds that Annie had conducted "an endless series of extramarital affairs" prior to his.

Guilty until proven innocent, Annie was crowned Golf's Bad Girl. In her mind, she deserved it. A year earlier, lonely from three months on the road away from David, who had steeped himself in his business, she'd been attracted to a charismatic and renowned sportswriter who was doing a profile on her. After taping a long interview in their hotel's bar, they were riding up to their respective rooms on the elevator when he surprised Annie with a kiss. He had led her to his suite, where they necked and eventually undressed, but, just as impulsively as she'd gone to his room, Annie guiltily bailed out moments before consummation, leaving him high and dry and landing herself on his shit list forever. When the bad-girl rumors began to fly, his column fueled them.

For the first time in her career, she developed a case of what golfers call the yips. Even with her ankle healed, she found herself botching easy putts and losing confidence in her always reliable chips. She'd have a superb round or two, then lose her touch and finish out of the money.

Johnnie Bridget, whose publicly controlled temper and attention to detail had made him an extraordinary coach, became increasingly distracted and edgier than usual after his nightly bourbons. David Strickland seemed to be developing into a monster with an appetite for any kind of publicity. He fought the divorce and stalked Annie on and off the course, one day making seemingly sincere statements to the press about his love for Annie, his contrition, and his desire to get her back, and the next night club-hopping with his new girlfriend, Rachel. Miserable, Annie sequestered herself between tournaments, refused to date, and tried to focus on her game. She was barely making expenses when Reebok, despairing of the negative publicity, let its deal with her lapse.

"I stink and I'm pathetic," Annie said one night in Johnnie's kitchen, after yet another poor showing in a western Massachusetts B-level tournament.

"Shush," he whispered mock-disapprovingly as he filled the dishwasher. "Your brain will hear you." It was something he always said when she put herself down.

"Sorry, Dad," she said, more discouraged than he'd ever heard her. "But this is killing me."

"Me, too," said Johnnie under his breath, slapping the dishwasher door shut. "I'm gonna take care of it."

"What?" Annie said, her brow furrowed, not sure she'd heard him. "What did you say?"

"Huh?" replied Johnnie, shaking his head as though to clear it. "Nothing, nothing, I didn't say anything. I'm goin' to bed."

A week later, David Strickland disappeared.

· · ·

David had been abducted from his house on a foggy night in Yonkers as his newest girlfriend, Rachel, slept. Rachel was not an official suspect, but the tabloids took care of that, adding her to the mix. The *World,* based on no evidence whatsoever, suggested that David had been sneaking out to a reconciliatory tryst with Annie the night he disappeared, painting a picture of a "bizarro love triangle."

Rachel had reported panicking when, after waking and finding David wasn't in bed, she called out for him. Running through their living room to the front door, she saw David being pushed into a black SUV by two men. In the misty darkness, she couldn't make out the SUV's license number or its exact make, though she testified that it looked like an Explorer. Hysterical, she called 911.

News of David's disappearance made the wire services on Sunday afternoon as Annie was in the final holes of what might have been her first LPGA win. She became increasingly distracted by ever-louder murmurings that seemed to be following her from hole to hole. Upset by the noise, Annie complained to her longtime caddie, Bix McCloud, who pointedly asked the crowd for quiet. After a poor drive off the sixteenth tee and wondering why all the talking around them hadn't stopped, Annie went to an official, who felt duty-bound to tell her what was being reported on television. Her last seven holes included five bogeys and were hastily covered live by ESPN and ABC.

The sports world intensified its obsession with Annie Bridget that afternoon. Some wrote of the bad girl getting her just deserts, but others described the beautiful, wild, possibly wronged wife, graciously playing her heart out under ever-mounting pressure. Walking away from the eighteenth green after a double bogey that lost her the match, she was approached by the ABC camera crew.

"How does it feel, Annie?" asked the sportscaster. "So near and yet so far."

"Hey, it's only golf," she answered, meaning it, fighting back tears. "I couldn't think of anything but David the last few holes. My heart goes out to Rachel, too." She started walking toward the clubhouse, struck by the enveloping aroma of fresh-cut grass.

"Any ideas about what could have happened?" the reporter said, trying to keep up with her.

"Couldn't we talk later?" urged Annie. "This is kind of a tough time for me." The reporter kept pace, his microphone still held out to her.

"To come *so* close to a big win and then miss an easy putt there at the end. What was going through your mind?"

Annie stopped walking for a moment and faced him. She was shaking. "I'm afraid I might say something that your parent company wouldn't want to hear on the air. *Please.*"

"Well, you heard that, Bret," said the reporter loudly into the mike. "Golf's Bad Girl has no comment."

"Do you think you might possibly cut me just the slightest amount of, how do you say in your language, motherfucking slack?"

"They'll just bleep that, Ms. Bridget," said the sportscaster in an irritatingly pleasant tone. Annie noticed with astonishment that the camera was still running. She had nothing left.

"My prayers are with them both," she said sadly, giving up. "I'm sure he'll be found. I'm sure there's a perfectly logical explanation."

And, of course, there was.

*   *   *

That night, Annie called her dad, who, instead of accompanying her as he often did, had stayed home with a bad flu.

"Have you heard?" she asked.

"I just saw it on the news," sighed Johnnie. "They said David was on his way to see you."

"Well, if he was," snapped Annie, "I sure didn't know about it."

"It'll be okay," said Johnnie. "They'll find him."

There was a silence.

"It really got to me, Dad. I wish you'd been there. I couldn't make a putt."

"Well, honey," he said distantly. "You know, sometimes . . ." He breathed a long sigh and coughed. More silence.

"Sometimes what?" she asked. He didn't answer. "Dad?"

No reply.

"Dad . . . what?" A terrible thought flashed at her. "You don't know anything about this—do you?"

"Don't be ridiculous, honey. You're upset. Let's not talk about it."

"Okay." Silence. "I was just . . . remembering . . ."

"Remembering what?"

"Just . . . stuff. Vito. Stuff we joked about once when you—"

"Joking is joking," interrupted Johnnie. "I gotta go."

"Dad . . . ? What's going on?"

"Nothing. Nothing, honey. I'm tired and it's just hard to feel sorry for that pathetic son of a bitch. But, hey, I'll say a prayer for him, too, okay? But talking about it won't do him any good."

It seemed to Annie that there was an unfamiliar edge in his voice, and it shook her. But she wasn't sure of anything, and she felt frightened to pursue it.

That night, the Voice started, waking her before dawn.

I am denial, it breathed into her ear as she rolled over, damp with sweat. *I come and I go.*

As the days passed, Annie did her best to put her fear aside and channel her energies into her game. She certainly didn't feel she was in denial. She had asked Johnnie and he had said no. That was that.

But the Voice followed her to her next two tournaments.

See no evil, hear no evil, it breathed. *Accomplice,* it said, with variations on that theme. She considered seeing a psychiatrist, but her experience with shrinks after her mother's death was that they only made things worse.

She failed to make the cut two more times.

After five months with no further leads, the story of David's disappearance began to recede into news limbo. The police found that his bank account had been zeroed out and his car had disappeared and they speculated that maybe David hadn't been abducted at all. Perhaps, the authorities suggested, he had fled the country, or even committed suicide, disappearing off a cliff or bridge somewhere.

When gasoline prices started to rise and unemployment did the same, and when a fresh sex scandal bloomed in the Senate, the story died and things quieted down for Golf's Bad Girl.

At the Pepsi Challenge in Orlando in early March, the Voice was silent and Annie showed signs of regaining her stuff, finishing ninth. Two weeks later at the LPGA Masters in

Woodside, Ohio, Voiceless for four days, her stroke was sure, and she found herself in the zone. Far from overthinking, and ignoring Johnnie's lifetime advice, she was stepping right up to the ball and forgoing her practice swing. She was incapable of a bad shot for the last two days.

Out of nowhere, there it was—her first major win, by four strokes.

A month later, in Texas, Annie wowed the golf world by taking her second straight LPGA major, the Ladies National Invitational. No Voice, no thinking. Reebok came back and renegotiated. *Sports Illustrated* and *Vanity Fair* sent reporters to do covers on her. Colin Farrell was photographed with her at a margarita-laden karaoke party following the tournament, and invited her to join him at Cannes as his date for the film festival. She declined—she was not, after all, officially divorced from the still-missing David Strickland—but photos of her and Farrell singing Britney Spears's "Drive Me Crazy" before a throng of party revelers sold out that week's *People*.

Four weeks later, behind by two strokes on the par-4 eighteenth hole in the final round of the Ladies Masters, Annie's second shot, a wedge from ninety yards out, struck the pin and was sucked down into the cup for an eagle. It tied a flabbergasted, devastated Gail Fahr, forcing a play-off. On the second hole of sudden death, Annie birdied a par 5 to steal the tournament—her third straight major win.

The Voice, it seemed, was gone for good.

• • •

"Annie Bridget: is she Golf's Bad Girl or its First Lady—or both? Hi, you're watching ESPN and I'm Bret Shayne along with my partner, Jack Maddox, coming to you from the gorgeous St.

John's Golf club in Hastings-on-Hudson, New York, just a short ride from Manhattan—but worlds away in atmosphere. This venerable club, this town, and, well, the whole sports world are here to watch as Annie Bridget is poised to tie Tiger Woods's seemingly unapproachable record of four straight major PGA wins. This young woman, just twenty-eight years of age, graced with movie-star looks and a swing as smooth in its way as Joe DiMaggio's, has had to endure, it seems, a life of tabloid headlines. But for these last few months, her past has been on pause and she has climbed right into this nation's—indeed the whole world's—hearts. I understand, Jack Maddox, that this tournament is being watched in almost a hundred countries, by men and women, golfers and nongolfers alike."

"Well, Bret, what Tiger Woods did for the world of golf a few years ago has reached juggernaut proportions as Annie Bridget is bringing people to this sport in numbers never before dreamed of. I heard this morning that club memberships for women are up something like 40 percent in the past few months, and I think we can lay that figure right at the feet of Annie Bridget."

"Well, Jack, men all over the world have been metaphorically laying their hearts at the feet of this remarkable young woman, who overcame the early, tragic death of her mother, endured a terrible ankle injury just as her career was starting to take off, and then was plagued by tabloid scandals, first when she left her husband and then when he disappeared mysteriously six months ago. They say these kinds of things only happen to movie stars, but if Annie Bridget weren't the best woman golfer in recent memory, she probably *could* be a movie star. Everything this young woman does these days, she does under the magnifying glass of the press. Ms. Bridget reportedly turned down $2 million to pose for *Playboy* last month. But hey, when you add up the endorsements and her recent winnings and the legend that she's creating for herself, who the heck needs *Playboy*?"

"Not that some people aren't disappointed"—Jack laughed—"but seriously, this is a young woman, Bret, whom no one can quite figure out. No new scandals, no late night appearances at the clubs, no new man in her life despite rumors of an affair with Colin Farrell and an apparent recent offer by the dashing Prince Aboud from the United Arab Emirates to make her his bride. Instead, she's been living like a sequestered Olympic athlete, taking daily lessons from her dad, coach, and mentor, Johnnie Bridget. Over the past few months, she's developed into one of the most disciplined players the LPGA Tour has ever seen. And how that discipline has paid off. Annie Bridget is just one round away from joining the ranks of golf's all-time greats."

"She's already joined those ranks, Jack, *but*—if Annie Bridget can hold her lead today, we will have witnessed one of the great feats in sports history."

"We understand that Annie just finished hitting a bucket of warm-up shots, signed a few autographs, and is heading to the clubhouse for her usual last-minute powwow with her dad and her longtime caddie, Bix McCloud. We'll be right back with the tee-off, so stay with us!"

· · ·

Johnnie looked pale and more tired than usual when Annie came face-to-face with him in the trailer that the club had provided outside its own locker rooms. Was something weighing on his mind?

Ask him. Ask him now. You have to know.

"Dad . . . what is it? Are you sick? You don't look so good."

No, don't ask. What you don't know won't hurt you.

"Couldn't sleep," he answered, looking up at her with his lopsided grin. "Nerves. It's nothing. Don't pay any attention." He was cleaning the heads of her woods with a whisk brush.

"That's Bix's job, Dad," she said, patting him on the back gratefully.

"Bix was hungry. Or nervous. Not that he'd ever let you see it. I sent him to get a sandwich," said Johnnie. "Besides, I like doing this." With a fingernail, he flicked a piece of mud out from the grooves of her 4-wood. "Reminds me of when you were a kid. Makes me feel like you need me."

"I do need you," she said, hugging him from behind as he worked. "Just having you around is great. You don't have to say anything if you don't want to."

"Just remember to breathe on the ol' backswing—"

Killer!

It rang in her ear, raspy and loud. Frightened, Annie turned to see where it came from before she realized with despair that it was the Voice.

"You know what?" she said, moving away, nervously grabbing an open Evian bottle and taking a quick slug. "No offense, Dad, but I kind of don't want to talk. I'm ready. I don't want to think. I just want to go out and do it. Come what may."

"That's my girl," Johnnie said, finishing up with the clubs.

Bix walked in. Tall and skinny, with a seventies Pete Rose crew cut and a perennial tan, Bix adjusted the yellow cardigan sweater he had worn in all three of Annie's previous wins. The temperature was hovering now at ninety, but Annie knew that Bix wouldn't surrender his sweater this afternoon. Bix was as superstitious as Annie was disciplined. Besides, Bix was Mr. Cool out there. Nothing ever made him sweat.

"Nice sweater," said Johnnie, brightening a little and turning Bix's baseball hat around on his head.

"You never know when it might turn chilly," said Bix, deadpan. Annie grinned in spite of herself.

There was a knock on the trailer door, which opened a few inches.

"Miss Bridget," called a solicitous young network assistant with a headset and clipboard, his eyes averted in case Annie was changing. "Your tee-off is in exactly three minutes."

Annie turned to Bix. "Go ahead. I'll be right out." Taking the hint, Bix nodded, grabbed her clubs, and left, closing the trailer door firmly behind him. Annie stared at her father.

"Dad?"

Johnnie turned to her. "Go get 'em, kiddo." He gave her a loose hug. "I'm so goddamn proud of you. Like your ma used to say, 'Come what may.'"

Annie looked into his eyes, which seemed strangely vacant. She wanted to talk to him, to ask him once and for all, but there was no time.

"You know who said, 'Come what may'?" asked Annie quietly, checking herself quickly in a mirror.

"Sure," returned Johnnie, bewildered. "Your ma."

"It was Macbeth," said Annie, turning back to him.

"I never read any of that stuff. Too busy skipping class to play golf. But your ma said it a lot."

"I remember."

Come what may, mocked the Voice.

"Did you . . . hear anything?" she asked almost hopefully, pulling on a new glove.

"Yeah," he said, matter-of-fact, as Annie's eyes widened. "Police siren, I think. Probably crowd control. You're gonna need it." She turned toward a sliding window and peered behind a crinkly beige miniblind. There was, indeed, the sound of a siren in the distance. She tried to smile and checked his eyes again. Nothing there.

He's a killer, you're his accomplice. Is that the police coming? Wouldn't you almost welcome it?

"Miss Bridget," called the assistant director from outside. "One minute. Really."

Annie patted her father on the back and opened the trailer door. Someone had just said it was ninety degrees outside. How could it be chilly?

You'll find out.

Annie was in a foursome with Gail Fahr, Janet Deeter, and Kelly Castile, a redheaded rookie who was only five strokes off the lead, and whose own natural good looks and appeal had made her a telegenic addition to the foursome.

As Annie strode to the first tee, she put on her best smile and waved to the crowd, steeling herself for the Voice. Bix grinned, and then, as he always did at the start of a match, winked, palmed her a tee, helped her out of her pale blue nylon Reebok windbreaker, and handed her a Nike 1 ball.

"I swear, Jack," oozed Bret Shayne from the broadcast booth, "it's like if Grace Kelly was reincarnated and took up golf. What a beauty. Can a journalist talk like that on national TV?"

"And what a talent," chimed in Jack Maddox.

"And—*hello!*—just look at that drive!" enthused Shayne. "Long and true and straight out there . . . it's gonna roll to— wow!—could be 265 yards . . ."

"Two seventy-five, Bret."

"And smack in the middle of the fairway. Oh, baby, we're under way!"

．　．　．

Through thirteen holes, the Voice had remained mercifully dormant. Annie still held a three-stroke lead over Gail Fahr and Janet Deeter, with young Kelly Castile another stroke off the pace. Annie smashed her drive over the churning twenty-foot-wide brook that split the two hundred yards between the white tees and the pin of the par-3 fourteenth. Her shot bounced onto the green as though divinely directed, landing six feet above the pin. The crowd let out a whoop. Annie nodded, exhaled, and leaned onto her 5-wood as she stood next to Bix and watched Kelly drive her shot long, over the pin, scattering the crowd. As the ball came to rest a few feet beyond the green, Annie noticed that someone in the crowd was waving his arms as though to attract attention. She squinted and saw that it was a tall, dark guy in a madras shirt. He seemed intent on distracting Gail Fahr, who was now teeing up her shot.

"Jerk," Annie whispered to Bix. "Somebody ought to tell him to stop waving his arms like that."

"Who?" asked Bix, his eyes fixed on Gail.

"That schmuck down there," said Annie. "Look at him. What a putz."

Gail swung and hit a low drive that bounced to the green and snuggled up close to Annie's, as though they were two balls on a pool table.

"Some concentration she's got," Annie said to Bix. "God, she's tough."

"Don't worry about her," whispered Bix as Janet Deeter set her ball onto a tee. "Just play your game and enjoy the beautiful day. You love the heat, remember?"

Heat? What heat? thought Annie, fighting off a chill. Her eyes went back to the guy who'd been waving his arms, but she could no longer spot him in the crowd. Janet hit a beauty of a drive, and suddenly there were three balls within five feet of each other, none of them more than seven feet from the cup, with Kelly's perhaps thirty feet away, just off the green.

As Annie and Bix walked toward the tee, Annie took a deep breath. No Voice.

Acknowledging polite applause, she approached the green and Bix handed her her putter. Comfortably warm for the first time since the round began, she slowly moved toward the hole, lining up the putt as Janet, Gail, and Kelly joined her. Annie felt a slight breeze on her back and turned around to let it cool her face.

Not twenty feet away, the man in the madras shirt waved again.

He looks like someone, Annie thought, turning away and ignoring him.

Look again, said the Voice.

Reflexively obeying, Annie turned and found herself staring into the once blue eyes of David Strickland.

But the eyes were no longer blue. They were gray, almost black, and his complexion was a pasty, sickly hue.

I'm here. It's me. You lose.

"Bix," Annie called, beckoning. Bix broke into his easy, purposeful trot and was by her side in seconds.

"Want the new putter?" Bix asked.

"Look behind me, over my shoulder," Annie urged quietly,

her eye seemingly on her ball. "Two o'clock." Bix obeyed. "Is that . . . David?" she asked.

"David?" repeated Bix, confused, still looking where she had indicated. "As in . . . Strickland?"

"Maybe it just looks like him. Is it?"

"There's . . . nobody over there who even looks vaguely like David, boss."

Annie turned around to see. The man was gone. She blinked and watched as Kelly Castile stroked her putt, from thirty feet and off the edge of the green. The green was incredibly fast, and for a second Annie felt relieved, knowing that the putt would have to be perfect not to overshoot the hole.

But the ball found the center of the cup for a birdie and Kelly was only three strokes behind Annie. The crowd roared.

"Hold on to your hats, folks!" exclaimed Bret Shayne on national TV. "I don't hear any fat lady singing yet."

Of the three remaining putts, Annie's was farthest from the pin. She moved in, determined not to overthink. Stepping right up to the ball and squaring her feet, she went into a deliberate backstroke.

Miss it!

Her putter caught a piece of green just before making contact with the ball. The clubhead twisted slightly, and the resulting glitch sent her putt to the right of the hole and rolling down the quick grass.

The crowd oohed.

"Man! It looked like a possible birdie for leader Annie Bridget, but something happened—the slightest hitch in her swing—and instead she's got herself a tricky uphill putt—I'd say ten feet—to save par."

Still away, Annie stepped up again, eyeing the precise route she wanted the ball to travel. She took a slow, even breath and gently stroked it.

I'll see you on the seventeenth. In the pond. I'll be waiting.

Her putt rolled straight for the pin, whirled around the rim of the cup, and dribbled out. Annie winced and reflexively looked back, but the man in the madras shirt was nowhere to be seen.

She tapped in for a bogey, after which Janet and Gail each came through with birdie putts.

Annie was suddenly just a single stroke ahead.

• • •

"Bix," said Annie as he took her putter and walked her to the fifteenth tee. "Stay close. Talk to me. Okay?"

"You always tell me to keep my mouth shut, boss."

"Beautiful day, huh?" she said, shifting her tone, smiling and waving to a gaggle of teenage boys who whistled when she looked their way. "Just keep talking."

"Okay . . . yeah . . . beautiful," said Bix, who hadn't become indispensable to Annie because of any sort of easy way with words. "Beautiful," he repeated, still wondering what was going on. "The, uh, greens seem to be running faster."

"This is one beautiful day," Annie said, ignoring him, speaking as though she had just noticed for the first time.

"You okay, boss?"

"Four hundred and fifty-five yards, par 5, huh?" she said.

"Yup."

"Whatta you think, Bix? Nine-iron? Sand wedge?"

Bix tried to smile. In his years with Annie, she had never once attempted a joke during a close match. Renowned for his cool, he felt a trickle of perspiration run down his side, as though a tiny faucet had opened. As they reached the tee, he handed her a driver.

Annie waited as each of the other three hit. Janet's sliced a bit, but Gail's and Kelly's were beauties, and all three were far onto the fairway. Annie bent over and placed her ball on the tee. She noticed now that she was trying *not* to look at anyone in the crowd. Not thinking of something was, she knew, tantamount to thinking of it.

"It's like a frickin' pink elephant," she said, unaware that she was speaking out loud. "Try not to think about *that*."

"Beg pardon, boss?" said Bix, bewildered.

The man in madras did not appear. She sensed him hovering in the wings, but she took a deep breath and hit a spectacular drive, outdistancing her rivals by thirty yards.

Keeping her head down and making nonstop conversation with Bix, Annie managed to par 15 and 16. But so did Gail and Janet, keeping them one stroke behind, with Kelly losing another stroke.

At the seventeenth tee, Annie looked out. There it was. The pond.

Come on. I'm waiting.

Trying to decide whether to hit a 3-wood or a 2-iron, she was interrupted again—but not, it seemed, by the Voice. It was strained, and higher-pitched than what she'd been hearing.

They just cut the grass on the green. Wait till you smell it!

Annie swung around to face Bix.

"Did you say something?" she asked, her voice rising more than she could control.

"No."

Without thinking, Annie turned to the crowd.

"Listen," she called out impulsively. "I have to ask you to please keep quiet. I know most of you are really polite, but will whoever is talking to me please give me a break!" The crowd shifted its collective weight. People glanced at each other, confused. A few looked angry. Annie blushed and tried to keep from losing any more control.

"Just play your game, Annie! We're with you," called a voice.

A real voice.

A woman's voice. Annie turned, smiled, and made a little wave. The woman waved back, giving her a thumbs-up.

You want to know why I sound different?

Annie shook her head, trying to will away the sound, and placed her tee.

I was castrated.

She stepped back and looked down at the pond. All I have to do, she insisted to herself, is get my drive over the water. Please, God, let it go over the water.

Bix handed her a ball, a tee, and her 3-wood.

"Two more holes, boss, and I'll buy you a lemonade," said Bix, backing away, as matter-of-fact as he could manage.

She rubbed the ball against the side of her skirt and looked at the pond as though concentrating on it might make things all right. She placed the ball onto a tee in one hand and plugged the tee into the soft turf as the crowd grew mercifully quiet.

Come what may!

Her head snapped toward the crowd.

Was it her mom? Her dad? The Voice? Don't be ridiculous, she thought. No thinking. Just step up and hit it.

She coiled into her backswing and let go.

The second her club struck the ball, she knew the contact was poor. She'd topped it. The ball spurted off the tee, low to the ground, bouncing hard, making straight for the pond.

"Uh-oh!" called out Bret Shayne on national TV. "She didn't want to do that! She's headed for the water hazard . . ."

The ball bounced a few yards in front of the pond, rolled, hit a small boulder that rimmed one side of the water, bounced again, and plunked into the sandy mud, an inch from the water's edge.

"Wow," sighed Jack Maddox. "I tell you, Bret, you hate to see this. This is a hole that Annie Bridget parred in each of the first two rounds and birdied yesterday. She's always owned this hole, but today, when she probably just needs to par these last two holes, well . . . she's got herself in real trouble. Her ball looks to be at the *very* edge of the water hazard—I guess you could say she's lucky there—it isn't actually *in* the water. But now the question becomes, do you take a drop and lose a critical stroke, or do you try to hit out of a terrifically bad lie?"

"She'll get wet if she decides to hit out of there, Jack. Let's see how she handles it."

Gail, Kelly, and Janet each hit drives well over the pond and onto the fairway beyond. The crowd cheered them, torn, it seemed, between rooting for their shaky leader or for the three possible spoilers.

Annie followed Bix down the slope toward the pond.

Come on, come on. I've been waiting.

The crowd was silent. As though marching to her execution, she felt another chill. The smell of fresh-mowed grass was everywhere as she approached the water. Was that a good sign? She didn't know. She didn't know anything. She saw her ball, gleaming wet, lying in a little crater it had dug for itself at the pond's edge. She'd have to put one foot in the water to hit out. Her decision was quick. There was no way she could take a penalty stroke. She'd have to play it. If she could choose the right club and somehow make a great shot—get close to the green—she could chip, then one-putt to save par.

"I'm thinking, dammit!" she said out loud. "Stop it!"

Bix looked at her, not knowing what to say. There were murmurs from the crowd.

"Uh . . . sand wedge, boss?" asked Bix carefully.

"Try your 9-iron, kiddo," advised a quiet voice out of nowhere. Annie turned, terrified. Her father approached, politely moving through the crowd, which parted for him.

Perfect! Both of you right here. Right where I want you.

"That's Johnnie Bridget," announced Bret Shayne. "We've seen him do this in the past when his daughter's been in a tight spot. He'll say a word or two to her, and it seems to calm her down. It's unusual, but, hey, what's usual about today? We saw him huddle with her during the first round when Annie Bridget's drive put her behind a tree on the thirteenth. Johnnie came out of the crowd, whispered something, and Annie proceeded to hit a beauty of a shot to par that hole."

"Well, let's see if Dad can help her now," said Jack Maddox. "Bix McCloud, Annie's caddie, is stepping aside. Some caddies wouldn't like this, but he and Annie seem to have an understanding. Let's watch . . ."

As Johnnie moved toward her, Annie tried to read his eyes.

Look down at your ball, Annie. I have a surprise for you.

Annie looked down as Johnnie reached her side. Her face went white and she recoiled.

"Oh, God! Oh, dear God!" she called out to her father, almost in a sob. "What have you done?" Johnnie stopped and looked down.

In the water next to her ball, Annie saw part of a man's hand and arm, slightly exposed beneath the surface of the shallow water. She screamed and looked up at her father. Just over Johnnie's shoulder, she again saw the even-more-emaciated face of David Strickland. He stood, leering, the flesh of his face rotting, his teeth black or missing, the madras in rags and barely clinging to his lean frame. He looked a hundred years older. He wasn't smiling.

Ask him. Ask your dad why he did it.

"How could you do this, Dad? I never asked you to do this!"

"Do what?" sputtered a bewildered Johnnie Bridget, trembling.

Bix looked on, holding Annie's club in his hand, unable to speak.

"Get out," she screamed at her father. "Get away from me! Get him out of here!" A tanned, powerfully built Asian security officer appeared from the sidelines and approached hurriedly.

"Is there a problem, Ms. Bridget?" he asked, keeping calm.

"Get out of here, Dad. I don't want to see you again. Ever."

"Honey—what *is* it?" begged Johnnie, tears in his eyes.

"I'm afraid you'll have to leave, sir," said the security man, carefully taking Johnnie's arm.

"Okay. Okay," said Johnnie, shaking, not wanting to make more of a commotion. "I'll . . . see you inside, sweetie. It's okay. It's okay. Just . . . take a deep breath."

"Get away!" Annie screamed again as the crowd completely

quieted. She looked down at the hand in the water. Was it moving? No. Yes. No.

Bix took a few steps toward her. "What can I do, boss?" he asked gently.

Annie looked down, terrified that Bix or, God forbid, the camera might see what she saw. Her head was swirling. How do I get through this? she asked herself. No thinking, she answered.

Get it off your chest, Annie.

"I want to stop play!" she called out suddenly. No one moved. She stepped away from her ball, turned, and looked directly into a TV camera.

"Cut to a commercial," she ordered in simple, deadly earnest.

The red light on the camera, however, stayed lit.

Bret Shayne knew that no TV director in his right mind would cut away from this.

Confess. Do it now.

Annie started to shake. "I'm going to . . . hit this shot," she said into the camera, "this *motherfucker* of a shot, and I'm going to finish this match, and then . . ." She broke off and took a breath.

No thinking!

"And then . . . I . . . have a statement to make. Someone might want to call . . . the police. There's something I've been carrying, for too long—and I need to talk about it. Come what may. I can't do this anymore."

She felt her shaking subside a little.

See? You'll feel better when you tell them.

She took the club from Bix, waded partway into the water, moved astride her ball, and, with one foot on dry land and one in the sand where she'd last stood on prom night, she closed her eyes and imagined where she needed the ball to go.

She inhaled, brought her club back slowly, and swung. Mud splattered her legs and skirt.

"What a shot, Bret! Oh, baby, is it possible that she did it?"

The ball traveled up and up, seeming almost to hover before it began its fall, bouncing twice, rolling, and finally stopping ten feet shy of the green, about twenty feet from the cup. The crowd stood silent for a moment, then broke into frenzied applause.

"Wow. Whatever Johnnie Bridget whispered to his daughter," said Bret Shayne, "whatever made her lash out at him— *whatever* happened, that young woman just reached down somewhere and came through with the shot of a lifetime. And you are watching it all *live,* folks. Stay with us!"

•   •   •

"We're back live from the world-renowned St. John's Golf Club where Annie Bridget has just made history, tying Tiger Woods's record of four straight major PGA wins, and earning herself a place in the annals not just of women's golf but in the *sport* of golf. If you're just joining us, Annie Bridget parred the seventeenth hole and just birdied the eighteenth on a *spectacular* eighteen-foot putt to win this event by a mere stroke over Janet Deeter, who led a brave charge that was joined by Gail Fahr, who finished two strokes off the pace. We're in the clubhouse now, where Ms. Bridget is on her way, apparently to make some kind of statement. As you can see, it's quiet here, not the kind of celebration you'd expect after such a remarkable achievement. While we wait, I'm told we have Tiger Woods with us via satellite from Tacoma, Washington, where he, like the rest of the world, has been watching. Tiger? Tiger, can you hear me?"

"Hey, Bret. You're loud and clear."

"Tiger, how do you feel?"

"Well, Bret, days like this just bring out the fan in me. I mean, what a round of golf, what a show of character—I don't know what *else* is going on, but Annie Bridget showed the world what she's made of today. It just speaks for itself, and, hey, I'm proud to share this record with her. I think she—"

"I'm sorry but we have to break away, Tiger. Thank you for your gracious remarks, but Annie Bridget, as you can see, has entered the clubhouse and is ready to make her statement. Down to you on the floor, Jack."

"Thanks, Bret. I think they're just adjusting her microphone, and yes, here we go . . ."

Pale, her eyes bloodshot but determined, Annie cleared her throat. Silence fell over the room. She opened her mouth to speak but stopped, shaking her head.

"We love you, Annie!" called a voice from the back, and the room broke into scattered applause that grew louder and more insistent. Annie took a deep breath and nodded, her face grim as she put up her hands for quiet.

"Thank you. Thank you. I wish I could enjoy this moment. But . . . the truth is that I haven't been able to enjoy much of anything really, not *any* moment of my life for the past six months since my husband . . . disappeared." She fought back tears, trembling. "I'm sorry, Dad. I wish this could just be my statement, my . . . confession. But it has to be yours, too." Her mouth twisted and her whole body seemed to vibrate.

"I . . . can't tell you how David Strickland died. But I can't live with this anymore. I thought I could just . . . not know. If I didn't ask, I wouldn't know. So I didn't. And that makes me almost as guilty as if I had done it. I can't talk anymore. I'm fucking delirious. Excuse me. I don't know what I'm saying. I'm so sorry. But . . . if you just . . . go down to the pond, the water hazard, on the seventeenth fairway, you'll find him. You'll find David. Sorry, Dad. I'm so sorry."

An LPGA official with a uniformed cop and a plainclothes officer stepped forward. The officer gently took Annie by the arm and started to lead her out of the room. Several reporters surged forward to follow. As the policeman held the door for Annie and turned his head to block the quickly following Jack Maddox and his camera crew, Annie saw in an instant what she knew would be her only chance.

No thinking.

Without a trace of hesitation, she reached for the policeman's pistol, jerked it from his holster, brought the service revolver to her head, and pulled the trigger.

• • •

It wasn't the pain behind her ear, it was the fact that she couldn't move. Or see through the bandages. She could only hear, and smell the antiseptic that was everywhere.

"Some people never come out of a coma, Mr. Bridget. Or, who knows, she could open her eyes and be talking in a few days. We just have to wait and see."

"But, okay, let's say she comes to, Doc. Will she . . . ever get up out of that bed?" Johnnie Bridget asked in a quavering voice.

"I don't want to get your hopes up, Mr. Bridget. There's been some damage to the brain, and there's so much swelling. We won't know until the swelling goes down. It could take days. She might just pull through, but—the truth?—the likelihood of her ever . . . walking again is, well, almost nonexistent. I'm sorry."

"Mother of God. Can I . . . bring anyone else in to see her?"

"Only relatives are permitted, Mr. Bridget."

"It's her husband."

"Oh. Of course. But keep it very quiet, please."

"Do you think . . . I mean, is it possible that she can hear us?"

The doctor exhaled. "Anything is possible, Mr. Bridget, but I seriously doubt it. I'll leave you alone. Nurse, you can let the other gentleman in. Five minutes, please."

Annie heard the doctor leave. Then footsteps and low whispers and the sound of a chair, maybe two, scraping across the floor to where she lay.

"Jesus," said the quiet voice of David Strickland. Then no one spoke.

"Tell her," ordered Johnnie.

"I . . . can't do this," said David. "I thought it might be a good idea. I'm sorry, Johnnie. I can't."

"You piece of shit. You owe her!" insisted Johnnie. "Sit down. If you won't say it, I will. This might be our only chance. She could be gone tomorrow."

"She can't hear us," moaned David. "What's the point?"

"Ah, Christ, shut up, you putz," hissed Johnnie.

She smelled a trace of bourbon as Johnnie drew closer. "Honey," he said in a softer tone. "It's . . . Dad. And David. I . . . we . . . have something to tell you."

She thought she heard a sob. She had never heard her father cry.

"Go on, for God's sake," Johnnie said impatiently. But David didn't speak.

"Oh, shit, forget it. Never mind! Sweetie. It's me. It's . . . Daddy. I need to tell you this, maybe it'll ease your mind, I don't know. Listen, I . . . I paid David to leave the country. I knew you wanted him out of your life and I'm your dad. I wanted to take care of you. But . . . I'm so sorry, honey. Just . . . so sorry."

Johnnie laid his head slowly onto the edge of the bed near Annie's face. David Strickland got up and left the room.

•   •   •

The days are long. One of her nurses, the one who talks to her, likes to watch TV. "Do you want to watch with me?" she asks in a singsong tone that makes Annie wish she could spit, or scream. "Of course you do!"

The nurse loves afternoon talk shows, *Ellen, Oprah,* and the local news. When her mind is awake, Annie hears it all.

It's afternoon. The nurse zaps on the set and gathers her knitting. A compassionate-looking doctor is a guest on *Maury.*

"Doctor," says Maury, "as an expert, can you shed any light on what might have been going on in this woman's mind? Why would a person confess to a crime she didn't commit? A crime, as it turns out, that was never committed?"

"Well, Maury, no one can really answer that question except Annie Bridget."

"Oh, dear," says the nurse, shaking her head disapprovingly and looking down at Annie. "Cover your ears."

"But from most accounts, Ms. Bridget probably won't ever speak again," says the host.

"Maury, some people's moment-to-moment anxiety is so

great that they spin worst-case scenarios about everything. Some of these people become agoraphobics—they literally can't leave their homes or neighborhoods for fear of what they *think* will happen. Logic doesn't help them. Therapy and medication can produce wonderful results, but . . ."

"Annie Bridget's therapy," suggested the host, "such as it was, was golf?"

"I think so. In order to control their world in any way they can, some people become great achievers. Intensely skilled perfectionists. Annie Bridget apparently believed that her father had had her husband killed. That was real in her mind. She felt she couldn't tell anyone. And that must have been a terrible burden, although in some perverse way, it may have also fueled her."

"She played golf like a champion. She *was* a champion."

"If she could do this impossible thing of hitting a tiny golf ball perfectly and then winning under what may have been the most intense pressure any golfer ever had to face— that was a way to fix her world. But it didn't work, finally, because in her own mind she was a don't-ask, don't-tell accomplice to a murder. That was real to her. Everything else was denial."

"Wow. So sad."

"It's just one possibility, Maury. I could be way off."

The nurse zaps off the TV. "Enough of that! Experts! What do they know? Shall I open the window, dear? Shall I? Of course I will!"

No! No.

The nurse turns a handle at the bottom of the window frame and opens it a few inches. Annie hears the sound of a loud motor and feels a slight breeze waft across her cheek.

"The noise will stop in a few minutes, dear," purrs the nurse kindly. "It's just the gardeners. They're almost finished. When they cut the grass, it leaves such a nice smell. Don't you think? Of course you do!"

THOSE GOOD DAYS

Tom Franklin

The first thing Mr. D. L. Philips did when they found the oil on his land was buy more land, cheap, and rent some bulldozers and hire some black guys to work under him, and within a year they'd built his famous golf course. It had 178 holes, and it took three or four days to play through, sometimes a week. He called it the Luna Gautreaux Commemorative Golfing Course, named for his girlfriend. Later he added "and Shooting Range" to the title when golfers started carrying arms to shoot snakes with. There was a swamp along the eastern rim of the course where the cottonmouths and diamondback rattlers came from, and poor black children kept sneaking over the chain-link fences and stealing, as decoration for their bicycles, the flags that marked the holes, so it became custom that dead snakes were wrapped around the flags— freshly shot snakes replacing rotting ones—to scare the thieves away.

Mr. D. L. built a giant house next to where the course began, a room and bathroom for each of his three boys, and a huge den. We were the nearest neighbors, half a mile south.

Me and the old man. He ran a lathe at the mill and I was in ninth grade for the second time.

If people wanted to play golf—and they always did, there were dozens of golfers every day—they got Mr. D. L.'s permission, provided they were white and could pay his fifty-dollar-per-head fee. The first year the course was open, rich people from all over Alabama came all the time, and Mr. D. L. rented them four-wheelers with racks welded on to carry their golf bags. At the other end of the course there was a gate with a guardhouse, and here sat Jimmy Younger, supposed descendant of the Youngers who rode with Jesse James. He had a jar on the windowsill for tips, but the two dollars in the jar were put in by Jimmy in the morning and taken out by Jimmy at night. His job was to take the four-wheelers people returned and make sure they hadn't been damaged and in a pickup truck drive the golfers back to their cars where they were parked on oyster shells by Mr. D. L.'s house.

· · ·

I was fourteen that year and friends with Mr. D. L.'s youngest boy, T-Bob, who was thirteen, and while we cared little for golf, we loved roaming the land and watching the rich people—and Luna—play.

The course started back in the woods behind Mr. D. L.'s house, kudzu clogging the trees and anaconda vines fit for Tarzan hanging down. It was eighteen miles long, the LGCGCASR, through the woods for several miles into an abandoned gravel pit of red clay that looked like a blood-drenched desert. A great butte rose in the center of it, the ninety-fourth hole up there in the middle, flag snapping in the wind. After you played through the pit, you came to the final eighty-four holes, spaced hundreds of yards apart in Mr D. L.'s cattle fields. There were great rolling hills and gaps and gullies and banks of earth, and there were sand traps, bunkers, in the shapes of all the southern states. The cows and bull were legitimate obstacles, and so were the ponds. Little stands of oak or pine made good hiding places for us boys. Sometimes the golfers stopped to pull in some of Mr. D. L.'s catfish and grill them on straightened coat hangers over a fire and eat them before playing on, and once, near Christmas, we saw Mr. D. L. get out of his four-wheeler with a rifle and aim into a giant oak tree stripped bare by winter. We crouched in the brush and followed the barrel of his .30-30 with our eyes and saw what he was shooting at: sprigs of mistletoe growing in the top of the tree. When it fell Luna ran after it and held it over her head so he would kiss her.

I was watching them until I noticed T-Bob watching me.

"What you looking at?" he asked.

"Nothing," I said.

•   •   •

But things lull, and end. For a year after the course was finished, even the lieutenant governor of Alabama came and played the first nine holes while flashbulbs popped and men in dark suits eyed the trees and the snakes on the poles and talked into their collars. But gradually people stopped coming. Mr. D. L. had lost interest in the sport shortly after completing the course and had stopped sinking money into it. If he hadn't removed the fifty-dollar fee a few months later and opened it to the poor public, the grass wouldn't have kept the footpath you followed, fresh snakes wouldn't have stayed on the flags. It would've become the jungle/desert/cattle range it was before the oil. But soon even the poor lost interest and Mr. D. L. had to let Jimmy Younger go. He sold the four-wheelers to a hunting club.

Now Luna alone played regularly, but she alone couldn't keep it going, and now cows, not golfers, moved slowly up and down the hills. They'd shit piles as big as cakes for the flies to lay their eggs into and piss great yellow streams onto the grass, wade neck-deep into the algae-green water of the ponds to chew their cuds, emerging to drag their heavy tongues over the dark brown salt blocks Mr. D. L. had ordered from the hardware store in Grove Hill. What he did to keep the course from going completely to pot was hire a colored man called Lucius to drive a tractor and bushhog the greens, and to keep hunters out. Lucius wore a big pistol strapped to his leg, sweat streaming from his black-black skin, his eyes and teeth gleaming from under the brim of his St. Louis Cardinals cap. He died one day when he bushhogged over a yellowjacket nest and, trying to jump off the tractor, firing the pistol in the air, got one of his legs caught in the blade.

He lay there for days, at last getting spotted by Luna as she played 48. She came to the house and locked herself in the bathroom while we boys went with Mr. D. L. to have a look, excited to see our first corpse. Mr. D. L. told us to stay in the truck as he wrapped his handkerchief around his nose. We could see Lucius lying in the grass, half under the bushhog, flies swarming. Mr. D. L. walked over and looked at Lucius, shaking his head. He poured a gallon of gasoline into the yellowjacket nest and used the truck's battery to jump-start the tractor and cranked it and pulled it a few yards off. He got a spade from the back of the pickup and buried Lucius there on the spot, pistol and all, for Lucius didn't have any family. He'd lived in one of the five barns on the course.

We went there next, and one after another we climbed the ladder into the dark hayloft where Lucius had lived. We saw his things, a mandolin with "Gold Fingers" carved into the back of its neck, a cigar box full of papers that Mr. D. L. tucked under his arm, some copper wire in a coil, a blue suit on a hanger, a coverless Bible, four or five hundred cartridges in a suitcase and, hanging in a frame on the wall, a picture of Jesus as a black man.

"Y'all boys want any of that stuff?" Mr. D. L. asked.

There were four of us, Mr. D. L.'s three sons and me. We shook our heads.

"Let's go, then," he said.

•   •   •

At the end of the next school year, T-Bob failed the ninth grade, and to stay in the same class as him I failed it, too, on purpose, which is harder than it sounds, especially when the vice-principal says, "We'll just bump you on up, see, 'cause it looks bad for a fellow to fail the same grade twice, reflects poorly on us all," but I called him a faggot and gave him the finger and spit on his desk so he sighed and closed my file and said, "Fine," and T-Bob and I would be together in school as well as on the golf course.

To celebrate we climbed back into Lucius's hayloft and stole the suitcase full of cartridges. We used gasoline syphoned from the last four-wheeler to make a giant fire in another of the barns and threw the suitcase in and waited. When the cartridges started going off we hid in an empty horse stall. It was like a war, especially when a bullet ricocheted about four times and lodged in T-Bob's calf. I helped him out as the fire spread and we watched the barn cave in.

We went back to Lucius's barn then, which was built like a dog-run house, split through the middle with rooms on both sides, haylofts over the rooms. It sat with its back against the woods, this barn, so the kudzu from the woods had already claimed the building and covered it and camouflaged it so it seemed part of the woods, its big front door, when opened, the mouth of a cave leading into a vast green mountain face. Lucius had picked it because he said the shade kept it cool. Grass from the field grew right up inside the front door, as far as the sun could reach, and after that there was soft dirt and several old easy chairs arranged in a circle. Once we'd asked Lucius what the chairs were for, since he'd lived alone and except for us never had visitors, and he'd said they were for spirits, for after haunting the woods all night the spirits are weary, Lucius told us, smoking his pipe, and they need a place to sit down and rest their feet before they go in for the day.

The two haylofts were accessed by ladders, the loft Lucius used for living quarters fairly clean, the other wild: dusty, rotting hay still on the floor, gaps in the walls where boards had come loose, rusty nails sticking out of the woodwork, ivy curling around the door and the gaps in the walls, having ventured in and, not finding the sunlight it needed to live, crept back out. After he died we stayed in Lucius's loft when we felt serene, but feeling wild as hair grew under our arms and between our legs we would clamber up the ladder to the other loft and light cigarettes and drink whiskey and with our rifles take potshots at birds in the trees skirting the fields.

Going out the back of the barn you went into immediately dark woods, kudzu hanging all over like chandeliers gone mad. We climbed the trees there behind the barn and went higher than the barn, looked over its peak to the hills where you could see the flags of the golf course still standing. We took boards from a woodpile in one of the barn's rooms and nailed ourselves a ladder up the steep back side of the tin roof, and we'd climb and lie on the peak looking at the green hills and at the dots that were cows, the grass of the greens growing high and turning brown in spots without Lucius to cut it back, the fancy irrigation system Mr. D. L. had installed no longer working, hairy tridents of bitterweed overtaking the bunkers. A mile away the gravel pit baked in the sun, the ponds drying up. Soon even the cows started dying.

After a while T-Bob and I were the only ones who went behind Mr. D. L.'s house, past the great iron gates into the woods. T-Bob still limped. We shot anything that moved. We shot a panther. We shot owls, hawks, deer, coyotes, coons, squirrels, dogs. We shot at each other once, after an argument.

Mr. D.L. had become interested in the stock market. He hired some fellows in suits who knew what they were doing and the group of them flew to New York City, where they made more money. "A mint," he wired. He liked it up there and stayed, letting Luna tend to the kids. With Mr. D. L. gone, T-Bob's brothers, Strump and Mike, used to take turns getting her drunk and trying to seduce her. T-Bob said when their daddy got home, he'd cream them, didn't I think so?

Yes, I said, turning away.

The thing was, I was in love with her.

•   •   •

The golf course jungled up even more, and Mr. D. L. didn't come back even after a month. There was plenty of money at home for Luna and the boys—Mr. D. L. saw to that—and Luna threw parties where she invited fifteen or twenty guys.

She drove to the next county, which was wet, and bought whiskey and beer by the case and pot by the pound—Jimmy Younger grew it somewhere out in the woods. If the deputies came, Luna did stripteases, but only to her bra and panties, and bribed them with free cases of beer. They'd give her a "warning" and drive away with their lights off. They began stopping by every night.

More cows died. T-Bob and I were led to their rotting carcasses on the fields by skyfuls of sailing buzzards, and we came over hills or out of woods to see ten or more of the huge black stinking birds with their bad posture and leathery heads lit all around the dead cows, some with their necks deep inside the holes they'd eaten in the cows' sides, others standing apart, as if on watch. We charged them and they hopped away on foot, their wings half-spread. We set the cows afire using gasoline and old tires to get the blazes going and watched them bake and pop in the sun, and we shot off the buzzards' heads with our rifles and holding our noses against their smell drenched them in gas and set them afire too.

Afterward we would go to Lucius's barn and climb into one of the lofts and drink from the cases of whiskey we'd stolen from the house. We would get drunk and sit brazenly in the spirits' chairs and call out to them to show themselves, expecting moldy skeletons, executed slaves, to show their rattling old bones. We stood in the chairs and tossed the bottles back and forth, juggled them, and broke the empty ones on the ground so that a terrible garden of broken glass grew between the chairs, and because we were barefoot, climbing along the walls became necessary to get to the chairs and to the ladders leading to the haylofts, and a game evolved. We would go all around that barn without touching the ground, the threat of

jagged glass great and growing greater with the hurriedly passing days and their sound of smashing glass, for if you fell you
would be impaled on the crystal shapes that rose from the dirt
like teeth.

We would arrive at the barn some days cold sober. There
would be dead animals in our wake, spent cartridges smoking
in the grass, our rifles left leaning against the outside wall. We
would jump and grab the jutting boards and nails and skirt
along the walls and fall into the spirits' chairs, and we would
each open a bottle of Jack Daniel's or Evan Williams or Jim
Beam or whoever Luna was buying that week, and we would
swig deeply, like old men, belching from the pits of our stomachs, and then we would race around the walls with the ground
a blur beneath us, tossing back great belts of the sweet whiskey
each time we passed the spirits' chairs, becoming drunker as
the barn spun around us and we it, stopping only to pick splin-
ters from our fingers with our teeth and to pour the stinging
alcohol on the drop of blood that appeared like something
summoned.

Sometimes we would collapse in one of the haylofts and
sleep eighteen hours, rising only to throw up or piss from the
doors, or we would pass out in the chairs, not even stirring if
one of our feet slipped from our fetal curl onto the floor
where the glass was, but waking to the cold stiffness of the
blood in the morning, the pain.

Nights were a blur. We went to Mr. D. L.'s house, the lights
there Las Vegas–like as drapes were ripped down by toppling
drunks and fires swayed like cobras from dropped cigarettes
or joints. We came in dirty from our crusades across the
course, stinking of whiskey and sometimes bloody, with
headaches and upset stomachs, and Luna would pounce

squealing across the room with her boobs flying out of her gown to embrace us.

"Hair of the dog," she would say, raising a bottle high above her head.

One night I got drunker than usual and ate some mushrooms I'd found growing in a patch of vomit in one of the upstairs sinks. Taking Luna's limp hand, I led her from the party smoke into another of the bathrooms. A man I'd never seen was passed out in the hot tub. Tears were streaming down my face. I looked into her eyes and said, "I love you, Luna. Will you marry me?"

"You're dead," T-Bob said. He was standing in the door.

We fought viciously through the house and out into the woods. It was dark. You could hear sounds from inside, music, whooping: Luna laughing. Bark split from a tree over my head and I heard the shot. T-Bob was good with a rifle, even at night. I aimed at where I thought his bullet had come from and emptied the chamber of my .30-30, working the lever action out of a bright instinct, my eyes suddenly clear, all sound fading from around me as if my blood flowed only through my head, where it was most needed. I hated Luna's whoredom, her drinking, her body odor, her stubbly legs and armpits. Why couldn't we get married?

I was out of bullets in no time but kept clicking the hammer on an empty chamber, *snap, snap, snap*. The blood oozed back through my body, to the places it usually went. I could breathe again.

"Luna," I said.

"No," T-Bob said.

He put the barrel of his .30-06 against my forehead.

He said, "I could kill you."

I said, "She's a whore."

He said, "I know it."

I said, "I love her."

He said, "You didn't hit nowhere near me."

He left me there and I felt my way into the woods. I knew them well enough, after all the times we'd slipped through them after the golfers. It used to be a game with us, in those good days, trying to keep quiet and listen to their adult conversation. We would catch green snakes in hedge bushes and sling them toward the golfers and watch them cringe. They would whip pistols from their holsters and fire into a snake's jumping body. They'd high-five each other and then lift the dead snake with a stick and drape it across the nearest flag.

But on the night of the mushrooms I got lost in the woods, for the woods are different after you lose your best friend. Mr. D. L. owned thousands of acres and I kept walking. The moon was high, shining and almost white through breaks in the dark cragged limbs, but clouds were massing. Something ran.

"Just a deer," I said, and stopped. I looked up and saw nothing except the blackness, not even the form of anything; even the moon was gone.

In the morning I came upon the gravel pit and climbed the butte. Hole 94 was there, full of rainwater and dead frogs. The flagpole lying flat. I was thinking how T-Bob and I used to run from hole to hole looking for frogs that had fallen in by accident. We'd gotten into the habit of carrying golf clubs with us, sometimes pretending they were swords, sticking them in our belts and drawing them, saying *en garde,* and fighting. If one got bent we'd get another out of Mr. D. L.'s den, where there were dozens of expensive clubs still in boxes. We would roam those woods and hills, sending great sticky mushrooms into puffy clouds with one swing. Sometimes we would obliterate the frogs from the holes, grinning at the *thwack* they made when they popped. We would charge barefoot through the grass when that golf course was in its heyday, hearing the occasional crack of a .22 when some golfer shot a timber rattler sunning on a rock, or the laughter of a hole in one.

But that morning when I was fifteen, after being lost all night, I climbed that butte and sat in the dirt and watched the sun come up, the white haze of trees in the morning fog, the ground damp from the night's dew, a rooster crowing from somewhere, gold rimming the horizon.

• • •

Summer ended.

T-Bob ignored me at school and I ate at the table with the colored boys, who ignored me too. I can report almost nothing about those days. I have no memory until the September evening when my old man came home from work and said he'd heard Mr. D. L. had come back. Unlocking the padlock on the Deepfreeze, where he kept his rum, he said they were leaving that very night, for New York.

"What about Luna?" I asked, rising from the table.

"He's leaving her here. Says he'll send for her later. Just him and the boys is going."

My fork clattered in my plate.

"Hey," the old man called.

I ran all the way over, leaping into the briars when their big Oldsmobile 98 shot past, heading the other way. At their house I ran through the tall grass and fell going up the porch steps.

Inside, Luna wore a housecoat. She was standing in the

middle of the floor with her face red from crying. She had a pistol in her hand.

"They left me," she said.

"Luna," I said, running to her and hugging her against me. I tried to kiss her, even though she smelled like whiskey and cigarettes and body odor. I took the gun out of her hand and ejected the clip and led her into the big master bathroom and while the tub filled I put her head in my lap and whispered how much I loved her. She sat up as if I wasn't there and filled a bong with a big bud and lit it and inhaled, the green water inside gurgling. Her eyes grew dreamy and she smoked more, then let me unbutton her housecoat. Underneath, she was naked. I led her to the tub and helped her in. There was a bottle of suds on the floor that I poured in. I couldn't find soap so I used shampoo to wash her.

From the medicine cabinet I found a toothbrush and toothpaste. I brushed my mouth into a foamy lather, then kissed Luna on the lips, licking her teeth. I brushed them for her. Washed her hair and face. We kissed. She stood dripping and I dried her with a clean towel.

"I love you," I told her. "Will you marry me one day?"

Her head moved. I told myself it was a nod. She fell asleep soon and I lay beside her, awake all night.

In the morning I began to clean the house, which took two days. I mowed the grass and drove Luna to Grove Hill and we bought groceries on Mr. D. L.'s charge account. She didn't say anything, just let me lead her among the aisles. She had a pipe that she kept hitting. In Wal-Mart we charged a VCR with one of Mr. D. L.'s credit cards and got a membership to a movie club in a drugstore. We rented nine movies and watched them together in the water bed.

Weeks passed. We watched every movie in that store, we ate in bed. Sometimes people from the old days of partying came by but we didn't let them in. The deputies came and asked me if Luna was okay.

"She's fine," I said.

"Can we see her?"

"No," I said. "She's got the morning sickness."

They looked at each other. "Is she . . . pregnant?" they asked.

"Yes," I said.

"Who's the father?"

"You're looking at him," I said.

The vice-principal called once, to see if anybody had heard from T-Bob or me. "No," I said, disguising my voice. "They're gone."

Lastly I heard from the old man. He called late one night to see where we kept the bacon grease.

After that it was just Luna and me, for a good long time.

•   •   •

October.

One morning before it got too cold I packed the camping gear I'd charged at the hardware store and Luna and I started hiking the course. She didn't want to but I lied and told her I knew where Jimmy Younger's pot patch was. The paths were grown so that we could barely follow them, kudzu everywhere, streaming up the flags and covering the snake skins as we walked through the tall trees. Most of the course's holes were full of dirt and water, and we kept walking, coming to a new hole every half hour or so, stopping there. We frightened a doe once and watched her bound away, through the foliage.

"Where is it?" she asked me.

"Not too far," I kept saying.

We came to the gravel pit and walked over the red clay, looking up at the butte. We camped on top of it, raising our pup tent and building a fire to heat our cans of Dinty Moore beef stew. After the sun dipped beyond the tree line we heard a coyote howling.

The next night we camped next to one of the ponds.

"How old you think I am?" asked Luna. It was the first thing she'd said all day.

"It don't matter," I said. "Love can't count. Love missed that day in school."

"You think they'll ever come back?" she asked me.

My heart was a fire stampeded by horses. "You want them to?"

She didn't answer. She said, "Did I ever tell you how I met Daniel Lester?"

I'd never heard what Mr. D. L.'s initials stood for. I said, "No."

"I was working in New Orleans. Hustling. These wealthy guys who'd used me before said they had a fellow they wanted me to treat right. Said whatever he wants, no matter how weird, I'm to give it to him. I'd been with lots of men, see, but nobody ever treated me like Daniel Lester. When I first saw him I didn't know what to think. This little bitty weird guy. These sideburns. But he was polite and gentlemanly. Took my coat. Mixed me a margarita.

"So after we, well, you know, *after*, we're watching TV and he asked me what I want out of life, and I go, 'I want some shrimp,' and he calls down to room service and they send up these giant shrimp cocktails. Then I say, 'How 'bout some champagne?' and he orders it. I see what he's doing, so I keep asking for things, and he keeps getting them. Finally—there's golf on TV—I look at the screen and go, 'I always wanted to learn to play golf.' 'That'll take a little time,' he says, but by that time he was ready to go again."

"Do you feel pregnant?" I asked.

Luna looked at me over her shoulder. "Do I feel *what?*"

In the pond a great catfish rolled. They would come to life at night, rising to the surface and showing their white bellies to the moon. Luna turned away from me and I crawled out of the tent, my fishing rod rigged. I put calf's liver on my treble hook and threw it into the water, sat waiting for the tug that meant breakfast. In the tent I could hear Luna crying softly.

"I'm forty-four," she called, "you fucking weirdo."

• • •

After I took Luna home I went to the barn where the tractor was and got it running and taught myself the use of Lucius's bushhog and, wearing a cowboy hat and a .44 Magnum on my belt, began cutting the weeds that had overtaken the course. I cut for a month, dawn to dusk. When I finished the grass, I rode the tractor to Grove Hill and picked up the two hundred flags I'd ordered. The old dude behind the counter didn't want to give them to me until I paid some on the charge account, but I said Luna would take care of it soon.

On the corner I ran into some guys from school, guys who'd once come to Luna's parties. They avoided me.

I took the flags home. Got a posthole digger and spent a week fixing the decrepit holes, digging out the tiny, delicate frog bones, the water, the grass. I weeded the bunkers, the southern states. I put up the new flags and, using a hand mower with a vacuum attachment, neatly trimmed the sod around the holes. Growing wild and watering from all the rain had benefited the sod—it was flowing and beautiful like grass over a septic tank and, cut back, looked as good as any course you saw on TV. I cleaned out Jimmy's guard shack and re-painted the walls, left a small combination lock hanging on the door.

The sun was tanning my skin dark brown; I hadn't had a haircut or shave in months. I jogged, my legs growing muscu-lar, my lungs expanding. I swam the catfish ponds, full of water now from the rain we'd been having. I teased the aging, ornery bull with a red towel, easily sidestepping as he lunged for me with his dull horns. I led the last living cow back to Mr. D. L.'s house and paid a black man to slaughter it, storing the meat in Mr. D. L.'s freezer. Luna and I sat on the sofa at night watch-ing ESPN: baseball, soccer, racing, golf. She was drinking again and smoking and would throw up in the mornings as I dressed for my day's work.

I turned sixteen.

I found some of Mr. D. L.'s blank checks in a drawer and forged Luna's name on one to a man for several head of cat-tle. The truck driver backed his rig to the gate behind the guardhouse. We shooed the fat beef cows down the ramp and out into the fields for the old bull to mount and further our herd. The truck driver talked me into buying a horse and I wrote another check and he delivered the big paint the next day and threw in a free saddle and I taught myself to ride.

I called the horse Big Steve. I set tees with dusty golf balls from Mr. D. L.'s den and played polo from horseback. Riding at a dead run, I would hang over his side and with a wood try to send the teed golf balls shooting away like bullets.

I rode Big Steve to the place where colored people lived, shacks on blocks behind dead trees, dogs asleep in the dirt road, fancy cars with chrome. A thin black girl braiding her grandmother's hair on a porch. Children gathered around Big Steve with their eyes round and their faces shiny from sweat. Their fingers touched Big Steve's flank gingerly, with respect.

"Any y'all know a man ain't scared of snakes?" I asked the faces.

"Mr. Haskew ain't," one said.

"Where's he live?"

They pointed me to a house across the road, an old colored man with wrinkled skin rocking on his porch. He wore a suit and hat despite the heat, suspenders. A cane rested across his lap.

I nudged Big Steve over the road and through the dirt of his yard. "Mr. Haskew?"

He nodded.

"Did you know Lucius, that used to work for Mr. D. L.?"

Mr. Haskew nodded.

"Would you like that job now? I'll pay you five thousand dollars a year and you can pick any of those old barns for living quarters. I'll supply you with a tractor and you'll bushhog all day."

"Six," he said.

"Seven," I said, and wrote him a check.

He nodded and stood. He was taller than Lucius had been, his eyes yellow and watery.

"Get your things," I told him.

He went in and a few minutes later came out carrying a cardboard suitcase and an umbrella and was followed by a girl called Inez, his daughter or stepdaughter. They walked behind

Big Steve and me, Mr. Haskew leaning on his cane. When the road forked I told them to keep going toward Dickinson and I'd catch up with them. Then I galloped off toward where Jimmy Younger lived.

• • •

I started spending nights on the butte. As the sun went down I sighted the surrounding area in my scope. I pegged a box turtle at one hundred yards as it moped across the cracked clay, saw its shell explode in a mist of red. I built a lean-to on the butte and took a gas grill up there for cooking. It was starting to get chilly, the leaves changing color, wrinkling, drifting to the ground.

Each day I rode out to talk with Jimmy Younger, listened to his stories of the James-Younger gang. How Jesse didn't really get shot, that he and Bob Ford had rigged the whole thing and killed a gambler who looked like Jesse and turned that man in for burial, how Jesse lived to be a ripe old age of a hundred one, that the history books were wrong, how Jesse went straight.

The last thing I'd tell Jimmy before I rode off was, "Don't let anybody in. You only let people out." Then I'd put a ten-dollar bill in his tip jar.

He'd say, "That's a big ten-four."

I'd gallop over to the barn where Inez was hanging out laundry. It wasn't Lucius's barn, for Mr. Haskew and Inez were afraid to stay near those spirits' chairs. Across the Negro community had gone stories of what came to sit and rest there at night, so they stayed in a littler barn, but Inez had given it a woman's touch: drapes, pieces of carpet she found somewhere, flowers in pots. When I stopped she had always done something new, put up a birdbath made from an old hubcap, a wreath woven from buzzard and turkey and owl feathers. Most of her teeth were missing and one of her eyes strayed. I stretched my legs in the saddle and looked proudly about the hills, the distant tree line, the soaring hawks, the dumb cows, the half-blind bull, thinking how fertile the land was. Then I'd ask Inez where Mr. Haskew was working today, and she would point.

Tipping my hat, I'd spur Big Steve into a run and we'd soon hear the buzz of Mr. Haskew's tractor. We'd ride out so he could see us; if he needed something he'd kill the tractor and I'd go over, but most of the time he just nodded or waved his cane.

When I went to Mr. D. L.'s house Luna would be red-eyed in front of the television, eating potato chips, candy bars, cookies, hamburgers, TV dinners.

"How you doing, darling?" I'd ask.

• • •

One evening after a solitary supper of catfish on the butte I went to talk to Mr. Haskew about it. He was sitting on a bench outside his barn cleaning his pistol. I sat and told him that Luna had lost her affection for me, how we never kissed since I asked was she pregnant. I lit my pipe and offered him my tobacco. He refused with a wave of his hand. He offered me a bottle of Jack Daniel's, which I accepted. I took a long swig, feeling dizzy. I started crying. He stood up holstering his pistol and limped into the barn, leaving me the bottle. Before long I heard the tractor cough to life. I was drunk but still knew it was too late in the day to start bushhogging. I heard Inez's steps coming up behind me. She walked barefoot around me wearing the dress she always had on, a blue one with no sleeves. I thought I ought to bring Inez some of the things that Luna never wore.

"You want a drink?" I asked.

She reached and took my hand and led me inside. We went into a little room with deer horns and cow skulls nailed to the walls. A bird's nest hung in one corner. Inez took the bottle from me and put it away. She bent down over me and undid my pants, took out what she found there. She lifted her dress with a rough scratching of material over skin and eased herself down onto me.

• • •

All good things end.

Luna was gone the next day, and then Mr. D. L. and his boys came home. I watched from the woods as they stabbed a For Sale sign into the yard of the house. They all wore suits. All smoked cigars. T-Bob had grown taller and had his hair cut short. The three of them went past the gate and into the golf course. They looked at one another as they saw its condition, no doubt having expected it to be a gnarled mess, a wilderness. They walked on. I kept pace with them, always a tree, a hill between us. Mr. D. L. took a tiny telephone from his pocket, opened it and talked to someone. Then they walked on.

Half an hour later I watched as Jimmy Younger drove up in his pickup. I watched as they talked and I knew he was telling them all about me. I watched as they started looking toward the trees, as Jimmy gave them all rifles. At Mr. Haskew's barn they told the old man and Inez to pack up and go.

Then they came looking for me.

I rode Big Steve over the hills and drew him up alongside

Lucius's barn and then turned him loose, watched him gallop off across the meadow. The closed barn doors were so overgrown with kudzu that I had to pry them open and slip inside and let them shut behind me. I slid my feet along carefully, avoiding the larger pieces of glass that were like spikes, and I moved toward the spirits' chairs. They were dark with cobwebs that sagged with the weight of dust, and sunlit cracks in the walls caught the swirls of dust I made by sitting. Taking off my boots, I picked diamonds of glass from the soles and drank from a bottle of Jim Beam. I left my socks hanging on the back of a chair and leaped and caught a ledge and swung hand over hand around the barn's interior, sure-handed and -footed as ever, hugging at times the wall while my fingers dug into cracks between boards and my toes clenched an inch-wide outcropping of wood: scaling the wall and moving through the rafters like a thing from the jungle, dropping easily into the spirits' chairs for shots of whiskey, then back up, around, flying through beams and over nails, feather-light, daring, unstoppable, shooting more whiskey as my speed picked up, going around until at last I crashed the empty bottle on the others and sprang from the chairs and rushed up the wall and through the rafters, and with a scrabbling of hands left red stripes across the board where my fingernails were ripped off, and the ceiling was falling away and there was weightlessness and a spray of noise like spindles of musical notes, then numbness: warmth.

For a long time. Till the door was slung open and Mr. D. L. and T-Bob and his brothers and Jimmy Younger stood there in silhouette, holding rifles. I couldn't move. They came forward.

DEATH BY GOLF

Jonathan Gash

T wo things in life matter: antiques and women. Get them right, you're a millionaire in paradise. Get them wrong, you'll be penniless like me. Should you be barmy enough to believe that there's a third essential, you've no hope. A man can survive two incurable ailments. Three—and one of them golf—you're into death, quite possibly your own.

• • •

The auction was pretty gruesome, even for a rainy Friday. There was the usual dross—old tables, wartime chairs, threadbare curtains, rusting garden implements. A few junk dealers spent a groat or two. Us antique dealers ignored the mounds of boots, jam jars, warped pianos and wonky wardrobes, scanned the dud paintings and made for the door.

"Here, mate." Joe Winter grabbed my arm. "You not bidding?"

"For what, Joe?" He nodded at a trio of old golf balls, Lot 206, with the indented surface that's supposed to make them fly faster, slower, whatever, like I cared. "Them? No good.

They're old, all right, but didn't you see who's over there?" I had more sense than point at the elderly gent waiting by the window.

"No," he lied. "Who is it?"

"That's Judge Wymond." I kept my voice low. "He's been hoovering up golfiana for twenty years. Spends like a drunken sailor. I'm broke."

"You've got to, Lovejoy," he said. "Please, mate."

I was in time to cadge a lift to the usual Friday drinking session in the Fox and Stork, hoping to collect the usual scuttlebutt. I'd hit a bad patch, living on crumbs from other dealers' tables.

•   •   •

Antique dealers are a clone of obsessive neurotics—correction: psychotics. A neurotic is to be helped and sympathized with. Psychos, you keep out of their way. Think of them as politicians with an ax. They're often antique dealers. This Friday night scene in the Fox and Stork will explain.

We meet in this ancient pub. Not from friendship, but to undermine each other's confidence by pretending that we've made some brilliantly profitable deals. Most of us are broke, trying not to buy the next round, hoping some other dealer will become maudlin enough to let their antique secrets slip.

The inn, old as the hills, is now so posh you've to call it a bistro, taverna or some such. This was a month ago, before the carnage. Until then, I'd thought golf was a "good walk spoiled," as that ineffable bore Bernard Shaw once cracked. It was his only witticism. I'll bet that he pinched it, just as he nicked Pygmalion. He should have been an antique dealer. Maybe he was.

•   •   •

It had been a hell of a day. Dandy Jack, filthy as a stoat and drunk as an autumn wasp, was leaning on the taproom bar complaining (not an all-time first) about auctioneers. A dozen other dealers were getting sloshed with the economical energy of the dedicated grumbler. I was still thinking about Joe Winter. Odd that he'd been so insistent, wanting me to bid for those golf balls. He's a gardener like his dad was.

"Gimbert's upped his commission to 15 percent," Dandy was grousing. "Rotten, like Sotheby's."

"Auctioneers are thieving parasites," Fluke agreed. He's a disheveled ex–army bloke, rotund and boisterous. He once tried to become an auctioneer but kept telling the truth, so he only lasted three days at Gimbert's in Long Melford.

"Did anybody notice that mad buyer? A right duck egg." Dandy stared morosely into his empty glass. No passing saint offered him a refill.

"That was Georgina's ex," Rowena chipped in. "She's a bitch."

Women get no concessions from Rowena. She hates other females. Reasons are obscure. She sits on a high stool because she has perfect legs, to rile other women and make us men sigh.

"Was it? I thought he was a snooker pro," Paltry said, buying himself a drink and ignoring Dandy's pathetic stare. "Must be a lunatic to pay that much for a glass paperweight."

Paltry's a scruffy giant of a man who deals in Georgian silver and Victorian oils. He smokes a pipe and is the only known antique dealer in East Anglia with a woman barker. She's called Poppy and is remarkable for loving him. Everybody keeps telling her that he treats her like dirt. She's beautiful and frighteningly frank. "Oh, I know Paltry's not worth it," she says, dazzling you with her smile, "but I love him, so there you go." She's married to a bookmaker's clerk in Winchester and goes home once a week. She was seated opposite Rowena, waiting patiently, ready to spring should Paltry signal that he wanted another glass. It's a rum world.

A barker, incidentally, is an antique dealer's sniffer-out of antiques. Every dealer has one. Think of a pilot fish questing ahead of a hunting shark. All barkers conform to a pattern, usually being habitual drunkards who assimilate news of antiques and other tat simply by leaning on some dingy bar all day. They learn by osmosis, I suppose.

"His name's Bill Porteous," Chris Laughton said. "Him and Georgina Porteous split because of That Fight."

Chris is colonial tribal artifacts and Great Civil War coinage, but is a better forger than he is an antique dealer. If you've got a genuine Zulu impi shield from the Battle of Rorke's Drift, take it to Chris in Sudbury. He'll pay you over the odds, then turn out a dozen fakes, all copied meticulously in genuine materials, and swamp the antique market. Like all skilled forgers, he makes money while cheating everybody else. Chris added complacently, "Bill Porteous has started an antiques shop near Georgina's. He's ruining her trade."

"The darling!" Rowena cooed, radiant at the thought of Georgina starving in some gutter. "I *do* hope he succeeds! She's a bitch."

"Good luck to him," George Arrance put in morosely. "My antiques shop lasted a fortnight."

Everybody knows the antique dealer's old adage: If you want danger, try sky falling with an umbrella, or Russian roulette, but don't do anything really risky like opening an antique shop. George had been talked into it by a meek little lady who wanted a quick sale for her Olde Tea Shoppe in Lowestoft. She'd taken him to the cleaners.

Then Velcro laughed, shaking his head. He's a New Zealand sailor who jumped ship, never again to leave our shores. He owns a shoe retailer's in Wellington. People keep writing asking when he's coming home. They send him monthly accounts and AGM reports but he bins the lot unread. Sometimes they even send him airline tickets, which he sells. When antipodean lawyers come a-stalking we tell them that we've never heard of him. Paltry misdirected the last lot to Manchester. Velcro bought him beer for a week for that kindness. Nice bloke, Velcro. He can drink a pint while doing a handstand, the sort of trick I really admire.

"Know what?" he said, helpless with laughter and almost falling off his bar stool. "We're a right load of plonkers."

Everybody scowled. Antique dealers hate being thought morons. They *know* they're genius level, way above the hoi polloi They're wrong, but don't tell them that.

"We're obsessed, see?" Velcro could hardly get the words out, rolling in the aisles. We waited threateningly. Chris roughly pushed him back on his stool.

No, we didn't see. He subsided, seeing the grim faces.

"Look," he said reasonably. "We think there's nothing in the world except antiques, right?"

Glances exchanged. "So?"

"Not counting Lovejoy. He thinks there's *two* things in the world—antiques and women. Right?"

They thought this over. I shrugged, because he was speaking the truth. Rowena gave me a fond smile. She'd wheedled a pair of gold and garnet Victorian nipple rings out of me the previous week for a song. Well, not a song, more of an encounter, but you don't betray a lady's confidence. These nipple rings are often sold as "large pendant earrings of unusual design" by dealers who haven't a clue. Victorian ladies journals carried advertisements for these intriguing jewels. It's a "silent" field for collectors, as the trade says, meaning waiting to be discovered. You can pick them up in flea markets for a tenth of what they're worth. Tip: They're almost always gold, even if the jewel is only garnet, because gold doesn't irritate tender skin like cheap alloys do. Chromium, used in alloys, irritates skin.

"So what, Velcro?"

"Well, think of collectibles," Velcro said, sobering.

"What about them?" Paltry said. "Somebody bid a fortune today for a Baccarat paperweight. Did you see it?"

"It was a fake," I said. They stared.

"It can't have been." Chris went gray. He had bid, and only dropped out when a determined stranger kicked in. "I examined it. Genuine Baccarats have silhouettes on the colored glass ends in the pattern. I saw a deer, a dog and a horse, all in black, so it must have been genuine."

"No, Chris. It felt wrong."

"What an escape!" Chris, badly shaken at his narrow squeak, tottered for a brandy. "I bid four thousand before I ducked out. It was dated 1848. That date's okay, isn't it?"

"Forgers can look dates up."

This is the trouble with antique dealers. They fix their minds on one minor clue and start celebrating. They don't think. My mind, on the other hand, is like a ragbag, full of odds and ends—like, Theodore Roosevelt got his pearl-handled revolvers from Tiffany's, and suchlike dross. Useless, until suddenly bits form a weird pattern to worry me sick.

"It looked genuine," a mellifluous voice remarked, starting this particular pattern.

We looked round. A smart-looking woman sat in one of the armchairs. We all knew she'd been listening, and had sussed her as a visiting dealer, which is why we were being cagier than usual. Wandering dealers come prowling the coast this time of year. I'd sensed money because everything she wore matched. She looked class. She'd followed us.

"Yes, dear," Rowena said in a voice of sleet. "We all saw your bungled attempts to bid."

The visitor ignored her. Bonny and cool, her casual manner showed that she could be as frosty as Rowena any day. Makes you wonder if convent schools teach some 101 course in social sniping. She had an American accent, so we knew instantly that she must be a millionaire. All Americans are.

"Are you one of those divvies?" she asked me, casually curious.

"Of course he is," Chris said. "I'm still narked, Lovejoy. You might have tipped me the wink that the Baccarat was a fake. I could have gone on bidding and wasted a fortune." He went pale at the thought. Other dealers shuddered.

"Not you, Chris," I said bitterly. He still owed me for a Spode dinner set. Two months, and not a penny. "You're too tight."

The rest chuckled. They love debt, in friends.

The exquisite stranger wouldn't let go. "You can detect genuine antiques without even examining them? I'd always thought it was a fable."

She lit a cigarette, pouting to release a plume of smoke into

the taproom air. Lots of symbolism there. We were all so mesmerized that nobody reminded her of the no-smoking rule
that had come in the previous Sunday.

"He's the only divvy in East Anglia," Chris said, anxious to
ablate my mention of his debt.

Ingratiation, but no money.

"So you can tell me whether that Staffordshire spaniel fig-
urine was genuine," she remarked. I watched her smoke rise.
Symbolism's a pest.

"I saw you buy it. You've been had."

She looked her astonishment through the haze.

"You didn't have time to examine it, Lovejoy."

"Tip it upside down, lady, and look inside." I was suddenly
tired. Dealers always blame me when they've been stupid. "It'll
be too thin-walled. Look with a probe light—you can get one
in a toy shop. You'll see no potter's finger dabs there. Genuine
figures should show them clearly. And the glaze's craquelure
will be even, not patchy. There are other signs."

"Told you!" Paltry said proudly. "Lovejoy's never wrong."

"Then why is he so shabby?" She was now well and truly
narked. "He looks off the road, worse than a tramp. If he's in-
fallible, why doesn't he make some stupendous finds of his
own?"

"Women, dear," Rowena purred. "Didn't you hear? You
were flapping your big ears hard enough. Lovejoy falls prey to
any coarse tart that happens by."

Which from Rowena . . . I said nothing.

The woman smiled. The radiance was brilliant, so warm we
didn't need the taproom's log fire. I felt myself go red. She
scrutinized me.

"Fern Margrave, Norwich, a dealer. I'm doing a sweep

through the Eastern Hundreds and need an adviser. I can pay a retainer plus expenses. Interested?"

"Starting when?"

"He means yes!" Chris exclaimed, desperate to see money come into the area instead of ebbing as usual. We dealers have this saying: Money in rather than money out. The others chorused agreement, except for Rowena, who was doubtless plotting some poison for the lovely newcomer.

She dazzled me with a look and remarked, "I'll remember your law about only two things in life, antiques and women. Quite a doctrine!"

"He's wrong," a voice said.

We all looked. There in the inglenook sat Bendix. You'd hardly notice him. In fact, we rarely ever do. Bendix is a quiet, reserved geezer, wears a waistcoat and watch chain. He's creakingly old, always wears his bowler hat. Black boots, crumpled suit, spends all evenings in the Fox and Stork sitting alone. Whenever you look at Bendix he's asleep. I could only remember hearing him speak a few times before.

"Wrong?" Paltry said, grinning. The village kids use their peashooters on Bendix's bowler hat. They bet who'll hit it first in three goes. He's harmless, just another dullard on the East Anglian landscape. Paltry winked at us and asked innocently, "What else is there besides antiques and women, Benny?"

"Golf," Bendix said quietly.

Crime doesn't come stealing in any quieter. I think I was the only one there who had the slightest feeling of foreboding as everybody instantly launched into golfing memorabilia we'd all missed at a million auctions and a jillion trunk sales.

As the evening ended, my new employer let me cadge a lift to my cottage. I ignored the others' knowing looks. She hadn't given Bendix a single glance. A small incident just made for my ragbag mind. It stayed in me, as we drove into the darkness.

• • •

"My husband's a waste contractor," Fern Margrave told me. She drove the night roads with decision, none of this bumping along with one wheel in the gutter. She scraped the hanging hedges with impunity. Her vintage Bentley could always get a respray. "Don't laugh, Lovejoy. Where there's muck, there's brass, people say."

I hadn't laughed. I knew of Margrave. "Where?"

"Locally. The old De Haviland place."

These ancient manor houses were once the centers of whole estates with thousands of acres. Over centuries they shrank, bits being nibbled off for that hunting lodge or this new housing complex. The final few hundred acres tend to sit in rural bondage, rimmed by motorways or shopping malls. They're subjects for historical societies. Wildlifers investigate the flora and fauna of the old forests. Bored broadcasters pretend delirium when some rare *Fritillaria* plant is discovered lurking in the undergrowth. Real estate developers point indignantly to the decaying mansion and lust after the two thousand houses they imagine building there and the profit they'll rake in.

"Does he bribe many?" I asked. Developers are known for it.

She smiled. "Of course!" She shot me a sidelong glance, hard as nails. "How else do you think I could indulge my hobby of antiques?"

A few minutes later she dropped me off at my cottage, making the usual response: "Dear God! You don't *really* live in that hovel?" etc., etc. I watched the motor drive away, a dark blob dragged through the countryside behind its cone of amber light. What had I got myself into?

I went in and brewed up, cut myself some cheese and a chunk of bread, and thought about Bendix, he of the bowler hat and frayed mustache. One thing you learn to spot in antiques is a setup. Tonight's coincidence gleamed like a moon in a mine. For Bendix had been the butler at the old De Haviland place before the manor house was closed up. And Fern Margrave's husband was the real estate man with his eyes on developing the whole estate. And I'd been pressed by Joe Winter, gardener, to bid for some old golfiana junk. His dad was once the De Haviland gardener.

Now, I know nothing about golf. Who does? And if Bendix had ever played a single round of golf I'm the pope. Bendix's eyes hadn't even flickered in her direction, but you can always tell.

Too many coincidences. Why had she dropped in at the Fox and Stork? And her husband ran a garbage disposal firm whose latest development was on the old De Haviland place. And Bendix was the De Haviland family's retired butler, who'd not spoken in the Fox and Stork since the Boer War . . . No, too many coincidences spoil the broth.

Next dawn I was up at six. I fed the blue tits their sunflower seeds and thumbed a lift into town as the town hall clock struck seven. I waited at the bus station near St. Alfege's church, and thought of golf and what it meant to antique dealers.

• • •

They say golf is the best game on earth. To me, it's yawnsville, even more pointless than synchronized swimming. Unbelievably, golf courses are burgeoning everywhere. If some derelict hospital grounds or some school's playing fields are sold off, sure as eggs some lunatic will spend millions to build a golf course.

Not only that, golfiana's a massive field for collectors. (I'm not making the name up.) The most valuable relics are ancient golf balls—featheries the most highly priced. In days before Dr. Paterson of St. Andrews, meaning pre-1845, you boiled feathers (one top hat full of goose down was the correct measure) to a soggy mess, then compressed each dollop. You squashed the blob into a hand-sewn leather sphere, and there was your golf ball. Of course, scoundrels now fake them. But if you find an original antique one, it'll buy you a house. Then came Dr. P. and his gutta-percha golf balls, made from the inspissated gum of the *Isonandra* tree—it's found in Malaysia and thereabouts. One old guttie ball will buy you another house. And if you can find one of those ancient wooden press gadgets the Victorians used to indent the balls with, you're talking a round-the-world cruise. Fakes abound, so watch out.

The clubs are as bad, or as good. Those made in the nineteenth century by some country blacksmith cost a fortune, especially if the shaft is glued intact with old catgut. Socket-jointed clubs came in about 1900, they say. The point is, golf memorabilia are mostly tat, of no interest except for the small incidental fact that they'll bring in a fortune. If they're funny shapes—like the toothed raker (seven prongs on an ash, hazel or American hickory shaft)—then you're into a year's cruising plus a freehold house. Daft, I call it, but if the world's crazy for such things who am I? It's a collector's world. The last thing I could recall seeing auctioned, golfwise, was a group of three golf balls made by one Coburn Haskell, who in 1900 first thought of making balls with a rubber inner core. Big deal. Or so I thought, until I saw the bidding rise like a lark and almost vanish off the map. I quickly realized that anything vaguely associated with golf is valuable until proved otherwise. Golfing teapots, if you can imagine such things, ashtrays, briar pipes, T-shirts, standishes and hat pins, even ladies' golfing shoes, go for a mint. Even poor quality golf paintings bring in four years' worth of income. There's only one way to prove a collectible's value, and that's by selling it so the money's in your hand.

By the time the bus came I was almost fainting at the aromas coming from the bus station nosh bar, but I'd only just got the fare. I stayed hungry, and reached the town council's rubbish tip by nine.

There stands Marjorie.

• • •

Now, I'm not knocking sports. They're great. I just think we should stop inventing them. Sport, not religion, is the opiate of the people.

"See," I told Marjorie when we'd got talking at the Council Recycling and Waste Disposal Facility, "if we didn't invent any more sports, we'd not keep losing at the Olympics, right?"

"What on earth are you on about?"

Marjorie is a superb example of perfect middle age. She stands all day long beside her grand Alfa Romeo motor—this week it was a bright cerulean blue—and watches people dump rubbish. Occasionally she leaches out a piece of dross, takes it home in her trunk, has it cleaned and sells it to antique dealers. A strange occupation, but if you stick at it as Marjorie does you can make a living. Council workmen help her if some crud proves heavy, but they wouldn't help the likes of you or me.

Marjorie has ample means of persuasion. She knows little about antiques, but acquires a dozen or so worthwhile collectibles every week—sewing machines, old telephones, glassware, pottery, pewter cups, treen (read old wooden implements) and cutlery. I like her.

"Well," I said, painstakingly working toward the subject of golf, "look at badminton. Look at lawn tennis, real tennis, soccer, darts, even snooker, for God's sake. Look at rugby. Polo. Bowls. We only invent them so we can lose. Cricket." I paused because I'd run out of sports. "Wasn't baseball in Jane Austen's *Northanger Abbey,* pre-USA?"

"What are you after, Lovejoy?" she demanded shrewdly.

That's the trouble with women. I find that they outmaneuver me without my realizing, but I try the same trick, they spot it a mile off. Her steady eyes kept hold of me.

"Nothing, Marj. Honest!"

"This hour of the morning?" A cold wind was coming off the estuary, the distant sea glinting cold as a frog. It was her best hour for finding worthwhile pieces of rubbish, she'd told me once, hence my arrival at cockshout.

"Well, all right." I tried to look crestfallen. "I'm after some golfiana. Got any?"

She usually assembles her gunge according to themes: old football boots that she'll pass off as worn by somebody once famous, or a broken cricket bat she can swear was used by a West Indian player at Lord's. She sells them to Empsom in Peldon Marsh, who says he's expert in suchlike gunge.

"In time for the new golf course?" She smiled. Not quite as dazzling as Mrs. Margrave's, but getting there.

"Is there one?" I asked innocently.

"That's the gossip."

A small estate wagon came bouncing over the ruts of the dump's lunar landscape. It carried a rusting lathe and worn tools.

"You've caught me out, Marjorie," I said ruefully. "That's it. I'm trying to acquire some golf sticks."

"Clubs. I once found a mashie niblick here, practically mint. And a cleek head, but the shaft had broken."

"Honest?" What the hell was she on about?

"Ferdie restored them to near-mint condition."

Ferdie's a local carpenter who sidelines in revarnishing old furniture and mending sporting trivia. She waved, smiling. The man unloading the estate wagon grinned and laid his dross out in a line for any passing lady to nab and load up into her splendid motor.

"I found an old, er, 3-iron once," I said lamely.

She laughed. "You haven't a clue, have you? They're old names for golf clubs. The mashie niblick's the modern 7-iron. The cleek's another. They changed to numbers about the 1930s. It's worth keeping a lookout." She drew her fur coat tighter round her against the wind. "An old persimmon-headed wooden club would buy you a freehold five-bedroom house on Margrave's new estate—when he gets round to building it." She grew reflective. "I've been wondering whether to transfer to his landfill, now it's got going."

I looked over the derelict landscape. "You'd leave here?"

"Margrave's new rubbish tip will be massive. Imagine the finds!"

"I heard Margrave was begging the local council for a single acre for a landfill." I was still questing.

She shook her head at my ignorance.

"He's been allowed to dump twenty thousand metric tons

of uncontaminated rubble there, Lovejoy. That means he'll bribe the council's inspectors to stay away—while he dumps ten times that much. And uncontaminated's a laugh." Not laughing now, though. "Lorries go where he tells them, any-where over the twenty-three hectares he's got his eye on. As-bestos, oil drums, toxic waste. He gets a backhander from every unauthorized wagon. He's already made a million from it." Her expression became pure scorn. I felt withered by her look. "The trucks dump a thousand loads a week. It's ever since the landfill tax came in—32,000 unauthorized sites in this creaking old kingdom, Lovejoy." She saw my look of dis-belief. "You can't teach me anything about rubbish. I had *you* once, remember?"

I swallowed the insult. "You telling me the truth, Marj?"

"Don't call me Marj. I pay the men to rescue the good bits and clean them up so they're safe to handle. Never heard of Brisket Wood in Hertfordshire? Margrave did it there too. Now it's a wonderful golf course, splendid clubhouse and all, built on contaminated illegal garbage."

"Why doesn't somebody report him?"

"They did. He got fined a few pence." She glared at me. "You know why? The council can't afford to excavate the rub-bish dump once the land's filled. It's cheaper to let the danger-ous contaminants lie covered by a golf course that pays revenue and employs people."

"Who's the golf king hereabouts?"

"Player, memorabilia collector, clubhouse owner, what?"

"Any of the above."

"You want Wymond, the Norwich judge. He was in town yesterday, buying old golf stuff. He employs three collectors hunting for his golf museum."

"Where is it?"

"He's going halves, him and Margrave, when there's enough infilled De Haviland land."

For a moment or two I thought hard. I'm pretty slow.

"Ta, Marjorie. I'll help you lift your garbage."

She laughed outright. "You're so gullible, Lovejoy! Since when did a woman ever lack help to lift anything?"

True, true. I said so long and trudged toward the road.

• • •

Bendix lived in a cottage down the River Deben estuary. There, folk frolic in yachts. The pubs are always full of talk about force nine gales and compass bearings, all very nautical. I got a lift from the vicar's wife. I said I was visiting an old friend's grave. She offered to help me find it. I told her no, ta, I'd manage.

"I do understand. Spiritual solace." She went all misty. "How sweet."

Which left me within a hundred yards of Bendix's place. I found him sitting on his veranda watching the water. Punts glided by. It was sickeningly serene.

"Wotcher, Benny." I plonked myself down. He didn't even turn his head. "Tranquillity like this gives countryside a bad name."

He turned to inspect me. "Countryside's the land's breath, Lovejoy. Vandals throttle it."

"Never seen you without your bowler," I said, surprised by his thin wispy hair, gray-white. "What was that crack about golf?"

"It's on the parlor wall, son. Bring it."

Apart from a broken mirror there was only a small water-color painting. I lifted it down and took it to him.

"I knew you'd come, Lovejoy. Recognize it?" As I tilted it for more light he cautioned, "Shade it from sun," as if we were in torrid desert heat.

"I know, I know," I said, narked, examining the painting.

Somebody had done it in the style of Victorian watercolorists, highlighting with pastels. The artist must have admired the Rowbothams, a family of old artists. Do the painting, then pick out the areas you need to show more brilliantly. Purists see this technique as cheating, but even great artists used the trick. It showed a landscape, a manor house in the distance, nearby a clump of trees and a small mound. So?

"Only worth maybe a week's wages, Benny."

"Any good?"

"No. Want to sell? I'll talk Shipshape into flogging it at some auction, if you like. Get you enough for a holiday weekend." I smiled at the thought. "Be waited on, instead of serving others, you being a butler and all."

He didn't speak. Squinting, I guessed, "The old De Haviland place at Horkesley?"

He nodded, watching a rowing boat slide through the reeds. Two ducks flew up angrily. The young couple saw Bendix's cottage, us both on his veranda, and decided to find somewhere else to snog. I waved sympathetically. They ignored us. The ducks settled down, miffed.

"When I worked there," Benny ruminated, "we had eighteen gardeners, thirteen full-time resident household servants, grooms."

Funny what a word does. You can't say the word "servant" now without getting neck prickles, because it proves you're fascist or something. The word's only legitimate use is in historical novels, "Ho there, Milady" and all that. But these old servants (sorry) don't have any such compunction. On the wall near London's Kings Cross Station is a small plaque recording the lifetime slog of an old Victorian geezer, nominating him as *A Trusty Servant of the Company.* He was Lord Somebody, no less. See? Prickles and all, I cleared my throat.

"Quite a crowd, Benny."

"Three months short of fifty years I served the family, from being fourteen. Apart from national service in the Malayan war." He almost smiled. "You have to say Ma-lay-si-an now."

"Right, Benny. Ta for the, er, visit." I rose and propped the framed painting against the wall, face inward. "See you Friday, eh?"

"That painting's of her grave, you see. He never saw me watching him bury her, after she was murdered." I sat down again. We watched two punts on the river, one energetically poled by a young laughing bloke, a seated girl squealing, while two oldsters in the other punt frowned at such levity. "Youngsters nowadays just don't think. They disturb the waterbirds. One moorhen had a broken wing last week. I got the bird people out to help it, all the way from Fingringhoe."

My feet were suddenly unwilling. What had he said? I picked up the picture and looked again.

"The river used to be much wider," Benny was rabbiting on in his dry voice. "Until the earthquake. Was it in 1883? It struck Colchester as well. I forget important dates."

There was a small mound depicted in burnt umber on yellow ocher, the tired watercolorist's trick to get shaded ground. It stood close to the viewer, so your eye tended to pass over it and look instead at the manor house, the drive, a coach drawing up to the broad steps by the ornamental balustrade. Was that just a clever deception or a beginner's fluke? It seemed to be shadowed by a grove of trees—larch, were they? I'm hopeless with Mother Nature.

"Broad-leaved limes." He answered my unspoken question, adding proudly, "One was planted by the lord lieutenant of the county." He looked at me with rheumy eyes. "It was an honor. We servants were allowed to watch the planting ceremony."

"How, er, kind."

Grave, though? I peered. The mansion was shown about a mile off. Undulating fields, a cow or two, fencing of thin wire done with pencil, a wash of cerulean blue but no expensive French ultramarine, directly from the paint box. The old adage is that true artists mix their own, never using what the colorman sells. The earth was painstakingly shown as disturbed—browns, umber, ocher, sienna, used, rubbed out, used again. Too meticulous, done by a rank amateur.

"Was this your first drawing, Benny?"

He nodded. "And last. You know, son, I'm glad they stopped motorboats using this stretch. Engines and vandals go together."

"Why didn't you report them—it—to the police, Benny?"

"One doesn't betray. Things were so different then. And what would have happened to the bab if I had?"

His obliquity was narking me. I pointed at features in his watercolor, trying to remember bits from the local newspapers. "Isn't there going to be a new putting green at this end of the estate? A furlong from the lane?"

"Yes. Developers want it. People will play there of a Sunday. I'm told putting is very popular with children." He paused while a punt went by. "I'm the last of the old servants who know. Teddy Winter, the gardener, was my friend. He died a fortnight ago."

"Teddy Winter? His son's Joe, the gardener at Gramphorn's Garden Centre?"

"Ted and I swore silence until only one of us was left, you see."

No, I still didn't see. There must be honor among thieves *and* servants. Different reasons, of course.

"And?"

He seemed so sad. "Now I've spoken to you, son. I sent Joe Winter with those old golf balls, hoping you'd buy them. Judge Wymond would outbid you. It would set you off hunting like you usually do, and bring things to light."

Nothing for it, so I asked, "What for, Benny?"

"Could you help make reparation?"

The way he said it meant reprisals, sanctions or something worse. One thing troubled me.

"Who's the rich bird? Mrs. Margrave? You heard her hire me. She's a Norwich dealer, coming through the Eastern Hundreds."

"What makes you think I know her?"

"Dunno."

But I did know. An exquisite woman draws everybody's eyes, other women's because they hate her on sight, men's because we're busy lusting after her legs. And if she's got money, or says she's an antique expert, then the one who takes no notice—in this case Benny—is definitely odd.

He sighed. "I'd better tell you. The lady in the grave is the De Haviland daughter, Thalia. Unwed, she had a child." He paused, stared frowning at some distant memory, then continued, "By a member of staff at the great house."

Decades ago, we'd have all been horrified at such dynamite scandal. Now we just wonder who the bab is, how it got on.

"I'm sorry if I give offense, son," he said quietly, like he was revealing some horrendous outrage. "But I'd best let you know."

"Why me, Benny?"

"Other dealers forget that it's people that matter, not furniture and pottery and money."

He was speaking heresy. Antiques and women first, and everything else nowhere. That was my law.

"Look, Benny," I said, uneasy at this turn in the conversation.

"Please, son. My illness doesn't give me long. I want it finished."

Suddenly I took a good look at him. He was a lot thinner. But how often did I actually stare at him on a Friday in his inglenook? His clothes hung on him. His hands looked transparent. I'd seen one of my uncles fade like this, from . . . I hated the idea.

"And Thalia?"

"She was . . . very beautiful." He halted. The word took him by surprise. Perhaps he didn't use words like that very often. "She had the baby in the east wing. Old Dr. Lambourne from Horkesley moved in during her last month. The baby was sent away and brought up elsewhere. Avoiding tittle-tattle is vital for society people."

I vaguely remembered hearing something about a daughter. A riding accident came to mind. Was it folklore, invented by a determined rich family, to cover up dreaded rumor?

"Judge Donald Wymond—only the family lawyer back then—was being put up for the council by the De Haviland family. He often stayed. The scandal would have ended his ambitions."

"What happened to Thalia?"

"She . . . died. There were tales, of course, below stairs. No way to stop those. Me and Teddy Winter were paid extra, to pass on funds silently for the child's education and upbringing."

"You're after revenge," I said, like pass the marmalade.

"Yes," he said simply.

"Then tell me who killed Thalia."

"I'm sure of the assassination, but not of the assassin." His eyes looked opaque. "You'll find out if it really was Wymond or not."

"Assassin" was an odd word. I would have asked more, but he started to nod off. His words were already blurred. I borrowed the fare home, brewed some tea for him and left him facing the river.

There was a motor by my cottage when I reached home, and a note from Mrs. Margrave that it was hired in her name for me to start the sweep.

The rest of that day I proudly drove my hired crate to visit anyone who might know of local historical scandals, and to dealers who were addicts of sporting memorabilia.

• • •

My most significant visit was to a golf club steward. Jocko was a beefy retired bobby who joked that his girth increased three inches a year.

"Free booze and grub, see?"

"Lucky you," I said enviously. "And free dossing, eh?"

The golf course was on a peninsula by the estuary. You

couldn't imagine a more peaceful—read boring—scene. Golf links stretched here and there, flags marking holes, people dragging those carts about, rain sleeting down. The clubhouse was vast, its walls adorned with trophies. Everything was clubs, emblems, coats of arms of societies. God but golf crazies have a lot to answer for. Imagine what the world could achieve if it stopped wasting time like this.

"Idyllic, isn't it?" he said mistily.

"Great, Jocko," I lied. "Marvelous sport, golf, eh?"

"The greatest. Did you know that Mary Queen of Scots shot a truly terrible round at St. Andrews when she played there?"

"Well, it was a bad winter."

He sighed. "What I'd give for one of her golf clubs. Did you hear that an old iron club went for an eighth of a million the other day?"

"Yes." I hate hearing about other dealers' successes, so I quickly changed to another lie. "Look, Jocko. I've got two funny-shaped clubs. Wood, stamped 'Morris' in capital letters. Any notion who'd give me the best price?" He gaped, speechless. I love the sight of greed. "They're not up to much. Some string's loose. I'll stain them when I get a minute."

"Don't touch them!" he shouted, then gathered himself. "Er, I wouldn't, mate. You say you've got two?"

Greed is the king of emotions. I watched Jocko with fascination. His hands started to tremble.

"I've a few letters to go with them," I invented recklessly. "I'm having difficulty milking the widow of her Spode trophy, though. Spode's always got a market."

"Please let me see them all," he said in a strangled voice. "I'll sell them for you. Promise."

"Who on earth to?" Casually I wandered across the lounge to look at some drab painting hung beside the bar. It showed hundreds of people watching some nerks putting in a torrential downpour. It looked like a copy of J. Michael Brown's 1913 painting of the thirteenth hole at St. Andrews. The original painting is pretty awful, even though it sold for a fortune, but this copy was sheer tat. This is what I mean about addicts. Some certifiable goon had actually paid to have Brown's picture copied. "Just look at this. Who'd give it house room?"

"I know, mate," Jocko said, overacting like mad and thinking this was his lucky day. "These golfers." I stared at his list of past club presidents and officers. "Once this bar gets crowded, they talk of nothing else. Drives me mad."

"Even got judges and doctors playing it, eh?" I indicated the list. "Old Doc Lambourne from Horkesley."

"Passed away years ago. Surly old sod."

"And Judge Wymond. He once sent me down for a month."

"Aye. Not all active, though. Judge Wymond's in Norwich now, but keeps up his membership. Big in the proposed new club, they say. Lots of our members are in the syndicate."

"Not my scene, Jocko." I made to leave as if disinterested.

"Can I take those old golf items off your hands, Lovejoy?" He was sweating at the prospect of losing a fortune.

"Honest?" I went all shrewd. "Don't think I'll give them away, Jocko. I know you're a mate, but I want a fair price. I've heard those golf collectibles are popular in some circles."

"I'll see you right, honest. There's a member I know who'd buy golf historicals, comes in on Fridays."

We struck a deal. I felt really good, giving him the chance of a lifetime like that. He'd sell the golfiana that I'd discovered in my friendly widow's attic, giving me a flat rate of 20 percent.

He'd show me invoices. I would certify the items as genuine. I would not attempt any restoration. He wanted to draw up a legal document there and then, trying to bribe me with malt whiskeys. I declined. I wouldn't use malt whiskey to do my teeth. Anyhow, all real antique deals are done on the nod. I felt I'd done him proud—if anything I'd said was true, that is. I'm always willing to help a friend.

I stayed up all night, to be ready for Fern Margrave in the morning.

• • •

It's one of life's most sinister truths that lawyers grab headlines while doctors, if they've any sense, don't. That interesting link stayed in my dull brain: Wymond was an old golfing partner of Dr. Lambourne. The judge was retired now and Lambourne deceased. With these facts in mind, I phoned Lisa—she of the foul language, M.A. (Sociology), and stringer for the local newspaper—asking her to suss out details of past tragedies at the De Haviland manor. I promised her money and a scoop.

"On a scale of ten, Lovejoy," she demanded, cold, "how would you score this particular promise?"

"Ten, love," I said. There was a brief silence.

"Are you really as sad as you sound?"

"Worse," I said. "Ring me, Lisa."

"Okay," she sighed, "but just this once get my name right. It's *Lizzza*."

Who can remember details, for heaven's sake? I tried to doze on my grotty divan bed. The phone went at two in the morning. She'd got photocopies from the old extinct *News Standard,* with reports of a young woman's accidental death. The coroner's court had waxed lyrical over Miss Thalia De

Haviland's tragic demise, caused by taking herbal remedies for a mild stomach complaint. The doctor—guess who—was highly praised for his attempts to resuscitate the poor lass. The coroner ruled that there was no suggestion of suicide. She had presumably awoken, drowsily taken the wrong medicine and passed away peacefully in her sleep. A mercy, said the coroner, and God rest her soul. The family mourned.

"Rumors kept surfacing, Lovejoy," Lisa told me, reading stuff out. "A lawyer reviewed the case and said it was all tickety-boo. The family expressed gratitude."

The coroner was promoted very soon after. And Wymond sailed on, so to speak, to pastures new. Local dignitaries were content, and all was well.

Until now, when poor Bendix started to die, and old Teddy Winter, his mate, passed away. Bendix wanted action before he went. I couldn't afford an Ordnance Survey map of the area, so made Lisa promise to drop one off for me in the morning.

"Is this the scoop?" she demanded.

"Tell you soon, Lisa. Don't forget the map."

• • •

The old De Haviland place still looked quite grand in the morning air, yet somehow it seemed to have shrunk, as if its brickwork was being whittled as the surrounding grounds dwindled. The trout farm was hived off, signs indicating where anglers could stand, and the oak wood had become some kind of nature reserve. Three distant pastures were now filled with bungalows, a milk float clinking around the cul-de-sacs. It took me a while to work out where Bendix must have been standing to paint his one contribution to world art so many years before.

The field was a mere paddock, a lone donkey contemplating the infinite. Twelve trees stood in a circle, with a thirteenth standing alone in the center. I wondered how long ago those had been planted so precisely. How fast does a tree grow? Could they shoot up to that height in thirty years? East Anglians say that trees planted in a ring, with one in the center, mark some ancient tribal king's barrow, from before the Romans came. Local farmers do it from superstition. I walked about the overgrown corner looking for Thalia's small tumulus. Finally I persuaded myself that I'd found it, where the grass seemed more tussocky than elsewhere, but wasn't sure because of the vicious brambles and hawthorns. Now, it's quite legal to bury a relative on your own ground. You don't need a religious service, free country and all that. There are even societies that will arrange burials in woodlands and on remote moors. Lisa had found no mention of the interment in her old newspapers.

It would have been quite okay—if Thalia died naturally, that is. And everybody at the time had said so.

Folding the map against the wind, I checked that nothing was marked for this corner. To the right, however, beyond the manor house was a series of huge new mounds, great bare swellings. I could hear engines revving and see puffs of diesel smoke. Margrave's rubbish dump was active. I drove my whining little motor to see.

Marjorie wasn't there, but a couple of workmen in orange jackets directed the arriving trucks. Vaguely worded signs announced that this was an "authorized disposal facility" run by J. T. Margrave & Co. It seemed a hell of an area. A bloke came over, stocky, gruff.

"Commercial or domestic?" he asked.

"Eh?"

"Commercial, you pay per truckload. Domestic rubbish you dump free."

"Why've you got four dumping spots instead of one?" I waited. His eyes narrowed. "This field's seventeen acres. I thought you blokes did it inchwise, not random." As I watched, a truck roared in, was waved to the far corner to shed its load of rubble. The driver handed an envelope to one of the workmen.

"You a clever dick? It's my orders."

So he was Margrave. I said I'd go to the council dump instead and cleared off. It was too early for a scrap, and anyway, I had to collect Mrs. Margrave. I was sure now that I was being had. I didn't blame Bendix, him being poorly and all.

The Margrave address was in what people call a leafy suburb. We all try to make our dingy streets sound like Los Angeles, dunno why. I knocked, and got admitted by some old dear who offered me breakfast. I brightened, but Fern Margrave swept in and said we had to be off. I obeyed.

•   •   •

There's something really odd about antiques. If you're broke, you see Rembrandts and Turners on every street barrow, a Wedgwood on every stall, and gorgeous women smile at you everywhere. If gelt's bulging your wallet, there's not a genuine antique anywhere, and the world's full of anonymous miseries.

Like now, chasing round the Eastern Hundreds. Antiques thronged the universe. Unbelievably, in seven hours we picked twenty worthwhile antiques. Two were genuine Meissen, though it was hard work having to keep explaining to Fern Margarve ("Yes, missus. The base is always covered with leaves and florals; the figure looks separately made," etc.)—God, did she argue. I got sick of her. I kept telling her the obvious: "No, missus, you can't trust the mark, because every faker on earth copied the Meissen crossed swords, including Derby, Worcester, Bow . . ." I must have saved her a king's ransom and earned her a fortune. Like, a set of Britain's lead toy soldiers, including the marching band, wasn't really antique, being only 1938, but I got it for the price of a meal. I had a hard time insisting that the boxed set would buy her a new motor. All I got was, "Toys?"

She got on my nerves, trying to stop me buying her a Wellington chest complete with Bramah locks.

"But it's so ugly!" she grumbled. "And the back isn't even polished. Nor are the insides of the drawers."

"Never are. Feel its weight, missus." And when she couldn't move it an inch, I told her sourly, "See? It's heavy Cuban mahogany. The wood's been impossible to get for the past hundred years. I've just earned you a year's profit. We'll do better if you shut up."

Even that didn't stop her. I'd never met a woman like her for guessing wrong and grumbling at the expense. "Remember, this is my money, Lovejoy," she kept saying, like I wasn't aware I was only getting groats. She was so unlearned in antiques that she even tried to twist a pewter flagon, to test if it was genuine. I grabbed it from her in the nick of time, cursing. She gave me the one bit of knowledge she'd picked up: "It should give a kind of cry, if it's genuine!" I set it back on the auctioneer's tray, muttering that she wouldn't like being twisted until she screamed. She stared at me after that and went quiet, but soon she was trying to scratch an ancient piece of jadeite jade with her diamond ring.

"Right, missus," I said in disgust. "That does it. I'm off. You're a frigging barbarian. You've no bloody right to touch any antiques. Toodle-oo."

"You can't leave!" she cried, making people all over the viewing rooms turn and stare. "Not now that—"

I froze. "Now that what?"

"Now that I've got a decent collection for my antiques shop."

She had to think a few moments before the words came out. I let myself be persuaded, and on we went. That convinced me: She was no antique dealer.

"North," I told her as we stowed our—her—purchases in the motor. "Norwich."

• • •

I left Fern Margrave to bid for the items I'd marked in the catalog of an antique auctioneer a few miles outside Norwich. I'd carefully selected five items above Lot 200. The fastest auctioneer only manages fifty-six an hour, so I'd got at least three hours to drive to Judge Wymond's home and get back in time.

The house was a rambling affair, gables and gargoyles, slates off the roof and the drive overgrown. I drove up, gave the car door a convincing slam and knocked like the clap of doom. A pale elderly lady let me in. Yes, the judge was in the drawing room. I gave him my name and found him reading. Lots of maps of East Anglia on his walls, including an old sepia aquatint I recognized. I explained I was doing an antique sweep for a lady dealer and had found things he might want.

"I take it you will be defrauding your client?" he said drily. "Using her resources to buy certain antiques, then slip them to another buyer? I had hoped you were going straight, Lovejoy."

That, from him?

"Look, sir," I said lamely. "If you're not interested . . ."

"You were at the Estuary Golf Club."

"Yes. Jocko told me about your new golf links."

"I overheard part of your conversation." He adjusted a hearing aid. It whistled, making him grimace. "Old age is a problem, Lovejoy. Faculties diminish."

"Here's my list."

He took the paper with an old man's tremble. All the golfiana I'd lied to Jocko about were there, with two or three last-minute extra lies. He quizzed me with a glance.

"You really do have golf clubs this rare?"

"They look and feel old. But I know nothing about the game."

"I'll take them, for the right price."

We argued for an hour, him driving me down and me moaning about being robbed. In the heat of the deal I quite forgot I hadn't got as much as a single old golf ball. When he offered a deposit, I said he could be trusted and I left. On the way out I asked the old dear if the judge had family living nearby. She prattled contentedly about him. I listened for as long as she wanted to chat, then drove to catch up with Fern Margrave.

Except I made a detour. I paused at the best of the specialist antique dealer's shops in Poulton and bought seven matching lithophanes, all genuine. I charged them to Mrs. Margrave. Hang the expense. I also bought a Victorian bangle, about 1860, with turquoise pellets, fragment diamonds and coral. These aren't favored by dealers now—fashions change—but they're beautiful things. You can take the central cluster out and use it as a brooch.

"Wrap them, please," I commanded airily. "I'll carry them under my driving seat for safety." I meant secrecy.

When I reached Mrs. Margrave, I was disappointed about her progress. She'd bottled out of all but one of the antiques I'd told her to bid for, and she'd even got confused about that and bought the wrong thing.

"Ancient parchment is sheep or goatskin," I told her wearily. "The manuscript you've bought can't be seventeenth century because it's simply cotton soaked in sulfuric acid and glycerin, then pressed out. You can do the same with ordinary paper in nitric acid. There's a modern watermark. See? It's a fake."

She filled up. "You're rotten to me," she sniffed. A couple of old dears who were passing clucked in disgust at me, oppressor of poor downtrodden women.

"Take no notice of him, love," one crone said sympathetically. "They're not worth it."

I waited outside for Fern to settle up at the auctioneer's table. The two elderly ladies went past. One said scathingly, "He's even made her pay! Rotten to the core."

Mrs. Margrave didn't even buy me a pastie on the way home. I was famished.

* * *

That night I penciled on the reverse of each lithophane and added a name. I got a spade from my neighbor's shed and drove to the corner of the De Haviland estate. There was no moon, so it was hard blundering to the right spot. I deliberately sidestepped where I guessed Thalia was lying, and started digging.

Honestly I'm never really spooked. But I've never been a lover of countryside. I mean, once you've seen rivers, trees, a couple of fields and a pond, what else is there? And things flit by in the darkness that I really think shouldn't be flying about at that hour. Towns are safer. In fact I'd go so far as to say that cities are innocent. Countryside scares me.

And there's another thing. Digging near somebody's grave is more than a mite worrisome. I mean, who knows what a corpse might be up to, alone down there in the earth? The idea was to make others discover Thalia, not me in the lantern hours like this. I paused for breath, clicked on my torch to check how much I'd dug, and there staring at me was a fox. We both yelped and leaped a mile. I dropped my flashlight and had to scrabble for the damned thing. The fox was gone. See what I mean? Countryside's not good for your health. My heart was going like a hammer. I made myself stop shaking and kept on. Deepest of all, I laid the bangle, its central cluster separate, then began replacing the soil. Somebody finding the cluster would hunt on for the matching piece.

The stink from the rubbish dumps was more noticeable at night. I worried about how deep to plant the lithophanes and finally decided that one foot down would do, give or take. I was tempted to smash one of the lovely 'phanes and leave the fragments scattered, but didn't. There are too many vandals about. I kept one back.

All remaining six I buried as near to Thalia as I had the nerve to do, then walked back to the motor. I'd cunningly labeled it *Beckholta Owl Watchers' Society Members This Way*, with a vague arrow, in case some cycling plod got suspicious. I drove home. Next dawn I was waiting for Marjorie at the council dump.

•   •   •

Professionals are great. You've got to admire them. Marjorie arrived in her grand saloon, wafting elegantly across the lunar landscape among the council trucks and early bin-loaders. The men all shouted greetings, some more cavalier than others. She did a Queen Mother wave, smilingly pulled up to the edge of the landfill. She alighted and simply stood, careful of her high-heeled shoes. I trudged across, avoiding puddles.

"Morning, Marj." I offered her the last of my lithophanes. She didn't move. I wiped it with a grubby hankie. She deigned to accept it.

"What's this?"

"Lithophane, love. Dealers call them Berlins."

She held it up to the light, smiling at the translucent picture impressed in the porcelain glass. "Very pretty, Lovejoy."

It showed a frolicking Pan among lovely shepherdesses.

"A kind of glass porcelain. Sometimes they're only four inches long, up to the size of a small windowpane. Used to be popular. Nobody recognizes them nowadays. Victorians put them in windows, vestibules, even had them in the bottom of drinking cups. You only see the picture when light comes through, see? Gone out of fashion."

"Why're you showing me?"

"I found it. Couple of days ago I went to the old De Haviland place, checking on an old watercolor somebody showed me. I noticed this sticking up out of the ground. I nicked it."

"And now you want me to do the rest of your dirty work?"

"Sorry." I went all crestfallen. "But you can charm the workmen. I can't."

She laughed, examined the lithophane. "We go thirds," she said. "Agreed? Me two-thirds, you get one. What's this writing say? Looks like *Forgive*."

I peered. "Forgive what, I wonder?"

Then I went to phone Lisa. Her scoop was on the way.

• • •

Three days later I sat with Bendix by his riverbank. I brewed him some tea and told him the tale. He had me read out the newspaper reports to him, even though I'd sent Lisa to tell him how she'd interrogated the workmen, made accusations against Judge Wymond and Dr. Lambourne. And how she'd worked out—she was thrilled at her cleverness—how the judge had decided to use an unscrupulous land developer, his friend Margrave, to cover the De Haviland estate with untouchable toxic rubbish, thereby rendering Thalia's grave cloaked in East Anglian soil forever. A golf course is sacred. It would remain undisturbed.

"She'll not print anything about you, Benny. She reported Teddy Winter as the last of the staff."

"Thank you." He smiled. I'd never seen him do that before. It was good, full of nostalgia. "I mean, for those things you wrote on the tiles."

"*Forgive me, dear Thalia, my murderous hands.* I think it's a quotation." I'd put one word on each lithophane. Pencil's best in soil. Ink is so easily degraded, not to mention easily dated. Graphite pencil isn't. Lisa had waxed lyrical how older generations, back to the ancients, had tried to provide pleasant vistas for their buried dead, only they'd used translucent alabaster.

We watched the boats on the river. I wanted to ask who Thalia's bloke actually was, but hadn't the courage. If he'd wanted to tell me, he'd already have said. I'd already guessed that Fern Margrave was Thalia's child. How come old Bendix and she had teamed up, though? And how would Fern Margrave square it with her husband? I felt too intrusive and closed my mind to it.

"I added his first name: Donald," I confessed.

Bendix winced and shook his head. "There was no relationship between him and Thalia."

"Well, it worked. They arrested Judge Wymond today," I told him. "Lisa's ecstatic. She says he's admitting everything." I felt uneasy. "I'll be in trouble with Mrs. Margrave, Benny. She'll bring a million lawsuits against me, using her like I did to expose Thalia's killing."

"You'll hear no more of it from her."

"Benny," I said, hesitant. "You know they're disinterring Thalia? And they'll do tests, to decide how she died?"

For a while he didn't speak. "Then we'll be buried together," he said finally. "Fern will see to it."

He said it as if to a child. I sat with him for an hour. He said he was fine. The district nurse would be along presently. I told him so long, and went.

Returning the hire motor the next day, I drove past the Margrave dump on the De Haviland estate. Police in lines walked slowly across the greensward. Others prodded the mounds of rubbish. A white canvas marquee covered Thalia's grave, a cluster of photographers and paparazzi loitering at the corner, stamping to keep warm and drinking from vacuum flasks.

Lisa was in the thick of it. I gave her a wave. She stared after me, didn't wave back, just watched me as I went by. A typical woman, full of suspicions when there's just nothing to be suspicious about.

ROOM FOR A FOURTH

Steve Hamilton

By Sunday morning, the rain had washed the blood away. The sun was finally coming out. It was a perfect day for golf, or at least it would have been if the course were open. I could see a couple of policemen on the twelfth hole as I drove in—it's a short par 5 running right along the entrance road, with a stream cutting across the fairway just in front of the tee. The water's just for looks, of course. It's not in play unless you really skull one. With a decent drive, you can roll a fairway wood right down the middle between the two sand traps. Two putts and you've got a birdie. It's one of the easier holes on the golf course, and with the tall marsh plants running down the right side, one of the prettiest, too. At least on the days when there are no dead bodies on it.

There were thirty or forty members milling around the clubhouse when I got there. They jumped all over me, assuming that as the assistant pro I'd know what was going on, who had found Old Sal the day before, whether the police had any idea who could have done such a horrible thing. More than a few of them wondering why the course was still closed. Old Sal would have wanted them to play—that was the common sentiment, anyway. He would have wanted the course open on such a beautiful day. The members would stay off the twelfth tee, of course, play the reds on that hole, maybe make it a long par 4. There was no reason why the whole course had to be closed. What better way to honor his memory?

I listened to that sort of thing for a while, nodded my head, told them I'd see what I could do. That seemed to make everyone happy. A couple of men started putting on the practice green.

The detective poked his head out of the bag room, gave me a little nod—the same man I had already talked to the day before. I was sure he'd want to sit down with me again, go over the whole thing one more time. Which was fine by me. Anything to help. But first, I had a little mission of my own.

I found the three men in the grill room—Anderson, Crowe, and Sabino—sitting together at their usual table in the corner. I went to the bar first, got myself a drink, agreed with Jenny behind the bar that yes, it was a terrible thing. And yes, it was good that we could all be together today, that we could all help each other get through it. "Everybody loved Sal so much," she said.

"You're absolutely right," I said. "I can't believe Old Sal is gone."

There was an empty chair at their table. I wandered over and sat down.

"Gentlemen," I said. "It's good to see you."

They seemed to have been in the middle of a serious discussion. Whatever they were talking about, they shut it right down and just looked at me with careful smiles.

"Do you mind if I sit for a moment?" I said.

They all looked at one another. "Of course not," Anderson said. "Please do." Anderson was the lawyer, so it figured he'd be the first one to speak up. He was a big man with a big golf swing. Before Sal straightened him out, Anderson was the most dangerous man on the course. He was the only member, in fact, who ever put a ball into the swimming pool.

"I'm sure you're all talking about Old Sal," I said. "And what a shock this whole thing has been."

"Of course," Crowe said. "It's good that you're here. I'm sure the members feel better." Crowe was a psychiatrist, so this kind of line was probably automatic for him. Crowe's swing had once been so fast, he barely had a backswing. Old Sal had slowed him down by making him hum the first four notes of Beethoven's Fifth Symphony while he was swinging. Whatever works, that was Old Sal's motto.

"It's unbelievable, isn't it?" I said.

"Unbelievable," Sabino said. "That's just the word for it. Here's to Old Sal." He lifted his glass. Sabino was a state assemblyman, so of course he had to make a little public ceremony out of it. Once truly awful, Sabino's golf game was perhaps Sal's most miraculous renovation project. Sabino's hairpiece, however, was beyond help. Today it looked like he had styled it with a sand trap rake.

"Here, here," I said as we all raised our glasses. "To Old Sal."

"Well, then," Anderson said. "We shouldn't keep you. I'm sure you have a lot of people to talk to."

"Oh, I don't know," I said. "I've already talked to everybody, I think. Although I'm sure I'll need to speak to the detective again."

"He asked you about Friday afternoon, of course," Anderson said. "Naturally, you were able to help him out? You know, with the chain of events?" Chain of events, he says. More lawyer talk.

"Yes," I said. "At least as much as I know. I mean, I was just in the pro shop all afternoon, watching the baseball game."

"Is that what you told him?"

"It was such a miserable day," I said. "All that rain. There were hardly any golfers on the course at all. Only a few diehards like you fellows."

Anderson shook his head. "Not diehard enough," he said. "If we had only stayed out there with him, I'm sure this wouldn't have happened. Whoever did this thing . . ."

"Wouldn't have had the chance if he wasn't alone?" I said. "Come now, you can't blame yourself for that. I would have quit after nine holes, too. I can't imagine why Sal kept playing in the rain."

"You know Old Sal," Crowe said. "A little rain wasn't going to stop him. He had a good round going, too. We couldn't convince him to come in with us."

"That's what I told the detective," I said. "On such a terrible day, with his friends all calling it quits like that, he must have really wanted to finish his round."

"We really should have made him stop," Sabino said. "Lord knows we tried. We kept yelling at him, even as we were on our way to the clubhouse. You probably heard us."

"No," I said. "Not that I remember."

"Well," Anderson said, "you did see us, at any rate. You saw us coming in after nine holes."

"No, I was watching the game," I said. I looked down at my drink and swirled it in the glass. "Like I told the detective, I couldn't be of much help. You know, in determining who was coming and going. And when."

I let that one hang in the air for a while.

"It's really quite incredible," I finally said, "when you think about it. The one day Sal plays the back nine by himself, that's the day somebody is hiding in the woods, waiting to beat him to death."

"Whoever it was," Anderson said, "he may not have been waiting for Sal specifically. He could have been waiting for any-body."

"I suppose," I said, just as Jenny came by to check on us. I ordered a round for everyone. When she had left, I leaned back in my chair and said, "There's something else that's been both-ering me. Maybe you can help me make sense of it."

"It was a madman," Crowe said. "It had to be. Who else could do such a thing? There's no use trying to make any sense out of it." Dr. Crowe, expert on the workings of the human mind. Especially the crazy ones.

"Perhaps not," I said. "But here's what I'm thinking. I know Old Sal was what, sixty-three years old? But he was a tough old bird, wouldn't you say? I bet he could put up quite a fight if he had to. He wouldn't go down easy."

"The killer must have snuck up on him," Sabino said. "From behind. Or maybe there was more than one!"

"A whole band of killers?" I said. "Lying in wait on the twelfth tee? I just don't see it. I think it had to be somebody he knew. Somebody who could have caught him off guard."

"Someone from this club, you mean," Anderson said.

"Someone from this club," I said. "Someone, or some per-sons, who really hated him. Or else had some other very good reason to want him dead."

There was a conspicuous silence. I looked out the window at the empty golf course. I didn't watch them think about it. I didn't watch them squirm. I didn't have to.

"Funny thing about that detective," I finally said. "He reminds me of that detective on the television show. Columbo—remember him? This guy even looks like him. Little short guy, wandering around like he's not quite sure what he's doing, asking all these crazy questions, driving people nuts. But then he'd always come up with all the answers. You remember that show?"

"I believe so," Anderson said.

"When I was talking to him down in the bag room yesterday, he didn't seem to know much about golf, but he was asking me all these questions about clubs."

"What kind of questions?" Anderson said.

"Mostly about the different kinds of clubs, you know, irons versus woods, the different shapes. It was like he already had this theory in his mind that Sal was beaten to death by a . . . well, this might sound crazy, but by a golf club. Like the forensics guys would come back with a certain type of trauma to the head, you know what I mean? So he wanted to see some examples. As a matter of fact, he looked in all of your bags." I rattled the ice cubes in my empty glass. "Where did Jenny run off to, anyway? I thought she was bringing us another round."

"He looked in *our* bags?" Anderson said. "Whatever for?"

"They were right up front," I said. "That's where you left them when you came in on Friday. You know, when you finished after nine. Tony had already gone home, so he didn't get the chance to clean them and put them away. Don't go anywhere, I'll be right back."

I went up to the bar and got the drinks. When I came back, all three men looked a shade paler.

"You know, I noticed something unusual, too," I said. "When we were looking in your bags, I mean. This detective, he's asking me all these basic questions about golf clubs, and I happen to mention that a golfer normally carries fourteen clubs in his bag. So wouldn't you know it, he actually counts the clubs in your bag—I think it was yours, Mr. Anderson— and there are only thirteen clubs there! Then he goes through the other two bags and oddly enough, in both of your other bags, thirteen clubs. Not fourteen. Very unusual. And then, of course, I happened to notice which clubs were missing. In all three of your bags, you didn't have your 7-woods."

"I can't believe you were actually rummaging through our bags," Anderson said. "What would possess you to—"

"I remember when Sal made you those 7-woods," I said. "He sure knew how to make a club, didn't he? For each one of you, he made it just right, custom fit it exactly to your game. Just the right weight. A little longer shaft on yours, Mr. Anderson, a slightly closed face on yours, Dr. Crowe. Absolutely perfect clubs to get out of the long rough out there. And boy, could you hit 'em. All three of you. I'm assuming you must have taken them out of your bags yesterday. You took them home with you for some reason, am I right?"

"Yes, that's right," Sabino said, perhaps a little too quickly. The other two men shot dark looks at him. "Tony usually does a good job of cleaning the clubs, but you know how it is when you have a favorite."

"Of course," I said. "Especially a custom-made club that— my God, what a terrible thought. Old Sal will never make another club. Anyway, you'll have a chance to talk about all of this with the detective. I'm sure he'll be up here to talk to you again, seeing as how you three were the last to see him alive."

"Of course," Anderson said. "Not that we'll have anything else to tell him. I hardly think he'll need to ask us about our clubs."

"You know the funny thing about those missing 7-woods?" I said. "I mean, excuse me, the 7-woods you took home with you yesterday? Aside from being the right club to hit out of the rough, they'd also be just the right club to kill somebody with."

"What are you suggesting?" Anderson said. "Are you suggesting—"

"Think about it," I said. "Your driver's the biggest club in your bag, but it's *too* big. You know what I mean? It's too clumsy, and hell, most driver heads these days are hollow. You could never get a good blow to the head with a driver."

"This is not funny," Sabino said.

"An iron is solid, but it's too small," I said. "You'd have to hit him just right. But those 7-woods he made you . . . solid, compact, but just big enough. Absolutely perfect for killing a man."

"This is absolutely absurd," Crowe said. "We don't have to sit here and listen to this."

"Fine," I said. "I'm going back downstairs. I think I need to talk to the detective. In the meantime, I suggest you go home and get those 7-woods. You know, just to prove that they weren't the murder weapons."

"Wait a minute," Anderson said. "Just wait one minute. We have to tell you something."

"What are you doing?" Crowe said.

"Are you nuts?" Sabino said.

"We have to tell him!" Anderson said. "We obviously have no choice."

"Tell me what, gentlemen?" I said. "Go ahead, I'm all ears."

Anderson took a quick scan of the room and then bent his

head down. "All right, listen," he said in a low voice. "We don't know where our clubs are. All right? We don't know. They're just gone."

"Oh, please," I said. "You're going to have to do better than that."

"We're telling you the truth," he said. "You have to believe us. Our bags are right where we left them on Friday. After playing *nine holes*! And then leaving! We didn't kill Sal, all right? We didn't do it!"

"But your clubs just happen to be missing . . ."

"Yes!" he said. "That's what we were talking about when you came up here. We didn't know what to do. We were thinking we'd just go down there and take our bags out of the room, but . . . I mean, it would look a little suspicious."

"I don't know," I said. "A minute ago, you said you took them home with you. Now you're telling me *this* story. I don't know what to believe anymore."

"Why in God's name would we kill him?" Crowe broke in, a little too loudly. The other two men cringed. "How could you even *think* that?"

"Oh, that's not so hard to imagine," I said. "Not after what he was doing to you."

That stopped them. All three of them looked away.

"Listen," I said, "I know how it works. Old Sal was a good teaching pro. And he certainly knew how to make a club. He got all three of you hitting the ball so well, especially with those 7-woods he made you, you started to *believe* in your games. How many times did you break 80 before Sal started working with you? Sabino, you couldn't even break 90!"

"This is good," Anderson said. "Are you suggesting that we killed Old Sal because he made us better golfers?"

I sat back in my chair. "No," I said. "You killed him because of what happened next. He went out with the three of you, and he let you beat him. A professional golfer. He's kind of old now, he can't hit the ball like he used to. But still, you beat the pro. And then you beat him again. You were probably hitting those new 7-woods out of the rough like butter, weren't you? And then maybe you had a bad round and you didn't beat him, but he took you out on the range and he worked with you, got you swinging the club again. And then you beat him the next time. You stomped all over him. And then finally, what happened?"

Nobody said anything. They were all staring down at the table.

"How much was it?" I said. "The first time? How much did you play for? 'Let's make this more interesting.' Is that what he said? 'I'll play all three of you. Three separate matches. Ten-dollar Nassau, automatic press on two down, and one down on 9 and 18.' Is that how it started?"

Silence.

"He let you win some money the first time. And then the second time. Cardinal rule of being a club pro, never play the members for money, but you didn't mind, did you? You took his money. Nobody was forcing him, right? It was all harmless fun. So he upped the ante. 'Let me try to win some of my money back, fellas.' How much did you start playing for? Fifty-dollar Nassaus? A hundred? How long did it take for him to finally beat you? How long until you owed *him* money? I'm sure it was always close—one good shot on 9, one clutch putt on 18. And then it started to add up, all those presses going at the same time. You gotta hand it to Sal, it can't be easy playing three matches at once, keeping all the bets straight and playing just well enough to win them."

Not a word from any of them.

"How did he keep you hooked?" I said. "Did he start giving you strokes? Did he give you little pep talks? 'Come on, guys! Start playing like you were playing last month! You'll win it all back in one round!' Lord knows, you're too embarrassed to tell anybody about it. You're not going to go to the golf committee and tell them you're losing money to the pro. You just keep playing and playing, and digging yourself into a bigger and bigger hole. Until what? How much did you owe him? What's the grand total?"

"Look . . . ," Anderson said.

"Give me the number," I said. "How much did you owe him?"

"He hustled us," Anderson said. "You're right, okay? He hustled us. We owed him money. A lot of money. We admit it, okay? But you have to believe us, we didn't kill him."

Sabino dropped his head into his hands. "This is such a nightmare."

"I gotta hand it to you guys," I said. "The whole setup, it began with those 7-woods. Kind of poetic justice to use those clubs to kill him. I'll give you points for style."

"What do we have to do to make you believe us?" Sabino said. "We didn't kill the man."

"You know who I feel sorry for right now?" I said. "There are two cops down on that twelfth tee again. They're on their hands and knees, looking for some kind of evidence, I guess. Something they might have missed yesterday. Wearing those hot blue uniforms, crawling all over that tee box. Of course you know what they're going to find. About eighty-thousand little broken tees. Then they'll start looking all over the golf course. And in the clubhouse. Maybe they'll get lucky and find something. Hell, maybe they'll even find the murder weapons."

I let that them work on that for a long, long minute. It seemed to hit all three of them at once.

Anderson was the first to find his voice. "You've got our clubs," he said. "You've got our clubs because . . ."

"Because you killed him," Crowe said.

"*You* did it!" Sabino said. "I can't believe it! *You* killed him!"

"Gentlemen," I said. "Please. Why would I kill Old Sal?"

"So you can take over as the head pro!" Sabino said.

"You know it doesn't work that way," I said. "You know how the members are. They'll go out and get some other old gasbag. In two months, I probably won't even be working here anymore."

"I got a better idea," Anderson said. "You killed him because *you* owed him money, too! A little friendly wagering between two golf pros? He had his hooks in you, too, didn't he?"

"Interesting theory," I said. "But you're forgetting one thing. Sal was an old man who made some extra money hustling gullible amateurs. He'd do it until he got kicked out of his club and then he'd go charm his way into a new one. That's what he did, guys. He's been doing this for years. The *last* thing he would do is play a real professional for money."

"Then why do you know about our clubs?" Crowe said. "You had to be involved in this!"

"Well, just for the sake of argument," I said, "let's imagine that Sal once hustled the wrong men. Let's say he hustled the last three men on Earth you'd ever want to hustle. Maybe, oh, let's say he hustled these men about seven or eight years ago. And they haven't forgotten about it. Let's say that once they finally found out that Old Sal had set up shop at another club, they made some . . . discreet inquiries into whether there might be someone who could cooperate with them in arranging a little impromptu reunion between Sal and his three old friends. If someone were to provide them with both the opportunity as well as the—what would you call it? The necessary 'tools' to make it a successful reunion? Needless to say, that man would be well compensated for his assistance."

"You set him up," Anderson said. "You set him up and you . . . You set *us* up!"

"I'm just speaking theoretically now," I said. "I'm not saying any of this really happened. But let's imagine if the police were to find those clubs today. Or tomorrow. *Your* clubs. All of them with the distinctive wear and tear you might find if you had happened to beat somebody to death with them."

"Whatever your game is," Anderson said, "you'll never get away with it."

"I can see it now," I said. "The most respected attorney in the city, taken to the police station for questioning in connection with the murder of Salvatore Burelli. Not to mention the most respected psychiatrist. And dare I say . . ."

Sabino closed his eyes.

"State Assemblyman Sabino," I said. "Imagine *that* press release."

"You're mad," he said. "You won't get away with this."

"The grand jury probably won't even indict you," I said. "It's just circumstantial evidence, after all. I'm sure your careers won't suffer in the slightest."

"I can't believe this is happening," Sabino said.

"On the other hand," I said, "maybe those clubs won't turn up after all. And maybe I'll even have a sudden recollection. 'Yes, detective. I'm sorry about the confusion, but I *just* remembered. I *did* hear those three men come in after nine holes. And I believe I saw them leave, too. Yes, yes, it's coming back to me now. They were long gone by the time Sal was killed. In all the commotion this morning, I just couldn't think straight. I'm sure you understand . . ."

"What is it you want?" Anderson said. "Surely those men have already paid you."

"If they did," I said, "then you know they must have paid me very well, thank you. Which would make me feel so generous in return, I'd just have to share my good fortune with you."

"What are you talking about?" he said.

"I was thinking," I said. "Now that Old Sal is gone, there's an open spot in your foursome. As soon as the course is open again, I think we should go out and play. All this money I've fallen into, and you played such a big part in it. It's only right that I give you a chance to win some of it."

"You're not suggesting . . ."

I looked out the window at the first tee. With any luck, the course would be open by noon. And what a perfect day it was to play a friendly round of golf.

"In memory of Sal," I said. "A little money game, for old time's sake."

MISS UNWIN
PLAYS BY THE RULES

H.R.F. Keating

Miss Harriet Unwin was a better governess than golfer. Indeed, she had never even heard of the game of golf until, in the late summer of 1888, she came into the employ of Mr. Mungo McMurdo, manufacturer of Mungo McMurdo's Marmalade, that well-known Scottish product made, all the more cheaply, in the East End of London. It was then that, to make her lessons for her charge, wee Margaret, more lively, she began to interest herself in what was, more than marmalade, Mr. McMurdo's overriding interest, this curious activity that was beginning to be seen as something rather more than croquet played not on the lawn but on the links.

The library in the tall London house was a not very large room, somewhat tucked away just below the servants' bedrooms. It was used by Mr. McMurdo more as a place where he would not be disturbed than as a room to read in. Mr. McMurdo was hardly a reading man, though his wife, almost a perpetual invalid, had a large collection of three-volume novels by such authors as Mr. Braddon and Mrs. Henry Wood. But Mr. McMurdo did possess one or two books about golf, and it did not take Miss Unwin long, in the mornings while he was away prowling his factory, to find out what there was to be found out about the strange game.

She learned that as long ago as the year 1618 King James I, because "no small quantitie of gold" left his kingdom "for bying of golf balls," had granted a monopoly for their manufacture. It went to one James Melvill in Scotland, where the game had originated (or possibly in Holland, though that was something not really to be spoken about). She discovered, too, that the object of the game was to strike a little ball with one or another of a variety of club-headed sticks until it could be induced to drop into a small round hole some considerable distance away. She sighed as she read that piece of information, though she knew it behooved her for little Margaret's sake to treat it as a great truth. She learned, finally, how the number of times the ball was struck had to be carefully counted, and that if there was a contest, the player who eventually made the fewest number of "strokes" was held to have won.

Before long, she had devised some games of her own for the benefit of lonely little Margaret, seldom seeing a mother who spent a great deal of her time in bed. Together they followed in imagination her father's progress, off every afternoon to "the links" out in the London suburb of Blackheath. Consulting the meticulously filled-in cards Mr. McMurdo had had printed, which Margaret had managed to beg off him, together they added up the number of strokes he had taken to get each of his little white-painted gutta-percha balls into each of Blackheath's seven holes. Then they worked out the average he had achieved over a week or a month. Margaret's arithmetic improved immensely, although—Miss Unwin could not help noticing—Mr. McMurdo's golf did not improve, however much he constantly affirmed that it had.

"Miss Unwin," Margaret even said once, "why has Papa crossed out that '9' and put in an '8'?"

Miss Unwin paused for only the shortest time before she replied.

"I expect when he had written down that figure, he recalled that it had taken him eight strokes and not nine before he had made that ball drop into the little flowerpot set in the earth there."

"Oh, Miss Unwin, I do wish one day Papa would take me to Blackheath so I could see those pots. They sound so sweet. I could put some wildflowers in them."

"Well, I am afraid he is hardly likely to let you go with him. You know how often he has said that the game of golf is much too serious an affair to have children watching him play it, or for the matter of that, to allow women anywhere near when it is being played."

"But, Miss Unwin, Papa said just last week that he did so badly at the fourth hole because there were some boys playing football in his way. He was very, very cross, you know."

"Perhaps he was right to be cross. However, that part of Blackheath is a common, open to all, so football is just another hazard that gentlemen playing golf there have to face."

Nor was arithmetic the only subject Miss Unwin taught her charge through the medium of the game, which in the privacy of her head she continued to think of as an exceedingly strange way of spending the time. Margaret learned, for instance, that gutta-percha was "a sort of juice or sap, called *gutta,* that comes out of a particular sort of tree in a faraway country named Malaya, where they call all trees *perchas.* When that juice meets the air, it gets hard in the way that rubber does coming from a similar tree, though gutta-percha has proven to get harder."

She explained to Margaret that gutta-percha had been found to be the ideal substance to be struck by any of the various "clubs" used in golf because of its property of bouncing. Then Margaret learned what it was that made some substances bounce well and others not so well, such as the balls made of feathers stuffed hard into little round bags of leather, until recent years the only ones available to the golfer. Margaret learned even the rudiments of economics when Miss Unwin told her that it had required many hours' work to make only a few of those old-fashioned balls and that in consequence they had cost some five times as much as the gutta-percha ones, familiarly "gutties."

"So a wealthy gentleman, like your papa, can afford now to use a new ball for each hole."

Miss Unwin did, however, persuade Mr. McMurdo to allow himself to be watched by his daughter while in the early evening he tested balls he had just bought by bouncing them time and again on the tiled floor of the hallway of the tall house, though when little Margaret had tried the effect of dropping one of them from the top of the stairs to bounce all the way to the bottom, she almost forfeited that privilege. And, of course, she received as well a stern lecture from Miss Unwin about the danger of playing on those unusually steep stairs.

"You might even be hurt so badly that you would have to go to the hospital, or even die."

"Oh, Miss Unwin, I don't think I would like that."

"Then just remember, it is dangerous to play on the stairs."

But eventually Margaret was restored to favor and admitted to the library to watch her father, with his own hands, rubbing emery paper across the surfaces of the iron heads of such of his clubs that were equipped with that metal instead of apple-wood or tough heartwood into which molten lead had been poured to give extra weight. Mr. McMurdo was so keen a golfer, however, that he would not allow Margaret, though she begged and begged, actually to touch any of the precious clubs while he oiled their long wooden shafts after making sure no fleck of rust would affect the accuracy of the iron-headed club he called his putter.

Miss Unwin had explained to little Margaret that "putter" was pronounced to rhyme with "mutter"—perhaps because of the way the verb "to put" was pronounced in Scotland—since this was the club that finally put the ball into the hole. So for days afterward Margaret went about *putting* her dolls back into their cupboard and asking if the nurserymaid was *putting* her newly ironed dresses into her wardrobe.

But Margaret also learned from her father the names of all his clubs—though it was Miss Unwin who taught her how to spell them—the driver for sending the ball the greater part of the distance to the hole, the cleek for lofting it over any obstacles that lay in its path, the brassie, with the strip of yellow metal under its head that made it so useful for getting out of the sandpits that were a prized hazard on the Scottish links which Mr. McMurdo visited on holiday. Then there was the driving iron with its metal head and beautifully whippy hickory shaft, the spoonlike baffy, much liked in Scotland for short approach work, the small-headed niblick, wonderfully helpful when a ball happened to land in a rut made by a cart wheel or in a deep sheep track.

"But, Miss Unwin," Margaret asked, pondering this new piece of knowledge, "if the wee ball gets stuck somewhere like that, wouldn't it be better just to pick it up and put it down where it would be easier to hit?"

It was then that Margaret learned about rules. That there were rules for the game of golf—one of which was that you could not, except in certain laid-down circumstances, improve the lie of your ball—and that there were, too, rules for the game of life.

"Some of those you know already," Miss Unwin told Margaret.

"Do I, Miss Unwin? I don't think I do. At least I can't remember any."

"But, of course, you can. What is the rule about the road outside?"

"Well, I know I must never go across from one pavement to the other without a grown-up being there. Is that a rule?"

"Yes, it is. And it is one you must never break."

"Never, Miss Unwin? Not even when I'm very old? Not even when I'm thirteen?"

"Well, yes, when your father thinks you are sensible enough, you will be able to cross the road on your own. But that may not be when you're thirteen. It may be sooner, or it may be later."

"So rules can change, Miss Unwin? You don't have to obey them always?"

"Some rules do change, and there are even times when a rule may be broken. But, remember, if a rule is made up for a special purpose like the rules for golf, then it has to be kept to all the time, or otherwise the game stops being a game where everyone playing it knows what is to be done. But the rules of the real world have to be obeyed only while they make sense. Circumstances alter cases. You should remember that. So, go now and find your copybook. I'll write those words out for you, and you can copy them three times, as neatly as you can. *Circumstances alter cases.*"

• • •

It was only some three weeks later, just after Christmas, that little Margaret learned that in some situations no amount of mentioning circumstances could alter in any way a case that confronted golf-obsessed Mr. McMurdo. It happened when, coming home unexpectedly early one horribly stormy afternoon, his rain-wetted plus-four trousers, baggy though they were, clinging with desperate dampness to his legs and the long stockings below almost pulled down by the weight of water soaked into them, he overheard John, his own valet, and wee Margaret's favorite among all the servants, loudly lamenting.

The words complained of were these: *He'll come back in with his clothes soaked through and through, I know he will. And all because he's so set on that daft game of his.*

"I heard you, John," came the resounding voice of his master. "You dared to call golf a daft game. Golf! You said it was daft. Leave this house within the hour. You are discharged. Dismissed. Never let me see your face again."

Mr. McMurdo, of course, could not be brought ever to acknowledge that he had been unduly impulsive in turning away his valet. He even declined, with angry vigor, to send to the employment agency for a replacement. It was not that he was not given opportunities enough to admit he had been overhasty. But wee Margaret, of whom he was insofar as his nature allowed fond, was told when she kept asking when "poor

John" was coming back to "mind your own business, miss." Nor did Mrs. McMurdo's faint pleas from the sofa where she lay feebly reclining have any more effect.

"But, Mungo, John was the only man in the house, since last Easter, when you sent the butler away because he told the maids to clean your golf things after you had come back from Scotland."

"Am *I* not a man, my dear? And a better man a thousand times than that English rascal who had no more idea of the game of golf than—than—than—whom I deservedly dismissed. Why are you moaning and puling about the lack of a man on the premises? In the drawer in my desk, as you very well know, I have always kept a stout life preserver. I can deal fast enough with any rogue who dares enter my home. I tell you that."

"But—but, Mungo, you are not always at home to beat down those men with that life preserver or one of your golf sticks."

"Golf sticks! Golf sticks! Have you gone mad, woman? First, they are not sticks: they are clubs. Golf clubs. And, second, I would no more use the least of my clubs, not even that old-fashioned baffy, to strike at any intruder, even if it were a black Hottentot."

And off he stormed. To Blackheath and its seven holes, stretching across the common where the hazards were as much nursemaids wheeling their charges in perambulators as gorse bushes, footballers, cart ruts or the treacherous shallow pit just before the first hole where many extra strokes were often needed before a gutty could be got within putter range of its ultimate destination.

· · ·

Trouble enough. But there was worse trouble, much worse, shortly to come. It arrived just before Easter. Easter was the time when Mr. McMurdo, year upon year, took a holiday in his native Scotland. To play golf. And, more than just to go out onto the links morning and afternoon, weekdays and Sabbath, he went at Easter to Scotland to trounce, over twice nine holes, his cousin, Ian McMurdo.

Ian had been his opponent, on the links and off them, for as long as either of them—Ian was a few days the elder—had been able to wield a club and sink a putt. He had been Mungo's rival, and enemy, because owing to those few days of seniority, he had inherited all the McMurdo family wealth and was able to live a fine, prosperous life without having to spend a single day in a factory down in London making marmalade. A bachelor, he could go out onto the links in any one of the daylight hours to play a match against his neighbor, aged Mr. Angus Todd, writer to the Signet, whom he was sure to beat, so slow was the old retired lawyer. When Angus Todd was safely back in his armchair by the fire, Ian McMurdo could go out again and again to practice his distance-carrying strokes with his driver, his approaches with the cleek, his final shots with his putter across the smooth turf round the hole, even the trick of using his niblick to get cleanly out of the waiting natural sandpits that were a special hazard of the Scottish links. And, worse, he could teach himself to lay a wicked stymie blocking the way to the hole when an opponent, such as his cousin Mungo, had got his gutty to within a yard or two of success.

The first signs of things being amiss down in London came when Mungo McMurdo announced he was going to stay, as he usually did, at cousin Ian's house but that he intended to go there, a thing unprecedented, without a manservant.

"But, Mungo," Mrs. McMurdo wailed, "what will Ian think of you arriving at his grand house without your own man? As if you were a land agent or someone of that kind."

"If Ian doesna like it, he may lump it," Mr. McMurdo answered, becoming more Scots by the moment.

"But what about us? Are we going to have to *lump* being here without a man in the house at all?"

"You are," Mr. McMurdo replied.

And he strode out of the drawing room.

But Miss Unwin had been there all the while that this domestic spat had taken place, Mrs. McMurdo having exercised the privilege of an invalid to say in front of her daughter's governess things that should have been said only within the privacy of the bedroom, or even behind the bed curtains.

Miss Unwin, since she had heard every word of the dispute and was not going to pretend she had not, was quick, however, to do what she could to calm Mrs. McMurdo's not-very-justifiable fears.

"I do not think you need worry too much about burglars, ma'am," she said. "I have heard nothing of any attempts in the neighborhood."

"But—but, my dear, there is always a first time. Why, oh why, did Mr. McMurdo dismiss that man John? He was a very good servant. No one had had a word to say against him until he made that silly remark about golf. What shall I do if—if when Mr. McMurdo is away, someone, some wicked man, should . . ."

"Well," Miss Unwin said with brisk cheerfulness, "if that should happen, I know where Mr. McMurdo keeps that life preserver he spoke of, and I shall be quite ready to use it myself."

"Oh, but—but, Miss Unwin, you are a lady, or—well, you are a woman, and how could you take up that horrible little bludgeon with the nasty rounded end that I saw once in Mr. McMurdo's desk, and—and strike a man, even if he is a wicked burglar?"

"Then let us hope the occasion never arises."

But Miss Unwin had other thoughts than wondering whether she would in fact, in those unlikely circumstances, use her employer's life preserver. Mr. McMurdo's unexpected decision to visit his wealthy cousin without taking with him a manservant to see to his personal needs had confirmed for her certain hints she had gathered over the past few weeks. She had heard, for instance, Mr. McMurdo telling little Margaret that he had played all seven holes at Blackheath "just using a single gutty." He had seemed proud of the feat, but Miss Unwin already knew enough of the game of golf to realize that a gutty hacked at over not one but several holes would not, dents and scratches all over its painted surface, fly as true as one not used before. And gutties, she knew, cost no more than a shilling each, a sum that should have been well within Mr. McMurdo's means. Then, something quite different but as telling, she had seen within the past month a number of advertisements painted on the side walls of houses in the shopping streets for *Genuine Dundee Marmalade,* and she knew that this was a clear threat to Mungo McMurdo's Marmalade, made on the cheap in London's East End.

So the long and short of it is, she thought, that Mr. McMurdo may be dispensing soon with a governess for little Margaret. And the prospect of weeks without an income while she found another situation was not at all welcome. Let alone having to establish good relations with another small girl or smaller boy. She was well aware that in two, or perhaps three, of the houses where she had been employed her charges had stubbornly refused to accept the rules she thought it her duty to impose.

Then came the day of Mr. McMurdo's departure. And other mysteriously disquieting signs came to Miss Unwin's attention. While Mr. McMurdo's baggage was waiting unattended in the hallway for the carriage to come round, wee Margaret had been unable to resist giving her father's long, many-pocketed leather golfing bag a rummaging inspection, and, as she later told Miss Unwin, "Papa went off with only one dozen of his little gutties. I wanted really to keep one for my own, but there were so few I thought I had better not, and, you know, even one of the ones he took he must have just picked up where it had been lost somewhere on the lanks—"

"It is *links,* Margaret. Links. And I'm glad to hear you didn't take a ball out of that bag's side pocket. Did you go peeking into any of the other pockets? It would have been very wrong of you."

"Well, yes, I know that really, I suppose. But would that have been one of the rules that it's all right not to obey sometimes?"

"No, my dear, it would not. Stealing is stealing and is never right."

"Well, it was a good thing, then, that I thought I heard Papa coming downstairs and stopped looking in the pockets of that bag."

"I think we had better say that Providence intervened and saved you from punishment."

Miss Unwin turned to lead the way back up to her sole

pupil's schoolroom. And then a thought at the back of her mind came abruptly to the fore. A tiny unanswered question.

"But tell me, dear, how was it that you thought your papa had picked up a ball on the links at Blackheath. You know, that is not the sort of thing a gentleman does."

"Is that another rule, Miss Unwin?"

"Well, yes. Yes, I suppose it is. *Finders keepers* may be a saying the poor can follow, but it isn't a rule that should be observed by a gentleman who does not need more than he already possesses."

"Well, Papa must have felt he was a poor person when he saw that gutty, because it cannot have been his. It had two letters written on it, and Papa never writes letters on his gutties."

"No, he does not, though I suppose if he played golf with another gentleman more often, he would need to do that, so that they would know whose ball was whose if they had hit them out of sight. But I think, young lady, you had after all better pay for the sin you did not quite commit. So go to your desk and write out fifty times the letters you saw on that gutty."

Little Margaret did not cry as she wrote out time and again *A T, A T, A T.* But once or twice Miss Unwin heard a suppressed sniff.

•   •   •

The family in London had no news from Mr. McMurdo in Scotland. But this they expected. He was never one to waste a bawbee on what he thought of as unnecessary correspondence. In his continuing absence Miss Unwin went on with little Margaret's lessons, all the more important to her mind now because of her fears that Mr. McMurdo, back at home, would claim that his daughter no longer needed someone devoted to nothing but her education. She foresaw Margaret being left to the care of some poor relation of her mother's, who would do nothing to see that she learned what was worthwhile. And Mrs. McMurdo continued to move, late in the morning, from her bed to her sofa and early in the evening from her sofa to her bed, and did little else but repeat over and over again that the house was not safe without a man in it.

Then something happened which puzzled and alarmed Miss Unwin to no small extent. Early one evening, driven by Mrs. McMurdo once more expressing her fear of burglary, although there had been nothing to indicate there was any reason to expect an attempt, she repeated her somewhat rash claim that, if necessary, she would possess herself of the little knob-headed life preserver kept in Mr. McMurdo's desk, and, in extremis, bring herself to use it.

"Oh, but no," Mrs. McMurdo exclaimed. "No, you could not. A woman to—to—to use violence. No, no. You could not do it. You could not. We shall be attacked. We shall be robbed. And then what will Mr. McMurdo say when he returns?"

Well, what he ought to say, Miss Unwin murmured to herself, is, *I am the one to blame. I should never have dismissed John and the butler in the way that I did.* But she knew that, even in the unlikely event that a burglar might defy the presence of the patrolling constable outside, bull's-eye lantern casting a steady light where the street lamps were far apart, she would at least arm herself with the life preserver.

But will I in the end have the courage to use it? she asked herself. The courage to bring that heavy little bludgeon down on some intruder's head and knock him unconscious, perhaps kill him?

Mrs. McMurdo believes it is impossible that I, a mere

woman, would be able to use such a formidable weapon. But I know at least that there are many women in London, and all over the country, who are capable of violence. So much violence, on occasion, that murder is committed. There is something still to be thankful for that I was left an orphan in the workhouse, and learned there what the wretched will do if provoked enough, will do even without provocation.

So, as soon as she had seen Mrs. McMurdo trail off, accompanied by her maid, to her lonely bedroom, she went boldly, candle in hand, to the library. If I once have that little weapon in my hand, she told herself, I will know whether I can use it or not.

Taking a deep breath, she pulled open the drawer where she knew it was kept.

The drawer was empty.

Only in its deepest corner, as Miss Unwin peered and peered, was there to be seen the tiny key of the locked tantalus, that row of decanters in which Mr. McMurdo kept three kinds of whiskey for his private consumption.

Miss Unwin stood there motionless for a few moments. Then she decided that there was nothing to be done about searching for the possibly useful little weapon until she could summon the servants in the morning. She took her candle upstairs to bed. And slept soundly.

She learned nothing next day from her inquiries among the servants, nor did such attempts as she was able to make to look for the life preserver elsewhere in the house prove any more successful. She came to the conclusion then that in all probability Mr. McMurdo, having impulsively reminded his wife of the existence of the little bludgeon, must have decided to change its place of concealment, such as it had been.

•   •   •

Easter came and went. Life appeared to be going on much as usual. There was still no word from Scotland about when they might expect Mr. McMurdo back, but in other years, so Miss Unwin learned, he had stayed on as his cousin's guest for some long time, unable doubtless to tear himself away from the nearby links, so much better provided with differing holes to play than Blackheath's nursemaid-haunted seven.

But when they were informed of his return home, it was in somewhat extraordinary circumstances. A telegraph message was brought to the door.

COUSIN IAN UNFORTUNATELY DECEASED, it read. RETURNING IMMEDIATELY.

But when the master of the house set foot again within its doors, they learned little more.

"Poor Ian," Mr. McMurdo told his wife and Miss Unwin that evening in the drawing room. "He died in my arms, struck by a gutt—struck by a golf ball. A terrible thing, a terrible thing."

Mrs. McMurdo broke into sobs.

"There's no need for that," her husband said. "You never met the man in all the years of our marriage. It's no occasion to weep for him now."

"But—but—"

"Enough. The man's dead, and that's all there is to be said about it."

The *Morning Post* was conveniently beside his chair. He buried himself behind its crammed columns of social announcements and advertisements.

Miss Unwin sat in respectful silence next to Mrs. McMurdo's sofa, ready with a bottle of smelling salts. And she thought. First, that all her suspicions about the game of golf appeared to have been justified. How appalling it was that, in the course of trying to get one of those white-painted gutties into a distant little hole, a man had died, struck by another of those small balls propelled from afar by a swishing stroke of that club known as the driver.

Then it occurred to her that the terrible accident was likely to be a blessing for herself, little though she could welcome the way it had come about. But there was no gainsaying that, with the death of Mr. Mungo McMurdo's rich, unmarried cousin, her employer would now be able to keep her in his service. For a moment she asked herself whether it was right that she should benefit in this way from the death of that gentleman in distant Scotland. Then she decided that it would be much better for wee Margaret, almost without a friend in this little-loving house, to continue to receive her lessons from someone she knew rather than from a stranger.

Before long, Mrs. McMurdo, still wiping away occasional tears, announced that she was feeling so upset that she thought she ought to retire to bed. Miss Unwin accompanied her in her toiling ascent of the steep stairs and waited until she had seen Hetty, Mrs. McMurdo's maid, approaching the bedroom. Then she went to bed herself, early though it was. To bed, but not for a long while to sleep. The extraordinary events of the past few days went revolving and revolving in her mind. They seemed somehow so unlikely, and, always hovering, there was a small feeling of guilt that she herself had been relieved of the anxiety about finding a new position if an impoverished Mr. Mc-Murdo had dismissed her.

At last she told herself firmly that she was almost certain eventually to learn more about how Mr. Ian McMurdo had met his end than her taciturn employer had chosen to tell his wife. The *Morning Post* was bound to carry a full report of the inquest. After all, it must surely be the first time that any gentleman had been killed by a ball in the course of playing this new game of golf, new at least outside the realm of Scotland. Her resolution made, she succeeded at last in falling asleep. But that sleep was pervaded by the most extraordinary dreams.

Miss Unwin dreamed that she, a woman, was playing golf. And she was being wonderfully successful on the links. Every time she stood there, the fat leather grip of a club, be it driver, cleek or niblick, in her delicate feminine fingers, the gutty she hit seemed to fly to exactly the place she had aimed it. And this despite finding from time to time that she was playing, not with any orthodox club, but with a long extended version of the ruler she kept on her desk in the schoolroom and, on rare occasions, found necessary to bring down sharply on little Margaret's held-out palm.

Nor was her success as a golfer hindered by the extraordinary hazards that presented themselves in front of her, whether it was a tall brick wall, suddenly springing up, with on it in elaborately painted lettering the words *Genuine Dundee Marmalade* or sometimes *Genuine Juice of the Percha Tree,* or whether it was a Blackheath nursemaid in neat uniform standing with her mouth wide open ready to swallow the gutty. Nothing hindered progress toward whichever flowerpot hole she was aiming for, not even the big sprouting bunches of curious flowers which, she somehow knew, little Margaret had put into them out of mischief.

But morning came at last. One of the maids brought Miss Unwin her hot water. Breakfast was served as usual. Margaret was on her best behavior. The nightmares began to fade away.

The questions lying deep in Miss Unwin's head did not, however, fade away.

• • •

It was more than a week later, after Mr. McMurdo had gone back again to Scotland to give his evidence at the inquest, that the report appeared in the *Morning Post*. Miss Unwin was able to take advantage of Mrs. McMurdo's late hour of rising to get to see it first. She learned that her employer and his cousin had been out on the links on the day of the death as soon as it was daylight and that they had progressed as far as a hole known as the Devil's Breeks, because it was necessary in order to play it successfully to take one wide green path through the surrounding whins rather than another leading steeply down to a cliff overlooking the sea. The two cousins had, according to the evidence, both succeeded in driving their gutties a good long distance, far enough for them to end out of sight on the far side of the slight hill in front of them. As they left the tee from which they had made those pleasing long drives, Mr. McMurdo told the presiding sheriff, they saw an aged gentleman known to them both, one Mr. Angus Todd, come up to play his customary early morning round. They said to each other that there was little danger of a no-toriously slow player catching up with them. However, it seemed that Mr. Todd must have been playing more speedily than usual, because as the two of them stood on the far side of the rise discussing which of their gutties was nearer the hole, a ball came flying over and struck Mr. Ian McMurdo on the back of the head.

I did what I could for him, the witness stated, but I knew almost at a glance that the wound was fatal.

Aged Mr. Todd had then given his evidence, breaking down and having to be granted a respite when he said that the stroke he had played "must have been the best stroke I ever made." After he had recovered, he told how he crossed the brow of the hill and saw Mr. Mungo McMurdo kneeling beside the prostrate body of Mr. Ian McMurdo. The final evidence was produced by the police constable who had investigated the occurrence, who said a golf ball found "nae muir than twa yards frae the corpus" bore on it the letters *A T*. The verdict had followed. *Death by Misadventure.*

It was then that a tiny thought, no bigger than a wee gutty, rose up in Miss Unwin's head, there to stay.

• • •

When, a week later, Mr. McMurdo returned from having inspected his new property in Scotland, he proved to be full of plans.

"We shall move into poor old Ian's house," he announced. "I intend to sell the works in Shoreditch. They have not been paying well for some time. And now we shall be able to live the sort of life I should always have had."

"But—," said Mrs. McMurdo.

"But? But? What is there to say *But* about? Wait till you see the old family house. A wonderful place. Haven't I always told you it was a wonderful place? And so near the links. I shall be out there first thing every morning, I tell you that."

"But how shall I manage without Dr. George? No one knows more about my condition than dear Dr. George."

"Nonsense. Arrant nonsense. The doctors in Scotland can run rings round any English one. Of course, you'll come, and be glad of it. And wee Margaret will have the time of her life in the big house and all the grounds. A bonny place for a grow-ing girl."

"But—but what about her education?"

"There are dominies in Scotland more learned than all the schoolmasters in the whole of England, and good men on the links too. Good men on the links."

"But Margaret has been used to being given her lessons by a governess. I do not think she would welcome some harsh—what did you call them?—some harsh dominie teach-ing her."

"Well, then," Mr. McMurdo spluttered, making some sort of concession to feminine weakness, "Miss Unwin shall come up with us. Yes, that will do. That will do."

"No, sir," Miss Unwin said then. "No, I shall not be able to accompany Margaret to Scotland."

"And why the d—— not, ma'am? Do you want better wages? Is that it? Yes, I dare say that's it. Well, you can have them. You can have them. No one can say Mungo McMurdo is unwilling to pay for his daughter's care."

"No, sir. That is not my reason. But I think it best if I ex-plained it to you tomorrow. May I come to the library at, shall we say, half past nine?"

"But, damn it, I ought to be on my way to Blackheath by then. Perhaps the last time I shall play on those wretched seven holes."

"No, sir. You have always left the house, whether to go to the marmalade works or to play golf, at ten o'clock. That is why I suggested half past nine."

For a moment Mr. McMurdo looked as if he was going to explode in an outburst of rage. But something about Miss Unwin's calm demeanor seemed to penetrate to him.

"Very well. Very well, ma'am. Half past nine, and don't you be one minute later."

"I shall not, sir."

• • •

At half past nine next morning, on the dot, Miss Unwin knocked at the door of the library.

"Come in," a gruff voice issued from the far side of the forbidding mahogany.

Miss Unwin entered.

"Well, what is it you've got to say?"

Miss Unwin took in a single breath.

"It is this. I cannot go with you to Scotland because you have murdered your cousin, Mr. Ian McMurdo."

Standing facing her, Mr. McMurdo said nothing. A red flush of blood began to mount into his cheeks. But Miss Unwin knew that he had already realized that no amount of rage and bluster would counter the accusation she had made.

"Allow me to tell you," she said, "why it is that I know what I have said is nothing but the truth."

Slowly Mr. McMurdo sank back into the chair behind his desk.

"First," Miss Unwin said, "I came to realize some weeks ago that your business was no longer producing the financial returns it had once done. Marmalade made in Dundee was claiming an increasing share of the market. Then I heard from little Margaret that you had told her, boasted to her, that you had used just one gutty to play all the seven holes on the Black-heath links, and I realized that you were having to economize even when playing golf. Next, you declined in spite of your wife's earnest requests to find another manservant in place of

John, even to the extent of taking no one with you when you visited Scotland."

"But—but why should I have done? Ian—Ian had plenty of servants."

"Yes, and you grudged him his establishment and his wealth."

"I did not. I—"

"But, if you did not, why was it that among the few golf balls you allowed yourself when you left for Scotland, there was one with written on it the initials *A T*?"

"How the devil did you know about that?"

"It was not the work of the Devil, Mr. McMurdo: it was the providential curiosity of your own little daughter."

"Well, what if I did happen to have a gutty with those initials on it? They could have been—they could have got there in any one of a hundred ways."

"I do not think so. I think you marked it in that way so that, when you had struck your cousin down with the life preserver you took with you to Scotland in one of the pockets of your golf bag, you could drop that ball beside his body and make out that he had been accidentally struck by the one sent over the hill by Mr. Angus Todd, who, to your knowledge, went out to the links there every morning and, being a gentleman of some years, was a notoriously slow player."

Mr. McMurdo sat there in silence.

At last he came back to life.

"I think there is one thing you have forgotten, Miss Clever-sticks."

"Indeed?"

"Yes. This."

In a single swift gesture he tugged open the drawer at his

left hand, dipped into it and produced the very life preserver which Miss Unwin had accused him of using, with its neatly rounded end, to kill his cousin.

"No, Mr. McMurdo," she said, and her voice did not betray a single tremor. "No, sir, I do not think so. I would have hardly come to you, alone as I am, if I had not taken a certain precaution first. I have," she lied, thinking of how wee Margaret had once written out for her three times in her best hand *Circumstances alter cases,* "deposited a full account of everything I have said to you with a trusted friend."

With a dull thud Mr. McMurdo allowed the life preserver to fall back into its drawer.

"So . . . so it is to be the police?" he said, all fire gone.

"Perhaps. But I would not like to have it on my conscience that I was the one who made your wife a pauper, deprived of the income she will need to live the life she has been used to, and, above all, I am not ready to see little Margaret branded forever as having a murderer for a father."

Mr. McMurdo managed to look up for an instant.

"But what . . . ?"

"Mr. McMurdo, the stairs in this house are, as I have often warned little Margaret, dangerously steep. If you were to have swallowed the contents of one of those decanters in the tantalus over there and then, stepping out onto the landing, put your foot on one of those balls you call a gutty, a ball which I happen to have left on the floor there, then you would be almost certain to fall to your death."

• • •

When the inquest was held on the body of Mungo McMurdo, Esq., the verdict returned was *Death by Misadventure.*

A GOOD **** SPOILED

Laura Lippman

It began innocently enough. Well, if not innocently—and Charlie Drake realized that some people would refuse to see the origins of any extramarital affair as innocent—it began with tact and consideration. When Charlie Drake agreed to have an affair with his former administrative assistant, he began putting golf clubs in the trunk of his car every Thursday and Saturday, telling his wife he was going to shoot a couple of holes. Yes, he really said "a couple of holes," but then, he knew very little about golf at the time.

Luckily, neither did his wife, Marla. But she was enthusiastic about the new hobby, if only because it created a whole new category of potential gifts, and her family members were always keen for Christmas and birthday ideas for Charlie, who was notoriously difficult to shop for. And as the accessories began to flow—golf books, golf shirts, golf gloves, golf hats, golf highball glasses—Charlie inevitably learned quite a bit about golf. He watched tournaments on television and spoke knowingly of "Tiger" and "Singh," as well as the quirks of certain U.S. Open courses. He began to think of himself as a golfer who simply didn't golf. Which, as he gleaned from his friends who actually pursued the sport, might be the best of all possible worlds. Golf, they said, was their love and their obsession, and they all wished they had never taken it up.

At any rate, this continued for a few years. But then Sylvia announced she wanted to go from mistress to wife. And given that Sylvia was terrifyingly good at making her pronouncements into reality, this was rather unsettling for Charlie. After all, she was the one who had engineered the affair in the first place, and even come up with the golf alibi. As he had noted on her annual evaluation, Sylvia was very goal-oriented.

"Look, I want to fuck you," Sylvia had said out of the blue, about six months after she started working for him. Okay, not totally out of the blue. She had tried a few more subtle things—pressing her breasts against his arm when going over a document, touching his hand, asking him if he needed her to go with him to conferences, volunteering to pay her own way when told there was no money in the budget for her to attend. "We could even share a room," she said. It was when Charlie demurred at this offer that she said, "Look, I want to fuck you."

Charlie was fifty-eight at the time, married thirty-eight years, and not quite at ease in the world. He remembered a time when nice girls didn't—well, when they didn't do it so easily and they certainly didn't speak of it so fluently. Marla had been a nice girl, someone he met at college and courted according to the standards of the day, and while he remembered being wistful in the early days of their marriage, when everyone suddenly seemed to be having guilt-free sex all the time, AIDS had come along and he had decided he was comfortable with his choices. Sure, he noticed pretty girls and thought about them, but he had never been jolted to act on those feelings. It seemed like a lot of trouble, frankly.

"Well, um, we can't," he told Sylvia.

"Why? Don't you like me?"

"Of course I like you, Sylvia, but you work for me. They have rules about that. Anita Hill and all."

"The point of an affair is that it's carried on in secret."

"And the point of embezzlement is to get away with stealing money, but I wouldn't put my job at risk that way. I plan to retire from this job in a few years."

"But you feel what I'm feeling, right? This incredible force between us?"

"Sure." It seemed only polite.

"So if I find a job with one of our competitors, then there would be nothing to stop us, right? This is just about the sexual harassment rules?"

"Sure," he repeated, not thinking her serious. Then, just in case she was: "But you can't take your Rolodex, you know. Company policy."

A month later, he was called for a reference on Sylvia and he gave her the good one she deserved, then took her out to lunch to wish her well. She put her hand on his arm.

"So can we now?"

"Can we what?"

"Fuck."

"Oh." He still wasn't comfortable with that word. "Well, no. I mean, as of this moment, you're still my employee. Technically. So no."

"What about next week?"

"Well, my calendar is pretty full—"

"You don't have anything on Thursday." Sylvia did know his calendar.

"That's true."

"We can go to my apartment. It's not far."

"You know, Sylvia, when you're starting a new job, you really shouldn't take long lunches. Not at first."

"So it's going to be a *long* lunch." She all but growled these words at him, confusing Charlie. He was pretty sure that he hadn't committed himself to anything, yet somehow Sylvia thought he had. He had used the company's sexual harassment policy as a polite way to rebuff her, and now it turned out she had taken his excuse at face value. The thing was, he did not find Sylvia particularly attractive. She had thick legs, far too thick for the short skirts she favored, and she was a little hairy for his taste. Still, she dressed as if she believed herself a knockout and he did not want to disabuse her of this notion.

(And did Charlie, who was fifty-eight, with thinning hair and a protruding stomach, ever wonder what Sylvia saw in him? No.)

"I'm not sure how I could get away," he said at last.

"I've already thought that out. If you told people you were playing golf, you could get away Thursdays at lunch. You know how many men at the company play golf. And then we could have Saturdays, too. Long Saturdays, with nothing but fucking."

He winced. "Sylvia, I really don't like that word."

"You'll like the way I do it."

He did, actually. Sylvia applied herself to Charlie's needs with the same brisk efficiency she had brought to being his administrative assistant, although she was clearly the boss in this situation. He made a few rules, mostly about discretion—no e-mails, as few calls as possible, nothing in public, ever—but otherwise he let Sylvia call the shots, which she did with a lot of enthusiasm. Before he knew it, a few years had gone by, and he was putting his golf clubs in his car twice a week (except when it rained, which wasn't often, not in this desert climate) and he thought everyone was happy. In fact, Marla even took to bragging a bit that Charlie seemed more easygoing and re-laxed since he had taken up golf, but he wasn't obsessive about it like most men. So Marla was happy and Charlie was happy and Sylvia—well, Sylvia was not happy, as it turned out.

"When are you going to marry me?" she asked abruptly one day, right in the middle of something that Charlie particu-larly liked, which distressed him, as it dimmed the pleasure, having it interrupted, and this question was an especially jar-ring interruption.

"What?"

"I'm in love with you, Charlie. I'm tired of sneaking around like this."

"We don't sneak around anywhere."

"Exactly. For two years, you've been coming over here, having your fun, but what's in it for me? We never go anywhere outside this apartment. I don't even get to go to lunch with you or celebrate my birthday. I want to *marry* you, Charlie."

"You do?"

"I looooooooooooove you." Sylvia, who clearly was not going to finish tending to him, threw herself across her side of the bed and began to cry.

"You do?" Charlie rather liked their current arrangement and, given that Sylvia had more or less engineered it, he had as-sumed it was as she wanted it.

"Of course. I want you to leave Marla and marry me."

"But I don't—" He had started to say he didn't want to leave Marla and marry Sylvia, but he realized this was probably not tactful. "I just don't know how to tell Marla. It will break her heart. We've been together thirty-eight years."

"I've given it some thought." Her tears had dried with suspicious speed. "You have to choose. For the next month, I'm not going to see you at all. In fact, I'm not going to see you again until you tell Marla what we have."

"Okay." Charlie lay back and waited for Sylvia to continue.

"Starting now, Charlie."

"Now? I mean, I'm already here. Why not Saturday?"

"Now."

Two days later, as Charlie was puttering around the house, wondering what to do with himself, Marla asked, "Aren't you going to play golf?"

"What?" Then he remembered. "Oh, yeah. I guess so." He put on his golf gear, gathered up his clubs and headed out. But to where? How should he kill the next five hours? He started to head to the movies, but he passed the country club on his way out to the multiplex and thought that it looked almost fun. He pulled in and inquired about getting a lesson. It was harder than it looked, but not impossible, and the pro said the advantage of being a beginner was that Charlie had no bad habits.

"You're awfully tan," Marla said two weeks later.

"Am I?" He looked at his arms, reddish brown, at least up to the hem of his golf shirt's sleeves. "You know, I changed suntan lotion. I was using a really high SPF, it kept out all the rays. But a little sun can't hurt."

"When I paid the credit card bill, I noticed you were spending a lot more money at the country club. Are you sneaking in extra games?"

"I'm playing faster," he said, "so I have time to have drinks at the nineteenth hole, or even a meal in the restaurant. In fact, I might start going out on Sundays, too. Would you mind?"

"Oh, I've been a golf widow all this time," Marla said. "What's another day? As long"—she smiled playfully—"as long as it's really golf and not another woman."

Charlie was stung by Marla's joke. He had always been a faithful husband. That is, he had been a faithful husband for thirty-six years, and then there had been an interruption, one of relatively short duration given the length of their marriage, and now he was faithful again, so it seemed unfair for Marla to tease him this way.

"Well, if you want to come along and take a lesson yourself, you're welcome to. You might enjoy it."

"But you always said golf was a terribly jealous mistress, that you wouldn't advise anyone you know taking it up because it gets such a horrible hold on you."

"Did I? Well, if you can't beat 'em, join 'em."

Marla came to the club the next day. She had a surprising aptitude for golf and it gave her extra confidence to see that Charlie was not much better than she, despite his two years of experience. She liked the club, too, although she was puzzled that Charlie didn't seem to know many people. "I kind of keep to myself," he said.

The balance of the two months passed quickly, so quickly and pleasantly that he found himself surprised when Sylvia called.

"Well?" she asked.

"Well?" he echoed.

"Did you tell her?"

"Her? Oh, Marla. No. No. I just couldn't."

"If you don't tell her, you'll never see me again."

"I guess that's only fair."

"What?" Sylvia's voice, never her best asset, screeched perilously high.

"I accept your conditions. I can't leave Marla, and therefore I can't see you." Really, he thought, when would he have time? He was playing so much golf now, and while Marla seldom came to the club on Thursdays, she accompanied him on Saturdays and Sundays.

"But you *love* me."

"Yes, but Marla is the mother of my children."

"Who are now grown and living in other cities and barely remember to call you except on your birthday."

"And she's a fifty-nine-year-old woman. It would be rather mean, just throwing her out in the world at this age, never having worked and all. Plus, a divorce would bankrupt me."

"A passion like ours is a once-in-a-lifetime event."

"It is?"

"What?" she screeched again.

"I mean, it *is*. We have known a great passion. But that's precisely because we haven't been married. Marriage is different, Sylvia. You'll just have to take my word on that."

This apparently was the wrong thing to say, as she began to sob in earnest. "But I would be married to you. And I love you. I can't live without you."

"Oh, I'm not much of a catch. Really. You'll get over it."

"I'm almost forty! I've sacrificed two crucial years, being with you on your terms."

Charlie thought that was unfair, since the terms had been Sylvia's from the start. But all he said was, "I'm sorry. I didn't mean to lead you on. And I won't anymore."

He thought that would end matters, but Sylvia was a remarkably focused woman. She continued to call—the office, not his home, which indicated to Charlie that she was not truly ready to wreak the havoc she was threatening. So Marla remained oblivious and their golf continued to improve, but his new assistant was beginning to suspect something was up and he knew he had to figure out a way to make it end. But given that he wasn't the one who had made it start, he didn't see how he could end it.

On Thursday, just as he was getting ready to leave the office for what was now his weekly midday nine, Sylvia called again, crying and threatening to hurt herself.

"I was just on my way out," he said.

"Where do you have to go?"

"Golf," he said.

"Oh, I see." Her laugh was brittle. "So you have someone new already. Your current assistant? I guess your lofty principles have fallen a notch."

"No, I really play golf now."

"Charlie, I'm not your wife. Your stupid lie won't work on me. It's not even your lie, remember?"

"No, no, there's no one else. I've, well, reformed. It's like a penance to me. I've chosen my loveless marriage and golf over the great passion of my life. It's the right thing to do."

He thought she would find this suitably romantic, but it only seemed to enrage her more.

"I'm going to go over to your house and tell Marla that you're cheating."

"Don't do that, Sylvia. It's not even true."

"You cheated with me, didn't you? And a tiger doesn't change his stripes."

Charlie wanted to say that he was not so much a tiger as a house cat who had been captured by a petulant child and then streaked with a Magic Marker. True, it had been hard to break with Sylvia once things had started. She was very good at a lot of things that Marla seldom did, and never conducted with enthusiasm. But it had not been his idea. And, confronted with an ultimatum, he had honored her condition. He hadn't tried to have it both ways. He was beginning to think Sylvia was a little unstable.

"Meet me at my apartment right now, or I'll call Marla."

He did, and it was a dreary time, all tears and screaming and no attentions paid to him whatsoever, not even after he held her and stroked her hair and said he did love her.

"You should be getting back to work," he said at last, hoping to find any excuse to stop holding her.

She shook her head. "My position was eliminated two weeks ago. I'm out of work."

"Is that why you're so desperate to get married?"

She wailed like a banshee, not that he really knew what a banshee sounded like. Something scary and shrill. "*No.* I love you, Charlie. I want to be your wife for that reason alone. But the last month, with all this going on, I haven't been at my best, and they had a bad quarter, so I was a sitting duck. In a sense, I've lost my job *because* of you, Charlie. I'm unemployed and I'm alone. I've hit rock bottom."

"You could always come back to the company. You left on good terms and I'd give you a strong reference."

"But then we couldn't be together."

"Yes." He was not so clever that he had thought of this in advance, but now he saw it would solve everything.

"And that's the one thing I could never bear."

Charlie, his hand on her hair, looked out the window. It was such a beautiful day, a little cooler than usual, but still sunny. If he left now—but, no, he would have to go back to the office. He wouldn't get to play golf at all today.

"Who is she, Charlie?"

"Who?"

"The other woman."

He sighed. "There is no other woman."

"Stop lying, or I really will go to Marla. I'll drive over there right now, while you're at work. After all, I don't have a job to go to."

She was crazy, she was bluffing. She was so crazy that even if she wasn't bluffing, he could probably persuade Marla that she was a lunatic. After all, what proof did she have? He had never allowed the use of any camera, digital or video, although Sylvia had suggested it from time to time. There were no e-mails. He *never* called her. And he was careful to leave his DNA, as he thought of it, only in the appropriate places, although this included some places that Marla believed inappropriate. He had learned much from the former president and the various television shows on crime scene investigations.

"Look, if it's money you need—"

"I don't want money! I want you!"

And so it began all over again, the crying and the wailing, only this time there was no calming her. She was obsessed with the identity of his new mistress, adamant that he tell her everything, enraged by his insistence that he really did play golf in his spare time. Finally, he thought to take her down to the garage beneath her apartment and show her the clubs in the trunk of his car.

•   •   •

"So what?" she said. "You always carried your clubs."

"But I know what they are now," he said, removing a driver. "See this one, it's—"

"I know what's going on and I'm done, I tell you. The minute you leave here, I'm going to go upstairs and call Marla. It's her or me. Stop *fucking* with me, Charlie."

"I really wish you wouldn't use that word, Sylvia. It's coarse."

"Oh, you don't like hearing it, but you sure like doing it. Fuck! Fuck, fuck, fuck, fucking!"

She stood in front of him, hands on her hips. Over the course of their two-year affair she had not become particularly more attractive, although she had learned to use a depilatory on her upper lip. What would happen if she went to Marla? His wife would probably stay with him, but it would be dreary, with counseling and recriminations. And they really were so happy now, happier than ever, united by their love of golf, comfortable in their routines. He couldn't bear to see it end.

"I can't have that, Sylvia. I just can't."

"Then choose."

"I have."

No, he didn't hit her with the driver. He wouldn't have risked damaging it, for one thing, having learned that it was rare to have a club that felt so right in one's grip. Also, there would have been blood and it was impossible to clean every trace of blood from one's trunk, according to those television shows. Instead, he pushed her, gently but firmly, and she fell back into the trunk, which he closed and latched. He then drove back to the office, parking in a remote place where Sylvia's thumping, which was growing fainter, would not draw any attention. At home that night, he ate dinner with Marla, marveling over the Greg Norman Shiraz that she served with the salmon. "Do you hear something out in the garage?" she asked at one point. "A knocking noise?"

"No," he said.

It was Marla's book club night, and after she left, he went out to the garage and circled his car for a few minutes, thinking. Ultimately, he figured out how to attach a garden hose from the exhaust through a cracked window and into the backseat, where he pressed it into the crevice of the seat, which could be released to create a larger carrying space, like a hatchback, but only from within the car proper. Sylvia's voice was weaker, but still edged with fury. He ignored her. Marla was always gone for at least three hours on book club night and he figured that would be long enough.

•   •   •

It would be several weeks before Sylvia Nichols's body was found in a patch of wilderness near a state park. While clearly a murder, it was considered a baffling case from the beginning. How had a woman been killed by carbon monoxide poisoning, then dumped at so remote a site? Why had she been killed? Homicide police, noting the large volume of calls from her home phone to Charlie's work number, questioned him, of course, but he was able to say with complete sincerity that she was a former employee who was keen to get a job back since being let go, and he hadn't been able to help her despite her increasing hysteria. DNA evidence indicated she had not had sex of any sort in the hours before her death. Credit card slips bore out the fact that Charlie was a regular at the local country club, and his other hours were accounted for. Even Marla laughed at the idea of her husband having an affair, saying he was far too busy with golf to have time for another woman.

"Although I'm the one who broke 90 first," she said. "Which is funny, given that Charlie has a two-year head start on me."

"It's a terrible mistress, golf," Charlie said.

"I don't play, but they say it's the worst you can have," the homicide detective said.

"Just about," Charlie said.

THE HOARDER

Bradford Morrow

I have always been a hoarder. When I was young, our family lived on the Outer Banks, where I swept up and down the shore filling my windbreaker pockets with seashells of every shape and size. Back in the privacy of my room I loved nothing better than to lay them out on my bed, arranging them by color or form—whelks and cockles here, clams and scallops there—a beautiful mosaic of dead calcium. The complete skeleton of a horseshoe crab was my finest prize, as I remember. After we moved inland from the Atlantic, my obsession didn't change, but the objects of my desire did. Having no money, I was restricted to things I found, so one year developed an extensive collection of Kentucky bird nests, and during the next an array of bright Missouri butterflies preserved in several homemade display cases. Another year, my father's itinerant work having taken us to the desert, I cultivated old pottery shards from the hot potreros. Sometimes my younger sister offered to assist with my quests, but I preferred shambling around on my own. Once in a while I did allow her to shadow me, if only because it was one more thing that annoyed our big brother, who never missed an opportunity to cut me down to size. Weird little bastard, Tom liked calling me. I didn't mind him saying so. I was a weird little bastard.

When first learning to read, I hoarded words just as I would shells, nests, butterflies. Like many an introvert, I went through a phase during which every waking hour was spent inside a library book. These I naturally collected, too, never paying my late dues, writing in a ragged notebook words which were used against Tom at opportune moments. He was seldom impressed when I told him he was a *pachyderm anus* or *runny pustule,* but that might have been because he didn't understand some of what came out of my mouth. Many times I hardly knew what I was saying. Still, the desired results were now and then achieved. When I called him some name that sounded nasty enough—*eunuch's tit*—he would run after me with fists flying and pin me down demanding a definition and I'd refuse. Be it black eye or bloody nose, I always came away feeling I got the upper hand.

Father wasn't a migrant laborer, as such, and all our moving had nothing to do with a fieldworker following seasons or harvests. He lived by his wits, so he told us and so we kids believed. But wits or not, every year brought the ritual pulling up of stakes and clearing out. His explanations were always curt, brief, like our residencies. He never failed to apologize, and I think he meant it when he told us that the next stop would be more permanent, that he was having a streak of bad luck bound to change for the better. Tom took these uprootings harder than I or my sister. He expressed his anger about being jerked around like circus animals, and complained that this was the old man's fault and we should band together in revolt. It was never clear just how we were supposed to mutiny, and of course we never did. Molly and I wondered privately, whispering together at night, if our family wouldn't be more settled had our mother still been around. But that road was a dead end even more than the one we seemed to be on already. She'd deserted our father and the rest of us and there was no bringing her back. We used to get cards at Christmas, but even that stopped some years ago. We seldom mentioned her name now. What was the point?

Like the sun, we traveled westward across the country all the way to the coast, though more circuitously and with much dimmer prospects. I'd made a practice of discarding my latest collection whenever we left one place for another, and not merely disposing of it but destroying the stuff. Taking a hammer to my stash of petrified wood and bleached bones plucked off the flats near Mojave, after the word came down to start packing, was my own private way of saying good-bye. Molly always cried until I gave her a keepsake—a sparrow nest or slug of quartz crystal. And my dad took me aside to ask why I was undoing all my hard work, unaware of the sharp irony of his question—who was he to talk? He told me that one day when I was grown up I'd look back and regret not treasuring these souvenirs from my youth. But he never stopped me. He couldn't in fairness do that. These were my things, and just as I'd brought them together, I had every right to junk them and set my sights on the new. Besides, demolishing my collections didn't mean I didn't treasure them in my own way.

We found ourselves in a small, pleasant, nondescript oceanside town just south of the palm-lined promenades of Santa Barbara and the melodramatic Spanish villas of Montecito, where the Kennedys had spent their honeymoon a few years before. By this time I was old enough to find a job. Tom and I had both given up on school. Too many new faces, too many new curricula. Father couldn't object to his eldest son dropping out of high school, since he himself had done the same. As for me, having turned fifteen, I'd more or less educated myself anyway. It was a testament to Molly's resilient nature that she was never fazed entering all those unknown classrooms across this great land of ours. My responsibility was to make sure she got to summer school on time and to pick her up at day's end, and so I did. This commitment I gladly undertook, since I always liked Molly, and she didn't get in the way of my schedule at the miniature golf course where I was newly employed.

Just as California would mark a deviation in my father's gypsy routine, it would be the great divide for me. Whether I knew it at the time is beside the point. I doubt I did. Tom noticed something different had dawned in me, a new confidence, and while he continued to taunt me, my responses became unpredictable. He might smirk, "Miniature golf . . . now, there's a promising career, baby," but rather than object, I would cross my arms, smile, and agree, "Just my speed, baby." When we did fight, our battles were higher-pitched and more physical, and as often as not, he was the one who got the tooth knocked loose, the lip opened, the kidney punched. Molly gave up trying to be peacemaker and lived more and more in her own world. It was as if we moved into individual mental compartments, like different collectibles in different cabinets. I couldn't even say for sure what kind of work my father did anymore, though it involved a commute over the mountains to a place called Ojai, which resulted in us seeing less of him than ever. The sun had turned him brown, so his work must have been outside. Probably a construction job—so much for his touted wits. Tom, on the other hand, remained as white as abalone, working in a convenience store. And Molly with her sweet round face covered in freckles and ringed by wildly wavy red hair, the birthright of her maternal Irish ancestry, marched forward with the patience and hope that would better befit a daughter of the king of Uz than a carpenter of Ojai—which our dear brother had by then, with all the cleverness he could muster, dubbed *Oh Low.*

• • •

The change was gradual but irrevocable, and would be difficult if not impossible to describe in abstract terms. To suggest that my compulsion to hoard shifted from objects to essences, from the external world's castoffs to the stuff of spirits, wouldn't be quite right. It might even be false, since what began to arise within me during those long slow days and evenings at work had a manifest concreteness to it. Whether my discovery of glances, fragrances, gestures, voices, the various flavors of nascent sexuality, the potential for beautiful violence that hovers behind those qualities, came as the result of my new life at Bayside Park, or whether it would have happened no matter where I lived and breathed at that moment, I couldn't say. I do know that Bayside—that perfect world of fantastical architecture and linked greens and strict rules—was where I came awake, felt more alive, as they say, than ever before. I who'd loved lifeless things was now reborn.

The first time I laid eyes on the place was early evening. Fog—which seasonally rolled in at dusk, settling over the coastal flats and canyons until early afternoon the next day—was drifting ashore like willowy, ghostly scarves. I wore my best flannel shirt and a pair of jeans to the interview. My head was all but bald, my old man having given me a fresh trim with his electric clippers, a memento filched from one of his many former employers. Even though it was late June and the day was warm, I wished I'd brought a sweater, since the heavy mist down by the ocean dampened me to the bone. I could hear the surf once I crossed the empty highway, and I started thinking about what questions I might be asked during my interview and what sorts of answers I'd be forced to make up to cover a complete lack of experience. There was a good chance I'd be turned down for the job. After all, I was just a kid who had done nothing with his life beyond collecting debris in forests and fields and reading novels and other worthless books. Weren't I so bent on getting clear of our house, pulling together money toward one day having a place of my own, unaffected by my shiftless father and moron brother, I'd have talked myself out of even trying. Tom called me a loser so often that, despite the contrarian waters running deep in me, I knew he wasn't altogether wrong.

As I approached the miniature golf park, I was mesmerized by a ball of brilliance, a white dome of light in the mist that reminded me of some monumental version of one of those snow shaker toys, what on earth are they called? Those water-filled globes of glass inside which are plastic world's fairs, North Pole dioramas, Eiffel Towers that, when joggled, fall under the spell of a miraculous blizzard. What loomed inside this fluorescent bell jar was a wonderland, a fake dwarf-world populated by real people, reminiscent of snow globe toys in other ways, too. The fantastic impossible scenes housed in each, glass or light, were irresistible. I walked through a gate over which was a sign that read *Bayside—For All Ages*. What lay before me, smaller than the so-called real world but larger than life, was a village of whirling windmills and miniature cathedrals with spires, of stucco gargoyles and painted grottoes. A white brick castle with turrets ascended the low sky, its paint peeling in the watery weather. Calypso's Cave, the sixth hole. A fanciful pirate ship coved by a waterfall at the seventh. And everywhere I looked, green synthetic alleys. All interconnected and, if a bit seedy, very alluring.

A result of lying about my age, background, and whatever else, I got the job. When asked at dinner to describe what kind of work was involved, I told my father I was the course steward. In fact, my responsibilities fell somewhere between janitor and errand boy. Absurd as it may sound, I was never happier. Vacuuming the putting lanes; scouring the acre park and adjacent beach for lost balls and abandoned golf clubs; tending the beds of bougainvillea and birds-of-paradise; spearing trash strewn on the trampled struggling real grass that lay between the perfect alleys; skimming crud out of water traps and ornamental lagoons; retouching paint where paint needed retouching. If Bayside were a museum—and it was, to my eyes—I was its curator. The owner, a lean, sallow, stagnant man named Gallagher, seemed gratified by my attentiveness and pleased that I didn't have any friends to waste my time or his. Looking back, I realize he was quietly delighted that I hadn't the least interest in playing. What did I care about hitting a ball into a hole with a stick?

That said, I did become an aficionado, in an antiseptic sort of way. Just as I had about the classifications of seashells or the markings of dragonflies in times past, I read everything I could about the sport in the office bookcase, surrounded by framed photos autographed by the rich and famous who played here long ago. The history was more interesting than I imagined. In the Depression they used sewer pipes, scavenged tires, rain gutters, whatever junk was lying around, and from all the discards built their Rinkiedinks, as the obstacle courses were called, scale-model worlds in which the rules were fair and the playing field—however bunkered, curved, slanted, stepped—was truly level. Once upon a time, I told Molly, this was the classy midnight pastime of America's royalty. Hollywood moguls drank champagne between holes, putting with stars and starlets under the moon until the sun came up. One of the earliest sports played outdoors under artificial lights, miniature golf was high Americana and even now, though it had a degraded heritage, was something finer than people believed.

• • •

My favorite trap in the park was the windmill, which rose seven feet into the soggy air of the twelfth green. Its blades were powered by an old car battery that needed checking once a week, as its cable connections tended to corrode in the damp, bringing the attraction—not to mention the obstacle—to a standstill. One entered this windmill by a hidden door at the back, which wasn't observable to people playing the course, indeed was pretty invisible unless you knew it was there. Gallagher had by August learned to trust me with everything except ticket taking, which was his exclusive province when it came to Bayside, and about which I could not care less. So when, one evening, a couple complained to him that the windmill blades on 12 weren't working, he handed me a flashlight, some pliers, a knife, and explained what to do. The windmill was at the far end of the park and I made my way there as quickly as possible without disturbing any of the players.

Once inside, I discovered a new realm. A world within a world. Fixing the oxidized battery posts was nothing, done in a matter of minutes. But then I found myself wanting to stay. What held me was that I could see, through tiny windows in the wooden structure, people playing, unaware they were being watched. A girl with her mother and father standing behind, encouraging her, humped over the white ball, her face contorted into a mask of concentration, putting right at me, knowing nothing of my presence. One shot and through she went, between my legs, and after her, her mom and dad. They talked among themselves, a nice, dreary, happy family, in perfect certainty their words were exchanged in private. It was something to behold.

I stuck around. Who wouldn't? Others passed through me, the ghost in the windmill, and none of them knew, not even the pair of tough bucks who played the rounds every night, betting on each hole, whose contraband beer bottles I'd collected that very morning. It became my habit, from then on, to grab time in the windmill during work to watch and listen. I found myself particularly interested in young couples, many of them not much older than I was, out on dates. Having avoided school since we came West, and being by nature an outsider, my social skills were limited. The physical urgency I felt, spying on these lovers, I sated freely behind the thin walls of my hiding place. Meanwhile, I learned how lovers speak, what kind of extravagant lies they tell each other, the promises they make, and all I could feel was gratitude that my brand of intimacy didn't involve saying anything to anybody. The things I found myself whispering in the shade of my hermitage none of them would like to hear, either. Of that I was sure.

One evening, to my horror, Tom appeared in my peephole

vista. What was he doing here? What gave him the right? And who was the girl standing with him, laughing at one of his maudlin jokes? He had a beer in his pocket, like the toughs. His arm was slung over the girl's shoulder, dangling like a broken pendulum, and his face was rosy for once. They laughed again and looked around and, taking advantage of being (almost) alone, kissed. At first I stood frozen in the windmill whose blades spun slowly, knowing that if Tom caught me watching, he'd beat the hell out of me and back at home deny everything. But soon I realized there was nothing to fear. This was my domain. Tom could not touch me in my hideaway world. Much the same way I used to trespass his superiority with those words lifted out of books, I offered him the longest stare I could manage. Not blinking, not wincing, I made my face into an unreadable blank. Pity he couldn't respond.

Work went well. Some days I showed up early, on others left late. Gallagher one September morning informed me that if I thought I would be earning overtime pay I was mistaken, and he reacted with a smiling shrug when I told him my salary was more than fair. "You're a good kid," he concluded. And so I was, in that what he asked me to do I did, prompt and efficient. Players, it turned out, were more irresponsible and given to vandalism than I'd have assumed. Given the game had so much to do with disciplined timing, thoughtful strategy, a steady hand and eye, what were these broken putters and bashed fiberglass figures about? Perhaps I'd become an idealistic company man, but the extensive property damage Gallagher suffered seemed absurd. I helped him with repairs and thought to ask why he didn't prosecute the offenders; we both knew who they were. Instead, I kept my concerns to myself, sensing subconsciously, as they say, it's best not to call the ket-

tle black. After all, Gallagher surely noticed my long absences
within the precincts of the park and by mutual silence con-
sented to them, so long as I got the work done.

In my years of wandering far larger landscapes than Bayside I had learned where the birds and beasts of the earth hide
themselves against their enemies and how they go about imposing their will, however brief and measly it may be, on the
world around them. All my nest hunts and shell meanderings
served me well, though here what I collected thus far were fantasies. I can say I almost preferred the limitations of the park.
Finding fresh places to hide was my own personal handicap, as
it were. And since this was one of the old courses, ostentatious
in the most wonderful way—a glorious exemplar of its kind—
the possibilities seemed infinite. They weren't, but I took
advantage of what was feasible, and like the birds and crus-
taceans whose homes I used to collect, having none myself to
speak of, I more or less moved into Bayside, establishing
makeshift berths, stowing food and pop, wherever I secretly
could. Like the hermit crab, I began to inhabit empty shells.

• • •

The girlfriend's name was Penny. Penny for my thoughts.
Thin, with sand-colored hair that fell straight down her back to
her waist, she had a wry pale mouth, turned-up nose, and
brown searching eyes, deep and almost tragic, which didn't
seem to fit with her pastel halter and white pedal pushers. The
haunted look in those eyes of hers quickly began to haunt me
and, as I watched, my bewilderment over what she was doing
with the likes of Tom only grew. In life many things remain
ambiguous, chancy, muddled, unknowing and unknowable, but
she seemed to be someone who, given the right circumstances,

might come to understand me, maybe even believe in me. I developed a vague sense that there was something special between us, a kind of spiritual kinship, difficult to define. Molly was the one who told me her name. She said they had taken her on a picnic up near Isla Vista, and that Penny had taught her how to pick mussels at low tide. Very considerate of Tom, I thought, very familial.

Meantime, he and I were never more estranged. Our absentee father kept a roof over our heads but was otherwise slowly falling to pieces, a prematurely withering man who spent more time after work in taverns, communing with Scotch and fellow zilches. Molly had made friends with whom she walked to school these days, so I wasn't seeing much of her, either. Always the loner, I was never more solitary. Time and patience, twin essentials to any collector, were all I needed to bring my new obsession around. So it was that I took my time getting to know Penny, watching from the hidden confines of the windmill, the little train station with its motionless locomotive, the Hall of the Mountain King with its par 5, the toughest hole on the course. Having wrapped her tightly in my imaginative wings, it was hard to believe I still hadn't actually met Tom's friend.

He, who returned to Bayside again and again with some perverse notion he was irritating me, would never have guessed how much I learned about his Penny over the months. Anonymous and invisible as one of the buccaneer statuettes on the pirate ship, I stalked them whenever they came to play, moving easily from one of my sanctuaries to another, all the while keeping my boss under control, so to say; Gallagher, who had grown dependent on me by this time. She was an only daughter. Her father worked on an offshore oil rig. Chickadee was the name of her pet parrot. She loved a song by the Reflections with the lyric "Our love's gonna be written down in history, just like Romeo and Juliet." Peanut butter was her favorite food. All manner of data. But my knowing her came in dribs and drabs, and the fact that what I found out was strictly the result of Tom's whim to bring her to Bayside began to grate on me. I needed more, needed to meet her, to make my own presence known.

How this came about was not as I might have scripted it, but imperfect means sometimes satisfy rich ends. The first of December was Tom's birthday, his eighteenth. As it happened, it fell on a Monday, the one day of the week Bayside was closed. Molly put the party together, a gesture from the heart, no doubt hoping to bring our broken, scattered, dissipating family into some semblance of a household. When she invited me, my answer was naturally no until, by chance, I heard her mention on the phone that Penny was invited. She even asked Gallagher to come. Thank God he declined. Molly and a couple of her friends baked a chocolate cake, and the old man proved himself up to the role of fatherhood by giving Tom the most extravagant present any of us had ever seen. Even our birthday boy was so overwhelmed by his generosity that he gave Dad a kiss on the forehead. Molly and I glanced at one another, embarrassed. Ours was a family that didn't touch, so this was quite a historic moment. If I hadn't spent most of the evening furtively staring at Penny, I might have thrown up my piece of cake then and there.

It was a camera, a real one. Argus C3. Black box with silver trim. Film and carrying case, too. The birthday card read, *Here's looking at you, kid! With affection and best luck for the future years, Dad and your loving brother and sister.* My head spun from the hypocrisy, the blatant nonsense of this hollow sentiment, but I put on the warm smiling face of a good brother, ignoring Tom while accepting from his girlfriend an incandescent smile of her own, complicated as always by those bittersweet eyes of hers, and said, "Let's get a picture." Tom's resentment at having to let me help him read the instructions for loading gave me more satisfaction than I could possibly express. We got it done, though, and the portrait was taken by a parent who arrived to pick up one of Molly's friends. The party was a great success, we all told Molly. That Argus was a mythical monster with a hundred eyes I kept to myself. Although the idea of stealing his camera came to me that night—Tom would never have used it anyway—I waited a week, three weeks, a full month, before removing it from his possession.

With it I began photographing Penny. At first my portraits were confined to what I could manage from various hiding places at the park. But the artificial light wasn't strong enough to capture colors and details in her face and figure, and of course I couldn't use flashbulbs, so the only decent images I managed to get were on the rare occasions when she played during the day, often weekend afternoons, and not always with Tom. I kept every shot, no matter how poor the exposure, in a cigar box stowed inside a duffel in a corner of the windmill along with the camera. During off-hours I often took the box, under my jacket, down to some remote stretch of beach and pored over the pictures with a magnifying glass I'd acquired for the purpose. Some were real prizes, more treasured, even cherished, than anything I'd collected in the past. One image became the object of infatuation, taken at great risk from an open dormer in the castle. It must have been a warm early January day, because Penny wore a light blouse which had caught a draft of wind off the ocean, ballooning the fabric forward away from her, so that from my perch looking down I shot her naked from forehead to navel, both small round breasts exposed to my lens. The photo was pretty abstract, shot at an odd angle, with her features foreshortened, a hodgepodge of fabric and flesh that would be hard to read, much less appreciate the way I did, unless you knew what you were looking at: her uncovered body laid out on that flat, shiny piece of paper. Thinking back to those heady times, I realize most pornography is very conventional, easily understood by the lusting eye, and certainly more explicit. But my innocent snapshots, taken without her knowledge or consent, seem even now to be more obscene than any professional erotic material I have since encountered.

Things developed. I made the fatal step of finding out where Penny lived. Her house was only a mile, give or take, from ours. It became my habit to go to bed with an alarm clock under my pillow, put there so that only I would hear it at midnight, or one or two in the morning, when I'd quietly get dressed and sneak out. These excursions were as haphazard as what I did at the park, if not more so. I took the camera with me, and often came home with nothing, the window to her bedroom having been dark; or worse—her lights still on, the shade drawn, and a shadow moving tantalizingly back and forth on its scrim. But there were occasional triumphs.

Milling in a hedge of jasmine one moonless night, seeing that the houses along her street were all hushed and dark, I was about to give up my siege and walk back home when I heard a car come up the block. Tom's junker coasted into dim view, parking lights showing the way. The only sound was of rubber tires softly chewing pebbles in the pavement. Retreating into the jasmine, I breathed through my mouth as slowly as I could. Penny emerged from the car many long minutes later and dashed right past me—I could smell her perfume over that of the winter flowers—and let herself into the house with hardly a sound. Good old cunning Tom must have dropped his car into neutral, as it drifted down the slanted grade until, a few doors away, he started the engine and drove away.

The lateness of the hour might have given her the idea that no one would notice if she didn't close her shades. Or maybe she was tired and forgot. Or maybe she was afraid to make any unnecessary noise in the house that would wake her parents. She lit a candle, and I saw more that night than I ever had before. To say it was a revelation, a small personal apocalypse, would be to diminish what happened to me as I watched her thin limbs naked in the anemic yellow, hidden only by the long hair she brushed before climbing into bed. How much I would have given to stretch that moment out forever. Though the camera shutter resounded in the dead calm with crisp brief explosions, I unloaded my roll. After she blew out the candle, I retreated in a panicked ecstasy, dazed as a drunk. When I woke up late the next morning, I didn't know where I was, or who.

The film came out better than I hoped—the blessing that would prove a curse, as they might have written in one of those old novels I used to read. The pimply kid who handed me my finished exposures over the counter at the camera shop, and took my crumple of dollars, asked me to wait for a minute.

"How come?" I asked.

Not looking up, he said, "The manager's in the darkroom. He wanted to have a few words with whoever picked up this roll. You got a minute?"

I smiled. "No problem."

When he disappeared into the back of the shop, I slipped out as nonchalant as possible and walked around the corner before breaking into a run, until I reached the highway and, beyond, the golf park.

Gallagher mentioned I was even earlier than usual, not looking up from his morning paper in the office. I explained I wanted to do some work on Calypso's Cave if he didn't mind. He said nothing one way or the other. Toolbox in hand, I hurried instead to the windmill, wondering what kind of imbecile Gallagher thought I was. Nothing mattered once I spread the images in a fan before me in the half-light of my refuge. Other than having to pay for them to be developed, these new trophies were just as virtuous, as pure and irreproachable, as any bird nest or seashell I'd ever collected—perhaps more innocent yet, I told myself, since nothing had been disturbed or in any way hurt by my recent activities. The camera shop had a fake name and wrong phone number. Everything was fine. To describe the photographs of Penny further would be to sully things, so I won't. She was only beautiful in her unobservance, in her not-quite-absolute aloneness.

•   •   •

Spring came and with it all kinds of migratory birds. This would normally be the season when our family meeting— which the old man called, as we might have expected, one Sunday morning—meant the usual song and dance about moving. Out of habit, if nothing else, we gathered around the kitchen table, Tom thoughtfully drumming his fingers and Molly with downcast eyes, not wanting to leave her new friends. Whatever the big guy had to say, I knew I was staying, no matter what. I was old enough to make ends meet, and meet them I would without the help of some pathetic Ojai roofer. I could live in the windmill or the castle for a while, and Gallagher would never know the difference. Eventually I'd get my own apartment. Besides, where was there left to go?

He came into the room with a grim look on his heavy brown face. "Two things," he said, sitting.

"Want some coffee, Dad?" Molly tried.

"First is that Tom is in trouble."

"What kind of trouble?" my brother asked, genuinely upset.

Our father didn't look at him when he said, "I might have thought you'd make better use of your birthday present, son."

Tom was bewildered. "I don't know what you're talking about." He looked at me and Molly for support. Neither of us had, for different reasons, anything to offer. Surely it must have occurred to my dear brother that his having misplaced his fancy birthday present and kept it a secret would come back to haunt him. On a lark, I'd started using his name when I went to different stores to have the film developed. Seemed they caught up with their culprit.

"Much more important is the second problem."

We were hushed.

"Your mother has passed away."

No words. A deep silence. Tom stared at him. Molly began to cry. I stared at my hands folded numb in my lap and tried without success to remember what she'd looked like. I had come to think of myself as having no mother, and now I truly didn't. What difference did it make? I wanted to say, but kept quiet.

"I'm going back for a couple weeks to take care of everything, make sure she's—taken care of, best as possible."

It was left at that. No further questions, nor any answers. However, when we put him on the flight in Los Angeles, Tom having driven us down, I could tell my brother remained in the dark about that first problem broached at the family meeting. Dull as he was, he did display sufficient presence of mind not to bring it up when such weightier matters were being dealt with. The old man, waving to us as he boarded his flight, looked for all the world the broken devil he was becoming, or already had become.

Things moved unequivocally after this. Mother was put to rest and her estranged husband returned from the East annihilated, poor soul. Molly withdrew from everybody but me. Penny and my brother had broken up by the time summer fog began rolling ashore in this, my year anniversary at Bayside. It fell to me, of all people, to nurture family ties, such as they were. To make, like an oriole, a work of homey art from lost ribbons, streamers, string, twigs, the jetsam of life, in which we vulnerable birds could live. I had no interest, by the way, in mourning our forsaken mother. But for a brief time, I tried to be nice to the old man and avoid Tom.

Which is not to say that my commitment to Penny changed during those transitional months. I continued to photograph her whenever I could, adept now that I had come to know her routines, day by day, week by week. Instead of hiding from her at Bayside, or downtown, or even in her neighborhood where sometimes I happened to be walking along and accidentally, as it were, bumped into her, I stopped and talked about this or that, when she wasn't in a hurry. If she asked me about Tom, I assured her that he was doing great, and changed the subject. Did the Reflections have a new hit song? I would ask. Did she want to come down to the golf course, bring some girlfriends along, do the circuit for free? She appreciated the invitation but had lost interest in games and songs and many other things. Rather than feeling defeated, I became even more devoted. My collection of photographs throughout this period of not-very-random encounters and lukewarm responses to my propositions grew by leaps and bounds. I enrolled pseudonymously in a photo club that gave me access to a darkroom, where I learned without much trouble how to develop film. Hundreds of images of Penny emerged, many of them underexposed and overexposed and visually unreadable to anyone but me. But also some of them remarkable for their poignant crudity, since by that time I'd captured her in most every possible human activity.

The inevitable happened on an otherwise dull, gray day. Late afternoon, just after sunset. The sky was like unpolished pewter, and late summer fog settled along the coast. I was down near my windmill, loitering at Gallagher's not-great expense, with nothing going on and nothing promising that evening, either, except maybe the usual jog over to Penny's to see what there was to see, when, without warning, I was caught by the collar of my shirt and thrown to the ground. I must have blurted some kind of shout or cry, but remember at first a deep exterior silence as I was dragged, my hands grasping at my throat, through a breach in the fence and out onto the sand. The pounding in my ears was deafening and I felt my face bloat. I tried kicking and twisting, but the hands that held me were much stronger than mine. I blanked out, then came to, soaked in salt water and sweat, and saw my brother's face close to mine spitting out words I couldn't hear through the tumultuous noise of crashing waves and throbbing blood. He slapped me. And slapped me backhanded again. Then pulled me up like a rough lover so that we faced each other lips-to-lips. I still couldn't hear him, though I knew what he was cursing about. Bastard must have been following me, spying, and uncovered my hideout and stash.

What bothered me most was that Tom, not I, was destroying my collection. He had no right, no right. None of the photographs that swept helter-skelter into the surf, as we fought on that dismal evening, were his to destroy. Much as I'd like to sketch those minutes in such a way that my seizing the golf ball from my shirt pocket, cramming it into his mouth, and clamping his jaw shut with all the strength I had, was a gesture meant to silence not slay him, it would be a lie.

Lie or not, Tom went down hard, gasping for air, and I went down with him, my hands like a vise on his pop-eyed face. He grabbed at his neck now, just as I had moments before, the ball lodged in the back of his throat. A wave came up over us both in a sizzling splash, knocking us shoreward before pulling us back toward the black water and heavy rollers. Everywhere around us were Penny's images, washing in and out with the tidal surges. Climbing to my feet, I watched the hungry waves carry my brother away. I looked up and down the coast and, seeing no one in the settling dark, walked in the surf a quarter mile northward, maybe farther, before crossing a grass strip which led, beneath some raddled palms, to solitary sidewalks that took me home, where I changed clothes. In no time I was at work again, my mind a stony blank.

• • •

Whether by instinct or dumb luck, my having suppressed the urge to salvage as many photos as I could that night, and carry them away with me when I left the scene where Tom and I had quarreled, stood me in good stead. Given that I had the presence of mind to polish the Argus and hide it under Tom's bed, where it would be discovered the next day by the authorities when they rummaged through his room looking for evidence that might explain what happened, I think my abandonment of my cache of portraits was genius. Clever, at least.

Clever, too, if heartfelt, was my brave comforting of Molly, who cried her eyes out, on hearing the disastrous news. And I stuck close to our paralyzed father, who walked from room to room in the bungalow we called home, all but cataleptic, mumbling to himself about the curse that followed him wherever he went. Though they had not ruled out an accidental death—he disgorged the golf ball before drowning—our father was, I understand, their suspect for months. A walk on the beach, man-to-man, a parental confrontation accidentally gone too far. In fact, their instinct, backed by the circumstantial evidence of his having been troubled by his estranged wife's demise, given to drinking too much, and his recent rage toward his eldest kid over having taken weird, even porno snapshots of his girlfriend, led them in the right direction. Just not quite. Molly and I had watertight alibis, so to speak, not that we needed them. She was with several friends watching television, and Gallagher signed an affidavit that I was working with him side by side during the time of the assault. Speculating about the gap in the fence and faint, windblown track marks in the sand, he said, "Always trespassers trying to get in for free," and, not wanting to cast aspersion on the deceased, he nevertheless mentioned that he'd seen somebody sneaking in and out of that particular breach at odd hours, and that the person looked somewhat like Tom.

Our father was eventually cleared. Turned out Sad Sack was

a covert Casanova with a lady friend in Ojai. This explained why our annual rousting had not taken place. He need not have been shy about it, as his children would prove to like her; Shannon is the name. Whether Gallagher'd been so used to me going through my paces—efficient, thorough, devoted—that he improved on an assumption by making it a sworn fact; or whether he really thought he saw me at work that night, ubiquitous ghost that I was; or whether he was covering for me, not wanting to lose the one sucker who understood Bayside and could keep it going when he no longer cared to, I will never know. Gallagher himself would perish a year later of a heart attack, in our small office, slumped in his cane chair beneath those pictures of stars who gazed down at him with ruthless benevolence.

The initial conclusions reached in Tom's murder investigation proved much the same as the inconclusive final one. They had been thorough, questioned all of Tom's friends. Certainly Penny might have wanted him dead given how humiliated, how mortified, she was by the photographs that had been recovered along the coast. Asked to look through them, she did the best she could. While she did seem to think Tom had been with her on some occasions when this or that shot was taken—they were all so awful, so invasive, so perverse—she couldn't be sure. Given that he was present in none of the exposures, that the camera used was his, and so forth, there was no reason to look elsewhere for the photographer. Penny had a motive, but also an alibi, like everyone else.

None of it mattered, finally, because good came from the bad. Our family was closer than ever, and Dad seemed, after a few months of dazed mourning, to shake off his long slump. He brought his Ojai bartender girlfriend around sometimes, and Molly made dinner. Penny, too, was transformed by the tragedy. Before my watchful eyes she changed into an even gentler being, more withdrawn than before, yes, but composed and calm—some might say remote, but they'd be wrong, not knowing her like I did. It was as if she changed from a color photograph to black-and-white. I didn't mind the shift. To the contrary.

●　●　●

The morning Penny came down to Bayside to speak with me was lit by the palest pink air and softest breeze of late autumn. I'd been the model of discretion in the several years that followed Tom's passing, keeping tabs on Penny out of respect, really, making sure she was doing all right in the wake of what must have been quite a shock to her. Never overstepping my bounds—at least not in such a way as she could possibly know. Meantime, I had matured. Molly told me I'd become a handsome dog, as she put it. Her girlfriends had crushes on me, she said. I smiled and let them play the golf course gratis. Why not? Then Penny turned up, unexpected, wanting to give me something.

"For your birthday," she said, handing me a small box tied with a white ribbon. There was quite a gale blowing off the ocean that day and her hair buffeted about her head. With her free hand she drew a long garland of it, fine as corn silk, away from her mouth and melancholy eyes. It was a gesture of absolute purity. Penny was a youthful twenty-one, and I an aged nineteen.

I must have looked surprised, because she said, "You look like you forgot."

She followed me into the office, where we could get out of

the wind. All the smugly privileged faces in Gallagher's nostalgic gallery had been long since removed from the walls and sent off to his surviving relatives, who, not wanting much to bother with their inheritance of a slowly deteriorating putt-putt golf park, allowed me to continue in my capacity as Bayside steward and manager. Like their deceased uncle—a childless bachelor whose sole concern had been this fanciful (let me admit) dump—they thought I was far older than nineteen. The lawyer who settled his estate looked into the records, saw on my filed application that I was in my mid-twenties, and further saw that Gallagher wanted me to continue there as long as it was my wish, and thus and so. A modest check went out each month to the estate, the balance going to moderate upkeep and my equally moderate salary. What did I care? My needs were few. I spent warm nights down here in my castle, or the windmill, and was always welcome at home, where the food was free. And now, as if in a dream, here was my Penny, bearing a gift.

I undid the ribbon and tore away the paper. It was a snow globe with a hula dancer whose hips gyrated in the sparkling blizzard after I gave it a good shake.

"How did you know?" I asked, smiling at her smiling face.

"You like it?"

"I love it."

"Molly told me this was your new thing."

"Kind of stupid, I guess. But they're like little worlds you can disappear into if you stare at them long enough."

"I don't think it's stupid."

"Yours goes in the place of honor," I said, taking the gift over to my shelves lined with dozens of others, where I installed the hula girl at the very heart of the collection.

Penny peered up and down the rows, her face as luminous as I've ever seen it, beaming like a child. She plucked one down and held it to the light. "Can I?" she asked. I told her sure and watched as she shook the globe and the white flakes flew round and round in the glassed-in world. She gazed at the scene within while I gazed at her. One of those moments which touch on perfection.

"Very cool," she whispered, as if in a reverie. "But isn't it a shame that it's always winter?"

"I don't really see them as snowflakes," I said.

"What, then?"

Penny turned to me and must have glimpsed something different in the way I was looking at her, since she glanced away and commented that no one was playing today. The wind, I told her. Sand gets in your eyes and makes the synthetic carpet too rough to play on. In fact, there wasn't much reason to keep the place open, I continued, and asked her if she'd let me drive her up to Santa Barbara for the afternoon, wander State Street together, get something to eat. I was not that astonished when she agreed. Cognizant or not, she'd been witness to the character, the nature, the spirit of my gaze, had the opportunity to reject what it meant. By accepting my invitation she was in a fell stroke accepting me.

"You can have it if you want," I offered, taking her free hand and nodding at the snow globe.

"No, it belongs with the others." She stared out the window while a fresh gale whipped up off the ocean, making the panes shiver and chatter as grains of sand swirled around us. I looked past her silhouette and remarked that the park looked like a great snow globe out there. How perverse it was of me to want to ask her, just then, if she missed Tom sometimes. Instead, I told her we ought to get going, but not before I turned her chin toward me with trembling fingers and gently kissed her.

As we drove north along the highway, the sky cleared, admitting a sudden warm sun into its blue. "Aren't you going to tell me?" she asked, as if out of that blue, and for a brief, ghastly moment I thought I'd been found out and was being asked to confess. Seeing my bewilderment, Penny clarified, "What the snowflakes are, if they're not snowflakes?"

I shifted my focus from the road edged by flowering hedges and eucalyptus over to Penny, and back again, suddenly wanting to tell her everything, pour my heart out to her. I wanted to tell her how I had read somewhere that in some cultures people refuse to have their photographs taken, believing the camera steals their souls. Wanted to tell her that when Tom demolished my collection of adoring images of her, not only did he seal his own fate, but engendered hers. I wished I could tell her how, struggling with him in waves speckled with swirling photographs, I was reminded of a snow globe. And I did want to answer her question, to say that the flakes seemed to me like captive souls floating around hopelessly in their little glass cages, circling some frivolous god, but I would never admit such nonsense. Instead, I told her she must have misunderstood and, glancing at her face bathed in stormy light, knew in my heart that later this afternoon, maybe during the night, I would be compelled to finish the destructive work my foolish brother had begun.

GRADUATION DAY

Ian Rankin

We flew into Scotland on some carrier called Icelandair, which was a good and a very bad start to proceedings. Good, in that I hadn't booked the flights: our travel arrangements had been Mike's responsibility. During the drive to the airport, he'd kept telling us how he'd got this "great deal": Boston to Glasgow via Reykjavík, business class, of course. Their idea of business-class food was raw fish—lots of raw fish.

"Where am I, Japan?" the Boss kept saying.

So the good news was, Mike had not endeared himself to our employer. The bad news was the fish.

There were four of us. Mike and the Boss, plus Pete and me. You better call me Micky. Or if you prefer a little formality, Mr. Dolenz, seeing how he was my favorite Monkee. I loved that show, still try to catch the reruns and have most episodes on tape. What follows is by way of a true story, with names and maybe one or two incidents changed to protect the guilty. So there's me—that's Micky—plus Mike and Pete. Then there's the Boss, of course, but I can't bring myself to call him

Davy. "Davy" just isn't his style. So maybe he should stay "the Boss."

Mike thinks he's the suave one, Mr. Sophistication. He does his job, but always with the air of thinking there could be something better for him out there someday. He thinks he's the brains of the outfit, too. The Boss's right-hand man.

Pete is just the opposite. He wears expensive clothes, but they don't sit right on him, and I swear, he buys a new pair of shoes? They're scuffed in the first hour. It was the same when we were kids: new pants, new shoes, Pete had worn them in big-time by sundown. Pete is not overendowed in the intellectual department, but he is the approximate size of an abattoir door. Even the business-class seat proved a little troublesome for him, and when the steward turned up with the food, Pete was the usual soul of diplomacy.

"I can't eat that crap," he said. Instead, he gorged on the snacks and some fresh fruit, the latter being maybe the first time I ever saw him eat something that didn't come in a wrapper or container of some kind.

"Careful, Pete," I told him. "That stuff's actually good for you."

He had the headphones on and couldn't hear me.

Meantime, I tried the fish, but only when the Boss wasn't looking, and I have to tell you, it was fine, and not even all of it was raw. I read in the magazine that it was traditional, but kept the news to myself. Mike, meantime, who'd made sure he was sitting next to the Boss, kept staring down at his own plate, knowing if he ate any he'd start getting looks from his neighbor. Whenever Mike glanced over in my direction, I made sure I was chewing.

We landed in Scotland late afternoon, to discover that our

final destination, the ancient city of St. Andrews, wasn't anywhere nearby. In fact, it was on the other side of the country
and, studying the map we'd been given at the information desk,
was actually in the middle of nowhere.

"We'll take a cab anyway," the Boss said. But Mike had another suggestion.

"What if we rent a car? We need transportation while we're
there, right?"

"We can take cabs."

"What if there aren't any?"

"Jesus, Mike, it's got this huge university. It's the home of
golf. We're not talking some hick town here."

"Actually," the woman at the information desk piped up in
a heavy Scotch accent, "St. Andrews isn't all that big. I went
there on holidays once when I was a child. Just a few thousand
people . . ."

Well, that's what I think she said. We just stared at her, then
at each other, shrugged eventually. As we moved off, searching
for Avis or Hertz, the Boss mumbled:

"We're not still in Iceland, are we?"

"The signs are all in English," I pointed out.

"Yeah? Then what language was she speaking back there?"

It was raining outside, not torrential but pretty good. We'd
got through Customs and Passport Control, so should have
been starting to relax, but we knew we couldn't do that till we
were on the road. I was pushing one cart. It had my bags, plus
Mike's and the Boss's. Pete had another cart to himself, two
cases on it. Just clothes and stuff, unless someone got real
nosy and happened to notice the weight. Then maybe they'd
take their search a little more seriously and find the false sides
and our personal firearms. Mike had taken care of the auto,

and we were loading the cases into the back. Bit of a squeeze in the trunk.

"Biggest one they had," Mike said, but the Boss's look said he had work to do before he got back on his good side.

"Got a great deal on it, too," he added.

"Probably means it runs on raw fish," the Boss grumbled.

Not that the Boss was tight with money or anything, but the business hadn't had its best year: lots of competition from new start-ups, established suppliers and clients a little rocky. Lean times made for financial constraints. The Boss had talked of traveling to Scotland alone. It took a lot of persuading that this was not a good idea. All those new competitors meant you never knew when someone might decide to take a try at whacking you. The farther the Boss traveled from home turf, the greater the risk. This was the argument we used. Then he balked at the idea of four of us.

"Who you going to leave behind?" I'd told him. His look had given me my answer: Pete. My own look had asked a silent question: what if we need a fall guy? If there was trouble ahead, a patsy could always come in useful.

Back when Mike had been getting us transportation, I'd gone to the head, returning by way of a little book and newspaper concession where I'd spent the first of my British money on a guidebook. As we drove slowly out of the airport, I started to read it.

"They drive on the left here," I reminded Mike.

"Contrary sons of bitches."

The rental desk had provided another map, and the Boss was trying to make sense of it. He passed it back to me.

"Designated navigator," he growled.

So it was me, Micky Dolenz, who ensured the show went

on, guiding Mike as he gripped the steering wheel like he was trying to choke a repayment out of someone.

· · ·

We didn't do too badly in the end, though the roads left much to be desired. The last twenty, thirty miles, it was two-lane stuff, tractors and delivery trucks, and all these switchbacks. The Boss kept saying he should have brought the motion-sickness bag from the airplane. When I looked over toward Pete, who was sharing the backseat with me, he was gazing out of his window.

"Fields and trees," he said quietly, as if he knew I was watching. "That's all there is out there."

And then suddenly we started seeing coastline. "That's St. Andrews, gentlemen," I told them. Then I started reading from the guidebook. The Boss turned in his seat.

"It's not a city?"

"Just barely qualifies as a town," I replied.

Mike was shaking his head. "I don't like this."

"You don't like what?"

"Middle of nowhere . . . small town . . . We're going to stand out."

The Boss stabbed a fat finger into Mike's ribs. "The travel was your responsibility. How come you couldn't do what Micky did, buy yourself a guidebook? That way we'd've known what we were dealing with."

"Forewarned is forearmed," I agreed. When Mike looked at me in the rearview, I knew he wanted to give me a forearm of his own, right across my mouth.

Our hotel was the Old Course, and was easy to find, practically the first thing you saw as you drove into town. When we were shown to our rooms, Pete went to the window.

"Nice grounds," he said.

"That's the golf course, sir," the bellhop informed him.

And Jesus, I suppose it was beautiful—if you like that sort of thing. Me, I prefer the pool hall: cigar smoke and brightly lit tables, jokes and side bets. That's pretty much how I got started in the business. By the time I was seventeen, the Boss—then just approaching forty—said I'd spent so much time in pool halls, I could run one standing on my head. So he gave me one of his to manage, and Pete, who'd always hung around with me, hung around until he was part of the business, too.

"How could we have lived so long and not seen this, Micky?" Pete asked as the bellhop left with some more of my British money. Something else I'd learned in my guidebook: they didn't like it in Scotland if you called them English. "British" was okay, mostly, though the book's author had hinted that things might change with the Scottish Parliament and everything.

"I don't know, Pete," I said. "Boston's not so bad."

He looked at me. "It's not the world, though."

"Only world you and me are likely to know, pal," I told him.

Just before dinner, I took a look in the hotel shop and came up with a couple of local books, one about golf and one about the town. This last had a good long section on the university, so I was able to tell the Boss a few things as we ate. There seemed to be a lot of our fellow countrymen in the dining room, and during the course of the meal, at one point or another, practically every one of them made the same gesture: gripping an invisible club and swinging it. They were illustrating some smart play they'd made, or maybe some unsmart one.

We were the odd ones out. I noticed there was almost a uniform: either loud sports shirts or woolen V-necks. We weren't dressed that way. We were dressed normally.

"That's interesting, Micky," the Boss kept saying. At first I thought he was being ironic, but he wasn't: he wanted to know what I knew about the place. Pete wasn't taking much of it in. He kept craning his neck, trying to see past the other diners, trying to spot more countryside through the darkening windows.

Mike arrived just as we were being served coffee. "I don't like it," he said. He was in full bodyguard mode now, and had forgone dinner to "check out" the town. "It's a security nightmare," he added. "Know how far the nearest hospital is?"

"For the love of God, Mike," the Boss snarled. "There's not going to be any hit!"

"Couldn't pick a better place for one," Mike argued.

"This is a family thing, Mike," the Boss went on. "I appreciate your concern, but do us all a favor and *lighten up!*" The Boss made sure his words had hit home, then tossed his napkin onto the table. "Now, you going to eat something or what?"

But Mike shook his head. Bodyguards didn't have time for thoughts of food. Instead, he concentrated on giving the other diners steely glances, which they, having drunk wine and port and whiskey, didn't even notice. Me, I had the inkling Mike would be placing an order with room service before the night was out.

It had been Mike's job also to book the accommodations, which was why I was sharing with Pete down the hall while the Boss and Mike had their own rooms next door to one another.

"Some mix-up in the reservations," was Mike's explanation, and now that the hotel was full, we couldn't do much about it.

"Never mind, Mike," I said, "at least the room for two saves the business some money, right?"

"Right," he said, unsure how serious I was being.

The hotel was full not just because St. Andrews remained, as the book said, "the Mecca of golf," but because it was graduation time at the university, and this, I guessed, was where the richer parents, people like the Boss himself, stayed while they were in town for the festivities, festivities which were due to begin the following morning with some service in the chapel.

The Boss fully intended to be present at this service, since his daughter would be in the choir. Even though it meant us rising at what our body clocks would tell us was something like three in the morning.

Yes, we were in St. Andrews because the Boss's only child was graduating with honors or distinction or something in some subject or other.

"If only her mother could have been here," the Boss said, enjoying a brandy after his coffee. Then he stared off into the distance, maybe thinking pleasant thoughts from the past, thoughts of the way his wife, Edie, had been . . . up until the time she'd run off with her tennis coach. We'd never been able to trace the pair of them, or the few hundred thou Edie had "misappropriated" from the business in the form of cash and jewelry.

"We get lucky, maybe she'll turn up," Mike said, patting his jacket. It was Hugo Boss, the styling described as "unstructured." Fashion was definitely on Mike's side, helping disguise the bulge of a shoulder holster.

"You not drinking, Micky?" the Boss asked. I shook my head. Before setting off from Boston, I'd read a magazine article about surviving long hauls. Lay off the booze and take some melatonin before bed. The magazine had been left behind by someone in the pool hall. It's amazing the things I've learned down the years in places like that.

* * *

Next day Pete's jaw dropped further when he saw the medieval chapel, probably the oldest thing he'd ever seen in his life. I thought he was going to break his neck, staring up at the ceiling and the stained-glass windows. He'd already been out exploring before breakfast and told me about it afterward in our room. I'd offered him the guidebook, but he'd shaken his head. Never a great reader.

The service wasn't too long. A couple of hymns and two reverend gentlemen in charge. They both made speeches. You could tell the university professors: they were dressed in robes, and we all had to stand while they were led into the chapel. The rest of the congregation appeared to be students and parents. The choir was upstairs, positioned in front of the organ. Beautiful music; I couldn't make out Wilma's voice, but I could see her. She had a cape on, too; all the choristers did. She smiled down at her father, and he smiled back. There were actually tears in his eyes, and I handed him a fresh handkerchief. Mike didn't notice: too busy eyeing the crowd.

Afterward, we waited outside for Wilma. The day was clouding over, growing cool. Wilma came around the side of the chapel and broke into a sprint, nearly pushing her father over as she hugged him.

"Dad, I'm so sorry I couldn't come to the hotel last night."

"Hey, you had to practice, I understand." He pushed her back a little so that he could look at her. "And you were fantastic. I was so proud of you, Wilma."

There was one of the other choristers standing just behind her. He turned his head to Mike and offered a smile. Mike scowled back, perhaps hoping to persuade him to be on his way. Wilma suddenly remembered he was there.

"Oh, Dad, I want you to meet a friend of mine. This is Freddy."

Freddy had thick dark hair and a pale, round face; looked a bit like he'd walked out of a sixties movie set in swinging London. But then he opened his mouth.

"A real pleasure to meet you, sir."

"Fellow American, eh?" the Boss said, shaking Freddy's hand.

"Freddy's graduating, too," Wilma explained.

"Well, congratulations, son."

Only now did Wilma seem to notice the rest of us. We got our pecks on the cheek and a few words. I'd wondered about Wilma and Mike once or twice, but she didn't seem to treat him any different from me or Pete.

"We better go get changed," Freddy told her. She looked down at her robe and smiled.

"See you for lunch, Dad," she said, hugging the Boss again.

"Twelve-fifteen at the hotel," her father reminded her. She nodded. Wilma's graduation ceremony was midafternoon, followed by a garden party and something called Beating the Retreat. Next day there was a graduates' luncheon, parents invited. We were booked on a flight out first thing the morning after that.

After Wilma and Freddy had gone, the Boss turned to us. "I don't need you guys till later." He looked at Mike. "And I certainly don't want to be sharing a table and my daughter with you over lunch."

Mike nodded. "We'll take one of the other tables."

But the Boss shook his head. "You'll make yourselves scarce, understood?"

So that was us, dismissed. "I don't like it," Mike said as soon as he had me on my own. "It's just the moment they'd choose for a hit."

"Can we skip to the next track on the CD?" I asked.

"You mean you're going to go along with this?" Mike's eyes narrowed, as though he thought I might be cooking something up.

"Mike, we've flown halfway round the globe to be here. I'd like to see a bit of the place."

"Sightseeing? What's to see?"

"Open your eyes, Mike."

"My eyes are open, friend. It's you that's walking around blind."

I just shook my head. "I want something to tell the guys back home."

"Such as?"

I shrugged. "I don't know . . . Such as playing a round of golf at St. Andrews." Until then, the thought hadn't occurred to me, but Mike's disbelieving laughter sealed it for me. And when I suggested it to Pete, he was more than agreeable. Which left Mike out in the cold.

"Well," he said, "I wasn't too comfortable about that Freddy guy. Think I might do some background . . ." Like he was still in the neighborhood and only had to tap a few skulls to get some answers.

Meantime, Pete and I took a stroll down to the golf course. The hotel had already explained that St. Andrews was a public course, and probably not expensive by American standards, but that its popularity was a problem. Too many people wanted to play, which translated as a raffle for the day's start times. However, if we wanted to risk it . . . In any event, a few showers seemed to have kept some people away and there were a couple of cancellations. We managed a slot late afternoon, which gave us time to visit the pro shop.

Pete was disappointed to find that "pro" was short for "golf professional" and that all they were going to sell him there were clubs, shoes and stuff. His second disappointment came when he discovered there were no plus fours. I think the cold and the rain were getting to him, because by the time we'd rented our clubs and shoes, and bought a tartan cap apiece along with some balls and tees, he was in one of his fouler moods.

"Ever played this game?" I asked him as he hauled our clubs—one set between us—toward the first tee.

"Watched it on TV," he replied.

"Then you're practically an expert."

Now, if you've ever been to a golf course, you'll know that the pockets are a good distance apart, and not with only flat green baize between them. The wind was whipping across us, and the little boxes on my scorecard didn't make any sense. As the gulls screeched overhead, I remembered that there was some ornithological aspect to the game: birdies and eagles and stuff. I also knew that the wooden clubs were for the initial tee drive, and that a putter was what you used in miniature golf.

"You don't know the game either, huh?" Pete said.

"Always meant to learn."

"Well, I can't think of a better time or place."

"You okay, Big Pete? You seem a bit down."

He seemed about to say something, then just shook his

head and mumbled something about jet lag. We were at the first tee now. Some players just ahead of us were marching up the fairway.

"They got wheels with their golf bags," Pete complained.

"Wheels were extra. You tote them the first nine, I'll tote them back, okay?"

"You mean we're playing sixteen holes?"

"Eighteen, Pete," I corrected him.

"We'll be here all day."

"Fortunately that's exactly how long we've got."

He bent down and pushed his tee into the turf. "I wanted to see the harbor again."

"Plenty of time for that," I promised, following his example with the tee and the ball. Pete was selecting one of the two woods. "Don't we wait for them to get out of range?" I asked, pointing to the golfers ahead of us. Pete shook his head and got ready to swing his club.

Now, some might put it down to beginner's luck, but me, I think it was a force much darker. Because Pete whacked that ball and it sailed up into the sky, perfectly straight and long. Very long.

I traced its trajectory with my eyes and watched it bounce off the head of one of the other players. As the man dropped like a stone, I watched Pete raise a hand, cupping it to his mouth and hollering, *"Fore!"* Then he turned to me and smiled. "That's what you do."

The player was being helped to his feet by his two playing partners. I couldn't make out their faces at this distance, but they were wearing loud sweaters. Also, they were looking at us. As I say, the pockets are pretty far apart, and we had to wait awhile for the men to reach us. The guy Pete had whacked, he'd had a lot of time to calm down during that walk. He didn't calm down, though; he just looked angrier and angrier. Even the sight of Big Pete didn't cause him to rethink any strategy he might have formed. There was a lump on the top of his head that looked like one of the gulls had laid an egg in the nest of his hair. He was swearing at us from about eighty yards out, his fellow players just a few steps behind.

"You stupid . . . I swear I'm gonna . . . of all the . . ." But then he stopped. And if we'd been walking, we'd probably have stopped, too.

Because we knew him, same as he knew us.

"How you doing, Blue?" I asked.

"Unbelievable," Blue said with a scowl. I didn't think he was answering my question.

• • •

They were Beating the Retreat when we caught up with the Boss. It was on the lawn in one of the college quadrangles and seemed to consist of some bagpipes and drums. Guests were huddled beneath umbrellas.

"Where the hell did you get those hats?" the Boss scowled.

"They were Mike's idea," I lied, seeing his displeasure. "He said we'd blend in more. Listen, Boss, we've got some bad news."

"Bad news," Pete agreed, drawing out the first word.

"What's wrong?"

I led the Boss a bit farther away from the merry sound of cats being skinned alive. "Guess who we just bumped into on the golf course?"

"Tell me."

So I told him. Blue had been about to enjoy a round with

his colleagues Buck and Manolito. Turned out that their boss, Big John, was in town, too.

"That's too big a coincidence," the Boss said.

I had to agree with him; thing was, I didn't know what else to say. But then Mike came up, looking feverish. "You'll never guess. I could give you a thousand years, and you'd still never guess."

It seemed that his inquiries had borne fruit.

"You've discovered that Freddy is Big John's son?" I told him. He looked thunderstruck.

"Just as well you're not the betting type, Mikey," Pete told him with a grin.

• • •

Okay, I need to explain a couple of things here. One is that the mob no longer exists. It was destroyed in a series of high-profile court cases. Everyone saw it happen on TV, so it must be true. The cops and journalists turned their attentions to other criminal gangs. I say this to make you aware that when my boss and Big John met that evening, it was just two businessmen having a chat. Though Big John operated out of Miami, the two men (having so many interests in common, after all) knew one another, had met many times in the past.

This leads me to my second point, which is that while Big John and my boss know one another, this is not to say that they are exactly on friendly terms.

The meeting took place on neutral territory: a disused putting green down by the seashore. Pete knew the place, having passed it during one of his exploratory walks. There were the eight of us. Blue had his head bandaged. Mike asked which doctor he'd used, but didn't get a reply. Our two employers walked toward one another and exchanged a brief hug.

"Funny we have to come all this way to meet again," Big John said.

"Yeah, some coincidence," my boss replied. "I didn't know Freddy was here."

"Likewise myself with Wilma."

"What's he studying?"

"Economics. And Wilma?"

"I don't know what it is exactly," the Boss conceded. "It's got the words 'Moral' and 'Philosophy' in it."

"So what's she gonna do now? M.B.A.? Harvard?"

A shrug. "She says she wants to teach."

"Teach?" Big John frowned. "Teach what?"

"Teach the thing she's been taught."

Big John smiled. "No disrespect to Wilma, but that sounds like some sweet scam."

I could see the Boss bristle at this. "So Freddy's going to Harvard?"

"That's the plan."

"Not according to what Wilma told me," the Boss said.

Big John opened his arms. "That's why we had to meet, sort things out."

"Wilma tells me they're in love. They're already living together." Another shrug. "The kids are happy, I say let them stay happy."

Big John's eyes grew colder. "And I say not."

"I hope we're not going to have a problem here," my boss said quietly. I could see Blue and Mike sizing one another up. Same with Manolito and Pete. Buck . . . well, I've always sort of liked Buck, few times we've met. The pair of us were too busy listening to do any measuring. But it was Buck who made the outrageous suggestion.

"If you don't mind me interrupting," he began, "we've already got Blue here needing some sort of recompense, not so much for his injuries as for losing out on that round of golf."

"What are you saying?" Big John asked.

"I'm saying it's not unknown for either of you two gentlemen to enjoy a bet. We could incorporate that bet into a game of golf. That's all."

Big John looked at my boss. "How about it? I know you can play."

"You against me?"

Big John shook his head. "All of us. Make it a bit more interesting."

If the Boss had looked at me, he'd have seen me shaking my head. These guys lived the year round in *Florida*. Nothing for them to do all day but drive practice balls and Porsches. But my boss, he wasn't looking at anyone but Big John. Then he thrust out his hand.

"You got yourself a bet," he said.

• • •

Mike spent the rest of the night on the phone, asking his contacts back home about the handicap Big John and his men might be expected to play off. Mike and the Boss could play, but as for Pete and me . . . well, you saw us in action, right? When Mike got off the phone, he had copious notes.

"Big John is a 7-, 8-handicapper, Blue's a 5."

"Meaning what?" I asked.

Mike rolled his eyes. "Meaning they'll expect to play only that many shots over par."

"Each hole?" But Mike didn't even grace that one with a response.

The Boss was thoughtful. "I'm a 4, you're a . . . what, Mike? An 8?"

"A 7," Mike stressed. He studied his notes again. "Manolito's played before, but never really got into the game. But Buck can play. So they've got three players against our two."

"Hey," I interrupted, "you didn't see Pete's tee shot. We may have a natural here."

"And how about you, Micky?" the Boss said. "You gonna let the team down or what? Get back to that practice room."

The practice room was our hotel room. Both beds had been hauled out into the corridor, giving us space for a few swings. Some golf pro had been found, and money had changed hands. When I went back into the room, he was helping Pete with his grip. This had been going on for the best part of two hours. I shook my head and went back into the corridor. Wilma was standing there.

"This isn't the way things work anymore," she said, her eyes sad.

"Your father knows that, Wilma."

"They can't stop us from living together, loving one another, by playing a round of goddamned golf!"

"Your father knows that, too: didn't he tell you as much?" I knew he had. I'd been there at the time. "But the thing is, it's like a gauntlet was laid down, you know? Your father had to pick it up."

"Not for me, he didn't."

"You're right, he's doing this for himself." I put my hands out, palms upward. "But maybe for all of us, too."

"It won't change anything," she said.

I nodded, telling her she was right. But I knew I was lying. If we lost tomorrow, Freddy would be spirited away somewhere, some university in the boondocks. He'd be where Wilma couldn't find him. Watching the tears form in her eyes, I knew we had to win. I walked back into the practice room and picked up one of the books on golfing rules and etiquette.

If I'm being honest, I was looking for a loophole.

• • •

My last hope was, we wouldn't get a tee time. But we did: early morning, right after breakfast. The format was simple: each team member took a turn at hitting his team's ball. We also agreed to make it the best of nine holes rather than the full eighteen. Big John teed off for his side, the Boss for ours. As they walked down the fairway afterward, the Boss asked Big John where he was berthed.

"Rented a beautiful big house just outside town. All services provided. How about you?"

"The Old Course Hotel."

"What's it like?"

"Pretty good."

"I'm sure it is," Big John said, his tone almost adding the words "for a hotel."

Pete took the second stroke and overhit it. That was when we decided he should maybe tee off at the second hole.

When my turn came, I had to chip onto the green, but rolled it right off again and into a bunker.

"Just as well we're playing hole by hole," Mike hissed at me afterward as we walked to the second tee. "We lost that one by three strokes."

By dint of a massive tee shot from Pete, we managed to

draw the next hole. Then at the third, Manolito, who was losing more interest in the game the farther we moved from the town's female population, put the ball into some deep rough, from which it took Big John's players two more strokes to get it back onto the fairway. Although we took three putts, we still won by a single stroke, Big John's own massive saving putt stopping about an inch and a half from the hole.

It was all square as we walked to the fourth. "Still shooting pool?" Buck asked me. I nodded. "Then it's just as well it's golf we're playing."

I smiled. "How about you, Buck? Life treating you fair?"

"It's tough all over," he said. But I knew it wasn't. Miami didn't have the same problems Boston did. Big John had made peace with the Cubans. This had allowed him certain avenues of diversification. First time my boss and Big John had met, they'd done so in a state of parity, a state which could no longer be said to exist.

Blue played a spectacular 3-iron at the fourth. I knew the clubs now, thanks to a long night with the pro. I could even use them, in a rudimentary fashion. But if Pete's deficiency was his inability to hit the ball at anything short of full power, then mine was more a matter of accuracy deficiency. That ball . . . it seemed to have a mind of its own, I swear. A putt of fifteen feet ended up curving away from the hole until it came to rest nine or ten feet to the left of where I'd been aiming.

"It's called the run of the green," Buck told me between holes. "A local caddie, someone who's played the course all his life, they know it like they know the creases, slopes and hangs of their wife's body."

That's when I knew Big John's team hadn't spent the previous night with a pro, but with a caddie . . .

We drew the fourth, lost the fifth and sixth. Buck had an elegant, easy swing, which I tried copying until Mike hissed that I looked like I was auditioning for Fred Astaire. Mike himself hadn't played a bad stroke yet, said something about teaching Tiger Woods everything he knew, then made the slightest adjustment to his leather driving glove.

When we won the seventh, it was in part because a cell phone went off just as Blue was taking his shot. The cell belonged to Big John, so they could hardly complain when Blue sliced his stroke and the ball got lost in more thick rough. The wind was growing stronger, and our tactic of having Pete tee off was beginning to lose efficacy. The problem was, he hit the ball too high, where the wind caught it and toyed with it, sending it literally off course. But at the eighth we were saved by another glorious shot from Mike, who took a 4-iron into the rough and brought the ball out and in a nice line with the pin. Manolito, meantime, had contrived to find a stream which, according to Mike, shouldn't have been a problem until the back nine. So they dropped a shot, and Buck had to play across the line of a foursome who were on their way home. They looked like locals to me, and just shook their heads. They'd probably seen lousier shots in their time, and maybe worse etiquette, too.

It ended up all square as we went to the ninth.

"Just the way I like my baseball," I told Buck.

"Except when it's the Red Sox, right?"

I couldn't disagree with him there.

The Boss hit a sweet tee shot, then reached into the pocket of the golf bag and brought out a pakamac. The rain was coming down now. Someone had once told me they did most of their business on the golf course. Well, that's what we were doing out there, too. No place for small talk. My own short exchanges with Buck had earned frowns from both captains.

Pete, despite our encouragement, hit the ball another mighty swipe which sent it sailing past the green and off to the right. Somehow he missed two bunkers and left Mike a manageable chip, which he decided to take with an 8-iron. It landed sweetly about three feet from the hole, but the ball had arranged for some spin, and rolled back a further five or so feet. An eight-foot putt. Buck, meantime, had putted to within four feet of the hole, only to watch Big John's tap-in roll around the lip of the cup and pop back out again.

So instead of putting to save the match, suddenly I had a chance to win it. An eight-foot putt in the wind and rain, here on the Old Course at St. Andrews. There was no pressure on me, no pressure at all. The pin was already out. I walked around the other side of the hole and crouched down, measured the line with my putter, the way I'd seen it done. Then back around to my ball again, crouching again, closing one eye to peer at the lie of the green, those curves and slopes . . . And something happened. The closer I got to the ground, the easier the putt looked. They started laughing at me as I angled my head, my hair getting wet as it touched the shorn grass.

"He going to knock it in with his nose or what?" Big John asked.

I got up again, brushed myself off and smiled back at him. "It's regarded as good manners to keep silent during a player's stroke," I recited.

"Why, you little punk . . ."

But the others could see that I had a point. Blue touched his boss on the arm, and Big John quieted, grinning a wider grin when he remembered that he was about to win. Me, I just looked at Buck and gave him a wink, then got down on my knees behind the ball, shimmying back until I could stretch out full length. I turned the putter around and imagined the golf ball was a straight black into the center pocket, the putter's rubberized grip a freshly chalked cue tip. I slid it back and forth a few times, until it felt right in my hands. Adjusted my elbow ever so slightly . . .

Big John was complaining now, his voice rising. I ignored him, ignored everything but the pot. Hit the ball cleanly and watched it roll into the cup. As I got to my feet, there was laughter. Mike was patting me on the back. The Boss was clapping. Pete sent one of the clubs spinning dangerously through the air.

I walked across to where Big John was still scowling, still yelling that I was a goddamned cheat.

"Look at the rules," I said. "Or ask a good caddie."

Then I went back to my team to celebrate.

• • •

Of course, by the time we'd finished that round, Wilma and Freddy, as I'd thought they might, had fled: just packed their things and gone. They'd turn up sooner or later, I didn't doubt, once the dust had settled.

We were due to leave before dawn next morning: the long drive back to the airport. But that didn't stop us partying into the wee sma' hours: champagne and malt whiskey, old stories and even a couple of songs. The Boss looked at me with new respect, and I got the feeling maybe I was about to graduate to something better . . . When I woke up, Pete was standing by the window, just staring out at the dark and silent world. No sodium glare, no sirens.

"You okay, old pal?" I asked him.

"Never better," he assured me.

Next time I awoke, he was gone. We drove out of St. Andrews without him. There was no question of us hanging around, looking for him. The Boss wanted to get back home and start spreading the word about the game. Besides, as I tried to explain, I didn't think Pete wanted to be found. There was a lot of world out there for him to explore. Me, I had a warm pool table waiting, and maybe a story of my own to tell.

LUCY HAD A LIST

John Sandford

This was the way you won the Open.

This was the way you won a million dollars.

This is what you *did*.

Lucy had a list, and she was sticking to it.

Every morning, in the back bedroom, braced on the tinny, oil-canning floor, looking into a full-length mirror she'd bought at the Wal-Mart, Lucy did a hundred grips and a hundred turns. She'd grip the club and check alignment, start the turn and check her intermediate position in the mirror. When she was satisfied, she'd continue, let her wrists cock, hold at the top and check the final position. Then she'd start over.

She was on the eighty-fourth turn when the screaming started. The screaming didn't affect the drill. Strange sounds came off a golf course, and besides, she'd do a hundred reps if the trailer burned down around her. At ninety-nine she hadn't even paused to look out the blinds.

On her hundredth turn, she checked her form in the mirror, nodded at herself and relaxed. She was a middle-sized girl, lean from walking and working out, deeply tanned, dishwater blonde with a pixie cut. She was sweating a little, and wiped the side of her nose on her shirtsleeve. She was dressed in a navy-blue golf shirt and khaki shorts, with a Ping golf hat. Her blond ponytail was threaded through the back of the hat.

She put the weighted club in the corner of the bedroom and walked down the central hall to the kitchen. Her mom was digging in a toaster with a fork, talking to it around a lit Marlboro, letting it know: "You piece of shit-ass junk, you let that outta there."

By some mistake, the television was turned off, so the screaming outside sounded even louder than it had in the back. Mom, still talking sticky-lipped around the cigarette, glanced sideways at the screen door and said, "Goddamned golfers," and turned the toaster upside down and banged it on the counter.

Lucy looked out through the screen, across the six-foot strip of grass that served as the front yard, past the corner of the Tobins' double-wide and over the fence, across the end of the driving range and the east corner of the machine shed, and judged the screams as coming from the first fairway. "Don't sound like drunks," she said. She corrected herself. *"Doesn't."*

"Yeah, well, fuck 'em anyway," Mom said. Lucy's mother knew about golfers, having had a number of hasty relationships with them over the years, including one with Lucy's father. Lucy knew little about him except that he was a 6-handicap and, under pressure, had a tendency to flip his hands at the beginning of his downswing.

"Duck-hooked me right into the county maternity ward," her mother told her. "Not that I didn't love you every minute, sweetheart."

Lucy would have liked to know more, but never would. She

had two photographs of him, taken with a small camera, reds and greens in the photos starting to bleed: her mom and dad in their golf clothes, standing near the ball machine on the driving range, squinting at the camera, sunlight harsh on their faces. Her father had been murdered by a man named Willis Franklin, who at that very moment was probably sitting on a barstool at the Rattlesnake Golf Club, not five hundred yards away, having gotten away with it.

"How did this happen?" her mother asked, peering into the toaster. "That sonofabitch is *welded* in there."

"I told you, you *cannot* put frozen flapjacks in a toaster; it don't work," Lucy said. "When they thaw out they get sticky and they sink down and grab ahold of them little wires at the bottom . . . Ah, shit." She was tired of hearing herself talk about it; and a little tired of correcting her own grammar. She did it anyway: "*Doesn't* work," she said. "*Those* little wires."

Her mom looked up: "You been pretty goddamn prickly lately."

"I'm headin' out; see what's going on," Lucy said. She rattled through the golf bags stacked in the corner and pulled out her putter.

"Dinner at 5:30," Mom said.

"Yeah." Like it made any difference what time they fired up the microwave. "I'll be back before then, probably for lunch. I got a couple of lessons; then I gotta run into town."

Lucy took her putter, which she called the Lizard, and stuck five balls in the pocket of the golf vest she'd designed herself and produced on Mom's pedal-driven Singer—a sports-activity vest that sooner or later would be stolen by those sons-ofbitches at Nike, she didn't doubt, and somebody would make a million bucks, but it wouldn't be her. She went out the door, the Lizard over her shoulder, the new Titleists clicking in her vest pocket. On the step, she automatically touched her pocket again, didn't feel the book. "Shoot."

She went back inside: "Forgot my list," she said.

"Heaven forbid," Mom said. She'd given up on the toaster and was looking through the litter in the kitchen for her Marlboros. "Got to clean this place up," she muttered.

Lucy went back to the bedroom, got the little black book from the dresser and headed out again, out the door, past the Tobins' place, through a hole in the fence and past the machine shed, where Donnie Dell was poking around the mower blades on an aging orange Kubota tractor. He called, "Hiya, Luce," and she raised the putter and called back, "What's all the hollerin' about?"

He shook his head: "I don't know. Too early to be drunks." She kept going and he called after her, "You gonna be around?"

"Maybe tonight," she called back. "Right now, I got a lesson with Rick Waite and his wife."

"Okay. Maybe, uh, I'll stop by. Later."

She smiled and kept moving. Donnie Dell was taking some kind of ag course over at UW–River Falls; a college boy. She knew exactly what he wanted; he'd been coming around for a month, ever since he got hired. What he didn't know, but that she did, was that he *was* going to get some, but not for a week. That's when he came up on her list, and she'd hold to it.

But tonight, tomorrow, the next day—uh-uh. She was busy.

•   •   •

She was passing the end of the machine shed, heading toward the putting green, when she saw one of the Prtussin brothers

trotting down the first fairway. The sight stopped her. Dale Prtussin was forty-five years old and weighed upwards of 250
pounds. None of it was muscle, and seeing him run was like
watching a swimming pool full of Jell-O in an earthquake.
He'd once eaten one of his own salads and come down with
food poisoning. The major symptom was projectile vomiting
and she'd seen him *walk* to the john in midspasm.

Up the fairway, at the top of the hill, just shy of the 185-
yard marker, a half dozen golfers were gathered around the
sand trap that guarded the inside elbow of the dogleg. They
were all looking into the trap. Lucy went that way, twirling the
putter like a baton.

• • •

One of the golfers, an older guy named Clark who always pretended to be taking an avuncular interest while he peered down
her blouse, frowned when he saw her coming, held out a hand,
and said, "This isn't for you, young lady."

"Don't make me hurt ya," Lucy said, pointing the putter
handle at his gut. Harley Prtussin said, "Howya, Luce?" as she
came up and looked in the sand trap. The first thing she saw
was the ball that somebody had driven into the lip of the
bunker; then she saw the nose in the divot.

"Holy shit," she said. She was gawking. "What's that?"

"Stevie," Prtussin said.

"Stevie? Is he dead?" All right, that was stupid. "How'd he
get in there? Who found him?"

"Somebody must've put him in," the avuncular golfer said.

A golfer named Joe said, "I found him. Swung at my ball
and felt the club hang up; I guess, Jesus . . . I guess it was his
nose."

She looked again at the ball in the lip of the bunker. "What'd you use, a 7-iron?"

"Yeah." They all looked down toward the green.

"Never gonna clear that lip from there with a 7-iron, not with your ball flight," Lucy said.

"I played it a little forward in my stance," Joe said.

"Good thing," Prtussin said. "If you'd dug in hard with a wedge, you'da really fucked up his face."

They all looked back in the hole where Stevie's nose stuck up, like a picture of the Great Pyramid taken from Skylab. One of the golfers shook his head and said, "Boy," and another one said, "Not something you see every day."

Prtussin said to Joe, "After you're done here, come on back to the clubhouse and I'll give you a rain check."

"You closing the course?"

"No, no . . ." Couldn't do *that*.

"Well, I'll just go on . . ."

"I think the cops are gonna want to talk to you, Joe."

Joe scratched his head and looked down toward the first green. Nothing but blue sky and light puffy clouds and maybe a one-mile-an-hour wind. The fairway was freshly mowed and smelled like spring golf "Ah, heck. You think?"

• • •

They all stood around looking at the nose, and then a cop car turned in the drive, stopped for a minute at the end of the parking lot, so the driver could talk to Dale Prtussin, who'd just come out of the clubhouse. Dale got in the backseat and the car bucked over the curb and headed up the hill through the rough.

The nose sticking out of the sand looked *austere,* Lucy

thought, plucking a word from her pre-sleep vocab list. White and semiplastic. Like a priest's nose when the priest is pissed off at you. The cop car rolled up and Jamie Forester got out of the car, hatless, remembered Dale in the back, popped the back door, and they both got out and Jamie said, "Everybody move back."

Everybody took a step back and he looked in the trap, nodded, said, "Everybody stay back." He had his hands on his hips, looked at the nose for another five seconds, then shook his head and said, "Man-oh-man," walked back to the car and called in.

• • •

Mitchell Drury arrived five minutes later. Drury was a member of the club and the lead investigator for the St. Croix County sheriff's office. Half the people around the bunker said, "Hey, Mitch," when he got out of his brown Dodge. He looked around, then said to Forester, "Everybody who wasn't here when he was found, get them out of here." To Dale Prtussin, "You and Harley better stay." He caught Lucy's eye, showed a half inch of grin and said, "Heard about the Ladies'. Congratulations."

Lucy nodded, and Drury turned back to the sand trap, all business again. Forester shooed them all away from the trap and back down the fairway to the first tee. At the bottom of the hill, Wade McDonnell, a retired mailman who worked as a ranger, was waving people off the tee. When Lucy went past, he asked, "They take him out yet?"

"Nope. Can't see nothing but the nose." She corrected herself "*Anything* but the nose." *The Businesswoman's One-Minute Guide to English Grammar and Usage.*

"You taking off?" McDonnell asked.

"Got the Waites."

McDonnell looked sympathetic. "Good luck."

"That ain't gonna help," Lucy said. Corrected herself: "*Isn't* going to help. Rick's got the reflexes of a fuckin' clam." Thought about deleting the *fuckin'*, but decided to let it be; that was just golf talk.

The Waites were unloading their fly-yellow Mustang when Lucy came up, and wanted to know what was going on; and then both of them had to walk up to the first tee to look up the hill and bitch at McDonnell about not being able to go on up to the bunker to look at the nose.

"It's a free goddamn country," Rick Waite argued.

"Tell that to Mitchell Drury," McDonnell said.

"Fuck a bunch of Mitchell Drurys," Waite said.

"Tell *that* to Mitchell Drury," McDonnell answered.

More cops arrived and drove up the rough to the trap; then a panel van from the St. Croix County medical examiner's office. Everybody from the bar was milling around the first tee by that time; and as players came off the ninth green and eighteenth, they joined the crowd.

Then nothing happened for a long time, the crowd waiting in the sunshine and the vanishing morning dew—always a few of them bleeding off to the bar, returning with beers and rum-Cokes. Lucy wandered off to the practice green, pushed a white tee into the ground three feet from one edge, and began practicing lag putts across the width of the green. Sixteen of twenty had to stop past the hole, but not further than seventeen inches past. Twenty minutes later, Rick Waite came over, his wife trailing, and said, "Might as well do that lesson," and Sharon Waite said, "Dale told us you shot a 68 up at Midland Hills in the Minnesota Ladies'."

Lucy said, "It shoulda been a 67, but I lost discipline on number 8 and three-putted."

"That happens to everybody," Sharon Waite said.

"Fuckin' shouldn't," Lucy said.

"But you won going away," Waite persisted.

"The Ladies' isn't the Tour," Lucy said. "They don't give you that stroke on the Tour." She turned away, and behind her back, Sharon Waite looked at her husband and shook her head.

• • •

Halfway through the lesson, Lucy told Rick Waite that "Your biggest problem, you're sliding your hips. Every time you go to swing, you slide your hips to the right. Then you got to slide them back to the left, for the club to come down at the same place that it started. That's too hard. You gotta rotate your hips instead of slidin' 'em. Like you're standin' in a barrel."

She demonstrated, but Waite shook his head. "I can't *feel* that," he said. "I gotta *feel* that before I remember it. Gimme a tip that'll make me *feel* it."

Lucy looked at him for a minute; behind him, his wife—who was a better natural golfer than her husband, but didn't much care for the game—shook her head.

"I'll give you a tip," Lucy said. "When you set up, your dick is pointing at the ball. Keep it pointing at the ball. If you rotate, it'll point at the ball. If you slide, it'll point at your right shoe. Think you can feel *that*?"

Behind him, Waite's wife was biting the inside of her cheeks to keep from laughing. Waite looked at his shoe and said, "Shit, honey, my dick is usually pointing at my left kneecap." His wife made a rude noise.

From the range, they could see up the hill to the crowd

around the sand trap. People—cops—were crawling around the trap, and then a couple of guys hauled a black bag out of it. "Body bag," Rick Waite said.

"Poor old Stevie," Sharon Waite said. "Must've put it in the wrong place one time too many." Her eyes cut to Lucy: "Don't mind my mouth, honey."

"No big deal to me," Lucy said. "Stevie and me didn't get along all that well." She caught herself: "Stevie and *I*," she said.

• • •

The medical examiner's van went by a minute later, but the cops stayed up on the hill. Lucy finished the lesson, got the twenty bucks from the Waites and walked back to the trailer, twirling the Lizard. Her mom was around to the side in a lawn chair with a reflector under her chin and a damp dishcloth over her eyes. "I'm taking the truck," Lucy said. "Back in an hour."

"Get some oranges at County Market," Mom said. "Them real tart ones."

"I'll put it on my list," Lucy said. She took the notepad out of her vest pocket, clicked the small ballpoint and added *Oranges* to her list for Tuesday.

• • •

Shamrock Real Estate was located on First Street in the town of Hudson, along the St. Croix River, in a flat cinder-block building that had been painted brown. Lucy parked in front and went in through the front door, the screen slapping behind her. The reception area smelled like nicotine, and held a desk, chair, computer and a beat-up faux-leather couch that might have been stolen from an airport lounge; there was nobody at the reception desk, and never was, because there'd never been a receptionist. Two small offices opened off the reception area. One was dark because nobody worked out of it. A light shone in the second, and Michael Crandon, who'd been reading a free paper with his feet up on his desk, leaned forward to see who'd come in.

"Me," Lucy said, leaning in the office doorway.

"How you feeling?" Crandon asked. He dropped his feet to the floor. He was too old for it, but his brown hair was highlighted with peroxide and gelled up.

"You got it?" Lucy asked.

"You got the cash?"

She dug it out of her shorts pocket, a fold of bills: "Two hundred dollars." She dropped it on the desk, as though she were buying chips in Vegas.

He handed her two amber pill bottles and a slip of paper. "Pills are numbered," he said. "Take the big one the first day, the small one the second day. Read the instructions."

"Better be good, for two hundred dollars," Lucy said.

"They're good."

"Be back if they aren't," she said.

"Have I ever sold you any bad shit?"

Lucy shook her head: "You don't want there to be a first time," she said, her mouth shifting down to a grim line.

Crandon gave her his square-chinned grin; but he wasn't laughing.

• • •

When she left the real estate office, she put the pill containers in the truck's glove compartment and headed back up to Second Street and then out onto I-94, across the St. Croix Bridge into Minnesota, off at the first exit and south to the Lakeland library, which was in a strip shopping center a mile south of the exit. She parked in front of the post office, got a clipboard off the truck seat and carried it down to the library.

The library had a couple of small computers tucked away in the back. She brought one up, typed for a few minutes and printed out the paragraph. Then she took out a couple of rubber Finger Tips, the kind used by accountants and bank tellers, fitted them on her thumb and index finger, pulled the envelope out of the clipboard, printed that, wiped the screen and shut the computer down. Handling both the paper and the envelope with the Finger Tips, she slipped them back in the clipboard and carried them out to the car.

The town of River Falls was back across the St. Croix and another fifteen minutes south of Hudson. She drove on down, elbow out the window, the wind scrubbing the fine hair on her left forearm, past all the golf courses and cornfields and dairy farms and yuppie houses. She went straight to the post office, sealed the envelope using a corner of her shirt dampened with Chippewa spring water, stamped it with a self-sticking stamp and dropped it in the mailbox.

Looked in her book, at her list.

Good. Right on schedule.

• • •

Back home, Lucy put the oranges in the refrigerator; Mom yelled from the back of the trailer, "Lucy? That you?"

"Yeah."

Mom came out of the back, her face wet, as though she'd been splashing water on it. "Why didn't you tell me about Steve?"

"I figured you'd find out soon enough," Lucy said. "Didn't want to make you unhappy."

"Jesus Christ, Lucy, I needed to know." Her voice was coarse; she'd been crying.

"So you know," Lucy said. "I got the oranges."

"Jesus Christ, Luce . . ."

Lucy brushed past Mom and went into the bathroom, closed the door and looked at the two yellow pill bottles and the piece of paper. The paper carried handwritten instructions, which looked as though they'd been xeroxed about a hundred times. She read the instructions, then read them again, then opened one of the bottles, took out the pill, looked at it, bent over the sink, slurped some water from the faucet, then leaned back and popped the pill.

Everything would be better now. She flushed the toilet and went back out into the hall, could hear her mother in the bedroom; she might have been sobbing. "I'm taking my clubs," Lucy called out.

Mom blubbered something, and Lucy picked up her clubs, then put them back down and went to the bedroom door and spoke at it.

"Can I come in?"

More blubbering, and she pushed the door open.

"I thought . . . I'm sorry, Mom, but I thought you were all done with that man."

"Well, I *was* all done," Mom said; her eyes had red circles around them. "Mostly. But I wouldn't want that to come to him. Being killed like that."

"Is there anything I can do about this? For you?"

"Naw, I'm just gonna sit around and cry for a couple of days. You go on."

"I mean, you aren't . . . pregnant or anything."

Now a tiny smile: "I ain't that stupid, honey. He never was a good bet."

"All right." Lucy nodded. "I'll be back for dinner."

∙ ∙ ∙

The first fairway was empty, except for some yellow tape around the bunker. Lucy swerved away from the course and the practice green and crossed the driveway to the clubhouse. She dropped her bag in the office and looked out into the restaurant area. Jerry Wilhelm was sitting alone at the bar, smoking a cigarette and staring at a glass of beer; Perry, the bartender, was standing in the corner looking up at the TV, trying to tune it with a remote. Lucy drew herself a Diet Coke, then went around and slid up on a stool next to Wilhelm.

"You talk to the cops yet?" she asked.

"Waitin' right now," he said. "Mitch is downstairs with Carl Wallace." He looked at the stairs that went down to the basement party room. "Jesus, Luce, you shoulda seen him when they took him out of that sand trap. Stevie. Like to blew my guts. He was all . . . gray."

"Glad I didn't see it," she said, and tipped back the glass of Diet Coke.

"Rick Waite told me about your dick-pointing tip. You get that from Stevie?"

"Shoot no; the only way Stevie's dick ever pointed was straight out."

"How would you know about that?" Wilhelm asked.

"He used to tell me about it," Lucy said. "Though I didn't believe but half of what he said."

"Shoulda believed about a quarter of it."

"About old Satin Shorts? Guess you'd know about that."

"Mary? Really? No, I didn't hear that one."

"Shoot, Jimmy, it was all over the club," Lucy said. "Give me some of those peanuts, will ya?"

As Wilhelm pushed the bowl of complimentary peanuts at her, he said, "I thought him and your ma . . ."

"That was over two months ago." Christ, they couldn't think Mom did it? Of course they could, she thought—Mom and Stevie . . . "Two months ago . . . Where you been, boy?"

Wilhelm shrugged. "Working, I guess. Heard about your scholarship. You're going to Florida?"

"Yup. I'll give it two years anyway."

"Well, good luck to ya. You're the only person ever come out of this club might make it as a pro," he said.

"I'm gonna try," she said.

"It's on your list?" Her lists were famous.

She finished the Diet Coke and touched her vest pocket: "Yup. It's on my list," she said. She pushed away and touched his shoulder. "Good luck with the cops; Mitch is a pretty good guy."

"Thanks," he said. She could feel his eyes on her ass as she walked away. Nothing to that, though. That was just normal. And the mission had been definitely accomplished.

•   •   •

If Lucy let it all out, held nothing back at all, and was hitting on a flat surface without wind, she could drive one of her Titleists three hundred yards, and maybe a yard or two more—not to say that she knew exactly where it would go under those conditions. Backing off a little, she could average 272 yards and keep the ball in the fairway.

Good enough for the Tour.

But the Tour didn't pay for long drives; the Tour paid for low scores. So though she hit her three buckets of balls each morning and evening, she'd devoted most of her practice in the last year to the short game—and specifically, the game within thirty to sixty yards of the pin. Anytime you were standing in that gap, one of two things happened: you screwed up, or you were a little off, or a little short, on your second shot to a par 5.

So the next shot would either make par, if you'd screwed up, and therefore keep you in the game; or give you a birdie on the par 5. Both of those things were critical if you wanted to win on the Tour, and in the calendar in the back of her list book, she'd blocked out two months of thirty-six practice, two-and-a-half-hour sessions on Rattlesnake's par 3, twice a day. Get up and down every time from thirty to sixty, she thought, and you rule the Tour.

• • •

As she walked out to the par 3, she let her mind drift to the coach at the University of Florida. He'd come up to see her, and they'd played a couple of rounds at Bear Path, over in the Cities. At the end of the second round, he'd given her a notebook and said, "Write this down."

"A list?"

"A list," he said. He was a tough-looking nut, brown from the sun with pale blue eyes and an eye-matching blue Izod golf shirt buttoned to the top. "This is what I want you to do."

Over a Leinenkugel for him and a Diet Coke for her, and cheeseburgers with strips of bacon, he'd given her thirty putting drills and thirty more short-game drills.

"How long?"

"At least two hours a day," he said.

"I do six now," she said.

He looked at her, saw she was serious and said, "Then don't quit, if you can stand it."

"If it'd put me on the Tour, I'd do ten," she said.

"We're gonna get along just fine, Lucy," he said through a mouthful of cheeseburger. "You do two hours a day, I'll put you on the Tour. You do six hours and I'll put you on the leader board in the Open. Whether you win or not . . . that depends on what you were born with."

She looked flat back at him: "I been playing"—she didn't say *for money,* but rubbed her thumb against her fingers in the money sign—"since I was twelve," she said. "You give me a six-foot putt for two hundred dollars with forty-three dollars in the bank, and I'll make it every time."

He leaned back in his chair and smiled at her: "You're giving me wet panties," he said.

• • •

She'd decided on this day to work on the ninth green on the par 3. The ninth was slightly raised all around, a platform, with steep banks climbing six feet up to the green. The pin was near the back, and she walked around behind the green so she'd be coming in from the short side; and she'd use nothing but the 7-, 8- and 9-irons, punching short shots into the bank, letting the bank and the rough slow the ball down, so it'd trickle over the top and down to the pin. This was not a common approach. Most people would try to flop the ball up to the pin, as she would, most of the time. But sometimes you couldn't do that—like if there was a tree nearby—and then you needed something different.

She was hard at it, punching an 8-iron into a spot two and a half feet down from the top of the platform, trying to control the ball hop, when she realized somebody was coming up behind her. She turned and saw Mitchell Drury.

Mitchell. He must've been forty, she thought. But you sort of thought about him anyway, looked him over, even if you were seventeen. That weathered cowboy thing, with the shoulders and the small butt.

"Lucy," he said. His face was serious; usually he'd do a movie-star grin when he was talking to her—he knew women liked him. Not this time. "Gotta talk to you."

"Sure thing. About Stevie?" She sat back on the bank next to the green and he plopped down beside her.

"Yeah . . . um. You know, I mean, everybody knows, he was seeing your mom."

"C'mon, Mitch. That was over two months ago."

"Over for your mom?" His eyebrows went up.

"Yeah, *over.* It ain't the first time she's had a romance out here—Christ, she's only thirty-eight. I'm surprised *you* ain't been knocking on the door."

"Hmm," Mitch said, his eyes cutting away.

Lucy thought, *Holy cow.* "Mitchell," she said.

"Don't ask," he said. "But besides *that* . . . you're sure. About Stevie."

"I'm real sure," she said. "That motherfucker dropped her like a hot rock and she cried for four straight days. She's crying right now. But she never would have done anything about it." She looked up the hill toward the bunker. "Nothing like that."

"All right . . . She been out playing lately?"

Lucy shook her head. "Not much. Didn't want to run into Stevie, I think. Take the chance."

"All right," he said. He stood up. "I gotta talk to her, though."

"How was . . . umm, I mean, was he shot? Stabbed? What?"

He shrugged. "I'll tell you, it's gonna be in the paper anyway . . . but I'd be a little happier if you didn't pass it around."

"Sure."

He looked both ways, as though somebody might be sneaking up on them, then said, "His skull was crushed."

"*Crushed?*" She shook her head. "Like with a car crusher? Like squashed?"

"No, no. Like somebody hit him in the temple with a driver."

She sat back. "Oh."

"What, *Oh?*"

"Nothing. I was just trying to think who I'd seen him playing with. But when I think about it, I ain't seen him playing with nobody, much. Mary Dietz a couple times, John Wilson last week."

"He have something going with Mary?"

Lucy shrugged: "I don't know. Might of just been playing lessons."

"Somebody else mentioned . . . I thought Mary was seeing Willie Franklin."

"Don't know about that, either," Lucy said. "Tell you the truth, Mitchell, I been a little out of it, ever since that letter come in from Florida. Gettin' ready."

Drury nodded. "Good luck on that, Luce," he said. Now he gave her the grin. "You're the best to ever come out of here. I think you'll go the whole way."

"That kinda talk'll get you a free lesson," Lucy said, grinning back.

Drury laughed and said, "May take you up on that."

Lucy stood up, brushed the grass off the seat of her pants and said, "Mom didn't have nothin' to do with it, Mitchell. Not a fuckin' thing. She's too kindhearted. I think you probably know that."

He might have blushed and he said, "Well, yeah, that's sorta what I think. See you later, Luce. Don't worry too much about your mom."

Lucy went back to hitting balls at the embankment. The first four or five hit too hard and trickled past, and she observed herself for a moment. Adrenaline. She had *this* feeling, *this* much adrenaline. Had to remember it: *this much* would get you nine feet past the pin . . .

Her mind drifted away from golf, just for a second or two. She'd made a lot of grammatical and usage errors when she spoke to Mitchell.

And that was good.

• • •

She thought about going back home. Mom probably could use some diversion. But she tarried at the putting green, trying again to make a hundred six-foot putts in a row. The drill was simple enough—you putted all the balls from the same spot, and after five or six, you could see a little pathway developing in the turf. If you could keep the balls in the pathway, you had a chance. But as the number went up, the stress built . . .

After two false starts, she made forty-eight, and missed on the forty-ninth when she saw Dale Prtussin hurrying toward her. "Howya, Luce? Did I make you miss?"

"Nah. Lost my focus."

"How far did you get?"

"Forty-eight in a row. Forty short of my record."

"I'm sorry . . . Listen. I hate to talk business like this, with Stevie not even in the ground, but do you think you could take over for him? For the rest of the summer, until you get to school? I mean, you aren't that experienced, so I couldn't pay you everything I gave him—"

"How much?"

"Six hundred a week, salary. You'd have to run the cash register in the mornings, starting at six o'clock, seven days a week. And you know, all the group lessons and supervise the school tournaments, but shit, it's not nothing you haven't done."

She nodded: "Start tomorrow?"

"That'd be good. I'll have Alice put you on the regular payroll, and you got a group lesson tomorrow at four in the afternoon. The ladies from 3M."

She poked her putter handle at his gut: "You got it, Dale. And thanks. It'll help me out at Florida, having a little bankroll of my own."

"Glad to do it," he said. But his tiny eyes were worried: "This is a bad day at Rattlesnake, Luce. Old Stevie was sorta an asshole sometimes, but nobody ought to go like that."

"Who's the hot name in the suspect pool?"

He shook his head. "Isn't any pool . . . yet. But, uh . . . never mind."

She raised her eyebrows. "Come on, you got somebody in mind?"

He looked both ways, like Mitch had earlier, and said in a hushed voice, "I'd like to know where Willie Franklin was Saturday night."

She looked away. "Didn't see him—and I wouldn't even want to say anything about that. You know, my daddy."

"I know; but I say the sonofabitch did it once, and if he can do it once, he can do it twice."

• • •

That night, Lucy did her vocab list, then lay in bed and thought about Willis Franklin, the man who'd shot her daddy. A group of men from Rattlesnake had been deer hunting, the weekend before Thanksgiving, up in Sawyer County. Out of tree stands. Franklin came running into the hunting shack, late in the day, and said he'd just found Lucy's dad dead on the ground, under his tree stand. Shot in the heart.

The body was taken into the coroner's office, and when it was examined by some state medical people, it was found to have a broken neck and small debris punched into the skin of the face—he'd been knocked right out of the stand.

Unusual. You'd have to be shooting *up* to hit him.

Then, blind luck, they'd found the remnants of a bullet in the tree, and metallurgical tests matched it to the fragments of metal found in the dead man's sternum. There was just enough of the slug left to match rifling marks made by Willis Franklin's gun. Franklin had denied shooting the rifle at all during the afternoon, but then admitted it, saying he was afraid of what he might've done. Said he wasn't even sure he'd done it—he'd been driving deer toward the stand, had one jump up close by, a buck with a big rack, and snapped an uphill shot at it . . . missed . . . and found Lucy's dad five minutes later.

That was all fine, except that Franklin had been after Lucy's mom like a bloodhound, until her dad stepped in and took her away. And Willis was a man known to have a foul temper and was not a man to forget. There was a trial, but nothing came of it: just not enough evidence, and the jury cut him loose. A tragedy in the woods, a few people said. A few more said, darkly, *murder* . . . And that was how Lucy learned the story.

Lucy thought about it all—her dad, Willis Franklin and Stevie—and allowed herself to snuffle over it for a few minutes. She tried to switch her mind over to the Tour, as she usually did, but it didn't work: she just kept seeing the dark shape of her father falling out of a tree stand, a bullet in his heart.

She'd never known him. By the time she first heard the murder story, she was seven years old, and her daddy had been moldering in the ground for seven and a half years.

• • •

Lucy did the early morning cash register, and when Dale Prtussin came in at ten o'clock, walked back to the trailer, found her mom reading the paper. "Gotta do my grips," she said, and went on back to the bedroom. The grips and turns took a half hour, and then she was back in the kitchen. "You're still going to the Pin-Hi's this afternoon, aren't you?" she asked.

Her mom nodded. "Yeah. No point in hanging around here." The Pin-Hi's were a group of women golfers who played a circuit of eight courses during the summer. "Half the girls will have known Stevie—a couple of them in the biblical sense—and that'll be all the talk." She tried a smile again. "I got to protect my back."

"Did you talk to Mitchell?"

Mom nodded: "We had a good little heart-to-heart. Stevie was fooling with somebody, but it wasn't me. I'd heard maybe Satin Shorts—"

"That's what I heard. Mary."

Mom frowned. "And I heard a couple of weeks ago that

Willie Franklin . . . Ah, shit, I'm not even going to *think* about that." She forced a bright smile. "So what are you doing, dear? With your new job?"

Lucy shrugged: "Usual stuff. Pretty much run the place in the early mornings, until the Prtussins show up. Stevie's job."

"So that's something you can cross off your list," Mom said.

"What?"

"Getting a bankroll together for Florida. A month ago, you were talking about getting a night job with UPS."

"Yeah, well. Stevie wouldn't mind, I guess. If he'd known it had to be this way."

Mom snorted, poured two tablespoons of sugar into a new cup of coffee. "Bullshit. I'll tell you something about Steve, honey—knowing that you were going to the pros was eating him up. He had a half year on the Tits Tour and that was the best he'd ever do. No way he'd ever make it on the regular Tour, make it through Q school. He hated every move he saw you make. He hated you out there practicing every day."

"C'mon. He was always helping . . ."

"Baby, I've known a lot more men that you have, and I knew Steve for fifteen years," Mom said. "That man would have run you over with his car if he thought nobody would catch him. Some goddamn *chick* stealing *his* glory at Rattlesnake? I don't think so."

"Then how come you were . . . seeing him?" Actually, Stevie'd come over and bang Mom's brains out on the other side of a sixteenth inch of aluminum wall.

Mom shrugged. "Company. He was a good-looking man, and he could make me laugh. I don't got that many years left, with men coming around."

Lucy fished the Lizard out of the bag in the corner. "Maybe you ought to look for somebody steadier. Somebody who doesn't play golf."

Mom snorted again. "Like that might happen."

• • •

Lucy did the group lesson at noon, then two private lessons and then went back in and pushed Dale Prtussin out of the cash register station, even though she didn't have to. At three o'clock, she walked home. Mom was gone, and she went back to her bedroom, found the second pill case, blanked her mind and went into the bathroom, looked at the second pill, took a breath, bent over to suck water from the faucet, looked at the pill and popped it.

At four o'clock, she had the 3M women. They liked her, but they were all talking about Stevie. At five, she went into the bar, got a salad out of the refrigerator, ate it and then walked back home, twirling the Lizard.

At the trailer, she lay down, waiting for the pill to work; fetched Dan Jenkins's *Dead Solid Perfect* from her rack of golf books and giggled through the best parts, though Jenkins sometimes cut a little close to home—a little too close to the way she and Mom lived in their little trailer off Rattlesnake.

She was waiting for the pill when she heard a ruckus out by the fence line, and then somebody started banging on the door, the whole trailer trembling with the impact. She climbed out of bed and went to look. Donnie Dell, the boy from the machine shed, the college student she was going to sleep with in a week, stood at the bottom of the steps. His straw-colored hair was sticking out wildly from beneath his ball cap, like the Scarecrow's in *The Wizard of Oz.*

"What?"

"You hear?" he croaked.

"Hear what?"

"The cops arrested Willie Franklin."

Lucy stepped out the door. "You're shittin' me."

"I'm not shittin' you," Donnie said. His eyes glowed with the excitement of it. "They found blood in the trunk of his car. And a hair, is what people are saying. Jim Doolittle got it straight from the cops."

"How would Doolittle know?"

"Works up with the hospital . . . I'm tellin' you, he *knows*. Jim's over in the bar right now. The cops found blood in Willie's trunk, and they matched it. He's absolutely fuckin' toast."

● ● ●

That was a moment that Lucy knew she'd remember forever.

She might someday be an old lady with a mantel full of Open trophies, and maybe a big scroll from the Hall of Fame, and maybe five kids and twenty grandkids—but she'd always remember standing outside the trailer door with somebody playing a Stones record off at the other end of the park, and a car accelerating away from the club, and the crickets in the cinder-block foundations, and the smell of cut grass and gasoline coming off the course, the best smell in the world. The moment she'd heard.

"Thanks for coming, Donnie," she said.

"You coming over to the bar?"

"I'd like to, but I'm feeling not so good. I ate one of them fuckin' salads . . ."

"Aw, Jesus," he said. "You know better than that."

"I know, I know, but I was hungry . . . So . . . see you next week?" She touched his shoulder.

"Maybe catch a movie," he said.

"That'd be cool, Donnie," she said.

She went back to the bed, but ten minutes later, a car pulled into their parking space, the lights sweeping over her window. Too early for Mom, unless something happened.

"Goddammit," she said. She pushed herself up, went to the door. Mitchell Drury.

"Mitch?"

"Hi, Luce. Is your mom home?"

"No, she's got the Pin-Hi's over at the Hollow tonight. Donnie Dell was just here, said you arrested Willie."

He nodded: "I was coming to tell her. 'Cause it's so much like what happened with your dad."

"How'd you catch him?" Lucy asked, crossing her arms and leaning on the door frame.

"Got a note from somebody at the club—said they saw him running off the course with his bag the night Stevie disappeared. Looked like he was panicked . . ."

"A note? From who?"

"We're trying to figure that out," Mitchell said. "Anonymous. Kind of think it might be one of the schoolteachers. One of the profession guys. The language was . . . high-level."

"No shit," Lucy said.

"Had access to a computer and a laser printer. We'll find him, one way or another."

"What's Willie say?"

"Same thing he did with your dad—that he didn't have anything to do with it. Now he's got an attorney, and he's not saying anything."

"Well, fuck him," Lucy said fiercely. "Two people? Fuck him."

"That's sort of what I think. I was talking to . . ." Drury paused and took a half-step back. "You feel okay?"

"Ah, I got an upset stomach from one of the Prtussins' fuckin' salads," Lucy said.

"Well, uh, you got . . ."

He looked down, and Lucy looked down and saw the dark spot near her crotch. "Oh, Jesus." Her hands flew to her face. "Oh, God, I'm so embarrassed, Mitch. My period, I, God, it's early, God . . ."

"That's all right," he said hastily. "You go take care of it, honey. Tell your mom to call me at home whenever she gets in. I'll be up till midnight or later."

"Aw, jeez, Mitch . . ."

He was still backing away. "Take care of it, honey . . ."

• • •

She shut the door and got a Kotex from the box under her bed, strapped it on, pulled on a fresh pair of pants, then squirted ERA all over her stained underpants and shorts and threw them in the washer. She grinned at the thought of Drury's face: men would generally cut off their arms rather than have to deal with something like that, she thought.

Men.

Like that goddamn Stevie. Fuckin' Mom all night, then coming on to little Lucy in the shop. Holding her hips during the lessons, when he was showing her how to turn; hands on her rib cage, standing her up straight. Hands all over her. And more than his hands, down there in the basement room of the club, after he'd closed it down. He called her *tasty*, like she was some kind of fuckin' bun. Nobody knew because Lucy had to deal with stealing her mother's boyfriend; and Stevie had to deal with the problem of statutory rape, which he knew all about.

Then last week, when she told him she'd missed her period, out there on the fairway, he'd laughed at her: "So much for the fuckin' Tour," he said, and he turned away, laughing. If there'd been anybody else out there in the semidark, they'd have heard him, laughing, laughing, laughing.

The driver had been right there, poking out of her bag. She'd had it out in an instant, a lifelong familiar. Stevie'd started to turn when the clubhead caught him in the temple, and he'd gone down like a shot bird.

She'd buried him in the bunker, because it was convenient, and she had a lot of thinking to do; lists to make. She was back in the house before she noticed the blood on the club. She went out to wipe it on the grass when she noticed the taillights blinking in the club parking lot, and down on the far end, where it always was, the hulk of Willie Franklin's Tahoe. He never locked the back doors . . .

•   •   •

Mom was home by eleven and knocked on the bedroom door. "Okay in there?"

"Yeah. Gotta get up at five," Lucy called back.

Mom opened the door: "You heard about Willie Franklin?"

"Yeah. Oh—you're supposed to call Mitchell if you get in before midnight. He wants to talk to you about it."

"I'll call him," Mom said. "See you in the morning."

Lucy listened to her footsteps down the hall, then got up and looked at the latest Kotex. It was fairly bloody, but the flow seemed to be slowing. That's what the instructions had said: the onset would take a couple of hours, then the flow would be heavy for a couple of more, and after that, it would be more or less like a regular period. She switched pads and crawled back in bed.

This was what it took to go on the Tour, she thought. A fierce *determination:* nothing would stand in the way. A fierce *organization:* determination was nothing without focus.

And talent. She had all of that, Lucy did.

And her lists.

Her lists. Better do something about those. She reached across the familiar darkness, found her vest and took out the small book. She had matches on her bedstand, to light the evergreen-scented candle. She lit it, and in the candlelight, found the pages and carefully ripped them out.

One note said, *RU-486.* Ripped and burned.

Another said, *New job.* Ripped and burned, the paper flaring in the near dark.

A third one said, *Frame Willie.* Ripped and burned.

She looked at the last note for a while, the only note not written with a golf pencil. It had been written the week before, in pale blue ink. Girlie ink, she thought now.

It said, *Marry Stevie?*

No fuckin' way. Not at this stage of her career, she thought. A pro went it alone, until the money got big. Then she'd have her pick.

Marry Stevie?

A tear trickled down her cheek. Ripped and burned, the smoke smelling of damp pulp paper and evergreens.

But it was gone in a moment, and everything was back on track.

Lucy lay in the bed she'd made, and dreamed of lists.

UNPLAYABLE LIES

William G. Tapply

Mr. Mazza met me at the practice tee around 12:30, where I had his clubs and a bag of range balls waiting for him.

He held a folded-up bill between his fingers. "Big match today, kid," he said. "You know what I mean?"

I nodded. "Yes, sir."

"Important I beat this guy." He tucked the bill into my shirt pocket. "Matter of respect."

He reached into his bag and took out his driver. I teed up a range ball for him.

He looked at the clubhead. "You clean these?" he said.

"Yes, sir."

He squinted at the clubhead, then nodded. "Yeah. Course you do. You always clean the clubs. Good job." He tapped my ass with the head of his driver. "Big match. Big fuckin' match for us, understand?"

I nodded. He was talking about my tip.

Mr. Mazza then proceeded to pound out that entire bag of balls with his driver as fast as I could tee them up for him. He grunted and cursed and kept swinging harder and harder and hitting bigger and bigger hooks, and by the time he was done, he was drenched with sweat.

If he'd asked me, I would've told him that if he wanted to win this big match, he should work his way up through his clubs on the practice tee. Start with a few wedges, little half-swings, just making clean contact, then a couple of short irons, move on up through the middle irons, long irons, fairway woods, getting loose, extending his swing, finding his groove, and end up smacking a few with his driver.

I'd been carrying for Mr. Mazza for three years, and if he ever asked my advice, I could've taken six or eight strokes off his game, easy. Club selection, reading the grain on a green, deciding when to lay up and when to go for the pin. Stuff like that. Not to mention how to warm up before a match and how to change his grip to straighten out that hook. All he had to do was ask.

But Mr. Mazza wasn't the kind of guy who asked anybody for anything. He told people what he wanted, and he expected them to do it. And I'm not talking about just caddies.

· · ·

The first time I told my old man I'd carried for Mr. Mazza, he said, "Shit, son. Big Paulie Mazza? You gotta watch out for that guy."

"He's got a wicked hook, I know that," I said. "I spent half the day in the woods looking for his ball."

"That ain't what I meant. Mazza's a made man, a fuckin' wiseguy."

"Doesn't matter to me what he does for a living," I said. "I just carry his golf bag."

"Don't ever say nothing to him," said my old man. "Just

say 'yes, sir' and 'no, sir' to that guy. How much he give you?"

"Twenty," I lied.

"Cheap bastard." My old man held out his hand. "Let's have it."

I gave twenty bucks to him and kept the other thirty for myself. Whatever Mr. Mazza was, he wasn't a cheap bastard.

Every time I got home from the club my old man had his hand out to me. A few months after that first time, he said to me, "This Mazza, he likes you, huh?"

"I guess so. He always asks for me. I'm his regular caddie."

"I been thinking," he said. "Maybe it ain't such a bad thing, getting in good with him."

"I'm in pretty good with him."

"He ever talk about business?"

"Not to me. To the guys he plays with sometimes."

"You should listen," said my old man. "Maybe learn something."

"I listen."

"You do a good job carrying his bag," said my old man, "maybe he'll find something for you, get you started on a career. He's got connections."

"I do a good job," I said.

"I got a better idea," he said. "Why don't you mention to him that your daddy's between jobs right now? See what he says to that."

My old man had been between jobs for about ten years. "Sure, Pop. I'll mention it to him."

"Tell him I do what I'm told, know how to keep my mouth shut. Anything he wants, I can do it. Anything at all. You tell him that."

"Yeah, okay," I said.

I had no intention of mentioning my old man to Mr. Mazza.

I wouldn't've minded working for Mr. Mazza, though. I didn't plan to shine golf shoes and carry bags and say "yes, sir" for the rest of my life.

• • •

Mr. Mazza handed me his driver, and I gave him the clean towel I always carry in my hip pocket for him. Mr. Mazza sweats like a pig.

He dried off his face and hands, then stuffed the towel up under his shirt and wiped his chest and his hairy belly. "Remember what I said," he said. "Important match. Got it?"

"Yes, sir," I said.

When we got to the first tee, Skeeter Cronin was leaning on a golf bag talking with a fat, bald-headed old guy, must've been at least fifty.

Skeeter was a couple years younger than me, a skinny red-headed kid with pink, peeling skin and freckles all over his face and yellow fuzz on his upper lip. I'd carried with Skeeter a few times. He always complained about his old man, who was in prison. I told him that was better than having an old man never went out of the house, with his hand out to you all the time.

The fat guy wore sunglasses and had the stump of a cigar stuck in the corner of his mouth. I'd seen him around the club a few times. His name was Vaccaro. He didn't play much golf, but he liked to take blond women to the members' dining room, have long boozy meals, watch the girls play tennis in their little short skirts or swim in the pool while he sat there drinking gin and tonics. Sometimes he ate with a bunch of other men, talking and laughing and flirting with the waitresses, and afterward playing gin rummy for half the night.

Mr. Mazza went right up to him and hugged him and kissed both of his cheeks. "How you doin', Mr. Vaccaro?" he said.

Mr. Mazza didn't call anybody "Mister" that I knew of.

"Hey, Paulie," said Mr. Vaccaro, calling Mr. Mazza by his first name, I noticed. "You been practicing on me?"

"I whacked a few balls," said Mr. Mazza. "Gotta be at my best, have a chance against you, huh?"

"You can't beat *me*," said Mr. Vaccaro, "you got a serious problem. You wanna hit first?"

"Maybe we should flip for it."

"You go ahead, Paulie. Show me the way."

I handed Mr. Mazza his driver and a new Titleist and a white tee. He teed up his ball, straightened up, squinted down the fairway, took a couple of practice swipes, then looked at Mr. Vaccaro. "One mulligan each side okay with you?" he said.

"Mulligan?" Mr. Vaccaro laughed. "The fuck you talking about, a mulligan. We playing golf or tiddlywinks? Hit 'em where they lay, Paulie. Play by the fuckin' rules. That's what rules are for."

"Club rules allow preferred lies in the fairway," said Mr. Mazza.

"Yeah, and they put out them red tees for the ladies, too. Don't mean that's where you hit from."

"Sorry, Mr. Vaccaro." Mr. Mazza shrugged. "Strict rules of golf, then, huh?"

"That's it, Paulie. Strict rules. What good are rules, they ain't strict? What're you hitting?"

Mr. Mazza looked at his ball. "Titleist 3."

Mr. Vaccaro held out his hand, and Skeeter gave him a ball. "Dunlop 4," he said. "Buck a hole?"

"Fine by me," said Mr. Mazza.

A buck meant a thousand dollars. A thousand dollars meant about as much to those guys as a dollar did to me.

Mr. Mazza proceeded to hit his drive into the left rough about 250 yards out.

"You're a big hitter, Paulie," said Mr. Vaccaro as he teed up his ball. "You got that hook, though. You gotta get that hook under control. No sense hitting big if you don't have no control."

It was the first time I'd ever heard anybody dare to criticize Mr. Mazza's swing. I expected him to whack Mr. Vaccaro in the face with his driver, but all he did was mumble, "Yeah, I know. You're right. I'm working on it."

Mr. Vaccaro had a short little swing, all shoulders and arms, and I knew before I even watched the flight of his ball that he was a slicer. But he started it left, and it arced out there and plopped safely down in the middle of the fairway about 180 yards out.

"Good hit, Mr. Vaccaro," said Mr. Mazza, sucking up to him.

"Play within yourself," said Mr. Vaccaro. "Don't try to do more than you can do, you know what I mean?"

"I like to go for it," said Mr. Mazza. "Challenge myself."

"That's why you always end up in the rough, Paulie. Not smart. Not the way to win."

Skeeter and I set off ahead of the two men to try to find Mr. Mazza's ball.

"That guy scares the shit out of me," said Skeeter after we'd put some distance between us and them.

"Who?"

"My guy. Mr. Vaccaro."

"He's just a fat old shit with a slice."

"I don't like the way he looks at me," said Skeeter. "It's like he knows what I'm thinking."

"So don't think nothing," I said. "Just call him 'sir,' stay out of his line of sight when he's putting."

Skeeter found Mr. Mazza's ball under a bush, then headed back to meet up with Mr. Vaccaro. After Skeeter was out of sight, I gave our ball a nudge with my toe, giving us a decent lie and a line at the green.

When he got to me, Mr. Mazza looked at his ball, peered out to the fairway, then winked at me. "Looks like we got a lucky bounce, huh, kid?"

"Yes, sir," I said.

"Strict rules of golf," he muttered. "Hit 'em where they lay. So says Mr. Anthony Vaccaro."

He took a 7-iron, choked down on it, and punched the ball nicely out onto the fairway, leaving himself a half-wedge to the pin. Meanwhile, Mr. Vaccaro had laid up his second shot about fifty yards from the green. They both chipped on and two-putted for bogeys.

As we walked to the next tee, Mr. Mazza put his arm around Mr. Vaccaro's shoulders and said, "No blood that time."

"There's always blood, Paulie," said Mr. Vaccaro. He glanced at me and smiled, and I wondered if he knew I'd given Mr. Mazza's ball a kick. I didn't see how.

The second hole was a blind shot over a hill, so Skeeter and I went ahead to watch for where the balls came down. "Did you say anything to Mr. Vaccaro?" I asked Skeeter.

"Like what?"

"About Mr. Mazza's lie back there in the rough."

"I just say 'yes, sir' and 'no, sir' to that guy."

"And he didn't ask you about Mr. Mazza's lie?"

"Nope."

I didn't know Skeeter well enough to tell if he was lying to me.

The two men halved the first four holes, Mr. Mazza whaling out those long hooks into the rough, Mr. Vaccaro hitting his high little slices in the middle of the fairway. Whenever Mr. Vaccaro was out of sight, Mr. Mazza would roll his ball over with his club to make it sit up for him, and he'd mumble, "Club rules. Fuck him."

The fifth hole was a par 3 with water on the left, and naturally Mr. Mazza's 6-iron hooked down in the middle of it. When Mr. Vaccaro dropped a soft 4-wood about twenty feet from the pin, Mr. Mazza said, "Go ahead, pick it up. Your hole."

"You shouldn't give up so easy, Paulie," said Mr. Vaccaro. "Hit another one. You might hole it out. Anything can happen."

"A hole in one for a par?" said Mr. Mazza. "Fuck that. I concede."

Mr. Mazza evened up their match with a long putt, and a couple holes later Mr. Vaccaro went one up again when Mr. Mazza took two to get out of a bunker. Otherwise they kept halving them. Whenever Mr. Mazza hacked his way to a 7, Mr. Vaccaro would manage to miss a short putt, and if Mr. Mazza sank a long putt for a par, Mr. Vaccaro's chip shot would nestle up right beside the hole.

So Mr. Vaccaro was one up when we got to the seventeenth

tee. He teed up his ball, then said, "You better win this one, Paulie, or you're dead."

"So let's double the bet," said Mr. Mazza. "Make it interesting."

"Good," said Mr. Vaccaro. "Two bucks, then."

The seventeenth was a par-4 dogleg to the right with woods and out-of-bounds all the way down the left side and a big bunker at the corner about 180 yards out. With Mr. Mazza's hook, it looked like a disaster waiting to happen.

Mr. Vaccaro's usual high slice landed in the middle of the fairway and started rolling toward the bunker. "That go in the sand?" he said to Skeeter.

"Yes, sir."

"Well, Paulie," said Mr. Vaccaro to Mr. Mazza, "there you go. There's your chance."

Mr. Mazza looked at me. "Whaddya think, kid?"

"Sir?" It was the first time he'd ever asked me what I thought.

"Should I hit the driver?"

"No, sir," I said. "You should hit your 4-iron. Put it in the fairway, you'll have an easy seven to the green."

He patted my cheek. "Smart kid. Gimme the fuckin' driver."

"Yes, sir."

He took the driver and swung so hard he nearly fell down. His ball went way the hell out there over the bunker, and then the hook caught it and it curved into the woods, where it clattered and ricocheted around, bouncing off about five trees.

"Fuck," mumbled Mr. Mazza.

"You shoulda listened to the kid," said Mr. Vaccaro. "Go help 'em find their ball," he said to Skeeter.

Skeeter and I started down the fairway. When I glanced back, I saw that Mr. Mazza and Mr. Vaccaro were still back at the tee. Mr. Vaccaro was leaning his face close to Mr. Mazza's, and he was jabbing his finger at Mr. Mazza's chest. I could tell Mr. Mazza was mad by the way he kept clenching his fists, but Mr. Vaccaro seemed to be doing all the talking.

"Your guy's ball's probably out-of-bounds," said Skeeter as we approached the place where we'd seen it dive into the woods.

"The way it bounced around," I said, "it could be any-where. Could've come down in the fairway, even."

We started looking. I decided to look along the edge of the fairway. If his ball wasn't where he'd have a shot at the green, the match was over anyway.

Skeeter headed into the woods, and as I wandered around the edge of the rough, I kept an eye on him. After a minute, I saw him stop and look down. I pretended not to be looking, but out of the corner of my eye, I saw him stoop down quickly, pick up a ball, glance at it, and drop it in his pocket. Then he pretended to continue looking.

From where Skeeter found that ball, Mr. Mazza would've had an easy little pitch out into the fairway, and from there maybe a 9-iron to the green. With Mr. Vaccaro in that bunker, still short of the dogleg, we'd have a good chance to win the hole.

But if we couldn't find Mr. Mazza's ball, it'd be all over. And unless we looked in Skeeter's pocket, we'd never find it.

So I reached into my pocket, where I had some more new Titleist 3s, fished one out, and let it fall into the short rough right beside the fairway. Then I kept wandering around, pre-tending to look.

After a few minutes, Mr. Mazza and Mr. Vaccaro came along. "Find it?" said Mr. Mazza.

"Not yet, sir," I said.

Mr. Vaccaro glanced at his watch. "Lost ball, you got five minutes."

"Yeah," mumbled Mr. Mazza. "Strict fuckin' rules of golf."

Skeeter was still ramming around in the woods, pretending to look. Mr. Mazza and Mr. Vaccaro and I were standing right near where I'd dropped the ball. "Hey," I said, pointing at it, pretending to see it for the first time. "What's this?"

Mr. Mazza bent down. "That's mine. Must've got a good bounce off them trees."

"Come on outta there, kid," said Mr. Vaccaro to Skeeter. "We got it."

The two of them went over to the bunker and stood there waiting for Mr. Mazza to hit. I saw Mr. Vaccaro touch Skeeter's shoulder. Skeeter nodded and said something, and Mr. Vaccaro shrugged and glanced in our direction.

"Pretty lucky," said Mr. Mazza to me. "I guess I prob'ly shoulda hit that 4-iron like you said. But it worked out okay."

"Yes, sir," I said. "We got lucky."

Mr. Mazza then hit his best shot of the day, a nice high, straight 6-iron that settled down on the front of the green and rolled up to about five feet from the hole.

"Good shot, sir," I said.

"Keep an eye on that sonofabitch," he growled at me. "See he don't ground his club in the sand."

He didn't, but it didn't matter. It took him two shots to get out of the bunker, one more to lay up, and by the time he chipped onto the green, he was lying five to Mr. Mazza's two.

When Mr. Vaccaro got to the green, he went over and

picked up both his own and Mr. Mazza's balls. "Your hole, Paulie." He turned to say something to Skeeter, and as he started to walk off the green, he tossed Mr. Mazza's ball to him. "Match all even goin' to the eighteenth. Whaddya say? Want to make it five bucks?"

"Why the fuck not?" said Mr. Mazza.

I knew that was no big deal to those guys. But five thousand dollars on one hole?

I figured there was a big tip riding on this one.

Mr. Vaccaro and Skeeter were walking ahead of us up the path to the eighteenth green. Mr. Mazza was mumbling something about respect.

"Sir," I said to him, "why don't I wash your ball for you?"

"Sure, kid," he said, and he tossed me his ball.

When I went to put it in the ball washer, I saw that it was a Titleist 2, not the Titleist 3 he'd been hitting. I almost laughed out loud. It was the trick that James Bond had played on Goldfinger—swap balls on your opponent. By the strict rules of golf, if you hit the wrong ball, you lose the hole.

Skeeter had tried to win the seventeenth by pocketing Mr. Mazza's ball. Lost ball, lost hole, end of match. But I'd seen him do it and dropped another one.

Then when Mr. Vaccaro picked up Mr. Mazza's ball to concede the hole, he substituted a different one that looked the same if you didn't look too closely. If Mr. Mazza hit that Titleist 2, he'd lose the hole and the match and five bucks. It would look like he'd hit the wrong ball from the short rough on the seventeenth, and there was no way I could tell them that I knew he'd hit a Titleist 3 back there, because then I'd have to tell them that I'd dropped it.

On the other hand, Skeeter couldn't very well say he knew

I'd dropped a ball, because then he'd have to admit he'd picked up the original one.

I took another Titleist 3 from my pocket, gave it to Mr. Mazza, and tossed that 2 into the bushes.

Mr. Mazza had the honor on the eighteenth. "Whaddya think here?" he said to me.

"Four-iron, sir. Keep it in the fairway."

He cocked his head at me and grinned. "Yeah. Good idea."

He took his 4-iron and hit it right down the middle.

Mr. Vaccaro sliced his drive into the rough.

Mr. Mazza hit to the fringe, while Mr. Vaccaro had to punch out of the rough. But then he hit a nice iron to the middle of the green, and when Mr. Mazza chipped about six feet past the hole, they were both lying three.

Mr. Vaccaro was away. His putt stopped about a foot from the hole. He looked up at Mr. Mazza, who waved his hand. "That's good," he said.

Mr. Vaccaro picked up his ball. "Big putt, Paulie," he said. "Make this one, you win. Looks like you got a little break to the left. Hit it firm. You been leaving 'em short all day."

I was squinting along the line of Mr. Mazza's putt. It looked straight-in to me, and if he hit past the hole, he'd catch the downslope and who knows where his ball would end up.

Mr. Mazza came around to where I was standing. "Looks straight-in to me," he whispered.

"Me, too," I said. "Just don't hit it too hard. You come up short, worst thing happens, you tap in and halve the hole. Too long, it'll roll forever, leave you a tough one coming back."

Mr. Mazza patted my cheek. "You're a smart kid."

Then he went back, stood up to his putt, and dropped it in the middle of the hole.

"Congratulations," said Mr. Vaccaro. "Pressure putt. Looks like you win." He reached into the hole and took out Mr. Mazza's ball. He tossed it up and down in his hand a couple times, then held it up, pretending to notice something. I saw his mouth open and close.

It wasn't the Titleist 2 he expected to see.

Slowly he turned his head and looked right at me, and his eyes drilled into me from behind those sunglasses for what seemed like about ten minutes. Then he sort of shrugged and tossed the ball to Mr. Mazza. "Let's go have a beer, Paulie," he said. "Winner buys, huh?"

On the way back to the clubhouse, Mr. Mazza slipped me a hundred-dollar bill. "Good work today, kid," he said.

You don't know half of it, I thought.

"Same time tomorrow, huh?" he said.

"Yes, sir."

After I got his clubs cleaned and stowed in his locker, I took the back stairs up to the members' bar and got Judy, one of the waitresses, to change my hundred-dollar bill into tens and twenties so I could take care of my old man.

Mr. Mazza and Mr. Vaccaro were sitting at a table by the window that looked out at the tennis courts. Neither of them were watching the girls in their little white skirts, though. Mr. Vaccaro was leaning on his forearms with his face pushed forward, talking in a low snarly voice, and Mr. Mazza was kind of slouched back with his arms folded, looking down into his lap, nodding and shaking his head and shrugging, not saying anything.

"What's with them?" I whispered to Judy.

"Those two, I don't want to know," she said. "Something about trucks."

•   •   •

When I got home, my old man was waiting at the kitchen table with his hand out, as usual. I gave him a twenty and a ten.

"Hey," he said. "Good day, huh?"

"Mr. Mazza won a big match, tipped me extra."

The old man gave the ten back to me. "Here, son. Guess you earned a little something for yourself."

"Thanks, Pop."

"So tell me about this big match."

"We were playing a guy named Vaccaro, and—"

"Vaccaro?" said my old man. "Fat, bald guy, wears sunglasses alla time?"

I nodded. "So it came down to the eighteenth hole, and—"

"Wait a fuckin' minute," he said. "You talkin' about Anthony Vaccaro? T-Bone Vaccaro?"

I shrugged. "I guess so."

"You know who T-Bone Vaccaro is?"

"He's got a slice but keeps the ball in play. Cheats about as bad as Mr. Mazza."

"T-Bone Vaccaro's the man," said my old man. "The boss. You follow me?"

"No."

"Your Paulie Mazza, he works for Vaccaro. Vaccaro tells Mazza to go fuck himself, Mazza says, 'Yes, sir. Where, sir?' T-Bone Vaccaro owns half the cops and politicians in the state. I hope the hell you didn't cross him, son. You were polite to him, right?"

"Sure, Pop. I was polite."

But I cheated him, I thought. And he knew it.

• • •

The next day I was waiting at the practice tee with Mr. Mazza's clubs and a bag of range balls. He didn't show up at 12:30, like he always did, and he still wasn't there at one o'clock, his regular tee time.

Finally around 1:30, Mac, the caddie master, came out. "Bring them clubs back," he said. "Mr. Mazza ain't playing today."

"No? How come?"

Mac shrugged. "Sick or something, I guess."

"Mr. Mazza called in sick?"

"Nah. Mr. Vaccaro told me. Said Mr. Mazza wasn't feeling good. He wants to talk to you."

"Who?"

"You. Mr. Vaccaro's waitin' on the patio. You better put them clubs away and hustle your ass out there."

"What's he want with me?"

"I don't know," said Mac. "He don't look too happy, I can tell you that."

I lugged Mr. Mazza's clubs back to the clubhouse, taking my time, trying to think, trying not to panic, and by the time I got to the patio, I'd pretty much decided that the best thing was just to admit what I'd done and make sure Mr. Vaccaro knew that Mr. Mazza had put me up to it.

Mr. Vaccaro was sitting alone at the table with a glass of beer. He was wearing a straw hat and sunglasses, and he was puffing on a cigar and watching a foursome of women tee off on the tenth hole.

I stood there for a minute waiting for him to notice me.

Finally I said, "You wanted to see me, sir?"

He swiveled his head around slowly. "Sit down."

I took the chair across from him.

"You want something to drink?"

"No, thank you."

He looked back at the ladies, and without turning his head, he said, "I'm thinking I'm gonna start playing more golf. Three, four times a week, maybe. That match yesterday, I had a good time, you know?"

"Yes, sir."

He turned and looked at me. "That kid Skeeter, he's a pretty good caddie, huh?"

I nodded.

"Not as good as you, though."

I didn't say anything to that.

"Paulie Mazza," said Mr. Vaccaro, "he don't beat me yesterday if Skeeter's caddying for him." He took off his sunglasses. His eyes reminded me of a lizard's, dark and hooded and without expression. "I had my eye on you, kid. It was you beat me, not Paulie."

"I was only—"

Mr. Vaccaro held up his hand. "I want you, my personal caddie."

"Well, yeah, but Mr. Mazza—"

"Mazza gave up golf," said Mr. Vaccaro. "He ain't coming back. Forget about Paulie Mazza, understand?"

"Yes, sir."

"You're a good caddie, kid, but you don't wanna carry golf bags, give alla your money to your old man, for the rest of your life, you know."

I nodded.

"So," he said, "let's talk about the rest of your life."

THE SECRET

John Westermann

Things slow down here fast after Labor Day and die off completely by the end of September, which is tomorrow, Sunday, getaway day at Le Club Fantastique. The weatherman on the pro shop stereo has been calling for heavy rain starting tonight and continuing through the weekend. Municipal courses on Long Island will be jammed, anyway, with poor bastards dragging themselves through sodden, seven-hour loops. Here at East Hampton's fabulously private Le Club Fantastique, three hundred acres of grass and dunes between Montauk Highway and the Atlantic Ocean, it will be just me, folding pink sweaters and stacking Ping golf bags, closing things down from dawn until dark.

For the record, my name is Jay Swann, assistant pro at this Siberian outpost, as I was last season. The head pro and director of golf, positions no self-respecting tour caddie would accept, is my half brother Levon Greenbriar. Of course, Levon left town two weeks ago for South Florida, allegedly to find us an apartment and winter jobs. More likely he is sunning himself with a topless waitress by a motel pool. Like most employees of Le Club, there are reasons we work here and few of them are good. Twice I have scanned the PGA Web site for West Coast job openings, looking to go it alone. Twice I have changed my mind, admitting, accepting, that Levon is the rainmaker.

Hence my position bogged down in these northern latitudes. When members drop in to play on this penultimate day of the season, it will be me who hauls their clubs out of storage and sets up the carts, who trades golf tips for stock tips, who does not cringe at their guests. Me, Jay Swann, of average looks and questionable parentage, already thirty and still working for twelve dollars an hour, plus half of my lesson fees. Levon gets the other half. And Levon isn't even all that handsome or witty, but Levon has blond hair working and that year-round tan, and he can listen to hours of drivel to get where he's going.

For me, it's all about the game.

Before heading South, Levon informed me that our continued employment here, or anywhere else in golf, depended on Le Club's notoriously difficult membership accepting my final draft of Levon's annual report: my, his, explanation of the occurrences leading up to the crime that spooked the Hamptons this summer.

"Keep it short and uninformative," he said, leaning on the roof of his overloaded Subaru Outback. Levon had dressed in denim and black cowboy boots for the road, any sign he was a sissy golf pro hidden, any good-byes already said. "File that sucker as you turn out the lights. Finish upbeat, you know, like a lesson. Make me proud." He flipped down his metallic-blue sunglasses and vanished.

Today was the last good day to write the report, as tomorrow I was also on that southbound highway. I had only one foursome out on the course at the moment, Mr. Jason Kravitz and his three doofus guests. The surplus clothing stock was mothballed, the new clubs reboxed and stacked, the billing records up-to-date. I fixed a cup of instant coffee and sat in my comfortable office off the shop, fired up the desktop computer. Dear Sirs, I began, not to be sexist, but because the husbands are the members here, not the wives, even if the women are sufficiently offensive to qualify on their own. And then I froze, remembering that the members are not individually— nor as a group—easily pleased, which is how they got to be members here in the first place. They are very rich, and they have been blackballed everywhere else. You know who I mean. The people of whom it is often said, "Not for all the tea in China."

How rich? The initiation at Le Club Fantastique is $200,000, and you have to buy a bond. The annual dues and fees are another twenty-five grand. How gauche? If I were to get up from my desk and walk you into the floral-scented locker room to greet the tuxedoed staff, you'd see names on the lockers you'd know, but not from the world of golf. We've got three dot-com billionaires—Jason Kravitz is one of them—and a Pakistani newsstand operator who won Powerball. Most have closed up their summer homes and returned to their kiosks and their baseball teams, their paving companies and dental practices.

The staff and I have Le Club pretty much to ourselves these days, and a magnificent place it is. They spared no expense when they built this place three years ago. The clubhouse atop the preeminent hill is a copy of the White House, right down to the security measures. A uniformed stylist remains on duty in both locker rooms. The men have a Grill Room. The women have a Necessary Room. The house staff is obedient and docile, usually imported from Ireland.

I know because I dated two of them this summer.

The handsome young caddies in their fresh white overalls winter at Wesleyan, Columbia, Georgetown, and Brown. They will never be members here. Here is for losers.

The golf course is short, the fairways wide, and the greens slow. The signature features are all but unhittable by the members; only a good player making a bad swing or a moron with a wild driver can find any serious trouble. Thus we've got 7s strutting tall here who couldn't break 90 at Shinnecock or Garden City, not that they'd ever get invited to such illustrious venues. And why should their golf lives be any less phony than their public lives? Most members never take a lesson. Why learn a skill when you can buy a self-correcting, titanium-shafted 9-wood, or cheat? Like lousy parents, they apply but a millisecond of ill-considered influence, and then yell, "Be good, baby. Be as good as you look. Ah, hell. I'll take a mulligan."

I'm a purist, and I purely hate the members, though I hide it well, or I have up till now. And nobody liked the victim, anyway, which is definitely par for this course.

Ah, yes, the victim, the sticky part of the report. Everything else would be smooth sailing, lies I've told before. What a grand season of golf and good fellowship we enjoyed, how much everyone improved, hosannas to the club champions and their beautiful new diamond rings, the planned course improvements, stay fit, see you in May, a tap-in for a schmoozer like me. It was only the disappearance of our member—and last year's D-Flight champion—Slingblade Beinstock that needed to be handled with care. (For a skinny little guy, Sling-blade could hurl his Odyssey prodigious distances when the wind was with him.)

"Jay? Are you on the counter, perchance?"

I spun around in my studded-leather chair to see Mr. Jason Kravitz leaning into my office, the dot-com geek in the midst of a spectacularly bad hair day. "Yes, sir. How was your round? Little windy?"

Mr. Kravitz gave me the deep frown of a man who thinks I really care how he played. "Only fair, Jay. Only fair. In fact, for a moment, dreadfully embarrassing."

"You didn't whiff one again, did you?"

"I wish I had, Jay, God help me. No, what happened is, one of my guests, big Wall Street guy, mergers and acquisitions, found some beer cans in a sand trap on the twelfth. Four, I think. Cans. Budweiser."

"Damn kids," I said. "Once the season ends they sneak in through that hole in the hedge, mostly at night. It's an unfortunate local tradition."

"That's no excuse, Jay. This land is for our exclusive enjoyment, whether we're actually here or not. And I don't enjoy the image of children drinking in our bunkers. I swear, winter can't come soon enough."

I had not the heart to tell him the man-sized break in the privet hedge was used by the locals to reach these snow-covered hills with their sleds. Somewhere, sometime, this guy Kravitz had taken a sales course that preached the cheerful repetition of the sucker's name. "I'll tell Emmett Bessler down in the security booth. Maybe they can double up the night watch."

"Good. Plus the greens were a little slow."

"What'd you shoot, sir?"

"Eighty, but it woulda been better if somebody'd thought to mow the damn grass."

"Yes, sir. Well, last day and all that. Breaking down and greasing the mowers. Now, do you want your golf clubs cleaned and packed to travel or will we be storing them here for the winter?"

Jason Kravitz shrugged his narrow shoulders as he turned for the locker room, showing me a bald spot I'd never seen before. "I don't know yet. Keep 'em out for now. I'll come back after my rubdown."

"Very good, sir."

And people wonder how a member here might have been the victim of a crime. Did the notion of a year-end tip never once cross his mind?

Anyway, it all started during the heat wave back in July, at the annual Sadie Hawkins Matches, where the ladies invite men other than their husbands to team up and scramble, the purpose being to stimulate sociability among the normally deplored. The rather austere Sarah Beinstock invited probationary member Jersey Joe Krumholt to join her team, and the new club hottie, Karen Krumholt, invited Sarah's husband, Slingblade, to join her. (In the interest of full disclosure, I freely admit I give Jersey Joe lessons now and then, but he's hopeless, both at golf and at club life, always showing up dusty, dressed in one of those faux athletic suits. My lessons have not helped him, but he says he enjoys our time together. I'm glad, because he carries a revolver on his ankle.) They set off in their golf carts from the first tee that Saturday morning with good spirits and high hopes, and large bottles of Absolut vodka. Somewhere on the back nine lightning struck; for they returned from 18 slobbering all over each other, laughing and grabbing ass. Their scorecard was illegible. They didn't care. They didn't even stay for the dinner-dance, just kept the team thing going into separate BMW station wagons, and then whizzed off from the gate of Le Club Fantastique in opposite directions.

Nothing happened, they told everyone the next day at the Sunday brunch. They just did it for laughs, to get everybody all worked up. Oh, such fun! No one believed them.

No one even cared all that much, except Levon, who had spent many pleasant hours alone with Mrs. Karen Krumholt while Jersey Joe was erecting a strip mall back West. Karen and Levon had met first at the club, where Levon adjusted her putting grip, then at the Krumholt summer house, where Levon tightened her stance. Levon believed he had developed a summer-long understanding with Mrs. Krumholt. I knew better, but I kept it to myself. I knew a lot of things I kept to myself this summer—besides the fact that Karen Krumholt hadn't totally fallen for Levon like the women at the last two clubs we'd worked. I also knew Jersey Joe and Slingblade had paid their wives to swap, and the wives liked it, both the swapping and getting paid. A win-win situation, I believe it was called by Jersey Joe.

Problem was, the inequality was built right in; and it wasn't long before Jersey Joe took to grumbling at our weekend lessons. Joe had a job running a construction business; Slingblade had a position as a GOP committeeman in Nassau County, New York. Few of Slingblade's several official titles required his actual attendance, and then only for an hour at a time. Slingblade thereby got the lion's share of the goodies.

Early August I heard that Jersey Joe had complained to

Slingblade after about a week of not being able to reach his own wife on her cell phone, like maybe they could come up for air?

After another long hot week away at his Camden job site, Jersey Joe made a bigger stink. Slingblade commiserated with him in the locker room one Sunday morning and offered to get him some public work in Nassau, the easiest money ever. Jersey Joe thought he was too heavily reliant on the country club for business already.

"You don't want a no-brainer, I won't twist your arm."

"In fact, let's call the whole damn thing off," said Jersey Joe as the two walked out to the tee, "even though I only nailed your Sarah twice."

"Fine. Five a side?"

"You're on. And don't cheat. And you'll leave my Karen alone? You know I know bad people."

"The same bad people I know, Joe."

"Answer me one question?" said Jersey Joe. "You took Viagra, right?"

Slingblade winked at Jersey Joe. "Once-in-a-lifetime chance like this?"

That night in the clubhouse dining room Jersey Joe told his wife that the men had decided the swapping was over. He took her velvet hands in his and said he was sorry he had so debased their wedding vows. He would make it up to her. Karen Krumholt laughed in his face right there at the table, then stood and asked if there was a lawyer in the room, announcing that she wanted a divorce, to better pursue Slingblade. "His nickname," she told everyone, "has nothing to do with him throwing his putter."

"Sit down," hissed Jersey Joe. "He's on the Viagra, you moron."

Karen Krumholt slapped Jersey Joe across the face and stormed outside to the clubhouse porch. She ordered the valet to summon a cab, and got to their rented summer house on Georgica Pond ahead of her husband, had his things packed and moved into a cheap suite at the ancient Hampton Arms before Jersey Joe honked angrily at the locked front gate. A call was then placed from the Krumholt home to the East Hampton police. The street was quiet when the first of three police cars arrived. Jersey Joe told me later he drove to Camden and spent the night on the couch in a trailer, unable to sleep. He told me he cried till the bricklayers showed up at dawn, which was too much information.

Two nights later, at the third annual membership meeting, the current members met in the west-wing library to winnow the list of probationary members who would be invited to move up in class, to buy an additional bond. This was usually a nonevent, as distinction and breeding were never considered. You could write the check, you made the cut. Not on this memorable night, though. When the name Joseph Krumholt was solemnly announced, and the ceremonial loving cup presented to each member by a waiter, Slingblade Beinstock dropped a coal-black marble into the mix.

"Holy cow," said President Shank Grucci. "That's a first for Le Club, breaking three years of tradition. You sure?"

"Not entirely because of him," said Slingblade. "His wife is bad news, too."

Shank Grucci turned to his hovering aide. "Draft a letter to Mr. Krumholt immediately. Application denied for cause: Wife bad news. Then go clean out their lockers. I don't want them dragging their chins around the pro shop Labor Day weekend."

Me and Levon stood in a corner and watched this small revenge in horror, both of us wondering how a little fun had got so out of hand.

• • •

Three nights later Sarah Beinstock called the East Hampton police to her family's oceanfront estate to report that Slingblade had failed to return from a Nassau County golf outing in Old Brookville. She felt certain her husband had fallen in harm's way, given the crumbling of our culture, and she cried real tears on the television news.

It took the local cops two days to zero in on the love swap at Le Club, and they scooped up Jersey Joe for questioning at his job site. But Joe had an alibi, as did his newly estranged wife. So did Sarah Beinstock, for that matter, who had been at the same charity luncheon as Karen Krumholt on the afternoon in question, although, reportedly, the two never conversed. Then everybody had a theory, from the sublime to the silly. Nassau Democrats promoted one theory that gained traction, that his life-long interest in municipal garbage had led Slingblade to some ill-gotten cash. He had always bragged that he was leaving public service with his pockets full. Not that I wanted to put something derogatory like that in the annual report. These members pay dearly to feel good about themselves and their fellows. They need the strokes.

The phone at my arm rang once, and I banged my right knee. "Pro shop. Swann."

"Em Bessler, main gate security detail. There's a Detective John Marks on his way up to see you."

I had the picture instantly. Old Emmett, in the front booth, wearing his generalissimo cap and golden epaulets, raising the black-and-white-striped barricade, saluting as the cops rolled past. "Because you told him I was up here, right? Emmett, how many times do I have to tell you—"

"Why? Did I—"

"That little puke Jason Kravitz wants a chunk of your ass, Emmett. Wants to bust you down to admiral."

"What now?"

"This time I'll let you be surprised." I hung up on the brain-dead security guard and quick-stepped through the near-empty racks of the pro shop and outside to the porch. A row of angry gray clouds raced past the portico from west to east, bound for the distant, churning ocean, as the wind, like most days here, merely howled. John Marks, the Suffolk County detective on the Slingblade missing persons case, the detective who had been leaving progressively nastier messages on Levon's answering machine, had stopped his black Caprice short of the parking lot and whipped his Big Bertha driver out of the still-open trunk. He was presently launching slices from our high-plains driving range.

"Start down with your legs," I told him as I approached from behind, "then accelerate your hands through the ball. You'll lose that big banana."

"Is that The Secret?" he asked, turning to me, exasperated.

"You mean is that the one key move to long powerful shots? No. But it helps." If that was The Secret, I certainly would not just up and tell Detective John Marks. I would not just give it away. No pro does. We rarely even mention The Secret to each other, fearful our social status and comfortable incomes would evaporate overnight."

"But there is a Secret?"

"If there was, you'd have to beat it out of me."

Detective Marks laughed, thank God. He regripped and addressed another ball, then looked back at me, and I'm thinking, Everybody wants free lessons. "Seen your buddy Levon today?"

I kept up my golf-outing smile. "The boss went South already. Couple of weeks ago. Rank has its privileges, you know."

"Kinda early, isn't it?"

"Not if you want a golf job. Levon don't feature flipping burgers."

Detective Marks wrinkled his nose, sniffed the salty wind like a retriever. "I guess I made a long trip for nothing. You heard from him since he left town?"

"Now and then, sure. Odds and ends for the club. Buncha the members waiting for some Steelheads™ to come in."

"Got an address on Mr. Greenbriar?"

"Nothing permanent yet. Why?"

"Not for nothing, kid, but I'm about to arrest a very rich and powerful man, and I want to make sure I'm right."

"What would Levon know? I gave Mr. Krumholt his golf lessons. But he didn't talk personal stuff. Just the NASDAQ."

"I say anything about Joe Krumholt?"

"No. I guess you didn't."

Detective Marks shook his head and winked at me knowingly. "Start down with the legs, huh? Let me try that. I'm hooked on this crazy game."

I nodded. "Aren't we all, my man, aren't we all?"

John Marks addressed a ball and swung hard, legs first, drilling it straight and true. His face lit up. "Damn. Can I try that again?"

"I am kinda busy. You know we're closing up."

"No problem, kid. But next time he calls, you tell Mr. Greenbriar to call me or I'm gonna go grab up his ass as a material witness. I like a free trip to Florida as much as the next man."

I put my hand to my throat. "You think Levon knows something about Slingblade Beinstock? Well, I'll be damned. Jesus, you work with a guy for two summers and . . ."

Detective Marks walked to his squad car and gently laid his Big Bertha next to his riot gun. "Looks like rain," said Marks, opening the driver's-side door. "Jesus, I hate rain, unless I'm playing golf, hitting it like that last ball. Then I don't mind." Marks leaned close to me, looked both ways. "Any chance I could sneak in a round tomorrow? I know you're closing up, but I wouldn't be in the way. Place should be empty, right?"

"Levon Greenbriar ain't gonna be here. I swear it."

"I know. I believe you. I love this game."

"We'd be honored."

• • •

I left work at six o'clock that evening and drove my dirty black Neon to the dirty Hampton Arms apartment I had shared that summer with Levon. I packed my dirty clothes in my duffel bags, threw out my mail, broke down my PlayStation. I drank cold coffee and grew nervous as I worked, the local twenty-four-hour news on my nineteen-inch television for background. As it got dark outside, I closed my blinds, feeling I was being watched. When I was ready, prepared to travel at a moment's notice, I walked down the main staircase to the dining room, intending to enjoy the last good supper I might eat for quite some time.

Jersey Joe Krumholt was at a table near the fireplace. He waved to me and I waved back.

"Join me?" he called across the half-filled dining room.

"Sorry. Getting something to go. How are things going?" I asked while signaling a waiter for a menu.

"You're joking, right?"

Actually I was just being polite.

"Let's put it this way, Swann. Drop dead."

Back upstairs in my room, I picked at my chicken salad sandwich and worried about what Jersey Joe Krumholt was doing out here alone. Pissed off, on a Saturday night. Wasn't he sick of this snobby town? Hadn't he suffered enough? I opened my window and kicked back on my creaky single bed, wondering where things had gone wrong this summer, deciding, as usual, the fault lay in the selection process, which was Levon's domain. See, at every club there are two—ten—women willing to betray their men at every opportunity. Levon left such women to the busboys, preferring for our purposes the wife on the edge—the seething little woman thinking hard about starting fresh. The foolish heart. Levon's theory was to find that one, tell her repeatedly that you love her more than life itself, and soon enough she'll be handing you her husband's fifties from her purse, then the keys to the kingdom. Then she wakes up one day and her jewelry box is light a few stones and the better artwork's off the walls. Any trouble, we're names without bodies; but they never ever complain, not to their husbands, their sisters, or the cops. They don't want to look dumb or loose. They don't even want to think it was us. And this way we—me and Levon—augment our meager salaries and enliven our workdays, spending every season under a different sun, harboring The Secret, yes, that Secret. The commercials are right: Us guys are good.

I fluffed up my pillow and thought of Amanda Kennedy from last summer, who skipped town in August unscathed, or her husband smelled a rat and they quit Le Club, we never figured out. I thought of the lean winter working we had endured, and the one to come.

I also thought some more about the report to the membership, if I even ought to bother:

Dear Rude Losers,

What a great summer for me and my staff! To make up for playing your bush-league golf course, we got to screw some of the wilder wives and swindle some of the dumber husbands. Your cheapskate swings, bad manners, and seriously funky hair weaves kept us giggling. The golf staff took a year-end survey. No Le Club member likes any other member of Le Club. All are agreed: You people suck. And what the hell is French about golf? Jeez.

Levon and Jay

•   •   •

I slept badly, then scarfed down a buttered roll and coffee outside a 7-Eleven on empty Montauk Highway at dawn. There were puddles in the parking lot, but it wasn't raining at the moment. Dismal, a nice day in Scotland. The full force of the threatened nor'easter was still hours away, high-wind and flood warnings going up for the low-lying areas. Hell of a day for Le Club staff to be loading moving vans, I thought. And way too early to shut down the club at all. The leaves on the trees along the highway were still green, with the best golf weather coming up, autumn in New York. But perhaps even more than playing it, the members loved their course simply sitting empty by the side of the highway, a flaunted jewel which could never be stolen.

I pulled my Neon into the wide driveway. Officer Emmett Bessler put down his coffee mug and activated the U.N.-approved security bar. He slid open the bulletproof window, no doubt to grill me about Kravitz, but I blasted right past him and up the hill. I parked behind the pro shop, near the door where we take deliveries, thinking all I needed from this dump were my magic wands and three pairs of golf shoes, but I ought to hang around, stick to the normal routine, finish upbeat.

I ran up the back stairs and said good-bye to my girlfriends on the kitchen staff, Bridget and Mary Katherine, then ducked into the main office, only to learn from our comptroller, Mrs. Whitney, that our final paychecks would not be cut until two o'clock; and that the annual employee gratuity drive had been discontinued for lack of member interest.

I went back down to my office and was about to call Levon when I wondered if the cops were monitoring the pro shop phone. And as I was thinking just that, Detective John Marks called. "Hey, Jay. I stopped and hit balls on my way home last night. Crushed 'em. Thanks for the leg tip. Still okay to play?"

My heart was hammering in my chest. "You been outside yet?"

"We got hours before the rain. I just checked with our air bureau."

"Your call," I said. "Where are you?"

"Down at the front gate. I brought my boss. Is that okay?"

My stomach flipped. "Absolutely. Come on up."

I met Detective Marks and Sergeant Tony Giordano in the pro shop, hooked them both up with complimentary monogrammed Le Club Fantastique rain gear, which I assured them they would need. They oohed and aahed at the opulence, the class, my generosity.

Marks even patted me on the back. "Mind if we poke around Levon's office? While we're here?"

"Nope. Not at all." I unlocked the wooden door next to my office and flipped on the track lights, showed them through Levon's empty file cabinet, the wide wooden desk holding the few written communications that had passed between us. It was easy to be smooth. I was innocent. And I was leaving, hopefully before they did. I said, "I hope it doesn't get too wet out there."

"Can we pay you?" asked Detective Marks, his mind back on golf, where it belonged. "Even under the table?"

"Don't be silly."

On the first tee I wrestled the wind with a Titleist umbrella as the homicide cops teed off, then I walked back into my office to catch my breath. My phone message light was beeping, Jersey Joe on the answering machine. "Pick up the damn phone, Swann."

I'd seen enough of Jersey Joe. I hated Jersey Joe. So I damn near fainted when Jersey Joe walked into the pro shop two minutes later, calling my name.

"What are you doing here, sir?" I said, leaning out of my office.

"I came to play golf on my last day of membership. Maybe my last day of freedom. My clubs are in my car. Go get 'em."

"But the detec—"

"The hell with them. I didn't do it. And I'm playing golf today." He lifted the cuff of his black polyester trousers to show me the snub-nose strapped to his ankle.

"I'll ready a cart."

"Put your clubs on it, too. I want a game. And let's play for decent money," he said. "A thousand bucks. Medal play. No handicaps."

Jersey Joe couldn't beat me at that game if I had a bullet in my brain. "Look, Joe, I don't want to—"

"Consider it your annual tip."

We teed off in twenty-mile winds and occasional light rain, conditions I can handle. I was up twelve shots in ten holes, and we were heading for the farthest corner of the course, near the infamous hole in the privet hedge, when the rain began to fall in earnest, like rain in Florida. Water pounded the roof of the cart and poured over the sides. This was senseless, unless Joe planned to shoot me dead. Glove soaked, arms and legs shivering, I turned to Joe and suggested a gentleman's draw. "Forget the thousand dollars."

"I'm being framed, you know, for the Slingblade thing."

"If you didn't do it, how are they gonna prove you did?"

"Lie. Scam. Talk to people who hate me, starting with my wife. People at the club, like you and Levon. Don't be so innocent, kid. I'm not buying it."

"She thinks you did it?"

"No, stupid, she thinks I had somebody do it. Plus the Suffolk cops are asking a judge to rip up all the new foundations in my Camden project. I'm ruined. Understand?" Joe grabbed his driver and bent over slowly to tee his ball on 13, a 130-yard par 3. I said nothing of his club selection, even as his ball sailed over the green and came to rest in Satan's Bum, the deepest bunker on Long Island.

"Take your mulligan," I said. Which he did. No member ever played from Satan's Bum, an unwritten club rule. Then I teed my ball and yanked my 8-iron in there with Joe's first ball. Of course, the pro gets no sympathy.

Joe dropped me off at the cavernous bunker's edge with my sand wedge and putter and drove off to bungle his next shot. Now, I'm not much for the supernatural, but I considered it bad mojo to dump one in Satan's Bum to close out my season. I narrowed my focus, determined to make a terrific recovery, show this fat-ass chump developer some golf. I climbed the wooden stairs down to the bottom of the pit and dug my cleats into the oddly squishy sand. My lie was decent, the ball sitting up. I laid my blade open, flared my left foot, and gouged mightily, blasting my golf ball high into the gray sky above the rim of the bunker; and also, with that one swing, slapping the bony remains of a human hand against the grassy wall before me, where it stuck a moment, then flopped down to the sand. I noticed the D-Flight championship ring right away. Then I heard Jersey Joe cry through the howling wind, "Great shot, kid. Six feet."

I climbed up out of the bunker and flashed thumbs-up. "Thanks. You have no idea."

I wanted to strangle my lazy half brother. The way Levon had told it, Slingblade's death was an accident, all cleaned up. On the day in question Levon had gone to the Krumholt house to resume the private lessons, and when Karen wasn't home, he took off his clothes, drew the shades in her bedroom, and hopped into bed. Just then Slingblade, who couldn't keep his word about anything, pried open the back door and started up the stairs. Both men knew Jersey Joe carried that gun and that grudge. They heard each other moving around; they scared each other. Levon said he found a wedge in the closet and used it on the back of Slingblade's skull as Slingblade crawled into the bedroom with a putter. But then Levon had also said he'd found the perfect place for the body, so who knew? My damn hands were shaking so badly I missed the putt, my first bogey of the round.

It was raining even harder when we passed the detectives at the point where the eighteenth and fourteenth fairways run side by side, and I noticed they were making great time for hackers. I left Joe at his ball and raced the cart across the wide, puddled fairway.

"How's it going?" I yelled to my drenched guests.

"Great. These suits are awesome."

"I'm with Jersey Joe Krumholt," I said. "Against my wishes."

"Yeah, we noticed."

"He's got a gun."

"He's got a permit," said Sergeant Giordano.

Detective Marks was beaming. "Forget Krumholt for a minute. He's *our* worry, isn't he? What's important is, it's working, the legs thing. I'm four over par and I've never broken 100."

"It's working for me, too," said Giordano. "Best round of my life. I owe you, kid, I've never had so much fun."

I said, "Then by all means, keep it rolling, boys. Finish strong." I just love a happy golfer, thinking he owns the answer, wishing everyone he ever knew was there to witness his mastery, mentally lining up victims. I pitied these poor policemen when they played a real golf course again, where the fairways were not so generous, the greens sloped and fast, and the bunkers placed where they could actually be hit. Their hands would tighten, their balls would find woods and rough and sand. The pressure would multiply; they had such high expectations. Then poof! All competence departs, and they are once again hackers, mired in triple digits. Such is the curse of Le

Club Fantastique. Golfers remember that for one day at that really exclusive club, they had it going on. "You're welcome to have a cold one at the clubhouse when you finish," I said. "Tell Woodward to put it on my tab."

Well, they couldn't thank me enough, of course, and the stuffy upstairs barman would complete the grease job. The detectives huddled under the roof of their cart and opened their wallets. They handed me PBA cards with their home phone numbers scrawled on the backs so we could do this again next summer.

Jersey Joe, of course, had an attitude when I got back to him. "Take me back in," he said. "Go play with your friends."

"What? I'm gonna ignore them?"

Joe shrugged, and counted out ten wet hundreds from his pocket for me, which I felt bad for taking. "Drive," he said, "I'm done with this place."

"Whatever."

I dropped Joe at the side door to the men's locker room and went into my office, dried myself with clean towels.

Then I sat down to write what I knew I had to write.

Dear Members,

It has been my distinct pleasure to serve your golfing needs this past season. Many of you showed dramatic improvement. All of you seemed to have fun. Stay in shape and watch the calendar. Opening day is only eight months away.

Best wishes,
Levon Greenbriar,
Director of Golf, Le Club Fantastique

I punched PRINT and carried the annual report upstairs, and as I looked out the window behind Mrs. Whitney, I saw the cop car in the parking lot. I hoped my having an open, ongoing, bar tab did not affect the release of my paycheck. I hoped I had not just screwed myself.

Mrs. Whitney handed me two paychecks, mine and Levon's.

"No open bar tabs?" I said, willing to pay with Jersey Joe's wet cash. "I believe I have a couple of police officers encamped at the bar."

"No you don't," she said. "Those gentlemen came in here to get some records. They're reading them right now in the library."

"Members' records?"

"Employees'."

I kept smiling and wished her a happy off-season, then took the back stairs two at a time down to the basement maintenance office. I locked the metal door, sat on a paint-spattered stool, and called Levon on his cell phone. I could hear someone splashing in the background, children squealing. Ah, the things we do for golf.

"I yanked one into Satan's Bum this morning," I said.

"You took a mulligan, I hope?"

"I wish."

I heard Levon light a cigarette. "Anybody see you? Or it?"

"Nope. And I was playing with Jersey Joe."

"Jesus Christ, are you kidding me? Only you would hit one in there on the last day of the year."

"Snap-hooked it, okay? The cops were on our ass."

"You got our paychecks?"

"Yup."

"Let's hear my annual report," he said. "And, Jay, if this

sucker's any good, we still might tee it up one more time at Le Club." Levon, if that was his winter name, no doubt figured if the cops busted Joe Krumholt for the Slingblade murder, we could squeeze in one more summer before the trial began.

I was not so confident. I read aloud to Levon slowly, without inflection. Just the facts. Well, two of them.

"Cool," Levon said after a moment, as if he were wrestling his conscience or sipping a lime-stuffed cocktail. "Very cool. Hey, Jay, I got us part-time jobs, okay? Teaching on the range, a little time in the pro shop. We start Wednesday, so haul ass."

"Where?"

Levon mentioned some fancy-sounding country club I'd never heard of in a tiny town I'd never heard of. No big whoop. They were all the same to me. Like I said, it's all about the golf.

Halfway through the pro shop I heard my answering machine take a call from Mrs. Whitney. She was sorry to bother me but I was needed back upstairs at once. Well, I don't have to tell you, I left my magic wands on the back of Jersey Joe's golf cart and jumped into my half-gassed Neon feeling like a man abandoning a child.

I skidded to a stop next to the squad car, saw the boys in blue had left it unlocked. I yanked the microphone from the radio and snatched the pair of cell phones from the dash, then got back in the Neon and raced down the hill. I stopped under the razor-wire awning at the security booth only because the barrier was made of heavy metal and my Neon is not. I leaned out my window and shook hands with Em Bessler, told the old man I was sorry I'd been hard on him lately, but that I'd deflected the beer-can complaints of Mr. Jason Kravitz.

He winked. "I know the pressure you're under, club full of flaming tyrants like this one."

"You got that right."

And then we both gazed wistfully up through the driving rain at the clubhouse, just as Detective Marks and Sergeant Giordano ran from the front porch and across the parking lot for their squad car. I noticed that they, too, had abandoned their golf clubs.

I said, "Oh, hell, Emmett, this cheapskate moron's been stalking me for golf tips. Can you keep him busy a few minutes? Like five?"

"Thinks you know The Secret, eh?" Emmett smiled greedily. "You share that little Secret with me, I'll shine him on. Otherwise, I think a lifelong security man like myself ought to be on the side of law enforcement, don't you?"

Not that tough a call, actually, when you think about it. He would take it out and try it. He would suddenly hit golf balls the way he always knew he could, and his life would mean something again. Small price for me to pay. And beggars can't be choosers. I made him lean close and whispered those three magic words in Emmett's ear and his eyes lit up with joy.

"Tell no one," I said.

"I'll take it to my grave."

And I believed he would, because most do.

The steel barrier rose and I raced out of Le Club Fantastique and into the anonymous storm, and, as I careened around a bend on Montauk Highway, I saw in my rearview mirror the homicide squad car skid to a stop at the now repositioned barrier. Detective Marks leaned out the driver's window, yelling at the booth.

A moment later the bulletproof window opened, and the

fringe of a golden epaulet whipped in the wind. Detective Marks jammed his shield in the face of Emmett Bessler, newly deputized guardian of The Secret; but the barrier did not budge.

I slid the new Dave Matthews CD into my dashboard and slowed down to the legal limit, lest I draw the attention of the highway patrol, never mind my pocketful of PBA cards.

I figured I had plenty of time. Em Bessler did dumb-ass better than most.

GOLF MYSTERIES

This list is alphabetical by author, listing the title, city, publisher, and date of the first printing. No effort is made to provide authors' real names in cases where they have used pseudonyms, variant titles, or reprints.

Adams, Herbert. *The Secret of Bogey House.* London, Methuen, 1924.

————. *The Golf House Murder.* Philadelphia, Lippincott, 1933.

————. *The Body in the Bunker.* London, Collins, 1935.

————. *Death Off the Fairway.* London, Collins, 1936.

————. *The Nineteenth Hole Mystery.* London, Collins, 1939.

————. *One to Play.* London, Macdonald, 1949.

————. *Death on the First Tee.* London, Macdonald, 1957.

Allen, Leslie. *Murder in the Rough.* New York, Five Star, 1946.

Anderson, W. A. *Kill 1 Kill 2.* New York, Morrow, 1940.

Ball, Brian. *Death of a Low-Handicap Man.* London, Barker, 1974.

Bartlett, James Y. *Death Is a Two Stroke Penalty.* New York, St. Martin's, 1991.

————. *Death from the Ladies' Tee.* New York, St. Martin's, 1992.

Bentley, E. C. *Trent's Own Case.* London, Constable, 1936.

Bernhardt, William. *Final Round.* New York, Ballantine, 2002.

Borissow, Michael. *The Naked Fairway.* Cranbrook, Kent, Cranbrook Golf Club, 1984.

Borthwick, J. S. *Murder in the Rough.* New York, St. Martin's, 2002.

Box, Sidney. *Alibi in the Rough.* London, Hale, 1977.

Bream, Freda. *The Vicar Investigates*. London, Hale, 1983.

———. *Sealed and Dispatched*. London, Hale, 1984.

Bruff, Nancy. *The Country Club*. New York, Bartholomew House, 1969.

Burton, Miles. *Tragedy at the Thirteenth Hole*. London, Collins, 1933.

Bush, Christopher. *The Case of the Green Felt Hat*. London, Cassell, 1939.

Cake, Patrick. *Pro-Am Murders*. Aptos, CA, Proteus, 1979.

Canning, Victor. *The Limbo Line*. London, Heinemann, 1963.

Casley, Dennis. *Death Under Par*. London, Constable, 1997.

Causey, James O. *Killer Take All*. New York, Graphic, 1957.

Chabody, Philip and Florence. *The 86 Proof Pro*. Jericho, NY, Exposition, 1974.

Christie, Agatha. *Murder on the Links*. London, John Lane, 1923.

———. *Why Didn't They Ask Evans?* London, Collins, 1934.

———. *Towards Zero*. London, Collins, 1944.

———. *The 4:50 from Paddington*. London, Collins, 1957.

Coben, Harlan. *Deal Breaker*. New York, Dell, 1995.

———. *Backspin*. New York, Dell, 1997.

Comfort, Barbara. *The Cashmere Kid*. Woodstock, VT, Foul Play, 1993.

Cooney, Caroline B. *Sand Trap*. New York, Avon, 1983.

Cork, Barry. *Dead Ball*. London, Collins, 1988.

———. *Unnatural Hazard*. London, Collins, 1989.

———. *Laid Dead*. London, Collins, 1990.

———. *Winter Rules*. London, Collins, 1991.

———. *Endangered Species*. London, Collins, 1992.

Corrigan, John. *Cut Shot*. Farmington Hills, MI, Sleeping Bear, 2001.

Crawford, Ian. *Scare the Gentle Citizen*. London, Hammond, 1966.

Cruickshank, Charles. *The Tang Murder*. London, Hale, 1976.

Cullen, Bob. *A Mulligan for Bobby Jones*. New York, HarperCollins, 2001.

Daly, Conor. *Local Knowledge*. New York, Kensington, 1995.

———. *Buried Lies*. New York, Kensington, 1996.

———. *Outside Agency*. New York, Kensington, 1997.

Daly, Elizabeth. *Unexpected Night.* New York, Farrar & Rinehart, 1940.

Devine, Dominic. *Three Green Bottles.* London, Collins, 1972.

Dexter, Ted, and Makins, Clifford. *Deadly Putter.* London, Allen & Unwin, 1979.

Dickson, Carter. *My Late Wives.* New York, Morrow, 1946.

Dods, Marcus. *The Bunker at the Fifth.* Edinburgh, William Hodge, 1925.

DuBois, William. *The Case of the Deadly Diary.* Boston, Little, Brown, 1940.

Duke, Will. *Fair Prey.* New Jersey, Graphic, 1956.

Dunnett, Dorothy. *Dolly and the Doctor Bird.* London, Cassell, 1971.

Durbridge, Francis. *A Game of Murder.* London, Hodder & Stoughton, 1975.

Elkins, Charlotte and Aaron. *A Wicked Slice.* New York, St. Martin's, 1989.

———. *Rotten Lies.* New York, Mysterious Press, 1995.

———. *Nasty Breaks.* New York, Mysterious Press, 1997.

Ellroy, James. *Brown's Requiem.* New York, Avon, 1981.

Engleman, Paul. *Murder-in-Law.* New York, Mysterious Press, 1987.

Fairlie, Gerard. *Mr. Malcolm Presents.* London, Hodder & Stoughton, 1932.

———. *Shot in the Dark.* London, Hodder & Stoughton, 1932.

———. *Men for Counters.* London, Hodder & Stoughton, 1933.

Ferrars, Elizabeth. *The Seven Sleepers.* London, Collins, 1970.

Fleming, Ian. *Goldfinger.* London, Cape, 1959.

Fletcher, J. S. *The Perilous Crossways.* London, Ward, Lock, 1917.

Flynn, J. M. *Terror Tournament.* New York, Bouregy, 1959.

Forse, Harry. *A Storm at Pebble Beach.* Farmington Hills, MI, Sleeping Bear, 2000.

Frome, David. *The Murder on the Sixth Hole.* London, Methuen, 1931.

Fuller, Timothy. *Reunion with Murder.* Boston, Atlantic Little Brown, 1941.

Furlong, Nicola. *Teed Off!* Edmonton, Commonwealth Publications, 1996.

Gibbins, James. *Sudden Death*. London, Collins, 1983.

Gray, Jonathan. *The Owl*. London, Harrap, 1937.

Gregson, J. M. *Murder at the Nineteenth*. London, Collins, 1989.

————. *Dead on Course*. London, Collins, 1991.

————. *Sherlock Holmes and the Frightened Golfer*. London, Breese, 1999.

————. *Death on the Eleventh Hole*. London, Severn House, 2002.

————. *Just Desserts*. London, Severn House, 2004.

Greig, Ian. *The King's Club Murder*. London, Ernest Benn, 1930.

Hallberg, William. *The Rub of the Green*. New York, Doubleday, 1988.

Hamer, Malcolm. *Sudden Death*. London, Headline, 1991.

————. *A Deadly Lie*. London, Headline, 1992.

————. *Death Trap*. London, Headline, 1993.

————. *Shadows on the Green*. London, Headline, 1994.

————. *Dead on Line*. London, Headline, 1996.

Hamilton, Patrick. *Hangover Square*. London, Constable, 1941.

Heller, Jane. *The Club*. New York, Kensington, 1995.

Highsmith, Patricia. *Mermaids on the Golf Course*. London, Heinemann, 1985.

Hunt, Richard. *The Man Trap*. London, Constable, 1996.

Hutchinson, Horace Gordon. *The Lost Golfer*. London, Murray, 1930.

Inigo, Martin. *Stone Dead*. London, Sphere, 1991.

Innes, Michael. *An Awkward Lie*. London, Gollancz, 1971.

Isleib, Roberta. *Six Strokes Under*. New York, Berkley, 2002.

————. *A Buried Lie*. New York, Berkley, 2003.

————. *Putt to Death*. New York, Berkley, 2004.

————. *Fairway to Heaven*. New York, Berkley, 2005.

Jamesson, Peter. *Unplayable Lie*. Farmington Hills, MI, Sleeping Bear, 2002.

Jardine, Quintin. *Skinner's Round*. London, Headline, 1995.

Jerome, Owen Fox. *The Golf Course Murder*. London, Hutchinson, 1928.

Kashner, Rita. *The Graceful Exit*. New York, Atheneum, 1989.

Gibbins, James. *Sudden Death*. London, Collins, 1983.

Gray, Jonathan. *The Owl*. London, Harrap, 1937.

Gregson, J. M. *Murder at the Nineteenth*. London, Collins, 1989.

———. *Dead on Course*. London, Collins, 1991.

———. *Sherlock Holmes and the Frightened Golfer*. London, Breese, 1999.

———. *Death on the Eleventh Hole*. London, Severn House, 2002.

———. *Just Desserts*. London, Severn House, 2004.

Greig, Ian. *The King's Club Murder*. London, Ernest Benn, 1930.

Hallberg, William. *The Rub of the Green*. New York, Doubleday, 1988.

Hamer, Malcolm. *Sudden Death*. London, Headline, 1991.

———. *A Deadly Lie*. London, Headline, 1992.

———. *Death Trap*. London, Headline, 1993.

———. *Shadows on the Green*. London, Headline, 1994.

———. *Dead on Line*. London, Headline, 1996.

Hamilton, Patrick. *Hangover Square*. London, Constable, 1941.

Heller, Jane. *The Club*. New York, Kensington, 1995.

Highsmith, Patricia. *Mermaids on the Golf Course*. London, Heinemann, 1985.

Hunt, Richard. *The Man Trap*. London, Constable, 1996.

Hutchinson, Horace Gordon. *The Lost Golfer*. London, Murray, 1930.

Inigo, Martin. *Stone Dead*. London, Sphere, 1991.

Innes, Michael. *An Awkward Lie*. London, Gollancz, 1971.

Isleib, Roberta. *Six Strokes Under*. New York, Berkley, 2002.

———. *A Buried Lie*. New York, Berkley, 2003.

———. *Putt to Death*. New York, Berkley, 2004.

———. *Fairway to Heaven*. New York, Berkley, 2005.

Jamesson, Peter. *Unplayable Lie*. Farmington Hills, MI, Sleeping Bear, 2002.

Jardine, Quintin. *Skinner's Round*. London, Headline, 1995.

Jerome, Owen Fox. *The Golf Course Murder*. London, Hutchinson, 1928.

Kashner, Rita. *The Graceful Exit*. New York, Atheneum, 1989.

GOLF MYSTERIES

This list is alphabetical by author, listing the title, city, publisher, and date of the first printing. No effort is made to provide authors' real names in cases where they have used pseudonyms, variant titles, or reprints.

Adams, Herbert. *The Secret of Bogey House*. London, Methuen, 1924.

———. *The Golf House Murder*. Philadelphia, Lippincott, 1933.

———. *The Body in the Bunker*. London, Collins, 1935.

———. *Death Off the Fairway*. London, Collins, 1936.

———. *The Nineteenth Hole Mystery*. London, Collins, 1939.

———. *One to Play*. London, Macdonald, 1949.

———. *Death on the First Tee*. London, Macdonald, 1957.

Allen, Leslie. *Murder in the Rough*. New York, Five Star, 1946.

Anderson, W. A. *Kill 1 Kill 2*. New York, Morrow, 1940.

Ball, Brian. *Death of a Low-Handicap Man*. London, Barker, 1974.

Bartlett, James Y. *Death Is a Two Stroke Penalty*. New York, St. Martin's, 1991.

———. *Death from the Ladies' Tee*. New York, St. Martin's, 1992.

Bentley, E. C. *Trent's Own Case*. London, Constable, 1936.

Bernhardt, William. *Final Round*. New York, Ballantine, 2002.

Borissow, Michael. *The Naked Fairway*. Cranbrook, Kent, Cranbrook Golf Club, 1984.

Borthwick, J. S. *Murder in the Rough*. New York, St. Martin's, 2002.

Box, Sidney. *Alibi in the Rough*. London, Hale, 1977.

Bream, Freda. *The Vicar Investigates.* London, Hale, 1983.

———. *Sealed and Dispatched.* London, Hale, 1984.

Bruff, Nancy. *The Country Club.* New York, Bartholomew House, 1969.

Burton, Miles. *Tragedy at the Thirteenth Hole.* London, Collins, 1933.

Bush, Christopher. *The Case of the Green Felt Hat.* London, Cassell, 1939.

Cake, Patrick. *Pro-Am Murders.* Aptos, CA, Proteus, 1979.

Canning, Victor. *The Limbo Line.* London, Heinemann, 1963.

Casley, Dennis. *Death Under Par.* London, Constable, 1997.

Causey, James O. *Killer Take All.* New York, Graphic, 1957.

Chabody, Philip and Florence. *The 86 Proof Pro.* Jericho, NY, Exposition, 1974.

Christie, Agatha. *Murder on the Links.* London, John Lane, 1923.

———. *Why Didn't They Ask Evans?* London, Collins, 1934.

———. *Towards Zero.* London, Collins, 1944.

———. *The 4:50 from Paddington.* London, Collins, 1957.

Coben, Harlan. *Deal Breaker.* New York, Dell, 1995.

———. *Backspin.* New York, Dell, 1997.

Comfort, Barbara. *The Cashmere Kid.* Woodstock, VT, Foul Play, 1993.

Cooney, Caroline B. *Sand Trap.* New York, Avon, 1983.

Cork, Barry. *Dead Ball.* London, Collins, 1988.

———. *Unnatural Hazard.* London, Collins, 1989.

———. *Laid Dead.* London, Collins, 1990.

———. *Winter Rules.* London, Collins, 1991.

———. *Endangered Species.* London, Collins, 1992.

Corrigan, John. *Cut Shot.* Farmington Hills, MI, Sleeping Bear, 2001.

Crawford, Ian. *Scare the Gentle Citizen.* London, Hammond, 1966.

Cruickshank, Charles. *The Tang Murder.* London, Hale, 1976.

Cullen, Bob. *A Mulligan for Bobby Jones.* New York, HarperCollins, 2001.

Daly, Conor. *Local Knowledge.* New York, Kensington, 1995.

———. *Buried Lies.* New York, Kensington, 1996.

———. *Outside Agency.* New York, Kensington, 1997.

Daly, Elizabeth. *Unexpected Night.* New York, Farrar & Rinehart, 194

Devine, Dominic. *Three Green Bottles.* London, Collins, 1972.

Dexter, Ted, and Makins, Clifford. *Deadly Putter.* London, Allen Unwin, 1979.

Dickson, Carter. *My Late Wives.* New York, Morrow, 1946.

Dods, Marcus. *The Bunker at the Fifth.* Edinburgh, William Hodge, 19

DuBois, William. *The Case of the Deadly Diary.* Boston, Little, Bro 1940.

Duke, Will. *Fair Prey.* New Jersey, Graphic, 1956.

Dunnett, Dorothy. *Dolly and the Doctor Bird.* London, Cassell, 1971.

Durbridge, Francis. *A Game of Murder.* London, Hodder & Stough 1975.

Elkins, Charlotte and Aaron. *A Wicked Slice.* New York, St. Mar 1989.

———. *Rotten Lies.* New York, Mysterious Press, 1995.

———. *Nasty Breaks.* New York, Mysterious Press, 1997.

Ellroy, James. *Brown's Requiem.* New York, Avon, 1981.

Engleman, Paul. *Murder-in-Law.* New York, Mysterious Press, 1987.

Fairlie, Gerard. *Mr. Malcolm Presents.* London, Hodder & Stoughton,

———. *Shot in the Dark.* London, Hodder & Stoughton, 1932.

———. *Men for Counters.* London, Hodder & Stoughton, 1933.

Ferrars, Elizabeth. *The Seven Sleepers.* London, Collins, 1970.

Fleming, Ian. *Goldfinger.* London, Cape, 1959.

Fletcher, J. S. *The Perilous Crossways.* London, Ward, Lock, 1917.

Flynn, J. M. *Terror Tournament.* New York, Bouregy, 1959.

Forse, Harry. *A Storm at Pebble Beach.* Farmington Hills, MI, Slee Bear, 2000.

Frome, David. *The Murder on the Sixth Hole.* London, Methuen, 193

Fuller, Timothy. *Reunion with Murder.* Boston, Atlantic Little Brown,

Furlong, Nicola. *Teed Off!* Edmonton, Commonwealth Publicat 1996.

Katz, Jamie. *A Summer for Dying.* New York, Avon, 2000.

Keating, H.R.F. *The Billiard Room Murder.* London, Hutchinson, 1987.

Kennealy, Jerry. *Polo in the Rough.* New York, St. Martin's, 1989.

Kenyon, Michael. *The Shooting of Dan McGrew.* London, Collins, 1972.

Knox, Bill. *The Man in the Bottle.* London, John Long, 1963.

Knox, Ronald. *The Viaduct Murder.* London, Methuen, 1925.

Law, Janice. *Death Under Par.* New York, Houghton Mifflin, 1981.

Lockridge, Richard. *Murder Can't Wait.* Philadelphia, Lippincott, 1964.

Loder, Vern. *Suspicion.* London, Collins, 1933.

Logue, John. *Follow the Leader.* New York, Crown, 1979.

———. *Murder on the Links.* New York, Dell, 1996.

———. *The Feathery Touch of Death.* New York, Dell, 1997.

———. *A Rain of Death.* New York, Dell, 1998.

———. *On a Par with Death.* New York, Dell, 1999.

MacVicar, Angus. *The Hammers of Fingal.* London, John Long, 1963.

———. *Murder at the Open.* London, John Long, 1965.

———. *The Painted Doll Affair.* London, John Long, 1973.

McCutcheon, Hugh. *Cover Her Face.* London, Rich, 1954.

———. *Brand for the Burning.* London, John Long, 1969.

McInerny, Ralph. *Lying Three.* New York, Vanguard, 1979.

———. *Cause and Effect.* New York, Atheneum, 1987.

———. *Body and Soil.* New York, Atheneum, 1989.

———. *Law and Ardor.* New York, Scribner, 1995.

McNab, Claire. *Death Club.* London, Allen & Unwin, 2001.

Manson, Will. *A Deadly Game.* New York, Caravelle, 1967.

Mavity, Nancy Barr. *The Fate of Jane McKenzie.* New York, Doubleday, 1933.

Melville, Alan. *The Vicar in Hell.* London, Skeffington, 1935.

Miles, Keith. *Bullet Hole.* London, Deutsch, 1986.

———. *Double Eagle.* London, Deutsch, 1987.

———. *Green Murder.* London, Macdonald, 1990.

————. *Flagstick*. London, Macdonald, 1991.

————. *Bermuda Grass*. Scottsdale, AZ, Poisoned Pen, 2002.

————. *Bermuda Play-Off*. Scottsdale, AZ, Poisoned Pen, 2004.

Miron, Charles. *Murder on the 18th Hole*. New York, Manor, 1978.

Moxley, Frank Wright. *The Glass Pond*. New York, Coward-McCann, 1934.

Moyes, Patricia. *To Kill a Coconut*. London, Collins, 1977.

Natsuki, Shizuko. *The Obituary Arrives at Two O'Clock*. New York, Ballantine, 1988.

Norton, Olive. *Now Lying Dead*. London, Cassell, 1967.

O'Kane, Leslie. *Just the Fax, Ma'am*. New York, St. Martin's, 1996.

Orason, Roy. *Five Iron*. Roseville, CA, privately printed, 1994.

————. *The Golf Twins/The Golf Heist*. Roseville, CA, privately printed, 2000.

Payes, Rachel Cosgrove. *O Charitable Death*. New York, Doubleday, 1968.

Philbrick, William Rodman. *Slow Dancer*. London, Hale, 1976.

Platt, Kin. *The Kissing Gourami*. New York, Random House, 1970.

————. *Murder in Rosslare*. New York, Walker, 1986.

Potter, Jerry Allen. *A Talent for Dying*. New York, Fawcett, 1980.

————. *If I Should Die Before I Wake*. New York, Fawcett, 1981.

Quirole, Pierre. *The Golf Links Mystery*. London, Mellifont, 1935.

Rinehart, Mary Roberts. *Tish Plays the Game*. New York, Doran, 1926.

Roberts, Lee. *Suspicion*. London, Hale, 1964.

Rocke, William Ireland. *Operation Birdie*. Dublin, Moytura, 1993.

Ross, Charles. *The Haunted Seventh*. London, Murray, 1922.

Ross, Jonathan. *A Time for Dying*. London, Constable, 1989.

Rutherford, Douglas. *A Game of Sudden Death*. London, Macmillan, 1987.

Sheils, Terry. *Par for the Corpse*. Electronic book, 2002.

Shore, Julian. *Rattle His Bones*. New York, Morrow, 1941.

Snaith, John Collins. *Curiouser and Curiouser.* London, Hutchinson, 1935.

Steele, Chester. *The Golf Course Mystery.* New York, Sully, 1919.

Stewart, Walter. *Hole in One.* Toronto, McClelland & Stewart, 1992.

Stout, Rex. *Fer-de-lance.* New York, Farrar & Rinehart, 1934.

Stuart, Ian. *Sand Trap.* London, Hale, 1977.

Tyler, Lee. *The Clue of the Clever Canine.* New York, Vantage, 1994.

————. *The Case of the Missing Links.* Santa Barbara, CA, Fithian, 1999.

————. *The Teed-off Ghost.* Santa Barbara, CA, Fithian, 2002.

Tyrer, Walter. *Such Friends Are Dangerous.* London, Staples, 1954.

Upton, Robert. *Dead on the Stick.* New York, Viking, 1986.

Various authors. *The Putt at the End of the World.* New York, Warner, 2000.

Wade, Don. *Take Dead Aim.* Farmington Hills, MI, Sleeping Bear, 2002.

Wales, Hubert. *The Brocklebank Riddle.* New York, Century, 1914.

Williams, David. *Unholy Writ.* London, Collins, 1976.

————. *Wedding Treasure.* London, Macmillan, 1985.

Williams, Philip Carlton. *The Tartan Murders.* New York, Knightsbridge, 1990.

Wynne, Anthony. *Death of a Golfer.* London, Hutchinson, 1937.

Zimmerman, Bruce. *Crimson Green.* New York, HarperCollins, 1994.